WRATH OF THE LOST

More Space Marines from Black Library

SONS OF SANGUINIUS
A Blood Angels omnibus containing *Flesh Tearers*
by Andy Smillie and many other stories

• MEPHISTON •
by Darius Hinks

BOOK ONE: Blood of Sanguinius
BOOK TWO: Revenant Crusade
BOOK THREE: City of Light

ASTORATH: ANGEL OF MERCY
A Blood Angels novel by Guy Haley

DARKNESS IN THE BLOOD
A Blood Angels novel by Guy Haley

DANTE
A Blood Angels novel by Guy Haley

THE DEVASTATION OF BAAL
A Blood Angels novel by Guy Haley

• DAWN OF FIRE •
BOOK ONE: Avenging Son
by Guy Haley

BOOK TWO: The Gate of Bones
by Andy Clark

BOOK THREE: The Wolftime
by Gav Thorpe

BOOK FOUR: Throne of Light
by Guy Haley

BOOK FIVE: The Iron Kingdom
by Nick Kyme

BOOK SIX: The Martyr's Tomb
by Marc Collins

• DARK IMPERIUM •
by Guy Haley

BOOK ONE: Dark Imperium
BOOK TWO: Plague War
BOOK THREE: Godblight

THE SUCCESSORS
An anthology by various authors

HELBRECHT: KNIGHT OF THE THRONE
A Black Templars novel by Marc Collins

THE HELWINTER GATE
A Space Wolves novel by Chris Wraight

WRATH OF THE LOST

A FLESH TEARERS NOVEL

CHRIS FORRESTER

A BLACK LIBRARY PUBLICATION

First published in 2023.
This edition published in Great Britain in 2023 by
Black Library, Games Workshop Ltd., Willow Road,
Nottingham, NG7 2WS, UK.

Represented by: Games Workshop Limited – Irish branch,
Unit 3, Lower Liffey Street, Dublin 1,
D01 K199, Ireland.

10 9 8 7 6 5 4 3 2 1

Produced by Games Workshop in Nottingham.
Cover illustration by Lorenzo Mastroianni.

A CIP record for this book is available from the British Library.

ISBN 13: 978-1-80407-340-7

Printed and bound in the UK.

To all those who supported me on this adventure, and those taken before the end, thank you.

For more than a hundred centuries the Emperor has sat immobile on the Golden Throne of Earth. He is the Master of Mankind. By the might of His inexhaustible armies a million worlds stand against the dark.

Yet, He is a rotting carcass, the Carrion Lord of the Imperium held in life by marvels from the Dark Age of Technology and the thousand souls sacrificed each day so that His may continue to burn.

To be a man in such times is to be one amongst untold billions. It is to live in the cruellest and most bloody regime imaginable. It is to suffer an eternity of carnage and slaughter. It is to have cries of anguish and sorrow drowned by the thirsting laughter of dark gods.

This is a dark and terrible era where you will find little comfort or hope. Forget the power of technology and science. Forget the promise of progress and advancement. Forget any notion of common humanity or compassion.

There is no peace amongst the stars, for in the grim darkness of the far future,
there is only war.

DRAMATIS PERSONAE

The Lords of the Flesh Tearers

Gabriel Seth	Chapter Master of the Flesh Tearers, Lord of Cretacia, Guardian of Rage
Appollus	High Chaplain of the Flesh Tearers, Master of the Lost, Keeper of the Tower
Harahel	Commander of the Honour Guard, Champion of the Chapter

The Fourth Company

Tanthius	Captain and Master of the Fleet
Teman	Lieutenant
Hanibal	Lieutenant
Dumah	Chaplain
Barachiel	Apothecary
Thuriel	Junior Apothecary
Paschar	Librarian
Hariel	Techmarine
Micah	Sergeant, Assault Intercessor squad
Adariel	Sergeant, Assault Intercessor squad
Daven	Assault Intercessor
Raziel	Sergeant, Assault Intercessor squad
Gathrix	Assault Intercessor
Castus	Assault Intercessor
Isaiah	Sergeant, Assault Intercessor squad
Kairus	Assault Intercessor
Toivo	Sergeant, Intercessor squad
Burloc	Sergeant, Intercessor squad
Castiel	Sergeant, Hellblaster squad

Tumelo	Sergeant, Hellblaster squad
Thanatos	Sergeant, Reiver squad
Angelo	Sergeant, Reiver squad
Kosmos	Reiver
Azariel	Sergeant, Eradicator squad, seconded from the Ninth Company
Castivar	Sergeant, Aggressor squad, seconded from the Ninth Company
Daeron	Venerable Dreadnought, emissary of Gabriel Seth

The Death Company

Gael Luciferus	Warrior
Helios Varro	Warrior
Aleksei Tamael	Warrior
Aurelius	Warrior
Tychos	Warrior

The Reclusiam

Kamiel	Chaplain
Israfil	Judiciar

Servants of the Chapter

Kara Étain	Shipmistress of the *Cretacian Justice*
Aesha	Adjutant and surgical lead
Reyan Abdemi	Armsman
Hakaar Vakhoni	Supervisor

The Children of Cretacia

Hakkad	Aspirant

PROLOGUE

The reliquaria's dark iron doors cast a long shadow over Reyan Abdemi.

Carved with tiny cuneiform detailing the blood-soaked history of Cretacia's angels, the chamber's door was usually guarded by two archangels clad in thick slabs of sacred metal. Celebrated veterans of the God-Emperor's sky-wars, their stature and aura of raw aggression never failed to set his heart racing and catch his breath in his throat. He had looked upon them with quiet awe, their heavy armour lending them a loose semblance to the statues of ancient war-gods he'd seen in countless Cretacian shrines.

Now the veterans were gone, with almost all their brethren.

In their place, two mismatched horrors of dark metal and greying flesh stood sentinel, their eyes lit by flat, murder-red stares. The thick coils of their arm-mounted light-casters glowed bright blue, harsh illumination grinding flashes of hot pain against his temples. Blood roared in his ears and his heart thudded a staccato rhythm against his sternum. He felt it echo in his knees and elbows. Like the angels, these new guardians had been known to kill those who failed to show the proper caution and respect.

A stone panel retracted on the nearest column, revealing a small square of clean black glass, like that left behind by the fire-mountains' eruptions. Reyan pressed his right hand on it, ignoring the sudden flush of heat and the faint green thread tracing around his fingers and palm. The glass hummed and grew hotter, burning his callus-thickened skin. A wince hissed between his gritted teeth, but he kept his hand pressed against the plate. Needles bit into the tip of each digit, the hungering device exacting a blood-price as tribute.

'Access granted,' a harsh, grating voice boomed.

The stone snapped back over the plate and the hideous, half-metal sentinels swivelled on their gimbal-torsos to face outwards once more. The ancient doors ground open and the soft flicker of torchlight spilled out. Reyan glimpsed human-sized shadows darting across the widening gap, the soles of barasaur-hide boots clacking sharply on rough stone punctuated by the supervisor's croaked orders. Wiping the blood on his ash-black fatigues, Reyan hefted his fire-caster and followed the scent of burned wood and fresh paint into the reliquaria.

He strode through the low light and carved stone. Galleries of granite pedestals and recessed alcoves held battered suits of metal armour, broken weapons, and banners stained with blood and grime in thin strands of white light. Cuneiform detailed the valiant deeds of angels fallen long seasons before his birth, their lines sharpened by mason-serfs through the careful application of hammer and chisel. The measured *clunks* knifed white-hot pain through his skull, but Reyan was grateful for it. The pain muted the silence.

Reyan had feared silence since the angels had left Cretacia.

The armsman walked further into the hall, absorbing the faint details of mosaics and frescoes where angels battled lithe, laughing monsters and shadows of fang, claw and dark flame. The artworks framed relics of warriors that had walked in the God-Emperor's time, their deeds captured in faded colour and eroded line. He read their legends, confusion prickling his mind. Several words had been used in a context that no longer made sense, while others held no meaning to him at all. Had their language evolved so much since the angels' arrival?

He dismissed the question as unimportant.

Reyan reached the farthest end of the reliquaria, pausing before a towering suit of armour, like that of the angels, but larger and more imposing. His eyes locked on the dull green of its inactive lenses, before scrolling along the crimson-and-black metal of its chest and arms. He read echoes of titanic struggles against unimaginable horrors in its scars, and ferocity finally unchained in the saw-toothed blades and bulky fire-casters attached to its fists. His gaze fell to the legend beneath it, written in elegant script that had no origin on Cretacia.

+They will die, you know.+

Reyan's heart seized. The voices were back, stalking his thoughts as they had done since the angels sailed away. They refused to leave him alone.

+Soon your beloved angels will meet their end.+

'No, please…' He silently begged the God-Emperor, master of the heavens and the stars, great ancestor to the angels. 'Cretacia cannot lose her angels.'

Cruel laughter echoed in his skull.

+The Anathema cannot save them, fool, and they will not survive what now comes for them. The Devourer will rend their flesh, and the Angels' Bane will take their strongest into his service. By blade or by blood-oath will he bring them to Kharnath's throne.+

Reyan screwed his eyes shut, white-knuckling his fire-caster. Visions of burning jungles and mountains ground to meal beset him, the scent of smouldering wood spiced by the spoiled-meat reek of the rotting corpses choking the rivers. His ears rang with the howls of red-skinned beasts with curved fangs and snarling, toothed saw blades that slaughtered his people for sport. It was the same whenever he closed his eyes.

Sleep was a refuge denied to him.

'Did you say something, armsman?' a cracked voice called.

Reyan spun wildly, searching for the speaker, heart pounding against his sternum. Had he spoken aloud? Or had the voices invaded the world beyond his skull?

'Or are you here for another lesson?'

Hakaar Vakhoni hobbled towards him and Reyan's heart settled to an even rhythm. Hakaar was a withered specimen, ravaged by time and servitude. Skin hung slack from his sparse frame. The tufted echo of a beard sprouted from his wattled chin. Age crooked his spine so much that his upper body resembled the cane he clutched in stiff, shaking hands, though his eyes gleamed with a fierce intelligence. Hakaar had been a formidable fighter in his time, a high chief of the armsmen before infirmity relegated him to maintenance.

'I learned all you had to teach long ago, old man.'

'Believe that at your own peril, lad,' Hakaar laughed – a wet, throaty rasp. He patted Reyan on the chest, the arthritic echo of old strength still clinging to the elder's hands. 'I could still humble you in the fighting pits without even breaking a sweat.'

The whispers throttled Reyan's laughter.

'If you say so,' Reyan said, flavouring the words with forced humour. The old man's eyes narrowed and Reyan flinched inside. Words slipped between his teeth like water through cracks in a dam. 'I know better than to steal an old man's fantasies.'

Hakaar scowled.

Reyan quashed the nervous wrench that twisted his stomach. The disrespect of an elder was a great offence among the clans, but his relationship with the old man had always risen above such tradition. The voices receded, though the scent of burned wood and decomposing flesh still circled his nostrils. Bile flooded his mouth.

A chuckle broke Hakaar's wizened scowl.

'Did the carvings catch your eye?'

Reyan nodded, swallowing the bile.

'No point trying to read them, lad,' Hakaar said, leaning heavily on his cane. 'The tongue of the first angels can only be read by their heirs. It is tradition, unbroken since they saved Cretacia and made her their heaven.'

Hakaar led him away from the heavy armour, towards a ragged banner of black cloth, easily three times his height. Blood and grime marked the fabric but failed to obscure the cup that brimmed with blood, the angelic killer, and the toothed saw blade and cerise droplet of the angels. Hakaar hefted an age-arched finger and pointed to the mural behind it.

Reyan gasped to see a crude reflection of the banner clutched in the metal hand of an angel. Tails of orange fire streaked blue skies, trees and mountains rendered in smears of grey and mixed green. A second angel, massive beyond reckoning, wore the same suit of heavy armour that had fascinated him moments ago, and stood at their head like a chieftain. Awe flushed through Reyan's veins to see them battling green monsters, thick with muscle and yellow-tusked, beside smaller, dark-skinned figures that could only be Cretacian warriors.

'Our ancestors painted this during the era of the first hunts,' Hakaar said. 'When they helped the angels raise their home. They say sky-fire rained upon the clans for seven days, that smoking rocks carved open the earth for the under-dwellers to emerge and spill our people's blood. It was only by the efforts of the angels that they were stopped.'

Reyan knew the story well.

His parents, like any other mated human pair on Cretacia, had used the threat of the under-dwellers and their dark cousins, the Night Terrors, as cautionary tales whenever he and his siblings misbehaved or shamed themselves. His people feared the monsters' return, even with the angels' vigil over Cretacia promising to keep them safe. They spat and spilled blood to ward against that dread event, hissing whenever they were invoked. Some clans even offered sacrifices at the sites of the ancient battles.

Reyan had visited the sites twice himself.

'Do you know why the angels left?' he asked the older helot, feeling absurdly childish for each breath he assigned to the question. He could not stop himself. He had to know why they abandoned Cretacia. 'Why only five remain to keep the vigil?'

Hakaar chuckled again.

'The angels do not entrust mere mortals with that knowledge, boy,' he said. 'Rest assured, they have left before. Twice in my lifetime they have all sailed into the stars to serve the God-Emperor. We thought them gone forever, but they endured His trials and returned to us with fresh trophies and new tales. This time will be no different, mark me.'

Reyan drew breath to speak when something heavy struck the reliquaria's door. The clamour of charging weapons and raised voices slipped through the narrow gap between the stone wall and iron portal. Artisan-serfs ceased their restoration efforts, casting fearful gazes at the door. Hakaar hobbled towards them, shouting for them to continue their work when the metal trembled again. Reyan's grip tightened on his fire-caster as he backed away.

The door crashed open and one of the monstrous half-metal guardians skidded along the stone floor, its torso ripped from its legs. Its light-caster was torn free, the stump of its shoulder leaking thick black fluid. The light vanished from its eyes, the silver grate of its lips rasping something akin to a death rattle. Reyan watched the artisans heft their hammers and chisels with growing terror. Had the under-dwellers risen with the angels' disappearance?

He shrank further back, clutching his fire-caster.

An angel charged into the hall. Reyan's relief caught in his throat when he saw the angel's armour was marred by fresh scars and simmering scorch marks. The angel was bareheaded and unarmed, his expression locked in a rictus mask of fury and old scars, streaked by dried gore. A vicious burn peeled back one cheek to expose stringy tendons and nubs of blackened bone. His eyes were pools of liquid black madness.

'Traitors!' the angel bellowed, closing on the serfs. Several fell to their knees, hands clasped or raised in fear, moaning protestations of loyalty through salty tears. Others were rooted to the spot, frozen by confusion or terror. 'Vile oathbreakers! Slaves to Horus! Upon which deck does your master cower?'

Then the killing began.

Reyan cowered behind the banner's plinth. Wailed pleas and shrieks pounded his ears, a nightmarish kaleidoscope of pain and terror punctuated by the dry snap of bone and the wet wrench of violated flesh. Vomit seared the serf's throat, spraying through the gaps between his gritted teeth to stain his thighs. The angel screamed demands for blood, for this Horus to step forward and account for his sins. Reyan knew no one by the name. It was not Cretacian, nor was it an angel name. An awful realisation settled on him, numbing his horror.

The angel had gone mad.

The angel had gone mad and Reyan was going to die.

Each thunderous beat of his heart was one step closer to the cold, quiet finality of the abyss. He wanted to stand, to fight, to die defiant and with honour, earning himself a place at the God-Emperor's side. But his muscles refused to obey. No matter that he willed strength into his body and steeled his thoughts with zeal, he could not move. He tried again and again, mouthing desperate pleas through the shrieks of dying men and women. It was no use.

He would die a miserable death at the hands of an angel.

'Brother!' a machine-altered voice snarled.

A second set of footsteps thudded against the stone. Slower and more measured, they broke the dissonant caterwauls of dying humans. Reyan winced at the clamour, even louder now than the din of slaughter had been. Guttural snarls and frothed curses met vulgarities native to Cretacia's equatorial clans, punctuated by the dry growl of toothed blades and the arhythmic clangs of blows. Reyan measured his life in the space between each beat his heart managed to complete. The adrenal cocktail of elation and dread soaring through his blood begged him to look, to watch death or deliverance approach.

He refused, kept foetal by fear.

Then there was silence.

It took several minutes for Reyan to summon enough courage to risk peeking around the plinth. He saw the second angel bear his unbalanced brother from the hall, away from the holy relics and without a single glance at the murdered helots. Blood gushed from a wound that curled from the first angel's back to his abdomen. His head lolled to one side and one arm was severed at the elbow. Reyan did not know whether he lived or if the other angel had killed him for defiling such a holy place.

Reyan emerged from behind the plinth, time populated by the breaths of dying men and women. The air was thick with the stench of blood and voided bowels. It clogged his nostrils, invisible fingers closing around his throat, constricting every breath. He vomited violently, scrabbling for breath between expulsions. He picked his way through the piles of pulped flesh and wet, glistening organs.

He found Hakaar near the door.

The old man's remains were pale from exsanguination, strips of torn connective tissue and ripped veins trailing from the stumps where one arm and both legs had been. Vital organs sagged through the ragged tear in his abdomen, a pungent mound of offal that pooled blood onto the carved stone. His skull was a cratered ruin of brain meat and bone fragments, his tongue lolling on his lower jaw. The circular blade and crimson droplet stitched over his heart was untouched by blood. Hakaar's cane was still clutched tightly in his left hand.

Nausea swelled Reyan's stomach, his throat threatening to close.

He vomited, clutching his sides. He was no stranger to death. It was unavoidable on Cretacia, culling the weak with every rise and fall of the sun. He had fought men and monsters since he could hold a spear. He had killed in battle. He had killed for food and self-defence, for jealousy and anger. More than a hundred tongues were stored in his cell, their owners' ghosts silenced by their removal. But the butchery the angel had inflicted was of a magnitude he had never seen before.

'Why did you do this?' he whimpered, staring at the relics befouled by the blood of his brothers and sisters. 'What offence had we given?'

Hakaar's voice answered him.

+None.+

'Then why do this?' Reyan snapped through hot tears, hand on Hakaar's heart. The old man's tongue rested on its bed of flesh and teeth. He would not take it. Reyan still wanted to talk to him. 'There must be a reason for it… for your death… It cannot be random!'

+What do you know of the angels in black?+

Reyan remembered everything.

The angels in black were a legend whispered between servants on the cold night watches. They were angels fallen to madness, driven there by endless war and the loss of beloved brothers. Reyan was ready to dismiss it as lurid fantasy, as he always had, but then he remembered the angel's eyes. The fury and despair he'd seen there.

'They are real,' he breathed.

+They have always been real.+

'The angel that killed you,' he said, connections flowering in his mind. 'Did this happen because his brothers were absent? He screamed for blood like an under-dweller, demanding one called *Horus* face him. What about that?'

+The Sacrificed King is of no consequence, boy. The blood is. It matters most to the angels. It is their shield and sustenance. It drew them to Cretacia in the time before, and the promise of an ocean to slake their thirst drew them back to the stars. Only direct offerings will prevent them drowning in it, and the angels here succumbing to madness.+

Realisation struck Reyan like morning light.

He drew his knife, an age-yellowed oviraktor tooth with a grip of wound human hair. He slashed it across his palm, clenching and unclenching his fist as crimson droplets seeped from the wound onto the serrated symbol on Hakaar's chest. Reyan ignored the pain in his palm, determined to keep the blood flowing onto the angels' symbol.

'Sons of Cretacia. Angels of Wrath.'

Reyan intoned their titles, recycling the words until his voice cracked. Crimson drops fell with each syllable that left his lips. Cretacian blood had drawn them here, Cretacian blood would bring them back.

'Sons of Cretacia. Angels of Wrath. *Flesh Tearers*.'

PART ONE

'Seth shares the uncompromising honesty my brother valued in his forebear. Amit courted censure often, but never wavered in his loyalty and service. Seth can speak whatever truth lives in his heart. I know he will not stint in his service to the Emperor, nor will his Chapter.'

– Roboute Guilliman, primarch of the Ultramarines

ONE

The *Victus'* Reclusiam was hot and dark, shrouded by a silence that was almost complete. The measured throb of plasma drives slithered through the carved granite of the apse. The snapping hiss of smouldering wood wafted from stone fire-bowls and flambeaux, weighing the air with a caustic incense. Black basalt cladded the adamantium bulkheads and carved menhirs framed the nave. Alcoves cut into the standing stones housed Chapter relics in shimmering stasis fields. A moat of volcanic sand staked with silver-steel honour blades divided the apse from the nave and transepts, their deck plates a grim mosaic formed from the plastrons of fallen captains.

To Dumah, it was a shaman's cave ripped from its primitive hellscape.

The Chaplain, his void-black Mark X Tacticus power armour embossed with fanged skulls rendered in gold and brass, crossed the narrow causeway that bridged the black sand, holding a relic chainsword reverently. Its black housing was sliced by two diagonal crimson stripes, and acid-etched with the names of fallen warriors. That honour roll stretched back to the strife of the Imperium's early foundation, and its kill tally reputedly exceeded that of several Chapters. It was a weapon, plain and pure, and the Flesh Tearers embraced the fact in its naming, an act of savage honesty Dumah could not help but admire.

They called it Severer.

Dumah carefully placed Severer on the mountings set in its niche, before unclasping the rosarius affixed to his belt and slotting the icon in another aperture. He made one quarter-turn with the icon, hearing the low hum of the stasis field powering to readiness. Dumah's eyes rested on the twin rows of monomolecular teeth, Severer's wrathful war-spirit calling to the sacred fury shackled in his own breast. Dumah relished the kinship he felt with the weapon, hands itching to lift it once more. He never felt a similar unity of purpose with the souls of Cawl's Mars-forged weapons.

He turned the icon after another moment of hesitation, sealing the chainsword in stasis and denying his desire to claim it. It mattered not that he knew the great deeds and valiant deaths of every warrior to wield it since Manakel, a vaunted hero of the IX Legion and a former High Chaplain of the Chapter. Appollus entrusted him with its protection and consecration. The preservation and protection of the Chapter's history and sacred relics was his calling, the crozius his staff of office. He would have it no other way.

Dumah moved away from Severer, casting his eye over the other artefacts locked in stasis. He admired reforged blades and suits of power armour with honour rolls longer and more illustrious than Severer, their surfaces engraved with Baalite sandscript. There were others Dumah privately considered distasteful – too Cretacian – in their primitivism. Razor-wire coils sported tongues ripped from the skulls of ork battle-chieftains, severed ears of aeldari witches, the scrimshawed bones and corrupted blades of Traitor Legion warlords, and chalices fashioned from the skulls of demagogues and despots taken by the Flesh Tearers during their long history. Some stasis seals were gene-locked and hexagrammically warded by the Chief Librarian, so their taint could never infect another loyal Imperial soul.

Some relics were famous throughout the Sanguinary Brotherhood.

He saw Slayer's Wrath, the stylised 'I' of the Holy Ordos still visible on the bolter's casing, and its exotic munitions stacked beside it. Sorrow's Genesis squatted on a block of grey stone three niches from the bolter, the Exsanguinator gauntlet renowned for its ability to restore mortally wounded warriors from death's embrace, though at terrible cost to their sanity and spiritual sanctity. The Gauntlet of Iron Wrath, black power fist of Chapter Master Korda, rested on a plinth of carved wood. Dumah sensed fury in its spiked ceramite plating, the same ferocity that had helped Korda carry the breach at the Siege of Phaeton, slaying an Iron Warriors' daemon prince and Dreadnought talon in the same hour.

Only one other artefact called to him as Severer did.

It rested on a black basalt ledge, silent in deactivation. A vellum honour scroll was set beside its haft of meteoric iron, ringed with spiked bands of gold. Its head was fashioned into the shape of a skeletal angel, wings spread wide in a frozen echo of flight. Dispersal studs for its disruptor field were cunningly woven between ribs and dark-iron feathers, the razor-edged wings of its ornate head capable of slicing flesh from bone or shattering power armour. At the angel's heart, the heraldic device of the Flesh Tearers was rendered in polished silver, a rare Baalite bloodstone set at its centre. A crozius arcanum, it had belonged to a hero and former High Chaplain. Dumah had inked the warrior's name on the honour scroll himself.

Carnarvon.

Brass censers leaked cleansing vapours onto the sacred metal, oils and unguents set on the ledge beside it ready for him to reconsecrate it to the Chapter's service. Dumah hefted the maul. It fit his hand as though forged for it. Its balance was perfect, the weight of the layered adamantium and gilded steel in its ornate head countered by a pommel carved to resemble a fanged, skeletal wight. Forgemaster Liscus had done exemplary work in his restoration, ensuring no compromise of lethality for artistry. Had Dumah been granted the High Chaplain's office, he would have eagerly accepted the weapon and borne it in battle, not left it here to moulder in safety as Appollus had.

The Chaplain lifted a square of cloth from a small wooden box on the ledge, dipping a corner in the first unguent and gently applying it to the maul's deactivated head. He intoned the First Litany of Reconsecration, dabbing the cloth again, the combination of word and balm purging any lingering impurities left from its exposure to xenos blood and the taint of the warp. The reconsecration rituals would take several hours, with numerous invocations and layers of unguent required to satisfy its venerable war-spirit, and ensure its purity was beyond question before its stasis-interment in the flagship's Reclusiam.

A secondary access hatch slid open.

Chaplain Kamiel and Judiciar Israfil entered, their black armour partially concealed by robes of supple leather coloured the earthen brown of sun-dried flesh. Israfil's executioner sword was mag-locked to his back, and Kamiel's crozius hung from his waist. Both wore their skull-faced helms, the lower half of Israfil's obscured by a square of brown leather he wore as a mask. They knelt in supplication before statues of Sanguinius and the Emperor erected in the transepts, paying homage to their father and their monarch. When their obeisance was made, they moved towards the chancel.

Dumah's vox-bead pinged.

'Cede your reconsecration duties to Kamiel and Israfil.' Appollus' normal angry tone was edged by either disgust or disappointment, Dumah was not sure which. *'Your attendance is required at a council in the personal sanctum of Lord Seth.'*

Dumah clutched the crozius tighter, unwilling to surrender it.

'Lord Appollus, you entrusted this duty to me,' Dumah said. 'I have scarce begun the required ministrations for Carnarvon's crozius. To interrupt the rituals of consecration would greatly dishonour this artefact, an offence incompatible–'

'I did not ask for excuses, Dumah!' Appollus snapped. Data screeded onto the Chaplain's retinal feed. *'Seth has demanded that you attend the council in his sanctum. That is an order, not a request! Kamiel and Israfil will sanctify my predecessor's weapon, and any further relics that require the rites. You will depart immediately.'*

Dumah reluctantly placed the crozius on the ledge.

'Yes, High Chaplain.'

He exited the Reclusiam without another word.

The dolorous clang of beaten metal welcomed Dumah to the upper levels of the command spire. The Chaplain exited the lifter, the red lambency of emergency lumens diluting on the osseous white of his skull helm and the silver traceries that charted recent battle-damage in his black ceramite. Sheets of opaque plastek obscured the route to the flagship's strategium and the personal sanctum of Lord Seth. They billowed on the stale, unfiltered oxygen wheezed into the suffocating heat of the corridor by damaged air-filtration units.

Dumah strode along the corridor, navigating between the plastek sheets and the mobs of thralls in heavy environment suits. Their hearts raced as he drew close, the dull thud of war drums reaching crescendo. He read exhaustion and malnutrition in their greying, sweat-greased skin and the hardened lines of their unremarkable features. They averted their eyes as he passed, tucking their chins to their chests, their focuses locked on the grinding machine tools showering the deck with orange sparks, and the acetylene hiss of arc welders fusing new sheets of plasteel to the bulkheads. The intense whine of metal shearing metal clawed his helm's auditory receptors and the stench of scorched plasteel filled his nostrils.

Several menials lay where they had collapsed, either killed or rendered unconscious by privation and the extreme heat. Dumah stepped over them as though they were not even there. He did not consider the act malicious, merely expedient. The menials lived brief, meaningless lives ruled by fear, selfishness and pain. That these menials had spent their lives serving the Emperor and Sanguinius earned them his recognition, brief thoughts he would not squander on the teeming trillions he would eventually sell his life to protect.

Dumah sighted the heavy iron doors of Seth's personal sanctum.

Carved with the sigil of the Chapter and framed by rust-veined scaffolding, the portal was guarded by two Terminators of the honour guard, their ceramite patched by grey repair cement and bonded sections of temporary reinforcement. The scent of old gore clung in the crevices, to the myriad trophies of xenos bone, carnelian chitin and flayed flesh secured to shoulder and thigh by brass chains. The bitter tang of charred ozone clung to the veterans, the air alive with the energies required to power the massive suits of battleplate.

'I have been summoned to attend a council with Lord Seth.'

The Terminator on his left inclined his helm, a piercing snarl of damaged servos and scraping ceramite. His storm bolter was drawn, its shot-selector switched to automatic fire, his power fist sheathed in crackling disruptive energies. The teeth of its underbite chainblade attachment were broken and chipped, the grey metal stained with age-darkened blood.

'You are expected, Chaplain Dumah.'

The doors opened and Dumah stepped through.

Seth's sanctum was simply furnished, with an arming rack and a small workbench set against one wall. An iron chair, sized for an Adeptus Astartes, was set slightly at an angle from it, and there was a small shelf with several sealed jars and old battle-trophies on it. Blood Reaver, the Chapter Master's infamous two-handed chainblade, rested on the workbench beside teeth tracks and a container stamped with the Technicarum's insignia. Two sealed hatches led to Seth's private arming chamber and his ablutions cell. The final fixture, situated in the centre of the chamber, was the hololithic planning table.

Five Flesh Tearers were gathered around it, all looking at him.

'I see you found time to attend,' Harahel growled in heavily accented Gothic. His Terminator plate was draped with grisly trophies, numbering far more than those of the warriors he had stationed outside. 'Did the Butcher not teach you that heeding your Chapter Master's summons is compulsory?'

Dumah bristled, more offended for himself than Lord Guilliman. He had received the summons from Appollus a mere thirty minutes ago, time he had spent in transit between the Black Tower and the command spire. His eyes found the High Chaplain lurking in the Terminator's shadow, his body set in an expression of raw, restrained wrath. Anger burned sun-bright, then Dumah snorted, admonishing himself for expecting support from his senior.

He bowed his head in a display of faux contrition.

'The Butcher taught me much, Harahel,' he said to the Chapter Champion. 'Not least that the duties of office are manifold and often keep their occupiers engaged. I do not recall any lectures in etiquette and protocol. Why? Do you seek some for yourself?'

Harahel laughed, a shotcannon's bark, and gunned his chainfist.

Dumah smiled and reached for his crozius.

'Enough!' Gabriel Seth snarled, slamming his fist on the table.

The master of the Flesh Tearers was an immense figure. Scars cut the natural contours of his square-jawed face, his expression rigid with the same restrained fury that bled from his High Chaplain. Seth's eyes locked with Dumah's, and the Chaplain felt himself grimace beneath the Cretacian's gaze, instantly regretting his flippancy. The Chapter Master exuded an aura of elemental aggression that sent a very human chill slithering down Dumah's spine.

Seth truly embodied the mantle *Guardian of Rage*.

'We do not have time for pointless bickering.' The words rode the predatory snarl that hissed between Seth's gritted teeth. 'We must resolve this matter, and quickly. There are wars that require our attention, and tyranid blood yet to be spilled.'

'My lord, the Fourth Company stands ready for your orders,' Tanthius said, and Dumah caught the ripple of eager impatience in the captain's voice, his scuffed and scarred Tacticus plate a visceral narration of wounds sustained in close assault. 'Upon which battlefield shall these monsters next taste our wrath?'

Seth keyed a number string into the hololith's data-pad.

The stuttering projection of a planet layered itself onto the table, a sphere of trembling light the colour of clean oceans. Its topography was shrouded in dense clouds and electrical storms. High Gothic script screeded beside it, detailing its classification as an extremis-grade death world, approximate lists of indigenous species, and its stewardship by Adeptus Astartes Chapter 082, claimed by Right of Conquest in M31.

Recognition clenched Dumah's stomach tight with disgust.

'Cretacia?' The second Primaris Space Marine breathed.

Apothecary Barachiel of the Fourth forewent his power armour for simple grey fatigues, ripe with the stench of his daily training regimen. A Terran veteran of the Indomitus Crusade, Barachiel had mentored Dumah, guided him towards his calling as a Chaplain and had saved his life on more than one occasion. The veteran's close-cropped silver-gold hair and beard framed age-creased skin the colour of cedar, his smile of modest joy flawed by a single scar.

'Home,' Harahel smiled.

'Almost twenty years has passed for Cretacia since we first sailed for Baal,' Seth said, affection colouring his voice with something like concern. 'Since Leviathan was defeated, we have received no astropathic hails, and those sent by the Librarians and astropaths of our own fleet continue to go unanswered. This silence cannot persist. It *will not* persist.'

Dumah fixed Seth with the impassive glare of his red optics. It did not take a genius to determine what Seth had in mind for them. He hated the idea already.

'My lord,' Tanthius began, choosing his words with care. 'The empyrean is wracked with tempests of a kind unseen for millennia. They blind Navigators and fragment astropathic cries as often as swallow entire battlefleets. Our communiqués could have been scattered in the turbulent tides or hampered by the chronometric anomalies unleashed by the Rift.'

'The captain presents a valid point, lord,' Dumah said. He did not want to sail for Cretacia any more than Tanthius, though he suspected the captain's reasons were wildly different to his own. 'The turmoil unleashed by the Great Rift has dimmed even the light of the Astronomican. If the Emperor's own might struggles to carry across the storm tides, what hope does any psyker, even the most puissant, have of successfully projecting an astropathic distress call?'

'It is likely Cretacia endures unharmed, my lord,' Tanthius

continued. Dumah looked at Barachiel, reading frustrated hope in his downcast features. His eyes narrowed, unsure why his brother would *want* to sail for Cretacia. 'The Indomitus Crusade secured the core worlds and suppresses heretic and alien encroachment in the Segmentum Pacificus. Should Cretacia cry out for aid, the lord regent's forces are better positioned to provide succour.'

'Cowards!' Appollus' strident voice was amplified by the vox-casters built into his skull-faced helm. The disruptor field on his crozius sizzled live. 'You dare dishonour the mark of Amit's chosen warriors with such a display of weakness? Pathetic!'

Dumah's teeth ground together, and his twin hearts thundered against his sternum, starving canids incited to frenzy by the promise of meat. He restrained himself from violence, barely. Tanthius did not. The captain roared and drew his blade, thumbing its activation stud. Coruscating arcs of lethal energy rippled along the sword's reforged length.

Appollus laughed and advanced on him.

Seth scowled and raised his hand. It was the only instruction Harahel needed.

The Champion forced his way between them, the enhanced strength of his Terminator plate throwing Tanthius into a bulkhead. The Primaris captain struck the plasteel with a thunderclap's force, one hand pressed to his helm as he sought to steady himself. Rage dragged bestial snarls from Appollus' lips as the High Chaplain pressed queries about the Champion's loyalty and parentage into the spaces between breaths.

'This childishness is done,' Harahel growled.

Tanthius snarled and lowered his weapon, deactivating it. Appollus glanced at Seth, then followed suit with a dry chuckle. Neither had the stomach to fight Harahel. The tension between the three vented like coolant from a ruptured hose.

'"Chronometric anomalies" aside' – Seth spat the words back at them – 'it is still years without a single communication from Cretacia.'

'What of our oath?' Tanthius snarled.

Seth's eyes narrowed.

'Our oath?' He seemed genuinely puzzled.

'We pledged to aid Dante in the purification of the Red Scar. We cannot depart with the war yet unwon. Would you see the Flesh Tearers shamed before the Golden Sons or the Angels Encarmine' – Dumah caught Seth's reflexive twitch at the mention of the aloof Second Founding Chapter – 'for sending warriors *away* from the war front?'

Seth glared at Tanthius.

'Our oaths to Cretacia predate any pledge I made to Dante. As for the Golden Sons and Angels Encarmine, I care not what quaint opinions they hold, or what they whisper in their blackest envy. *We* are Sanguinius' second sons, our blood most blessed with the sun-bright caress of his holy wrath. *I* am the Master of the Flesh Tearers, not Dante, nor any preening lord of our lesser cousins. Your vessel is already being prepared and your warriors have been alerted that they are to transfer aboard. My decision is final, *captain*.'

Tanthius nodded, beaten.

Barachiel's smile returned.

'Chancing the crossing from Nihilus to Sanctus is little more than suicide,' Dumah said. Seth's underhand moves infuriated him. He would speak his mind and damn the consequences. 'You would waste the lives of your warriors on a feat based entirely in deluded optimism? That is reckless even for you, Seth. If you are set on sending us to our deaths, then grant us the truth – why this fools' expedition to Cretacia?'

'You dare think to stand in judgement over my decisions,

Primaris?' Seth snarled, taking a step forward. Dumah stood his ground. 'I can smell the mother's milk still on your breath. Your rank may give you the remit to question me, to test me, but you have not served the Chapter long enough to be a worthy arbiter of my actions, or my soul.'

Dumah wanted to strike Seth, to crush his skull and tear the beating, bloody hearts from his chest. His fangs slid from his gums. Fury stung his blood, even as he calmed himself with slow, steady breaths. It would be little use to sink to Seth's level. He spoke in a low and measured voice, determined that his words be judged by their logic, not his fury.

'Cretacia is the birthplace of the muck that soils the honour of our Chapter in the eyes of the Angel and the Emperor. With Dante's fiat to recruit and tithe materiel from any world we see fit, what possible reason could we have to return to that accursed hellscape?'

Dumah expected Seth to rage, to curse and froth like a madman overtaken by a viral neuro-inflammatory. He imagined the Chapter Master snatching up his eviscerator to cleave him in half, or ordering Harahel and Appollus to tear him apart, a task both looked fully prepared to perform. Muscles tensed like steel cords pressed against Harahel's neck seals, and the teeth of his chainblade attachments tore the air with a dry, grating hunger. Appollus looked on the verge of apoplexy, shaking inside his black plate. Dumah expected Seth to do many things, but not the one thing he actually did.

Seth laughed.

'Perhaps the Angel's wrath does dwell in your kind too.' Seth's humour tapered away as suddenly as it appeared. 'Cretacia may be a worthless world, far from the salvation Amit once promised, but it is home. For me, and for this Chapter. It is the crucible of our fury and our flesh, the world won with the blood, sweat and wrath of our forebears. Not one of the worlds Dante offered us can lay claim to that distinction. If that cost must be exacted again to secure our home and our relics, then it is a price I happily pay.'

Dumah's hearing snagged on one word.

'Relics? There are relics on Cretacia?'

Seth nodded.

'We were forced to leave many honoured artefacts behind when we sailed for Baal,' Appollus growled. 'Some even date back to the Chapter's foundation, including Amit's own standard and his armour, the Crimson Plate. We had little time and brought only what we could use in battle. They were left in the custodianship of our serfs and a contingent of veteran Astartes.'

'The Crimson Plate…' Awe gave way to horror, which gave way to fury. 'What possessed you to consider those unwashed barbarians fitting custodians for the heirlooms of our Chapter?' Dumah resisted the urge to spit, so repugnant was the notion.

'When we sailed for Baal, it was to meet our deaths,' Seth growled. 'Not one Flesh Tearer expected to live beyond Leviathan's assault. We were scarcely two hundred warriors. Bequeathing our legacy to the people of Cretacia was more palatable than seeing it consumed by the tyranids or gathering dust as a hollow memorial in the Blood Angels' vaults, a monument to a legacy not their own, and one they could never understand.'

Dumah nodded, suppressing the anger stinging his veins. Though the notion of sacred relics left in the grubby, uncultured hands of ill-bred tribal savages was revolting, it was at least an understandable decision, one he may have made himself in their position. He looked to Tanthius and Barachiel, offering them his nod of affirmation.

'Then the Fourth Company alone will sail for Cretacia, and we shall recover these relics,' Tanthius said. He paused, before adding: 'And secure your home world.'

Seth smiled, his taut grin mirthless.

'I never said I would be sending you alone.'

TWO

The vessel chosen for their expedition was the *Cretacian Justice*.

An ancient strike cruiser of a pattern no longer manufactured in Imperial shipyards, she lacked the lethal grace and grandeur that had been her birthright. Generations of magi and artisan shipwrights had embellished her with supplemental weapons batteries, launch bays, expanded crew decks and enhanced armour. Her stern was a cityscape of battlemented minarets, palatial alcazars and revetments set over four engine stacks that slithered a low, pulsing throb through the deck. Each one was the length of a system-defence frigate.

She was an exiled queen, given leave to reclaim her domain.

Barachiel stood alone in one of those spinal minarets, in a small chamber adjacent to the primary apothecarion, watching the *Victus* hold orbit above a cleansed world. Fighters flitted around her hull on contrails of blue fire while escort vessels crowded her dorsal like grox calves seeking their mother's protection. Overlords shuttled supplies and Space Marines from the flagship. On the decks beneath his feet, Barachiel knew thousands of menials toiled to prepare the ancient, overworked plasma furnaces for the expedition to Cretacia.

Seth had not lied when he said their strike cruiser was already being outfitted for their voyage. Scarcely two Terran days had passed since the war council, and most of their supplies and equipment had already been transferred aboard. The Fourth Company was mere hours from breaking orbit above Kharthour, awaiting only the arrival of Seth's emissary from the *Victus*, and their final reinforcements from the reserve companies.

'My lord,' a small voice said behind him.

The Apothecary disregarded the sound, his mind fixed on the expedition the Fourth Company readied itself to undertake. The Flesh Tearers, reborn after Baal, were going home. *He* was going home. Not the home of his birth, the grim, dilapidated ecumenopolis accreted atop the ruins of the Emperor's dream, nor the cryo-vaults and surgical suites of the *Zar-Quaesitor,* where he had slept and suffered through much of the Imperium's tumultuous history. He was bound for the world his Chapter had called home since its earliest years. Such a voyage carried the ripe scent of myth about it.

Barachiel's mind turned to Terra, the world of his birth. Only the thinnest memories of it remained to him. The gnawing absence his stomach had once known. The refiltered air of the Terran underhives. The anguished cries of pilgrims robbed and murdered in the silent watches of the night. His last sight of the Throneworld had been from the spinal observation tower of a Navy battle cruiser when his crusade fleet had broken orbit from Luna.

It had left him thoroughly underwhelmed.

'My lord,' the small voice said again.

Barachiel turned, his gaze falling on an ash-robed thrall holding a data-slate.

The menial was female, scarcely into her adulthood if judged by the Terran calendar, the prime helix of the Apothecarion sewn over her heart. Her skin was a rich olive, its pigment not yet greyed by the years of exposure to false light that was a natural facet of life aboard Imperial warships. She possessed few visible bionic enhancements. Amber eyes watched him with detached curiosity, the cringing awe and fear that so many mortals greeted his kind with stark in its absence. He cocked an eyebrow, intrigued by the mortal's apparent bravery.

She offered him the data-slate, which he accepted.

'Your name, human?'

She blinked, surprised by the question.

'My lord?'

'You have a name, do you not? If you are to serve as my adjutant, I would know your name.'

Barachiel counted eight heartbeats between statement and answer.

'My given name is Aesha, my lord.'

Barachiel nodded and placed the data-slate on the desk, one in a small pile detailing combat and training injuries, medicae requisition orders and archival records. He would read it later. The mortal bowed and made to leave, freezing when he cleared his throat.

'My lord, is there any further service you require of me?'

'You supervised the initial provision of our apothecarion, did you not?'

'I did, my lord.'

'Then make your report to me.'

Barachiel ignored the rebellious twinge of irritation that tugged the back of his mind. Conversations with mortals were deeply uninteresting, too sanitised by their fear, awe, and the trivial concerns that plagued their brief existences. But Barachiel had learned much from the Lord Guilliman's example and shared his belief that conversation lent context to reports and could prove more informative than even the most detailed summarisation.

Silence stretched across seconds.

'Do not be timorous,' Barachiel said, allowing anger to ripple in his voice. 'I have not the time or use for an adjutant that cannot speak plainly to me. Do not call me "lord" either. I do not rule a city, nor govern a world. I am a warrior and a medicae, born in a gutter-sump on Terra. Gabriel Seth is your lord. Address me by name, or by my calling.'

Her eyes flicked to the side, then she drew a breath.

'No other trained medicae technician possesses my cranial enhancements. I, alone, was assigned to be your adjutant. What you ask is included on the slate, Apothecary.'

Barachiel laughed. This mortal *was* brave.

'I would rather hear it from you, adjutant.'

She adopted a more rigid posture, hands clasped behind her back.

'We have successfully completed installation of all the new apothecarion equipment transferred from the *Victus*. Our stocks of stimulants and soporifics are complete, and we have the means to synthesise more. There are some minor injuries sustained among the battle-brothers, including two that require surgery. I took the liberty of assigning medicae technicians to assist Brother Thuriel in both cases.'

Her initiative was impressive.

'The progenoid stocks are secure? The genesis chambers correctly installed?'

'They are,' Aesha said, the faint hint of a proud smile touching her lips. 'The archmagos dominus' medicae-priests have confirmed the genesis machines are functional and available for immediate use. Brother Thuriel has confirmed the gene-seed is pure.'

He nodded, pleased. They were his responsibility, necessary components to begin the Chapter's recruitment efforts on Cretacia. The journey was pointless without them.

'What of the additional stocks of vitae?'

Aesha looked at him, uncertainty blossoming in the uptick of her heartbeat. 'They... denied your request.' She paused. 'They have supplied a fraction of the original amount.'

Fingers curled to fists, accompanied by the whine of protesting armour joints.

'Did they provide an explanation?'

'My lord...' She hesitated once more, licking her lips. Barachiel needed no enhanced senses or extensive training in human physiology to recognise her trepidation. He ignored her slip back into the honorific – it was a minor irritant, and she was clearly distracted. 'I urge you to read the report. It holds a sensitive file coded with a vermilion-grade cipher and secured by a genetic encryption key. It may pertain to the denial of your request.'

Barachiel activated the slate, his fingers striking the hololithic keys projected onto his retinal feed. Its second layer of security demanded he enter a retinal scan and gene sample. He removed his helm to supply both, a web of thin red lines mapping his eyeball while its thin armature composed of sliding rods and sharp blades scraped blood and skin cells from his exposed cheek. The screen blinked green, and he opened the file. His brow furrowed and his expression grew thunderous.

'Where is the captain? Where is Chaplain Dumah?'

The human flinched at the sudden anger in his voice but recovered quickly. He met her eyes, catching the tint of activating cranial enhancements behind them. They flickered a faint orange. She stood ramrod straight, enunciating each word in a flat monotone, emotion and independent thought suppressed by the active cogitators implanted in her skull.

'Lords Tanthius and Dumah await the arrival of Lord Seth's emissary on the primary embarkation deck. Should I summon them here, lo– Barachiel?'

'Request their presence on deck eleven-aleph,' he said, drawing a small key shaped to resemble the prime helix of his office from an ork-hide pouch at his waist. 'Then purge all trace of that command from your data-spools, authorisation omicron-two-niner.'

'Compliance.'

Barachiel did not hear it.

He was already gone.

The deck Barachiel emerged onto did not exist on any official schemata.

He removed the key from its aperture within the lifter's control panel, mag-locking it to his waist, and replacing the tiny steel square he had taken from it. The microfilament emitters threaded into the metal unlocked the hidden decks aboard Flesh Tearers vessels for any Chapter officer. Barachiel, Tanthius and Dumah were the only brothers of the Fourth with access to this deck, and the only souls that could leave it. Though mortals dwelled there, any desire to leave was ruthlessly repressed.

The lifter doors slid shut, the slow grind of it ascending into the ship fading into the pulsing throb of the *Justice*'s plasma drives. There was no other sound, save rats and other vermin species scurrying behind the bulkheads or nesting in the piping.

Barachiel strode along the corridor, armoured boots clanging on the reinforced metal-mesh deck. Beneath the deck plates, he glimpsed the solid-red charging lumens of servitors in their coffin-sockets, ingesting the revolting nutrient paste made from their recycled waste and processed meat through opaque plastek tubes. He tasted it on the metronomic rasp of their breaths, a rhythm mirrored in the heartbeats of the menials staffing the deck. Several lined the corridor in tongueless silence, their wasted features making them a ghoulish guard of honour.

Dumah and Tanthius awaited him a little further down.

'What *urgent matter* requires our attention, brother?'

Dumah's voice was all challenge. His helm was mag-locked to his waist, revealing a face that had once been handsome. Its right half remained so, skin like carved alabaster framed by blond hair and an eye that seemed to shift colour with his mood. His eye was all that remained beautiful on the left half of his face. The flesh of his cheek was torn back to tendon and bone, the legacy of an ork warlord's chainweapon, hairless skin above his temporal bone rippled by burn scarring.

His features were half angel, half death's head.

'It *is* an inopportune moment to request an audience, brother,' Tanthius said, subtly reprimanding the Chaplain's zeal. 'Master Seth's emissary has barely arrived, and we have yet to brief the company's officers on our expedition to Cretacia.'

Dumah scowled at the mention of their new home world's name.

'Forgive my urgency, captain,' Barachiel said, gesturing for them to follow. 'Brother-Chaplain, rest assured that had I not deemed it an issue of the utmost importance, I would not have summoned you here. Please come with me, and I will explain.'

He led them towards one of the cells that faced the serfs' habitation units. The hatch was secured by a gene-lock, an aperture carved to admit the Apothecarion sigil situated above it. Barachiel placed his hand on the data-pad, allowing its needles to draw a measure of his blood as it scanned his palm-print and heart rhythm. He inserted his key and twisted it three times. The lock clunked, and the hatch groaned open on rusted mechanisms. The fusty scent of dust and old blood washed from the cell, clenching his throat tight.

They entered the cell.

It was small, furnished with a simple iron chair sized for an Adeptus Astartes and a small array of screens in one corner. A cruciform table dominated the chamber's centre, a polished chirurgeon hovering over it. Limbs folded like arachnid legs ended in sterilised blades, bone saws and modified reductors that fed vermin-chewed plastek piping to the large collection tank mounted in the farthest corner. The equipment was ancient and outdated. He had ordered much of it replaced the day he transferred aboard from the *Victus*.

'This is but one chamber of exsanguination. There are hundreds more.'

'You state the obvious,' Dumah said. 'Are we to tour secondary and tertiary medicae facilities next? Cut this theatre and get to the point.'

'The point, my dear brother, is that our stocks of vitae were drained by the Sanguinary High Priest and Master of the Logisticiam. They cited "the needs of the ongoing Angel's Halo campaign", offering as a counterproposal the rapid exsanguination of our flesh-tithe from Akathar, and the penitent thralls they transferred aboard two days ago.'

Dumah drew his combat knife, low light rippling along its serrated edge.

'Again, you are stating that which we already know. I did not see a problem when I reviewed the proposal. Nor did the captain. What problem does it present?'

Barachiel shot Dumah a dark look, before turning to Tanthius.

'Did either of you even examine the mortality rates?'

Tanthius shook his head. Dumah laughed, the bark of a starved jackal.

'I am no mere scrivener to be plagued by minutiae.'

Barachiel bristled at the insult. He was every bit the warrior

Dumah was, but he paid attention to the finer details. It was his remit as an officer of the Fourth Company. Rage sang in his blood, imploring him to draw the chainblade sheathed at his waist. He resisted the urge, forcing a thin-lipped smile. Scorn dripped from his every syllable.

'Perhaps you should concern yourself with the fine detail, brother. It might curtail the frequency with which you gawp like an ogryn whenever something outside your limited, linear expectations befalls us, like on Vorjun.'

Dumah moved for his weapon. Barachiel responded in kind.

'Enough!' Tanthius roared, interposing himself between them. 'I have already shamed myself before the Chapter Master with such a display, I will not tolerate it from either of you! Unless your words hold merit, remain silent. Explain yourself, Apothecary.'

'Certainly, captain.' Barachiel moved his hand away from the hilt of his chainsword, activating his vambrace's inbuilt holo-lithic projector. A range of graphs and charts layered themselves onto the nearest bulkhead. 'At the projected rate of consumption, it is likely we will exhaust the flesh-tithe in the first three weeks. Once they have been exhausted, we will be forced to institute a series of culls, including essential personnel – the medicae staff, the gunnery crews...'

'Reducing our combat effectiveness,' Tanthius finished slowly, as though tasting the logic in Barachiel's argument. 'Particularly should hostiles hold Cretacia.'

'Exactly.'

'Bah!' Dumah grunted. 'The menials exist to serve the Chapter. If that means they must be bled, then so be it. Bleed them. There are trillions in Sanctus that we can press into service as skilled or unskilled hands should the need arise. Dante granted us fiat to do so.'

'His ruling carries no weight in Imperium Sanctus, brother,'

Tanthius said. 'We cannot guarantee that any effort to impose a tithe will not meet resistance, or that we could overcome it with minimal losses. We do not have numbers to waste on futile efforts.'

Dumah grunted, waving his hand dismissively.

'What do you propose, Barachiel?'

'We limit each battle-brother to a stringent infusion of blood in their daily wine or food ration. I will expand initial exsanguination to include all viable non-essential crew under the guise of gene-purity testing, allowing time for blood to replenish between contributions. That will minimise *exsanguinem ad mortem* until between the eighth and tenth week, with a proportionate reduction in the mortality rate amongst essential crew. Overall detriment to our combat effectiveness will be minimal.'

Tanthius nodded slowly.

'That plan assumes that our brothers suffer the Thirst to the same degree,' Dumah interjected. 'They do not, and it presents significant risk to their mental and spiritual sanctity if they are consistently plagued by it. Such privation could result in a higher mortality rate among the menials than if we simply abided by the plan already put forth.'

'Brother, consider possibilities that exist beyond the simple and linear. If we are becalmed during the crossing, or delayed at any point in the voyage, the mortality rate will increase to totality if we have not carefully managed our resources. What service could a stranded vessel filled with mentally and spiritually pure warriors offer the Emperor?'

'Barachiel,' Tanthius growled in warning.

The Apothecary opted for a different approach.

'Forgive me, brothers,' he sighed. 'It is a bitter blow that we are removed from Lord Dante's crusade as it gathers pace. I share your disappointment, as will our brothers.' He turned to Dumah. 'I mean no insult, my friend, I truly do not. I am merely surprised by your seeming lack of desire to reach Cretacia. Of all the warriors aboard the *Justice*, I would have thought you would be most appreciative of its historical resonance and spiritual significance.'

Dumah's eyes narrowed. 'I am appreciative of both.' His monotone made a lie of the statement.

'Then why contest my proposal? It is the wiser course of action, as privation and hardship will stoke the wrath that is our Chapter's greatest weapon, allowing us to remain a combat-effective strike force while ensuring a ready supply of blood remains at hand.'

Barachiel saw Dumah begin to speak, before Tanthius overrode him.

'We do not have time for further debate.' His tone brooked no disagreement. 'You are the chief medicae officer aboard this cruiser, Barachiel. I will allow your recommendation, for the moment. However, should our brothers suffer as Dumah suggests, the original plan will be implemented with immediate effect.' He looked them both over. 'Am I understood?'

'Yes, captain,' they chimed in unison.

'Good. Now, let us greet Seth's emissary, and begin our voyage.'

THREE

Seth had sent a Dreadnought as his emissary.

Its venerable pilot, a Firstborn bearing the name Daeron on the scrollwork of his relic sarcophagus, had eschewed the company of his living brothers since their departure five days ago. He preferred the black oblivion of stasis-sleep in the Halls of the Honoured Dead, one amongst their ranks, the empty iron sarcophagi, and the carcasses of the war machines they were crafted for. Dumah found it difficult to blame him.

Interment within a Dreadnought's sarcophagus was a great honour, but also a costly one. Even the mightiest hero could succumb to insanity during the rituals required. Those who survived would endure a half-life that drained their sense of self and awareness of the world around them, until the past and present were merged as one, and they refought battles long concluded. Their suffering and absence from the daily affairs of the Chapter distanced them from its living warriors. Entire generations could pass between awakenings. They were a brotherhood apart, no different to the Chaplaincy, whose human faces were so often hidden behind the Emperor's leering death mask that they were too easy to conflate.

Dumah shuddered. Death was preferable.

He turned his mind from the absent war machine to the Fourth Company reciting their morning prayers. His brothers knelt on the polished granite of the nave, their unarmoured forms shrouded in black robes and lit by flickering flambeaux and the soft glow of lumens in the carved menhirs that framed the congregational space. Arranged by squad and rank, with senior officers and specialists forming the front row and sergeants delineating the central aisle, the Flesh Tearers raised their voices in praise of the Emperor and Sanguinius.

Their song echoed in transept and apse, the snarling edges of basso profundo registers unsullied by the delicate voices of choral serfs. It resonated on the chapel's curved walls, in the cupola of its domed ceiling. Wondrous stained-glass windows decorated the cupola like jewels on a prince's crown, depicting Sanguinius at every stage of his life, from the Baalite foundling that led his people against the mutants of his rad-ravaged home world, to the noble warrior-prince of the Imperium, soon to sacrifice his life to purchase his father's victory. The purity of the conjunction between lyric and artwork lifted Dumah's troubled soul.

This was his father's strength at its most potent and pure.

It was the closest to the primarch that he could ever be.

He raised an armoured hand from the lectern, a silent order for pairs of black-robed Reclusiam serfs to approach the assembled Space Marines. One serf swung a brass censer that trailed wisps of white smoke, the fragrant musk of oil and incense insufficient to mask the rich, salt-iron tang of Adeptus Astartes blood seeded into it. The second carried a bronze ritual dagger that drew thin red creases across the wrist offered by each Flesh Tearer. They caught the spilled blood in the small iron bowls carried in their other hands. Fear haloed the mortals in the sour stench of sweat, curdling the scent of fresh blood.

Dumah's lip curled over his angel's teeth.

When the blood was drawn and collected, the serfs shuffled in a slow procession from the narthex to the pulpit. They each poured their gathered measure into the first of three cast-iron bowls set at the pulpit's base. The divine scent of Sanguinius' holy essence grew more concentrated with every emptied bowl, and Dumah's augmented hearing caught the slightest quiver in his brothers' chant. He ignored it, his own mouth flushed with saliva. He thumbed a button artfully hidden in the lectern's lacquered wood surface.

Two servitors, their chem-bulked forms swathed in voluminous black robes, trudged from their coffin-sockets beneath the deck through a secondary access hatch in the apse. They circled the pulpit, murmuring the litanies of purity carved into their psy-scoured minds, offering him a deep bow at the compulsion of ingrained subroutines. They moved to the iron bowls, removing the lids from the second and third. They left the first, and its collected blood, untouched. Dumah's thirst curdled on the chemical stench that wafted from the second bowl, while the third flooded his neuroglottis with the charred remnants of a dozen distinct aromas. The Flesh Tearers' prayers reached their zenith as the slaves carried out their task.

Dumah raised his hand, and silence descended.

'Flesh Tearers!' Dumah bellowed. 'brothers of my blood! Rejoice, for this day is an auspicious one. We are a company reborn, our blood strengthened by fresh infusions from the reserve companies. Our fallen have been consigned to the sacred flame, their bones ready for interment in the Chapter ossuaries, their vitae blended with the incense we now inhale, that we may grow stronger through our remembrance. But we cannot linger on their memory, for we have a greater purpose.'

He paused, gauging his next move with an orator's practised care. His opening words had captured their attention. They laid the foundation for his sermon, one he hoped would raise his brothers' morale and banish the thoughts of exile that swept the Fourth Company like a plague. Dumah's eyes found Barachiel in the front rank beside Tanthius and his lieutenants, Hanibal and Teman. Annoyance flared in Dumah's breast at the slight upward curl of the Apothecary's lip. He had already guessed the angle Dumah's sermon would take.

He had provided it.

'Once more we bear the Emperor's illumination into the darkness. But this is no mere expedition, my brothers, for this voyage marks a turning point in the fate of our Chapter, and every son of the Great Angel granted the honour of standing here, in this chapel, should offer their most profound thanks to the Emperor and the blessed Sanguinius.'

Dumah allowed his gaze to wander over his battle-brothers.

The low light did nothing to conceal the varied shades of their skin, the gang tattoos, the tribal scarification and penal barcodes indicative of brutal former lives and origins across a score of different worlds. Such distinctions were meaningless. They were all second sons of the Angel, united by heraldry and the holy fury of their father that sang in their blood. The Flesh Tearers were the sons of many worlds, not one alone, and Dumah resented the potential for bias and change that might resurface within the Chapter once they reclaimed Cretacia.

'Before the toll of the twelfth bell, we shall break into the empyrean and begin our voyage to Cretacia. We will reclaim the home of our Chapter. The Blood wills it.'

'The Blood wills it,' the Flesh Tearers intoned.

Dumah read rage, frustration and disappointment in his brothers' micro-expressions, finding them reflected in his own hearts. He wondered briefly whether Sanguinius had ever misled his sons, whether he had engaged in the white lies that were the burden of leadership. He doubted it. The Angel was a numinous being, removed from such distinctly *human* flaws. Dumah cast aside the guilt wrenching his stomach at the lie he was set to peddle. There could be no flaw in his performance, nothing to suggest his own disgust at this exile concealed by lofty ideals.

He could not inspire his brothers if he appeared unconvinced himself.

'My brothers! Do not entertain thoughts of exile and censure. Allow envy and sorrow no purchase upon your hearts. Though we take leave of our brothers among the fleet, and of Lord Dante's crusade, we should rejoice for this grand opportunity. The Fourth Company sails in the shadow of myth, for not since the sundering of the Legion when Nassir Amit, the savage lord, sailed from Baal with the first Flesh Tearers has our Chapter made such a pilgrimage.'

Tension thickened the air. This was the moment.

'Reflect my brothers, upon the magnitude of this honour and who has offered us this opportunity. Master Seth has not sent the Second Company, nor the Third. Not even the veterans of the honoured First. He chose the Fourth Company because he knows that we will not only secure Cretacia but tame her as well. The world Amit once proclaimed our salvation will be made so. The Great Rift will not stop us and, whether we arrive as deliverers or conquerors, we will descend upon that world like angels of myth and remind its people that the Flesh Tearers still hold claim to their allegiance. The Blood wills it!'

'The Blood wills it,' his brothers answered in unison.

Silence settled on the chapel, and the only sound was the distant rumble of the ship's plasma drives. Dumah surveyed his brothers, silent, kneeling, waiting for the service to proceed. He met Tanthius' stare, the soft brown of his organic eye contrasting with the flat, inexpressive stare of a brass augmetic. He had lost the eye on Thracian Secundus, when the impetuous Veteran Sergeant Harox and his squad had broken the Flesh Tearers' line to slay a xenos cult leader. Scars networked his cheeks, another reminder of Harox, and the faint glint of sharp steel pegs grafted in place of natural teeth provided a stark contrast to his coal-dark skin.

'We are honoured by your words, Chaplain,' Tanthius said, rising to his feet. He was taller than Dumah, almost as broad without his power armour as Dumah was with his. He alone could speak without being directly addressed by Dumah. 'Perhaps you will administer the Rite of Battle before we enter the empyrean, and our voyage begins in earnest?'

'Of course, my captain.'

The Chaplain descended the stairs, turning away from the congregation to approach the servitors. They each held one of the larger bowls in rusting industrial claws. The first held the Flesh Tearers' blood, diluted with high doses of potent anticoagulants, curdling the rich scent with an obscene chemical odour. The second held a thicker, darker mixture, its texture almost gelatinous. Dumah recognised the faint scent of foliage and earth, flesh and animal fats mixed with chemically thinned blood drawn from the veins of fallen Flesh Tearers. The servitors had done their job well, and Dumah intoned the Litany of Purity as he prepared to administer the Rite. He approached Tanthius first, as was the captain's due.

Dumah dipped one hand into the viscous liquid of the second bowl, tracing cuneiform runes of strength, protection and steadfastness onto the captain's cheek and throat. His thirst flared as a finger brushed over the enticing pulse of Tanthius' carotid artery. It teased the Chaplain with thoughts of hot vitae pumped by a dying heart.

'May the spirits of the honoured dead grant you wisdom and their blood give strength to your sword arm in the battles to come. May the flesh of the world they fell to conquer gird you against the treachery of the alien, the heretic and the renegade.'

He mirrored the action with the donated blood, careful to ensure there was no cross-contamination in the glyphs or the hand used to mark them. The servitor offered Tanthius a small cup with a measure of vitae. He drained it, his angel's teeth extruding from his gums and small red flickers dancing in the depths of his remaining eye.

'May the blood of our father armour your soul against the weakness of your flesh and the darkness of your blood. May it grant you wrath in battle, that you may defeat the foe and bring honour to the Chapter. May the brothers who share your blood become your shield, and their willingness to shed their blood in your defence never be dimmed.'

'It will be as the Blood wills it, Chaplain Dumah.'

'As the Blood wills it,' Dumah responded.

Dumah moved to face Barachiel. He traced the protective runes onto the Apothecary's flesh, murmuring the same ritual warding as his mind turned to the relics abandoned on Cretacia. That the Crimson Plate was listed among them astonished him, as did the fact that its mere mention made Harahel and Seth so uneasy. Carnarvon's crozius was now interred within the *Justice*'s chapel, and remembering Appollus' bleak jest that the fallen High Chaplain had no further use for it brought the ghost of a smile to his lips. They were his mission, not Cretacia.

He moved to Hanibal and began the rite again.

* * *

Metal scraped against metal as Dumah parried a sharp thrust for his throat. He slammed the weighted haft of his crozius into his opponent's gut, savouring the wrenching snap of broken bone. He pressed his assault with an elbow that sent blood bursting from the warrior's nose and ended the sequence by spearing a punch to the solar plexus. The other warrior staggered, breathless and bleeding, his nose and right cheekbone a swollen, purpling mess.

Dumah broke from the combat, grinning.

'You should learn when you are beaten, Isaiah.'

'Never in this lifetime, Lord Chaplain,' the Assault Intercessor sergeant said, forcing stinging breaths into deep, even patterns through damaged nasal passages. Both combatants were stripped to the waist, skin sheened with sweat, the dull grind of broken bones twinned with the unpleasant itching sensation of them slowly rebonding. 'Certainly not by you.'

Dumah angled his crozius to defence.

'Such vanity. The Angels Encarmine lost a fine recruit in you.'

The assault sergeant growled at Dumah's deliberate glibness, angling his chainsword. Though its teeth were stilled, blood wept from fresh tears in Dumah's side, and one sliced through the burn scar tissue around his eye. Many had long scabbed over, wounds earned in earlier bouts crossing those accrued over five decades of blood and battle.

'I am a Flesh Tearer, lord,' Isaiah said, beginning to circle. He tipped the blade over in tight arcs, blood flecking the sand. Braziers piled high with burning coals circled the small arena, a handful of Flesh Tearers gathered in the tiers above to watch the bout. 'I have been since the Indomitus Crusade liberated Baal, and I will remain so until my dying breath.'

I would not be so certain, Dumah thought. *Not if the future lies on Cretacia. What then will become of the Angel's sons raised up from lesser worlds, like Isaiah and myself, when the Chapter world is restored to us?*

Isaiah drew the saw-toothed combat knife sheathed at his waist.

Dumah mirrored the action and his movements step for step, wrath searing his veins, stinging adrenal joy saturating his every muscle. Exhaustion infused his breaths with a thick coppery musk. His twin hearts beat hard against his sternum, war drums that wore down his carefully cultivated patience. He longed to hurl himself at Isaiah, to forego strategy in favour of brute force and fight as an avatar of the Angel's wrath. He envisioned tackling the assault sergeant to the ground, fracturing his skull with hammer blows of fist and forehead.

Such an impetuous attack would not beat the bearlike Isaiah.

'By his Blood was I made. By his Blood shall I endure,' Dumah hissed, the inexorable call to violence strangling his voice. Thick bands of pain pressed on his skull as he fought the compulsion woven into his blood. He would master his rage, not be subjugated by it.

'The Blood is my strength, and armour.'

Isaiah shot forwards, shoulder raised, chin tucked behind it.

Dumah met him head-on, feet crunching on the hot sand. He slipped under Isaiah's tight decapitation swipe, blocking the underarm thrust of Isaiah's skinning blade with his own knife, hammering his crozius into the sergeant's exposed ribs. Bone cracked. Blood sputtered from his mouth, splashing Dumah's scarred face. The Rage within burned bright, glutting on the hot, stinking vitae. A thunderous punch sent him staggering. The spiked guard of Isaiah's chainsword tore deep grooves into Dumah's cheek, strips of flesh hanging loose.

Isaiah pressed his assault, driving Dumah back with a swift series of ferocious strikes. The Chaplain parried, countering where he could. Isaiah blocked them easily, strikes melding into defensive strokes that evolved into counter-attacks. Hot breath sawed through the enamel grille of Dumah's gritted teeth, sweat dappling the hair that remained to him. He blocked the swift strike aimed to split him from clavicle to pelvis with his crozius' skull-topped head. The sly swipe of Isaiah's knife tore a wet flap of skin free from Dumah's forearm.

Black misted the depths of Isaiah's eyes.

Dumah roared, his own veins stinging with desire to answer the call of his father's blood. He envisioned clutching the sergeant's head in his hands, drinking his blood from the polished skull. The Chaplain hammered his head into Isaiah's forehead. Once. Twice. Thrice. His fourth blow smashed Isaiah's nose to wet gravel. The sergeant staggered after a fifth, the sixth parting his chainsword from his grip. The knife was shattered by a blow from his crozius. Isaiah's guard broken, the Chaplain smashed his weapon into the other Flesh Tearer's ribs, then slashed his blade for his eyes. It missed, carving a deep rent through the pocked cliff of the assault sergeant's forehead. Blood sheeted. Bone flashed white.

Isaiah was not deterred. His voice was a beast's snarl.

'I need no weapon to kill you!'

The assault sergeant roared and threw himself at Dumah, batting aside a heavy blow from his crozius. Dumah heard it shatter his forearm, though Isaiah paid the wound no more attention than a flea bite. The Flesh Tearers beat each other with bone-shattering blows, until Isaiah pivoted under one of Dumah's strikes, driving his foot into the side of his knee. Isaiah tackled him to the ground, and Dumah felt thin cracks web his ribcage. He tasted blood in his mouth, hawked up gobbets of it between broken teeth, infused with acid from his Betcher's gland. He channelled the pain, smashing his fists into Isaiah's ribcage. The assault sergeant continued hammering him with piledriver punches, death blackening his eyes further.

'Cease!' a voice demanded, Dumah could not tell whose. Red misted his sight, flashes of black armour and green fire accompanied by the smell of sulphur and hydraklorik acids. His hearts laboured; his lungs felt like wet sacks of river silt. 'The bout is won.'

Isaiah, breathless and bleeding, stood, then staggered to one side. Two warriors from his squad caught him before he fell. Another two hefted Dumah from the sand, carrying both combatants to the small medicae facility in the darkest corner of the chamber. Medicae-serfs and Barachiel's apprentice, Thuriel, awaited them. They bound their wounds, applied synth-flesh to flayed limbs and fused broken bones. The Flesh Tearers grimaced and grunted, the wrath spicing their blood subsided for the moment.

'You fought well,' Isaiah said, wiping blood from his eyes as one of the medicae-serfs stapled the flesh of his forehead together. 'As well as you spoke yesterday.'

Dumah snarled, the soporifics barely dulling his pain.

'Do not play to my vanity, brother.'

Isaiah snorted wetly.

'I was not. Many of our brothers were enthused by it, their fears allayed.'

The assault sergeant batted away the serf that sought to set his nose. He performed the deed himself, glowering at the serf that plunged a needle into his neck. The serf depressed the plunger, clear liquid evacuating into the Flesh Tearer's bloodstream. Dumah smelled the fear in the serfs' sweat, heard it in their heartbeats' roar. It spiced the blood. Dumah's throat itched with longing, despite the hot, fouling scent of welded bone and medicae narcotics.

'I performed the duty of my office, nothing more.'

For a moment, there was only the patter of human feet and their low whispers.

'You do not believe your own words, then?'

Dumah lapsed into silence, listening to the clash of blades outside.

FOUR

Barachiel stood over another brother wounded in training. Angelo lay on the surgical slab, rendered somnolent by high-dose sedatives, his armour carefully removed.

Clad in surgical robes, Barachiel watched the sergeant's life signs on the wall-mounted pict screens. They strayed dangerously close to non-existence, inducing panic in mortal technicians when the alarm bells blared null-sounds. Plastek tubing fed Angelo infusions of stimulants and synthetic chemicals, complementing those secreted in the Belisarian Furnace. Cawl's ingenuity had kept Angelo alive from the training halls to the apothecarion. Barachiel trusted it to continue doing so as he selected his scalpel and the chirurgeon peeled the black carapace from the sergeant's hiking chest.

It beggared belief they had only been in the warp three days.

Thuriel stood opposite him, likewise stripped of armour and clad in surgical attire. He took a tissue-fuser from the sterile tray beside him, setting to work on repairing Angelo's left calf muscle. It was a battered, blackened ruin of knotted cords and shredded meat, the flesh scorched and stripped from the limb. It was thick with small-calibre bullets and shrapnel, dark vitae spilling onto the surgical slab. An augmetic replacement had been requisitioned from the Technicarum, although Thuriel insisted he could save the leg.

Barachiel was willing to let him try, if only to teach him a lesson in listening.

The Apothecary made a long incision from Angelo's throat to his groin, peeling back the upper layer of flesh and the subcutaneous layer beneath from his torso. The thick cords of his enhanced musculature glistened wetly, protecting his fused thoracic shield from the apothecarion's hot air. Plastek tubes sucked away the excess blood that welled from his skinless chest into a purification drum, where it was cleansed of impurities and fed back into his body. A squirt of aerosolised counterseptic settled on the muscles before he started cutting through them. A pair of medicae-thralls came forwards with sterile clamps to secure them when he was done. Blood stained their overalls, their hearts thudding a nervous rhythm.

A thought-impulse triggered a whirring saw to descend from the overhead chirurgeon, the sharp grind of metal parting bone cutting through the subdued chatter of medicae-thralls tying off open veins, tending flesh wounds or extracting embedded shrapnel. Thrall-apprenta read his bio-signs from the wall-monitors. Aesha stood to his right, her nose wrinkling at the hot-bone smell that slipped beneath her surgical mask. The saw retracted, its work done, and a suction cup descended from the chirurgeon. It latched onto the bone and lifted it free.

Barachiel surveyed the ruin of Angelo's internal organs and cursed.

Fragments of the bone-shield stuck to the pulsing, quivering organs. Hot, sticky blood glued the shards in place. Angelo breathed through lungs that slowly filled with blood. Vitae leaked from small tears and jagged slices in the smooth muscles of his stomach, his intestines and bronchi, and the cardiac muscle walls, or through them. The hot scent nipped at his thirst, imploring him to feast. Angelo's preomnor was impaled by thick spines of shrapnel and his Larraman's organ had been pierced by a copper-jacketed bullet from a servitor's autogun.

'Fool,' Barachiel muttered, turning to Aesha. She looked to him, careful to keep one eye trained on the blood she suctioned clear from the Larraman's organ. 'Adjutant, make note that the sergeant is to only be discharged to resume full duties at my discretion.'

'Yes, Apothecary.'

'You cannot think that Angelo will attempt to immediately clear himself for duty and training,' Thuriel said, genuinely surprised. 'He is wounded almost unto death.'

Barachiel snorted, amused by the initiate's naïveté. He extracted the bullet lodged in the Larraman's organ with exaggerated care, whilst one of Cawl's medicae drained the blood from his lungs with a thin chest tube. It was the smallest repair among the litany that awaited him, and its enhanced clotting factor would be useful when repairing Angelo's other injuries. Aesha suctioned the blood as he applied the hot kiss of a tissue-fuser to the small, vital muscle. The smoky scent of molten flesh clogged his nostrils.

'You underestimate the sergeant's stubbornness,' Barachiel said slowly, withdrawing the tissue-fuser after several minutes. A thrall-apprenta applied a spray of counterseptic to the repaired organ, curlicues of grey steam rising from the scorched muscle. 'Or overestimate his intelligence,' he added with a wry grin, turning his attention to the preomnor. He counted a total of thirteen shards of dark metal. 'Our brother's enjoyment of the *extremis letalis* regimen is fierce and well-known. He will not stay far from training for long.'

Thuriel grunted. Barachiel resisted the urge to deride him.

The initiate had supported the lethal training regimens introduced to the Primaris Marines by Seth and his surviving Firstborn, initially. They had merits, that was a truth Barachiel could not deny. They honed the Flesh Tearers the way a whetstone did a fine blade, offering better preparation than the shadow-sparring and honour duels, blood games and live-fire drills practised by the other Chapters. They were a necessity, an unavoidable result of the terrible reality that gripped the Imperium. It needed fine blades and savage weapons to defend it.

What he struggled to understand was the zeal with which his brothers had committed themselves to the regimens. He disliked what it had roused in their hearts, the heightening of their natural aggression, their thirst for carnage and slaughter. He had felt its stirrings himself in the bleakest days of the Indomitus Crusade, a black mist that threaded thin bands across his sight, a dark cousin of the Thirst that had risen within him since his first full awakening as a son of Sanguinius. It had unsettled him then, as it unsettled him now to see his brothers cast aside even the veneer of discipline in favour of savagery. It had meant spending much time in the last seven years repairing injuries caused by his brothers' wrathful recklessness.

'Blood of the Angel,' Thuriel cursed, surrendering his vain attempt to save the leg. He lifted a bone saw from the sterile tray held by a medicae-servitor, pressing the activation stud.

Barachiel squashed the urge to roll his eyes, his attention on withdrawing the first shard from Angelo's preomnor.

'Angelo can suffer through the augmetic adaptation process,' said Thuriel. 'It will keep him away from the training halls, and our knives, for at least a few days.'

'I doubt Angelo has the patience to commit to any true rehabilitation,' Barachiel said, his voice softened by the bleakness of the jest. Angelo had little time for anything beyond the battlefield and the fighting arenas. He withdrew a thick triangular shard. It reminded him of a tooth of the *carcharodon carcharias* of Old Earth, a seaborne predator he had seen in illuminated holo-texts in Cawl's libraria. 'Curious, considering he commands a Reiver squad.'

Thuriel fixed the senior Apothecary with a questioning look, offence and mirth warring for dominance. He had served among the Reivers before his talents had brought him to the Apothecarion. Until his elevation to Apothecary, he would continue to serve with them. Sergeant Thanatos was a far more temperate leader than Angelo, and valued the junior medicae's attachment to his squad, where Angelo had mocked the idea outright.

'If he disregards his convalescence or the adaptation period, I will remove the bionic, cauterise the stump and send him to Dumah. He can watch from aboard ship or crew one of the gunships when we next bring the Angel's wrath to the enemy. That will teach him mindfulness,' Thuriel muttered darkly, the saw's steel blade grinding through bone. Osseous dust and blood misted from the cut, the thrall nearest to Thuriel wiping it from his eyes.

Barachiel grunted in agreement, using his steel forceps to remove another triangular piece of shrapnel from Angelo's second stomach. Aesha suctioned the blood clear while he brought the tissue-fuser to bear, sealing the wound with thin wisps of grey smoke and the gut-roiling stench of cooked flesh. He clamped them around a fourth piece, a needle-thin shard the length of Barachiel's hand, gently removing it. His eyes caught the trickle of blood from a puncture in the oolitic kidney. A female thrall-apprenta dabbed the sweat from his forehead whilst two of the senior medicae-thralls began work to repair the damaged organ.

'Do you believe Cretacia instilled this savagery in our Firstborn brothers?' Thuriel asked, depositing Angelo's severed leg into a large, empty tray. A medicae-servitor stumped over to bear it away for incineration. 'I have done little reading on the Chapter's home world and bear little recollection of my own.' The Necromundan gang-tattoo pulled tight beneath his eye. 'Its culture bears little tolerance for half measures and notions of morality. Both are considered irritants and distractions, weaknesses inimical to the survival of the self and of the clan. Its children are taught to kill from the moment they can stand.'

Barachiel blinked, momentarily wrong-footed.

'That much is also true of Baal or Naraka,' he said, gathering his thoughts as he removed another shard. It vexed him that he alone seemed interested in reaching the home world. Even Seth's envoy expressed little interest, and he was Cretacian by birth. 'Their children learn to forage and kill as soon as they are able, so that ineptitude or weakness of the individual does not harm the well-being of the collective. Yet those who ascend as Blood Angels and Angels of Light rise above the savage to become warriors worthy of Sanguinius.'

Barachiel turned away and busied himself with the surgery, tying off spurting veins and removing shrapnel from damaged organs. Where the damage was most severe, he cut the organs from their moorings, replacing them with cybernetic facsimiles to restore the full suite of the Emperor's gifts. Blood spattered his plastek surgical robes, and he cuffed the sweat from his forehead, the thrall assigned the duty too slow to react.

'For every Chapter that rises above it,' Thuriel said, carefully fusing artificial nerves to natural ones, 'another lowers itself to superstition and mysticism. Look to the Flesh Eaters and

Crimson Blades, or the Mortifactors of Guilliman's gene-line. They are savages given status unbefitting, their once-noble traditions infected by the fallacies of their home worlds.'

Barachiel signalled for a senior medicae to take lead.

He turned his full attention to Thuriel, still at work on Angelo's leg.

'It would make sense,' Thuriel continued. 'The sons of Cretacia channel the wrath of Sanguinius far easier than most because their world teaches them from first breath that to be wrathful and merciless is a virtue. Nassir Amit preached as much in the memoriam texts that Appollus holds so precious, and our brothers now emulate them, believing it the only way to live up to the name Flesh Tearer, and honour the savage lord who first bore it.'

The wet gurgles of surgical nozzles and the rhythmic beep of Angelo's biocodes were the only sounds for several long seconds. Barachiel met his initiate's eye, working to quash the anger that tightened his jaw muscles and set his blood aflame. Defiance lit Thuriel's gaze, even when fury made itself a lingering threat in the Apothecary's voice.

'You believe that our Chapter is thus?' He welded scorn to his fury, acutely aware of the thralls that bore witness to their masters' discord. 'Is that it, brother? You believe that our warriors are being changed by a world they have not yet set foot on? A world that is a mere name to many of them?'

Thuriel sneered. 'You see my point, whether you can admit it or not.'

Barachiel waited until Thuriel had returned his attention to the nerve-bonding process before reverting his own attention to the slab. Thuriel's point was annoyingly valid, chiming with Dumah's statement before they even set sail. His brothers had changed since the first days of the Indomitus Crusade. They were more wrathful and less reasoned, and their thirst for blood had risen in tandem.

These changes had increased tenfold since Guilliman brought them to Baal, bidding them exchange the sanguine red and winged droplet for the clotted crimson and the serrated saw blade, with no sign of easing. He thought of the mortals on eleven-aleph, strung out and strapped into the exsanguination devices to be bled like cattle, their lives sacrificed so that the Flesh Tearers could control the darkness that daily tore at their souls, weaponise it to preserve and protect the Imperium and its countless trillions.

It sickened him that it had always been thus.

'Cretacia will yield the answers to your questions,' he said quietly, as much to himself as to Thuriel. Something from Dumah's pre-warp sermon clicked in his mind. *The world Amit once proclaimed our salvation will be made so.* His mind churned with possibilities, and the sudden desire to visit the librarium. 'And may yet be the Flesh Tearers' salvation.'

Angelo's reconstructive surgery took another twelve hours.

'What do you mean you "cannot locate the texts"?'

The librarium serf quailed. A hunched and wrinkled thing, he was fussy in the way that scholars often were. Skin hung slack in wattles at his neck and jawline, and the scent of sweat was strong on his skin. The bones of his arms, shoulders and skull were all cleanly defined beneath the parchment-thin flesh. The echoes of juvenat treatments were visible in his wasted frame, for those who knew the signs. Barachiel knew them all.

He towered over the serf, clad in his full regalia as the Apothecary of the Fourth Company. He came armed, his chainsword mag-locked to his thigh and his Absolvor bolt pistol holstered at his waist. He disliked wearing the holster, its leather taken from the flagellated backs of two score Terran pilgrims. It was meant as a gift, a token of thanks from a crusade lord, and a touchstone to aid his remembrance of his former, forgotten birth world.

It repulsed him.

'My lord.' The serf bowed as much as the rheumatism in his back and shoulders allowed. He gasped in pain each time he slowly forced himself to straighten. Barachiel wondered how many times he could bow before the muscles seized. Not too many more, he fancied. 'The librarium has received a number of physical volumes and info-cores from the data-vaults of Lord Dante, from the *Victus* and from the Indomitus Crusade. We are still sorting–'

'Spare me your excuses,' he said, frustration boiling into his voice. 'I care nothing for them. I sent my adjutant here five days ago to inform you of my desire while I attended to the duties of my office.' He could not bring himself to speak of the exsanguination. 'I have seen the holo-picts from her mnemonic implants and assurances were given that the texts I required would be ready in time for my arrival. Now that statement is reneged.'

The serf wrung his hands like a war widow.

'A thousand pardons, great lord.' The thrall bowed again as Barachiel felt pity spike his irritation. 'The attendant who dealt with your adjutant was injured in an altercation two days ago and has been confined to a secondary medicae facility. Your request was passed to me only yesterday, and I cannot locate the texts he had sourced for you, nor can I speak with him to determine where he may have stored them in preparation.'

'Are you lying to me, serf?' Barachiel voiced the query without feeling, but he doubted the words as he spoke them. There was no baseline deviation in the serf's voice, nor between his words and behaviour. But he had to be certain. 'I can consult the medicae records to prove whether your word is good. Should it not be, it will be your last and greatest error.'

The man whimpered.

'Brother.' A hooded figure detached itself from the shadow of a bookcase. His Phobos armour was shrouded in cameleoline that shimmered as it sought to bend light and make him unnoticed. Motes of psychic power flickered in his eyes. 'Why do you intimidate my servants without good reason? What offence have they given?'

'Librarian.' Barachiel inclined his head to Paschar, noting the Codicier's rank badge above the warrior's primary heart. 'Well met, brother. I did not see you there, skulking in the shadows. For what reason would you wish to conceal yourself from me?'

Paschar shrugged.

'I did not wish to be seen. I value my privacy, the opportunity for quiet away from the fighting pits and the theatres of war. Now, what offence did my serf cause?'

Anger prickled Barachiel's mind. Paschar was a Librarian, an officer of the company, made junior by the hierarchy of respect unique to the Sanguinary Brotherhood. He quashed his rage beneath will's iron boot. It would serve no purpose for him to be wrathful.

'Himself, none.' Barachiel mimicked Paschar's nonchalant shrug. 'I have requested a number of texts concerning the Chapter's early history, and the conquest of Cretacia. There were assurances given that have now been broken.'

'The serf speaks the truth, as you well know.' The Librarian's knowing smirk told the Apothecary that he had heard everything. Anger tightened Barachiel's fingers into fists. 'I will personally source the texts you require. In the meantime, I suggest you come with me, brother. We are to exit the warp soon, and Tanthius will need us on the bridge.'

FIVE

The *Cretacian Justice* tore through a whirlpool of wretched light.

Coiling etheric energies haloed its adamantium hull, stretching it far beyond any true consideration of artifice or natural dimensions. Crooked tendrils lashed at its Geller field, the protective bubble of realspace that denied the warp its banquet of souls. Convulsions wracked bulkheads and decks across the storm-battered strike cruiser as it pulled itself free, tremulous groans of strained metal teasing slow, agonising oblivion in the thrashing immaterial madness of the empyrean if the hull should fail.

Dumah watched flocks of cyber-cherubs and servo-skulls flit across the bridge, pain pulling tight in his neck. His wounds from Isaiah were yet to fully heal, the synth-skin grafts still pale and puckered where they bonded to his natural flesh. Implanted vox-casters spilled the transitional choir's funereal chant into the crew pits like promethium on water. Serfs in ash-coloured tunics joined their voices to the chant, the faint blue data-screens lending an ethereal glow to their pallid flesh. Many had not left their stations in days, snaking tubes of bio-fluids and stimulants nourishing their starved bodies and removing their waste.

The High Gothic plainsong died away as the plasma drives powered the strike cruiser clear of the breach. The tremors weakened to dull rattles, the final echoes of their voyage in the empyrean subsiding into the natural ship-quakes caused by sub-light propulsion. Dumah allowed the strangled whispers of the command serfs to wash over him, punctuated by the sharp clack of haptic controls and the patter of supervisors' boots as they scurried through the monastic expanse of the bridge like frightened vermin seeking shelter.

Dumah stood to the left of the command throne, where Tanthius sat and scanned an incomplete holochart of the local system. Augur chimes echoed in the high arches and gothic rafters of the vaulted ceiling; another yellow icon added to the fuzzy green holochart with each echoing ping. Paschar and Barachiel were at Tanthius' right, each wearing full battleplate, the crimson and black contrasting starkly with the white and blue. Paschar's lighter Phobos-pattern armour was shrouded in refractive cameleoline robes, his force sword and heavy bolt pistol sheathed at his waist.

'Distance to the Mandeville point?' Tanthius asked.

'Five hundred million miles, Lord Tanthius,' the Master Augurium said, his voice a metallic rasp. Calculations screeded across his augmetic eyes. 'At the present rate of deceleration, it will take two Terran days at full propulsion to cross the system and reach the next Mandeville point. From there, it is two days sailing to the Rift. Polaris Station will serve as our halfway marker in crossing this system.'

Tanthius nodded.

'We are on schedule, Captain Tanthius.' Shipmistress Kara Étain stood on the step beneath the dais. A scarred Navy veteran, she still wore her Battlefleet Obscurus uniform, its creases sharply pressed, medals glinting under the banks of crimson lumens. Over the years she'd fought in the Flesh Tearers' reconstituted fleet, she had proven impetuous, outspoken and tough.

Dumah approved.

'My liege, shipmistress,' the Master Augurium called out. A vox-mitter thinned his voice to a nasal whine. 'Auspex has detected active reactor signatures consistent with multiple escort- and cruiser-class vessels operating near Polaris. There are several wrecks in the void, and numerous thermal blooms consistent with active lance and plasma weaponry.'

'Imperial?' Tanthius barked.

'Aye, lord. All vessels are broadcasting current Imperial signum-chains. Our archival records detail their assignments to the station's defence squadron, or local Navy patrols. The largest vessel is the modified Luna-class cruiser the *Herald of Virtue*.'

'Incoming hails?' Dumah asked, turning to the Mistress of Vox. Pain speared his left leg and his ribcage, the welded bones there still healing from his bout with Isaiah. He bit back the snarl from his voice as the mistress, a cybernetic construct of clicking calliper-like limbs, auditory receptors and neural interfaces, turned her ocular implants on him.

'No contact from any vessel, or the station itself, Lord Chaplain.'

'We may be beyond their scanning range,' the Master Augurium offered. 'If Polaris or the fleets have sustained damage to their auspex arrays or vox-towers, they may not be able to detect us, much less successfully establish communications.'

'We would have at least heard from the station, fool,' Étain said, before turning to face the Space Marines. Hunger burned in her eyes. 'My lords, I recommend we assume hostile or piratical intent for all vessels and Polaris and prepare for battle.'

The Space Marines looked to each other.

'You would deem this paltry handful a threat to us, shipmistress?' Dumah laughed. He enjoyed the frustration in her eyes. 'We are sons of the Great Angel, his wrath wrought in flesh and bone, sheathed in holy ceramite. We are more than a match for mere brigands.'

She flashed a wicked smile.

'To you, my Lord Chaplain, no threat at all.' She paused, her hands taking in the vast expanse of the vessel through the oculus, then moved it to her crew. 'To this cruiser, they may present a very real threat if they hold the station and its weapons are active.'

Dumah's respect for her grew yet another fraction. Humans with the tenacity to speak on equal terms to a Space Marine were exceedingly rare. Most simpered before the Angels of Death, intimidated by their raw power and presence. Étain had no such weakness. She had rapidly proved herself every bit as tenacious and fearless as Sanguinius' second sons, a Flesh Tearer in her heart if not in her body and blood. There was no higher compliment.

'Gunner?' Tanthius turned to the Master of Armaments for confirmation.

'The shipmistress' appraisal is correct, liege.' The gunnery officer was augmented almost to the level of the vox-mistress. What little flesh he possessed was heavily scarred and marked with penal tattoos. 'The orbital's weapon systems will crack this vessel's shields with sustained fire. Supported by a small fleet, they could annihilate us.'

'Brother Paschar.' Tanthius turned to the Librarian. 'What do you sense?'

The Librarian took three steps away from the throne, to stand at the very edge of the dais. He clasped his hands behind his back and closed his eyes, exhaling a long, heavy breath. Dumah stood behind him, his crozius drawn and held at the ready. Should the Librarian show corruption by the malign powers or alien witchery, it was his duty to slay the psyker.

Hoar frost rimed Paschar's armour. An unnatural cold misted the air around him. The dry snap of breaking ice cut through the low chatter of the bridge. The Librarian mumbled litanies of warding and protection, forked lightning streaming from his storm-blue eyes like electric tears. Dumah's stomach turned at the complex un-sound that fell from the Librarian's lips. Paschar grimaced, a grim, bestial thing. Blood dripped from his nose and eyes.

'Xenos,' Paschar said, his voice hoarse. 'The shadow of the hive mind falls across many of the vessels that circle Polaris.'

'Tyranids are aboard those vessels?' Tanthius' voice bled eagerness.

'Their collaborators, my captain,' Paschar said, slowly brushing the hoar frost from his gorget and cuirass. 'There are powerful psykers aboard the cruiser bearing the imprint of the hive mind. The station itself is shielded from my sight – its hexagrammic wards curtail any attempt at psychic probing or other empyreal intrusion.'

Silence endured for several seconds.

'Then we cannot count on it for support,' Tanthius said, then took a deep breath. 'It makes little difference. We did not choose this route because we knew it would be safe, or easy. We chose it because it would see us to our destination with the greatest possible speed, and not ferry us through a thousand warzones across Imperium Nihilus.'

'Is there no alternate route?' Barachiel asked, and Dumah was genuinely surprised to hear the caution bleeding into his tone. The Apothecary was the most fervent in supporting the swift return to Cretacia. Though he had objected to their route before, to hear doubt creeping into his voice at this juncture was a subtle reminder of the horrors they may yet face during the crossing. 'A more stable route to the true Imperium, free of xenos predation?'

'There is no route that does not require months of additional sailing,' Tanthius said slowly, staring into the void. 'We cannot allow this revolt to take a proper hold. Polaris may become an important resupply and docking station for merchant and military craft in the coming decades. It would be an ideal means for the xenos to spread their infection throughout Imperium Nihilus, and perhaps even back to the true Imperium.' He gestured to the wrecks twisting in the void. 'These vessels failed to contain it. It is now our responsibility.'

Dumah nodded, biting back a wince.

'I agree with our brother,' he said. 'These xenos have suffered many defeats these last months and seek to spread their corruption elsewhere. I propose immediate boarding assaults on the *Herald of Virtue* and Polaris. We cut off the cult's head, sever its limbs and deprive its heart's desire, then depart to let the humans finish off whatever remains.'

Paschar shook his head, his expression twisted by pain.

'I disagree,' the Librarian groaned, strength ebbing back into his voice. 'Our mission is to cross the Great Rift and discover Cretacia's fate. We cannot become embroiled in undue conflict that could potentially damage or destroy our vessel mere hours before we attempt the crossing. It would be foolish in the extreme to place such a risk on ourselves.'

'It is hardly undue, Codicier,' Dumah snapped.

'I agree with Paschar,' Barachiel said. 'We cannot afford damage or delay.'

'Nor can we afford to leave a potent threat behind us,' Dumah argued. 'As you stated, Barachiel, the slaves of the hive mind seek control over this orbital to infect any warships or rogue trader vessels that may pass through the conduit. We are Flesh Tearers, and we cannot allow this nest of xenos filth to endure when we are honour bound to eradicate it.'

'We should signal Lord Dante, or Lord Seth,' Barachiel suggested. 'Then we should run the gauntlet.'

'Signal Lord Seth?' Tanthius said, anger stolen by shock.

Dumah laughed and Paschar shifted uncomfortably.

'Do you seek their mockery, brother?' he said, switching to the tribal dialects of Baal Secundus they had learned as Unnumbered Sons. Barachiel had been his foremost tutor in the guttural languages. 'If so, then we should indeed run the gauntlet straight into the Rift, allow the enemy to infest this region like a cancer. But consider, is this not the perfect opportunity to expand our stocks of vitae? Would that not aid our mission?'

He grinned at the Apothecary's frustration.

'Their genetic base-code may be human,' Barachiel countered, snarling. 'But xenos taint rides within their blood, making it unsuitable for satisfying the Thirst. Would you stock our holds with tainted vitae, brother, just to satiate your battle-lust?'

'You have prattled on about duty to exhausting length before, Apothecary,' Dumah growled, wrath stinging in his veins. 'Is it not our duty to exterminate xenos where they lurk, to shield innocent souls from their vile predations?'

Barachiel said nothing, glaring at Dumah.

'The decision is made, brothers,' Tanthius said, cutting through the argument. He adjusted the holochart with quick movements of his hand. It narrowed to the void around Polaris Station. 'Shipmistress, position our escorts at maximum range, to provide support whilst you penetrate and then harass the picket line.' Étain grinned savagely. 'Paschar will scan each vessel to determine their allegiance until we launch our assault on Polaris and the *Herald of Virtue*. The Flesh Tearers will not flee from this fight.'

Dumah grinned and departed the bridge, to prepare himself for battle.

The Flesh Tearers were not alone in thoughts of the pending bloodshed.

Within the shadow it cast across the warp, an intellect vast beyond human imagination brooded. It was a frugal creature, its endless hunger governed by the arithmetic of deficit and surplus. The prey in red had left it with a significant deficit. It had expended billions of weapon-beasts upon their toxic, dry worlds, only to be defeated by them and their multihued kin. In a human, or any lesser creature, such thoughts would have been considered peevish.

The hive mind was not a lesser creature.

Among the trillion trillion facets of one of its sub-minds, it sensed motes of awareness that promised the red-prey's kin clad in crimson. The shadow twitched, seeding new psychic darkness over a dozen worlds. It considered the crimson-clad as responsible as the red, their brutish wrath accounting for a significant portion of its deficit. It coveted their fury, and the promise of new weapon-forms it heralded, but their part in its deficit was a slight it needed to see repaid.

The hive mind focused the smallest percentile of its intellect onto the relevant bodies. They were mongrel agglomerations of its gene-code and the prey's, a vile but necessary compromise to see its hunger sated. If it had emotions, it might have loathed the stunted caress of their minds, so impossibly different to the purity and singular focus of its own collective consciousness. It might have shuddered at their touch, or recoiled in disgust.

It did not.

Three facets stood out as its champions, its hopes of vengeance.

The first was the truest part of the hive mind. It flexed motes of empyreal power between fingers tipped by void-black talons. It watched its flock move between workstations, training weapons onto the crimson cruiser that powered ever closer. How it resented their weakness, their limited function in the plan of the great Star Children. They were unworthy of its prophetic message.

Protected by robed guardians with twin blades of venomous jade, the second facet tinkered with its technical apparatus. It relished the coming of the crimson prey, the chance to convert the warrior strain of this most vexing prey species. It looked upon the hailer staff of its office, a cruel smile pulling taut its lips. A chance to convert or kill, it reminded itself.

The third was a recluse, a revolutionary tired of adulation. It opened the scuffed iron box that contained its weapons, three six-shot pistols with depleted velonium rounds. It drew a sample of a frothing, murky green liquid from the glass alembic at its side to coat a bullet. The sickly stench of a highly potent bio-toxin filled its nostrils and a cruel smile tugged at its lips. Though the phage was limited, one coated bullet could kill a member of the warrior strain, beings this lesser mind considered as a false god's wrathful angels.

Its board set, the hive mind watched and waited.

The day before their launch passed quickly.

Dumah's cartolith plotted the route that ten Caestus-pattern assault rams cut towards Polaris and the *Herald of Virtue*. The pronged green icons were divided into two arrowheads of five, screened by servitor-manned fighter squadrons, decoy transports and melta torpedoes. Above the cartolith, his chronometer unwound towards zero, solid rounds and las-fire bracketing the heavily armoured prow. Isaiah sat beside him, the veteran warriors of his Assault Intercessor squad sharing their section. The tips of their chainswords were driven into the deck.

'Ready!' Isaiah roared as the counter hit two minutes.

Squad Isaiah braced themselves from within the support harnesses that shielded them from the kinetic forces unleashed by their craft's brutal attack pattern. They checked their weapons, locked in place facing the forward assault ramp. Dumah rechecked and cleared his heavy bolt pistol, his thumb depressing the activation rune on the haft of his crozius. The blood-red light of the compartment curdled on its carved bronze skull, the coruscating arcs of killing light painted a dull pink. It felt good in his hand, but not *right,* as Carnarvon's crozius had.

'Sixty seconds,' the servitor-pilot droned through a vox-grille implanted between the jaws of a skeletal angel. *'Primary weapons system firing.'*

Dumah felt the deck judder as the magna-melta fired, repeated each time it did so despite the ram's inertial compensators minimising its recoil. The mag-locks in his boots automatically increased under the ram's control, scant seconds before it struck the hull. Alert lights flashed and klaxons screeched their monotone wail. The magna-melta fired again and again, the ram boring like a blood-tic through layered adamantine and plasteel alloys to reach the warship's interior. The screech of tortured metal ground against his eardrums, the slam and crash of its forced entry threatening even his enhanced physiology.

'By his Blood are we made,' Dumah murmured. He felt his brothers' eyes clawing his back, felt their eagerness to shed blood spike at the thought of blessed Sanguinius.

He tensed at the sound of the prow frag assault launchers firing into the flaming ruin of whatever chamber the Caestus had come to rest in, savouring the thought of battle to come. He shivered at the hot flush of combat narcotics squirted into his veins, the roar of his brothers' chainswords fading into the thunder of his blood. Dumah's grip tightened on his crozius, the muted coughs of launching grenades fading beneath the groans of torn metal.

'By his Blood are we armoured, and by his Blood shall we triumph.'

'Five seconds.'

'We are wrath! We are fury!' his brothers howled.

'Breach. Breach. Breach,' droned the servitor-pilot. The support harnesses released, and the assault ramps thumped down.

The Chaplain roared and charged, squeezing a flurry of mass-reactive rounds into the clearing smoke. Hooded figures detonated like fleshy grenades, their tainted blood flecking the rusted bulkheads of the *Herald of Virtue*'s starboard promenade deck. His boots crunched on charred meat and splintered bone. Ichorous blood lapped at the ceramite, aggravating his thirst with quiet promises of renewal through the consumption of stolen life. His fangs threatened to burst from his gums, saliva stringing his teeth.

Alien shrieks of hate and pain snapped through the haze.

Bolts kicked from the muzzle of his heavy pistol, lighting the dank corridor with flashes of gold. More barked past his shoulders. Hybrids pitched forward in a tide of scattered limbs and shredded organs. Their xenos kin scrabbled through their hissing remains, mottled flesh resistant to the acidic blood that pocked the bulkheads and deck with smoking craters. Bullets and micro-organisms sparked and splattered on his armour, solid rounds hissing past his helm. Las-fire scorched neat holes in the brass and bone trim of his cuirass and pauldrons.

Then he was amongst them.

A purestrain's claws flashed towards his chest. Dumah dodged too late, its talons leaving deep gouges in his cuirass. Pain sang through violated flesh. Blood dripped from the tears. Its snapping jaws grasped at his helm, its ovipositor thrashing wildly. He hammered his crozius into its skull, grey meat and bone fragments sizzling on its disruptor field. Instinct urged him right, deflecting the suggestion of an ebon-clawed hand before it carved through his side. Brittle bones snapped like dried twigs, his empty hand curling around the hybrid's throat. He crushed its windpipe and hurled it at its kin.

'We seem short on numbers,' Isaiah chuckled. The sergeant dragged his chainsword across an aberrant's stomach, black innards spilling from the wound. He fired his bolt pistol, bolts ploughing into the press of its tainted kin. They disappeared in clouds of aerosolised blood. Limbs fell away. Organs slapped wetly on the deck. The survivors cursed in broken Gothic. 'We are too few to butcher these xenos *and* take the bridge.'

Dumah drew his combat blade, driving it into the head of a hunched acolyte with an autopistol and a dagger of alien metal. Another charged him, frothing oaths to its vile masters. Small-calibre rounds clinked against Dumah's armour, one punching through the ribbing at his neck. He tore its head off. Blood sprayed his visor, its sharp tang taunting his thirst. The Angel's wrath was a white-hot halo that nourished his soul, feeding his muscles with fresh energy. He laughed, bludgeoning two more with his crozius, relishing the dry crunch of bone.

'More blood to spill, more lives to reap.'

One of Isaiah's warriors fell, overwhelmed by a screeching pack of hybrids. None were even remotely human, their purple flesh and dark blue chitin shrouded in heavy robes of cerulean and orange. Blood jetted between his fingers as he clawed at his ruptured throat. His signum rune fizzled grey on Dumah's retinal feed. A purple-skinned beast squatted over him, tearing the progenoid from its nest of fibrous connective tissues with needle-like teeth.

It devoured the organ before Dumah's eyes.

'Die, wretches!' Isaiah snarled, his chainsword beheading the offending beast. He tore the heart from a second acolyte, pulping the vessel with a wet flex of his fingers. He howled something, his words slurred by black wrath, hurling himself into a chittering pack of the xenos abominations. 'For the Emperor!'

Dumah struggled to keep pace with Isaiah, shattering skulls with swift backhands and obliterating bodies with every sweep of his crozius. Isaiah snarled like a beast deprived of its meal. He cursed at the xenos cultists as traitors to the Emperor, vaporised meat jetting from the teeth of his weapon, his free hand slick with gore to the elbow. The Chaplain fought at Isaiah's back, shielding him from cowardly attacks and keeping the path that he carved open, but the sergeant appeared not to notice him, too intent upon the foes he ripped asunder.

Isaiah's second, Kairus, fought his way to Dumah's side.

'What madness has taken the sergeant?' Kairus asked. Blood trickled from wounds earned keeping the sergeant's pace. He dismembered a hooded acolyte with tight sweeps of his chainsword. Mass-reactive bolts sparked from his heavy pistol, obliterating kin-beasts in wet puffs of crimson smoke. 'Have these wretches deployed their damned psykers?'

'Nnnnh… nnnnh… *no*.'

Isaiah's grunt delayed Dumah's reaction by half a heartbeat. Void-black claws raked across his thigh, pain lancing through the muscle and meat. Soporifics squirted into his veins, warm tides that eroded the pain into nothingness. He beheaded the hybrid responsible, slicing a second from clavicle to pelvis. The horde was thinning, entire broods of acolytes and humanoid hybrids now little more than biological detritus staining the deck. Another Flesh Tearer fell, torn apart by a pack of acolytes and purestrains. Eight Intercessors remained.

'The psychic wretch no doubt remains on the bridge, directing the infestation with its strategos and kin-guard.' Dumah growled. 'It will not expose itself until victory is certain.'

'We cannot secure the bridge with only eight warriors,' Kairus said, gunning down a hissing acolyte with a burst of point-blank fire. Another leapt for him and died the same way. 'Where are Toivo and Burloc? Were they not supposed to breach along this corridor?'

'Toivo and Burloc were delayed making entry,' Dumah said, checking his cartolith. Their runes blinked, smaller and fainter than those belonging to him and Isaiah's squad. He tore an acolyte's spine from its back, its head ripping free with it. Scraps of flesh and torn nerves stringed the bone column, its distinctly alien features contorted in a hateful leer. 'Their assault ram took suppressive fire on final approach, forcing them to breach three decks below us. They fight to meet us.'

Dumah emptied his magazine into the slab-muscled chest of a monstrous hybrid with a simian's gait, heaving a square-faced hammer in three bony hands. Dark blood leaked from the craters punched into its flesh. Pain filmed the beast's gaze, its third eye a milky ovoid spread between its head and the twisted polycephalic twin fused to its cheek. He knew the magus, arch-prophet of the cult, could see him through its eyes, a fragment of its formidable will imparted to this creature, as it was to all those that shared its alien gene-code. It sensed their pain, and it felt their deaths. The hybrid dragged the hammer into a heavy overarm strike.

Dumah grinned and charged.

He dodged the first blow, reverberations slithering through his ceramite boots. His knife slashed through the beast's thigh, then along its chest, drawing a guttural growl and a spatter of dark blood. The void-black claws of its second right arm carved into his pauldron, dragging through the flesh of his shoulder. Blood beaded on black ceramite. Dumah slipped beneath the wide arc the hammer described, driving his crozius into the beast's knee.

The joint vanished in an explosion of flesh, blood and bone.

The abominant fell to one knee, casting aside the hammer to swing its claws at his chest and throat. Dumah avoided the swipes, or parried them with his crozius, stripping flesh from bone with every crack of its disruptor field. He caved in the beast's skull when it could no longer lift its arms.

The creature dead, he consulted his cartolith.

'Paschar and Thanatos are one mile ahead.' Dumah breathed heavily, dragging his knife through a wailing hybrid's throat. The muffled thud of a frag grenade tore through a pack and the Flesh Tearers cut their way forwards. 'Set the rendezvous at their position, then we push for the bridge and see our mission done. For the Angel and the Emperor.'

He did not hear Isaiah's confirmation, or the orders voxed to the other squads, instead immersing himself in killing. His crozius' disruptor field blasted meat from bone and limb from body. He relished the hot flush of serotonin that rewarded each rise and fall of his power weapon. Hybrids pressed him from all sides. Bolts reduced them to thick clouds of blood and aerosolised meat. Every death was a herald of what was to come for the magus.

Dumah would bathe in its blood before the day was done.

SIX

'Welcome, crimson-clad children of the False Emperor.'

Barachiel thundered through the corridors and passageways of Polaris, the wretched voice of the xenos predicant clinging to his ears. Its kin had offered little resistance thus far, only scattered packs of neophyte hybrids with lasguns and looted Astra Militarum-issue carapace. They were slaughtered, left for the vermin in halls darkened by unlit electro-sconces and smashed lumen-strips, the absence of light necessitated by their xenos-born sensitivity to it.

It was far from their only mark upon the station.

The Apothecary caught their pheromone stench in the foul tang of the bodily excretions that patched bulkheads with corrosion. Translations of anti-Imperial slogans in seventeen distinct Low Gothic variants, dialectic sub-branches and regional basilects were scraped onto his retinal feed. The cult sigil was artfully woven into gang marks and graffiti alike, two wyrms connected at the small of the back, one eye set in each direction.

Barachiel snarled at the blatant pastiche of the Imperial aquila.

'Illumination stalks your shadows. It waits for you.' The voice was corruption sweetened with honey, a confessor's kindness undercut by a serpent's hiss. He felt compelled to listen, to accept it as immutable truth. *'It longs to embrace you, deluded children of a false god, to grant you freedom and fellowship. You are alone, blinded to the truth by the wrath you hold as a precious gift, so deprived of voice and agency by your slave's yoke.'*

'Silence, xenos,' Barachiel snarled, shaking free of its glamour.

Twenty Flesh Tearers and Techmarine Hariel followed him towards Polaris' primary generatorum, their route guided by memories of the briefing holoschemata instead of auspex and cartolith. Arrowhead burrs of static rendered their inbuilt armour devices useless, a signal corruption generated by the malignant code seeded into the cult's transmissions. Even the vox was no longer reliable, their connections with Tanthius and the *Justice* severed moments after they entered the generatorum district. The cult wanted them cut off. It wanted them alone.

Barachiel grinned. It would be their final mistake.

The Flesh Tearers' thunderous footsteps echoed in the empty corridor, their heavy breaths sawing through sloped vox-grilles. Helm lumens tracked over sealed hatches and gantry railings, every warrior alert to the threat of ambush. One beam fell on a dusty gold sign with doggerel graffiti daubed over High Gothic print. Protective gear warnings were islands of red in the dull steel above the half-opened hatch.

Manufactorum Tertius. The translation scribed itself onto his retinal feed beneath the renditions of the cult's impassioned calls to arms and anti-Imperial dogma. He signalled two Flesh Tearers to open the hatch. They braced against it, their fibre bundles thrumming with the effort needed to force it open. Inch by inch, the door began to give.

'Mind your spacing,' Barachiel said. 'Watch for an ambush.'

Barachiel led the Flesh Tearers inside, weaving through lines carefully described by conveyance belts, ore processors and industrial machines. His Flesh Tearers spread out across the factorum floor, weapons panning, boots crunching on broken glass and thickened shards of plastek. The machinery's dull metal edges peeled flakes of white lacquer from his armour, revealing the gunmetal grey of bare ceramite. Vermin scuttled in dark corners, overshadowed by the hunched forms of the factorum servitors. Rot-blackened flesh and muscle tissue strung their bones, layers of decaying biological effluvia accreted atop rusted cybernetics.

'You believe yourselves angels, righteous deliverers of judgement and saviours of the Imperium's faceless masses,' the voice crooned, its relish unhidden. *'A falsehood your kind shroud yourselves in so you may continue defining yourselves as good. The true saviours walk with the people, teaching the truth to all that deserve it. You are monsters, polluters of mankind's sacred form, slaves to the whims of a deceitful god and a dying empire.'*

'You waste your breath, xenos,' Sergeant Adariel said, squeezing his blade's activation bar. 'We are monsters, aye, but we do not brainwash the unwilling to become parasitic hosts and slave-soldiers, nor do we pray to vile xenos or make pacts with them!'

'Then how do you explain your very being, Flesh Tearer?' It chuckled, a cruel and mellifluous thing. *'I know your kind. The Reborn Emperor whispered to me of blood-hungry savages forged from children given as tribute. He has tasted your dreams and knows the sins that you clutch in the dark chambers of your hearts.'*

'Vile xenos–' Barachiel began.

'Fear not, for they are not mine to tell. They are yours to endure, to seek forgiveness for. But you will never find it, not until your eyes

open to the holy majesty of the true Lord of Man, the Reborn Emperor, and the sacred illumination offered by his blessed avatars.'

'I will rip the lying tongue from your mouth, wretch,' Sergeant Tumelo snarled, his fingers tightening around his plasma incinerator. Desiccated tongues hung from a razor-wire coil twisted around one vambrace. Polished skulls clacked at his waist. 'Can you do nothing to curtail this offensive prattle, Techmarine? It becomes tiresome to hear.'

'The code is imbued with a chimeric nature in defiance of the sacred principles of the Lingua-technis.' Hariel's voice was a mess of soft metallic tics and burrs that drowned out the xenos creature's laughter. 'It imitates our armour's blessed info-emetics and renders them useless. I have isolated several code-strands to assist in crafting more specific purgatives.'

'Nothing can be done?'

'At the present juncture, no.'

'Filthy cowards.' Tumelo slurred the words. The Hellblaster kicked open a door to a small office. The plastek portal snapped off the hinges and he stepped inside. 'They besmirch our honour and the Emperor's name whilst cowering behind a communications signal.'

Barachiel followed Tumelo in. Dust gathered on the cogitator, filing cabinets and desk. A small, circular hololith displayed what he assumed were the foreperson's family picts. Food scraps mouldered on a cracked plate beside a mug of brackish water.

'Cunning should not be mistaken for cowardice.' Barachiel resumed his sweep of the manufactorum, passing beneath torn lumenator cables that swayed like entrails in a breeze. 'The cult only commits to action when it furthers their masters' agenda. They follow no other imperative. Strategy exists in every craven moment and every display of courage. Wisdom is knowing the enemy, death is underestimating them.'

'You quote the Codex, brother,' Tumelo retorted, shouldering aside a rusted factorum servitor. It crashed into a machine-press, the dolorous clang echoing in the cavernous space. 'We are no longer Greyshields, our fate governed by the Butcher's political machinations and his hidebound decrees. We are Flesh Tearers, the Angel's wrath writ in flesh and blood. Any consideration beyond how to best unleash that against our foes is meaningless.'

'Aye,' Sergeant Adariel intervened, his Assault Intercessors forcing open a secondary access hatch to the manufactorum. 'Their wiles will count for little when they finally find the courage to come against us. They will die, for none can escape the Angel's holy wrath.'

'You take Appollus too literally,' Barachiel said. Their fanaticism perturbed him. 'Wrath alone cannot rule our hearts. It must be tempered with wisdom, lest we become impotent caricatures enslaved to our fury, like the traitor World Eaters.'

'Why remain avatars of hatred and wrath when you can be reborn as angels of mercy and light?' It broke its silence, almost supportive in its argument. Barachiel's hearts howled a twin beat of disgust and fury, baying like hounds at the scent of prey. *'Learn to know the Reborn Emperor's love and mercy and become the champions of humanity that you have always claimed to be.'*

'You will learn the true meaning of the Emperor's mercy, wretch,' Adariel promised. 'I will teach it to you myself, when my axe tears the life from your tainted form and I drink deep of your veins. We are His champions, the Great Angel's wrath in its purest form.'

The predicant laughed.

'You cannot defeat his chosen, nor should you desire to. Rejoice at the coming of his children, for they will show his love by remaking us in his image. The Day of Ascension will dawn for all the faithful, while the faithless are left at the mercy of darker powers.'

'I will tear your head from your shoulders,' Barachiel spat, his father's blood striking a crescendo in his veins. His fingers curled around his weapons, the joints whining in protest. 'Then we will see who can be defeated, and who serves the darker powers.'

They exited the manufactorum, striding once more through the benighted corridors pocked by rust and graffiti. The dry scrape of claw against metal shadowed their passage, the quiet patter of bare feet accompanying it. Unease coiled through the muscles in his back and he felt predatory eyes crawl over his armour, assessing him for weaknesses. They continued unmolested, the predicant's voice hissing its true gambit in his ear.

'Foreswear your loyalty to the liar god of Terra and pledge yourselves to the Reborn Emperor. He welcomes all beneath his gaze and asks only that they kneel to him.'

'You will kneel before my axe, filth!' Hariel blared, burning away the corruption with sacred emetics. Their vox cleared, though auspex and cartolith remained compromised. 'We bow to none, save the Great Angel and the Emperor of Mankind!'

Guttural laughter followed the Techmarine's outburst.

'Blessed silence, at last. I never thought I would be glad to have it,' Intercessor Daven said drily.

Daven was the first to fall.

A bullet punched through his gorget, blood spurting from the tear. A second pierced his cuirass, puncturing his primary heart. A second warrior, one of Tumelo's Hellblasters, evaporated in a sun-bright sphere of blue-white fire, his incinerator's containment coils breached by a bullet. A ululating shriek tore through the dark and Barachiel spied the xenos shooter, a hunched, three-armed creature clad in beaten iron plate, a ragged serape and orange enginarium overalls. Its war cry was the first stone in a wall of screeched oaths and gunfire that slammed into the

Flesh Tearers. Cultists emerged firing from behind control panels and sheet-metal barricades, their dark, doll-like eyes aflame with a zealot's mindless hatred.

'For the Star Children!' they cried. 'For the Reborn Emperor!'

The Apothecary squeezed his pistol's trigger, a flurry of mass-reactive rounds ripping a pair of neophyte hybrids apart. Bullets peppered his greaves and plastron, las-fire scorching thumbnail-sized holes in the grimy white ceramite. Barachiel paid them little mind, emptying his magazine into a clutch of screeching cultists in stained enginarium overalls. They burst like over-ripe fruit and Barachiel weaved between the Hellblasters, the eye-watering bursts of their plasma incinerators immolating hybrids in wheezing puffs of irradiated ash.

Barachiel heeded only one guiding imperative: reach Daven.

Daven had wrenched his helm free, wheezing through peeling lips and bleeding gums. His face was a network of weeping blisters and sores. Barachiel plunged a narthecium needle into Daven's neck, his armour's advanced cogitators working to identify the poison that so debilitated his brother. Daven bucked, almost tearing the needle free. Bile spewed through gritted teeth, pink flecks in the froth evidencing dissolving organ tissue. Hair spilt from his scalp in thick clumps, the flesh already waxen and peeling.

The narthecium chimed its findings.

'Depleted velonium shells coated in toxicrene venom,' he snarled, reading the unique biological indicators from his vambrace-mounted screen. Daven's bio-signs were threadbare, his heartbeat and higher neurological functions beginning to fade. He selected the necessary counter-venom from his chemical store and injected it into the warrior's bloodstream.

Daven's convulsions quickened, the pink froth building around his mouth flecking Barachiel's chestplate and gauntlets. Sores swelled and burst across his face, greenish pus oozing down his cheeks and chin. His skin melted like wax, revealing muscles wasted away to blackened twists of hardened matter. His life signs fluctuated, seemingly at random, and the Apothecary rechecked the venom's genetic composition. The code was minutely different to the one his counter-venom was designed to negate. Both were distinctly Leviathan, but the venom showed signs of evolution, and that the genetic composition of the hive mind's creatures had reached a new iteration.

Daven's signum broadcast a tuneless flatline whine.

The Apothecary swallowed his frustration and closed Daven's eyes.

'He that may fight no more, grant him peace.' Barachiel's pack-mounted drill pierced the fallen warrior's throat. The wet wrench of violated flesh was followed by the crunch of his reductor pistol cocking. Plasmic fire glinted on its blessed housing as he put the muzzle on Daven's neck. 'He that is dead, take from him the Chapter's due.'

Barachiel squeezed the trigger, the wet *thunk* of progenoid extraction followed by the crisp *click* of a sealing cryo-canister. He let Daven's corpse slide to the deck, activating his retrieval rune so that when all was done his body and armour might be recovered and honoured. He slapped a fresh magazine into his bolt pistol, his chainsword's teeth churning the empty air, the wrathful call of Sanguinius' blood building in his veins. He craved the hot spatter of blood on his cheek, the faint and feeble resistance of flesh and bone as his blade parted them. He needed to kill, more than anything.

Barachiel hurled himself into the teeth of the enemy fire, ignoring the weak stings of bullet and las. They were nothing, flea bites in the face of the Angel's pure rage. His armour auto-senses swamped his retinal feed with reticules and bio-analytics, each set belonging to a different irritant. He squeezed bolts into a lumbering, three-armed aberrant, shredding it. Two more hybrids died, their heads vanishing in welters of blood and bone. He clubbed a bawling male, splitting its skull like an egg, emptying his magazine into another aberrant's chest.

It was not enough. It would never be enough.

'We are wrath,' Barachiel snarled, tossing a frag grenade into the barricades. Cultists vanished in black clouds of blood and meat. He sprinted past his brothers, breaking their line, and vaulted the barricades, crushing a scampering diminutive beast beneath his boots. 'We are fury!'

His chainsword decapitated a hissing acolyte with its first cut, disgust blooming in him at the pained moans its death elicited from its humanoid kindred. It appalled him that any human, even one compromised by the hive mind, could worship such vile creatures as deities, or the avatars of one. Their mourning whines only fed his rage, streaking his vision with black and red brushstrokes as he cut them down without mercy. They did not deserve to live.

A second hybrid, hunched and mewling in its hessian sack, lashed at Barachiel with a spiked whip of corded muscle, while a third drove him back with vicious swipes of its clawed hands. He parried and dodged each swipe, biting back rage-fuelled gasps when claws tore through his armour. Blood welled, beading on the ripped ceramite. The acolyte struck harder, faster, its animal hunger drawn by the droplets that fell from his plate. The black brushed tighter over Barachiel's vision as he thundered his helm into its bulbous skull. The hybrid staggered, dazed, and Barachiel dragged his blade through its arms and neck, stepping over it.

Sanguinius' wrath sang through him, and it was glorious.

The whip-armed acolyte lashed him again and again, directing its humanoid worshippers with its other, clawless arm. Fear bloomed in its eyes, desperation dripping from its jerky, insistent movements. He cut through any that dared get in his way, dimly aware of Adariel's Intercessors slaughtering their way forwards, hefting the second acolyte from its feet. He dodged reflexively as its vestigial third arm reached over its shoulder to paw weakly at his visor. His hand closed around its throat, and Barachiel relished every moment of fear that bulged its eyes before he pulverised its skull on the bulkhead.

He closed on Daven's killer.

Its exposed skin was almost translucent, the lower half of its face obscured by a strip of cloth, though its ridged forehead and wrinkled nose betrayed its tainted heritage. Smoke curled from its serape and its overalls were torn. The killer weaved between bolts and bursts of ionised plasma, spared death by its preternatural instincts. Bullets sparked from its three six-shot autostubs, shattering another Intercessor's eye-lens. The Flesh Tearer's final breaths bubbled into the vox. Barachiel's lip curled in rancid disgust at the alien gunfighter.

'Kelermorph,' he snarled, squeezing his trigger.

His bolts struck the bulkhead behind it, their fragments tearing through the cheeks of three neophyte hybrids. They collapsed, mewling and clutching their faces. Barachiel snarled, carving a path towards the creature. He shattered a hybrid's skull with a vicious backhand, disembowelled a screeching female in grimy overalls. An overarm swing bisected a gaunt elder from head to pelvis. Any that stood in his way died. He relished the hot squirt of combat stimulants in his veins, the dry snap of bone and wet crunch of torn flesh as his blade carved through limbs and opened bellies. Sanguinius called to him with every death.

Another Assault Intercessor, Tilonas, fell, velonium bullets punching through his eye-lenses and the seal at his gorget.

Barachiel cursed and shifted direction, drawn away from vengeance by onerous duty. The warrior's signum-rune fizzled grey before he could reach him, and even a cursory examination told him that the gene-seed was unrecoverable. Wrath seared his veins, a tightening circlet that squeezed all rational thought from the meat of his mind.

Sanguinius' call grew stronger.

Xenos worshippers threatened to surround him, to tear at him with milk-pale flesh and obsidian talons. They wielded pipes and socket wrenches, hammers and broken metal struts as bludgeons. He snarled and charged them, caring nothing for the pain, killing two for every blow they managed to land on him. The pain was nothing, brief kisses of fire amid the rage that scorched his nerves. It receded into the black mist that enclosed his vision as he hacked at everything about him, ending lives with every movement of his blade. He cut a pathway through the dross towards the kelermorph, panting by the time he reached the beast.

Barachiel swung his chainsword for its head.

The creature ducked beneath the strike, holstering one of its guns and drawing its jade knife. Bullets snapped from its remaining stub pistols, punching through his armour. Pain shrieked through his nerves and a chilling howl tore the air. Alert runes bleached his retinal feed, damage reports scrolling down his right eye. Barachiel disabled the function and drove for the beast with chainsword and bone-drill, howling in frustration as it evaded each and every strike. The creature moved with the supple fluidity of its fully xenos kin, a gift the hive mind only afforded its elite.

It shrieked in frustration as his blade sliced through one of its autostubs, severing its barrel just above the cylinder. It cast aside the ruined weapon, bobbing and weaving between futile attempts to decapitate or disembowel it, reloading its last drawn pistol with its second and third hands. It spun the weapon in one hand, an extravagant distraction as it tried to draw its holstered pistol. Barachiel's blade tore through its forearm, an arc of black blood trailing its wake. The kelermorph screeched, spinning away, its blood spurting onto the deck.

Barachiel met its glare and grinned.

'I hope that hurt, wretch.'

The Apothecary pressed his attack, driving the creature back to the generatorum control room. It deflected overarm strikes and lunging thrusts, using Barachiel's weight and fury against him. Xenos metal sparked against Mars-forged steel, filaments and chainteeth whickering free. Barachiel parried a swipe at his throat, too late, the tip dragging across the ceramite. He thrust for the creature's heart, but it curved beneath his blade, launching a rapid counterstrike that tore through the joint ribbing at his groin.

Pain screamed along his nerves, absent the acid bite of biotoxins. Barachiel had little time or inclination to ponder the absence, deflecting another ferocious series of strikes as the beast tried to drive him back. He parried and riposted, his sword-skill honed duelling several blade-masters among Dorn's knights. A blow with his chainsword's flat broke its wrist, the backswing narrowly missing its neck. Lactic acid bathed his muscles in fire as he swung again and again, each strike narrowly missing its mark. Sweat dappled his beard and rimed his gorget seal. The creature was too quick, its inhuman reflexes a match for his own.

There was only one way to beat it.

Barachiel allowed the blade to pierce his chest, a subtle twitch of his body causing it to miss his heart. Hot pain screamed through his flesh. The creature's eyes blazed with soured triumph as Barachiel's hand clamped around its throat. It struggled in his grip, its blade stuck fast. Its strength was prodigious, a fact belied by its lean, hunched physique, but it made no difference as Barachiel's blade licked outwards, a vengeful smile tightening his lips.

The creature fell, headless, hot blood jetting from the stump.

Barachiel dragged its blade from his chest, wincing slightly, wiping the blood from his visor, his stomach curling away from its fouled tang. He injected anti-venoms into the wound as a prophylactic before stapling it shut and applying temporary armour cement to the cracks in his plate. He kicked the kelermorph's corpse aside, activating the biocodes display on his retinal feed. They read as normal, the radioactive traces on the bullets enough to test his system, but not exert it. His eyes flicked up to see Hariel standing in the door.

The Techmarine looked to the kelermorph, then to Barachiel.

'I will ensure the reactors reach critical overload, Apothecary.' Hariel moved to the cogitator panel. Data cables snaked from ports concealed in his augmetics, plugging into the interface. 'The vox is fully functional, all trace of alien interference gone.'

'Thank you, Techmarine.'

Barachiel left Hariel to his labours, moving towards the fallen Flesh Tearers stacked beside the door. Daven's gene-seed was secure and Tilonas' had been destroyed, but there were still three viable progenoids to harvest. His bone saw revved in response to the thought, while Adariel and Tumelo secured the area and organised their survivors.

The vox crackled in his ear.

'Barachiel.'

'Teman.' Barachiel could hear the pain and fury clotting the lieutenant's heaving breaths. 'The generatorum is secure. We have three wounded and five dead. Have you taken the bridge?'

'We have, lord, and several brothers require your ministrations.'

'What of Captain Tanthius?'

Teman's hesitation lasted eight heartbeats.

'Slain, brother.'

SEVEN

Alarms trilled through the *Herald of Virtue*.

Dumah grinned as fresh foes swept towards the Flesh Tearers, now thirty strong after their unification with Paschar. The alarms brought the entire cruiser to full alert, thousands of creatures scrambling to sudden activity, driven by the single imperative coded into their genomes: protect the magus. Dumah sighted along his pistol, selecting a scuttling purestrain with mottled flesh and bladed forearms as his first target.

Its head exploded wetly.

Thanatos' Reivers, their grinning skull masks splashed with arterial spray, joined their fire to Isaiah's warriors and Castiel's Hell-blasters. Plasma bursts flash-boiled hybrids to dust and curls of steam. Mass-reactive rounds sprayed innards across bulkheads in arcing slicks, forcing those behind to scrabble over the dead. Dumah slapped a fresh magazine into his pistol and adjusted its selector to burst-fire. Bullets rippled across his plastron, entirely ineffectual. He sighted the muzzle flashes, bolts shredding the hybrids responsible.

'We are wrath! We are fury!'

Isaiah counter-charged the hybrids, pistol spitting death in gold flashes. He raged at them, a screaming dervish carving through them with wild abandon. Dumah emptied his clip into a shambling aberrant, its head vanishing in fronds of blood. Fury throbbed in the back of his mind. Isaiah's impetuous charge infuriated him, even as he relished the opportunity for slaughter. He rune-marked the access hatch at the far end of the corridor, transmitting it to the tactical displays of his three sergeants. Schemata marked it as directly feeding onto the bridge, and consequently their clearest path to the cult's magus.

'Secure the hatch. Castiel, supporting fire. Kairus, Thanatos, with me!'

Dumah charged the oncoming hybrids.

He gunned down three brood brothers in dishevelled Navy uniforms, more exploding as Isaiah and Thanatos' squads emptied their pistols into the oncoming horde. Paschar was at his side, spearing hybrids with coruscating arcs of crimson lightning. The stench of boiling blood and charred meat stirred Dumah's thirst as the Flesh Tearers broke the disorderly tide, trampling its front waves beneath ceramite boots.

Dumah smashed hybrids to ruin, bludgeoning them with his pistol grip or obliterating them with his crozius. Its disruptor field detonated flesh and powdered bone with each strike. Crumpled cracks of bolt shells exploding in flesh interspersed each beat of his hearts. Blood misted his visor, its salt-iron tang strong in his throat. Dumah let the Thirst free, angel's teeth extruding from his gums. He screamed for blood, drooling at the thought of its hot spatter on his face and tongue. Even the hybrids' tainted ichor would satisfy.

He would tear them limb from limb and drink his fill when none remained.

Paschar was a whirl of arterial-crimson plate and cameleoline, boiling beasts in washes of crimson fire. Its heat was like lava on Dumah's skin. He smashed another cultist aside, relishing the tortured screams of a creature more genestealer than man as Paschar peeled flesh from bone with twitching fingers. Dumah dodged the clumsy pecks of a metamorph's crustacean claws, thundering his visor into its snarling face. Its skull split with a sick crunch, and Dumah executed another of its brood with point-blank fire.

The Reivers swept past them, wielding serrated knives and bolt pistols with liquid elegance and relentless ferocity. Their short blades were perfect for close-range work, thrusting and cutting through the press like machetes through thick jungle. They followed Isaiah's squad towards the hatch, the Assault Intercessors carving a bloody path through the cultists. They tore throats with hands curled into killer's claws and chainblades that clove through chitinous exoskeletons and tainted human meat. Dumah stamped a survivor's head to meaty paste, dividing another at the waist with an upward swing of his crozius.

'They are pulling back!' Isaiah's voice was a garbled snarl.

'Let them!' Dumah growled, slitting another hybrid's throat. He scanned the corridor, recognising panic in their eyes, several fleeing from the rearmost ranks. 'They die when we set the engines to overload. To pursue them will take us away from our objective.'

'We cannot let them flee! These traitors must pay!'

Dumah smashed another aside, wrestling down the fury that boiled in his blood. It took much of his considerable willpower to resist the call for slaughter. Las-beams and bullets pattered against his plate. Flesh blistered and the bone detailing and brass trim were scorched black. Hybrids scattered in loose groups, firing from their hips or loosing boiling blasts over their shoulders. Xenoform kin scampered along walls or hauled themselves into aeration ducts, their lives bought through the sacrifice of their human slaves.

Rage smeared his vision with black, as the Thirst coloured it with red, but he was not so blinded that he did not see the deliberate feint in the movement. The hive mind had learned much about the Flesh Tearers in the years since Baal. It had studied their wrath, appraising its weaknesses, and how best to use them to its advantage. He forced himself to stop, slowing his pulse with deep breaths that purged the rage from his body.

'Do not pursue,' he snapped, as Isaiah and Kairus pressed forwards. Dumah moved to the access hatch, his crozius obliterating a bare-chested hybrid. Castiel's Hellblasters handled the rest. 'They seek to draw us from the bridge, into a prepared ambush site elsewhere.'

Kairus stopped, as did the rest of his squad. Isaiah alone forged on.

'Are you in the habit of allowing xenos scum to dictate your actions?' Dumah called.

Isaiah snarled, but ceased his pursuit, falling back to the access hatch. There were only twenty-seven alive, the gene-seed of the fallen preserved in Thuriel's cryo-canisters.

Dumah gestured to the access hatch. 'Get this open.'

Two Hellblasters forced the hatch open, their armour's servo-muscles squealing at the strain placed upon them. The metal groaned, faint light spilling through the cleft.

Dumah stepped in, rapidly scanning the tight, circular stairwell. It was patched with rust and graffiti, but otherwise clear. He took the stairs two at a time, sweeping every railing, subsidiary access point and aeration hatch. Breaths heaved through his stylised visor, and blood pounded in his skull to the beat of his twin hearts, pain a compressing band around it, a wet snarl building in his throat.

They reached the bridge without incident.

Dumah stifled his disappointment.

Castiel's Hellblasters stacked up on the farthest side of the hatch, Thanatos' Reivers and Isaiah's Intercessors behind him. Two braced against the hatch door, ready to pull it open.

'Do it,' Dumah ordered. The Hellblasters forced it open.

Dumah was the first through, squeezing a flurry of bolts into a chittering creature with a ridged forehead and crustacean's claws. One struck the hand flamer in its sole human hand, dousing it, and its kin, in liquid fire. They thrashed and screamed, lurching towards the Flesh Tearers, melting faces twisted by inhuman hate. Bolt pistols boomed, casting the metamorphs into the crew pits in sprays of burning limbs and blood. Gore spattered his armour, pooling in lacerations and dents, mingling with his own blessed vitae. His thirst pressed for satisfaction, something Dumah was more than happy to give.

'Slaughter them all!'

The Flesh Tearers ripped through the onrushing phalanxes, carried forward by their fury. Bolts reduced hybrids and brood brothers to shards of bone and strips of meat. Gouts of ionised plasma immolated them, or fountained sparks from overloaded consoles where they missed. Isaiah led his warriors into the beasts at Dumah's left, closing on the magus and its bodyguards. Chainswords sliced ribbons of tainted blood and flesh from the broodkin and hybrid leaders, while the magus summoned the unnatural powers gifted it by the hive mind. It was female, a cowl rising from its collar in mimicry of its masters' chitinous armour.

'Paschar!' Dumah led Thanatos' Reivers to the right, while Castiel's Hellblasters laid down a blanket of suppressive fire into the centre. Acolytes rushed them. 'Kill it!'

'You do not need to tell me that, Chaplain!'

Dumah snarled a wordless curse, bludgeoning an acolyte armed with a bonesword and a lash whip. Its broodkin darted for him, brandishing claws and looted repair equipment. Dumah laughed with joyous abandon, swerving aside the downward swing of a circular saw, cracking the wielder's head with his pistol grip. Blood splashed his visor. He batted aside a power hammer's overbalanced strike, crushing the creature's head between his elbow and a console. Its kin-beasts hurled themselves at him, eyes black with hate.

Claws raked along his breastplate, drawing deep grooves and runnels of blood. Bolts boomed inside the offending beast's torso, shredding it. Thanatos and Thuriel holstered their pistols, hacking two apart with their short blades. The Reivers carved apart mewling beasts and bare-chested fanatics, bloodcurdling roars issuing from their voxmitters. Dumah slammed his shoulder into another hybrid, sending it to the deck. He stamped its skull to mush. The Chaplain cut and thrust through its kind, slaying with every movement, screaming in the torturous moments between kills. He needed more. There had to be more.

An atavistic roar cut through the battle.

Dumah found Isaiah at the heart of the magus' kin-guard, wrenching the polycephalic head from a shambling aberrant. Another creature swung its mining pick towards the Flesh Tearer's head. Isaiah blocked the blow with his free arm, gripping the beast by its bicep and twisting the arm, wrenching it from its socket. Blood sprayed the deck and Isaiah caved its skull in with his fist. Its head a pulped ruin, he advanced on the magus.

The psyker-prophet siphoned power from its duel with Paschar, striking Isaiah with violet spears of psionic power. They sheared through flesh and armour alike, searing nerves and cauterising flesh. Isaiah ignored the smoking wounds, thundering forwards.

'Damn you, spawn of Horus! May you burn for your perfidy!'

Cold horror slithered down Dumah's spine.

Eight purestrains loped between Isaiah and the magus, their diamond-hard claws and bladed forearms slick with Astartes blood. Flesh Tearers lay on the deck around them, blood pooling in its subtle depressions. Dumah swallowed his rage, watching Isaiah hurl himself into the purii. They blocked and parried his blows, taking slow steps backwards. Isaiah chased after them, away from the bridge and the magus.

Dumah cursed, backhanding a cultist that dared strike him in his distraction.

'Slaughter these degenerates,' he barked at Thanatos and Thuriel. He could not focus on Isaiah, or what befell him, not while their duty remained undone. 'Castiel, cover me! I will support Paschar, and see this beast slain.'

They vox-clicked their assent.

Dumah charged the creature, carving himself a path through the remaining bridge crew. He ducked spears of psionic power and gouts of superheated plasma, powering through the radioactive ash and electrified corpses alike. He vaulted the railing around the command throne, sprinting the last fifty yards towards the magus, his crozius raised. He swung for the magus' head, disruptor lightning snapping hungrily for the creature's flesh.

It ducked.

Forks of purple lightning speared past his helm, scorching the bulkhead behind him. Dumah spun around, drawing and hurling his combat knife. The magus flexed its unnatural power, altering the knife's trajectory so it buried itself in one of the creatures still guarding it. Dumah again swung his crozius for the magus. It tipped the blow with its force stave, swiping at him with the jade dagger in its other hand. Alien metal bit through the softseal at his neck and blood seeped out. His free hand flashed up, pain stabbing into his throat.

Dumah pressed forwards, swiping at the magus with his crozius. One of its acolytes leapt forwards. He smashed it aside. Paschar bathed its broodkin in torrents of crimson fire, sloughing flesh from bone. He cleaved through purestrains with sharp chops of his force sword. Dumah pivoted aside, avoiding a spear of violet light. Its sheer proximity scorched his pauldron black, roasting the flesh beneath. Channelling pain into fury, a wordless howl tore from Dumah's throat. Rage threatened to smear his vision with black.

The Chaplain launched a devastating series of strikes that forfeited finesse for speed and strength. The magus pivoted and parried, thin cracks cobwebbing along its force stave with every blow it blocked. Tendrils of disruptive power set its robes aflame, scorching pale flesh black. Pain veined the magus' colourless eyes, though it refused to scream. Dumah felt the questing tendrils of its mind probing his mental defences. Blood trickled from his nose as he fought the urge to kneel and obey, pain pulsing hot flashes through his skull.

'I am a son of the Angel, pure and untainted.' The Litany of Fortitude fell from his lips without prompt, its familiar words bolstering his resistance. He wrapped his mind around the fury of Sanguinius, anchoring himself in the here and now with the white heat of its blessed touch. 'Neither the darkness within nor the enemy without shall supplant my will.'

The psychic pressure withdrew, fleeing the hurricane of hatred summoned by Dumah. He relished the frustration and too-human horror in the magus' eyes, a grin splitting his face. Taking advantage of its surprise, Dumah tore the combat knife from a fallen Intercessor, feinting a slash at the magus' throat. It moved to block the strike, frustration evolving into panic when it realised too late what Dumah intended.

His crozius powered into the magus' temple. Bone imploded

and flesh was scorched to ash by disruptor lightning. Blood sheeted its cheek. The creature fell, weak breaths bubbling through its shattered jaw. Dumah struck it again, and again. Metal buckled and groaned, scorched with soot. The magus' head was a gelatinous stain on the deck.

He forced himself to remain still for long seconds, expelling his fury in hard, copper-infused breaths. Sweat bathed his battered, abused body. His Flesh Tearers executed survivors with grim economy of blade and boot. Paschar stood with him over the magus' ruined body, breathless, his flesh drawn and pallid. Exhaustion ringed his eyes with black.

'What happened to Isaiah?' Dumah exhaled, retrieving his own blade from the hybrid's corpse. 'Could it be some facet of this psyker-wretch's power?'

'It is within their power to influence a mind, even that of one of our kind if the magus is particularly puissant,' Paschar admitted. He nudged the beast with the toe of his boot. 'Such beasts are rare, and I cannot confirm whether this was one, or what caused Isaiah's madness.'

'Then we find him and determine its cause ourselves.'

Paschar nodded and followed Dumah from the bridge. The magus' blood sizzled on his crozius and Dumah's thoughts turned to Isaiah's maddened howls.

He suspected he knew the answer already.

It took Dumah and Paschar almost two hours to close on Isaiah's signum-rune. The news of Tanthius' death reached them before the end of the first hour. Both maintained their silence, their focus entirely on the hunt. The time to mourn Tanthius would come later.

Isaiah's crimson icon pulsed on their cartoliths, in the corner of a refectorum in the lower levels of the command spire. The corridor outside was strewn with dusty skeletons, severed limbs and ruptured torsos. Tattered armsman uniforms clung to the bones, themselves gnawed by needle-like teeth. Dumah wondered whether these were the remains of those who had stayed loyal to the Imperium – betrayed, and massacred in the dark.

He crushed the question. It was unimportant.

He turned to Kairus, whose squad had accompanied them on the hunt.

'Paschar and I will enter alone. Secure the area and ensure that none follow. If we do not emerge, return to the *Justice* and make speed for Cretacia.'

Kairus bit back a pained gasp, forcing himself to speak. Bone-spines protruded from his abdomen, blood trickling from the punctures. They impaled two of his lungs, and his left hand was a mess of mangled flesh and plate. Thuriel had insisted he remain on the bridge, but Kairus had refused. Dumah allowed it when tensions threatened violence.

'My lord, he is our sergeant–'

'And I am your Chaplain,' Dumah snapped, refusing to allow him to finish. If Isaiah had succumbed to the Rage, he and Paschar stood the best chance of resisting its call. Even then, it was far from certain they could resist, but he refused to risk another's life in his stead. 'You will obey this command, acting sergeant, or see yourself censured.'

Kairus nodded. 'Aye, lord.'

Dumah turned to Paschar.

'I am ready, though I cannot be certain what awaits us in there.'

Dumah laughed. 'Nothing is certain save death, brother.'

They entered a refectorum, stepping over the broken furniture, pools of brackish water and mouldering food scraps. Isaiah stood in the farthest corner, facing the wall. He was still, murmuring, his chainsword snarling in one hand. His other arm ended at the elbow, a stump already scabbed over. His pauldrons had been ripped away. Dried blood sheened his cracked vambraces and the scraps of ceramite that remained of his plastron.

Dumah moved closer, his crozius crackling to life.

'Isaiah?'

The Flesh Tearer's head twitched towards him.

Hope bloomed in Dumah's hearts. In all his readings, Rage-stricken brothers rarely responded to their given names, the visions of the Angel's death consuming their identities entirely. He moved closer, allowing the crozius to dip slightly. 'Brother? Are you well?'

'Why, Horus?'

The demand tore from Isaiah's voxmitter. The Flesh Tearer moved like lightning, his blade screaming for Dumah's throat. Dumah parried the blow, staggering, his muscles' ache exacerbated by Isaiah's Rage-fuelled strength. He pivoted away, his mind racing, his anger soured by sorrow. Cawl insisted the flaws in their genome had been fixed, and yet here was the second reborn anew. He angled his crozius to guard, both hands on the grip.

Isaiah pursued him, raging.

'You betrayed our father! You betrayed the Imperium! Why?'

Dumah parried or avoided every blow that Isaiah sought to land. They were frenzied and uncontrolled, tragic echoes of Sanguinius' martial glory. Isaiah thrust with his stump the way one would wield a spear, then sliced with his sword, seeking to decapitate Dumah. The Chaplain parried the blow, driving his crozius into Isaiah's left knee. The sergeant staggered, blood lapping from the wound. Dumah quashed the nip of the Red Thirst, and the Rage that promised to brush his vision with black. He could not cede control, no matter that he felt it clawing at his mind, demanding entry, far more potent than the magus' power.

Dumah's neck muscles tightened as he forced it down.

He deflected the sergeant's maddened blows, chainteeth skittering off sanctified metal. They embedded themselves in his plastron and the bulkhead alike. Dumah suppressed the flash-pain that roared along his nerves, locking his crozius with Isaiah's snarling blade. Even defanged, Isaiah's weapon was still a sword, and more than capable of seeing him slain. The fallen sergeant frothed oaths and questions first given voice by their primarch in his final hours ten millennia earlier, pressing down hard on Dumah's defence.

He felt his wrists give slightly.

'Paschar!' Dumah snorted, forcing every ounce of strength into his defence. He tipped the muscles in his wrists, ready to off-balance Isaiah. 'Can you placate him?'

'His mind is shrouded in fire, Dumah. I cannot reach him.'

Dumah cursed, shifting his balance to allow Isaiah to overbalance. He thundered his helm into Isaiah's cracked visor. The fissures split wider, and Dumah saw a liquid-black eye glaring through a shattered eye-lens. It was madness given form and colour.

'Then stand aside, and I will deal with him!'

Dumah slipped under Isaiah's decapitating cut, the follow-up strikes coming within a breath of ending the Chaplain's life. An elbow connected with Dumah's jaw, shattering bone and loosening teeth. They tumbled from his mouth on a slick of blood, and Dumah worked his jaw several times, pivoting away from the raging sergeant. It was little more than wet silt in a fleshy sack, a painful reminder that Isaiah had been far too strong for him to grapple, even before the Rage blessed him with a shadow of the primarch's potency.

He struck at Isaiah's exposed flesh and damaged armour, bleeding away his might and protection with hammer blows and sharp jabs. Bones shattered. Flesh was scorched to muscle and sinew. Isaiah slashed and hacked at him, fracturing ceramite and breaking bones beneath, his fury renewed with every wound and missed strike. Pain twisted through Dumah's ribcage and his right arm, accompanied by the unpleasant itch of bones slowly reknitting.

He saw a break in Isaiah's guard and took advantage.

The Chaplain smashed his crozius into Isaiah's knee, the joint weakened by an earlier blow. It pulverised the muscles and socket-joint. Isaiah fell to one knee, a sorrowful whimper escaping his lips. Dumah's second blow reduced his wrist to scraps of gristle and splinters of bone. His chainsword broke above the quillons and Dumah was quick to snatch the broken blade from Isaiah's trembling grip. The sergeant fell backwards, breathing heavily.

'I die,' Isaiah panted. 'I die at my brother's hand...'

The pommel of Dumah's crozius connected with Isaiah's skull.

A moment passed, the silence broken only by the snarls of damaged armour.

'We should kill him,' Paschar said, raising his blade. 'He is a rabid animal, a stain upon the honour of the Great Angel and his descendants.'

Dumah almost killed Paschar where he stood.

'You will not harm him, nor any Flesh Tearer.' The words were bestial snarls beaten into a semblance of language. 'Know well, Librarian, this is the curse of all Sanguinius' sons, and it is no dishonour to succumb to it. We will remove him to the Reclusiam, and he will remain in my charge until I decree otherwise. Is that understood?'

'Surely it would be better to relieve him of misery? I would rather embrace death than suffer in the grasp of madness, whether in battle or by the Executioner's Axe, it would not matter. No battle-brother deserves to be shackled to so tortured an existence.'

'But that is not your decision to make. It is mine, and I have made it.' Dumah paused, allowing the words to sink it. 'Am I understood?'

'Yes, Brother-Chaplain.'

EIGHT

Barachiel arrived at the bridge three hours after the kelermorph's death.

Five Intercessors from Adariel's assault squad escorted him, led by the burly sergeant himself. He flatly refused to allow another to do it, ceding temporary command of his squad to Tumelo. Barachiel was honoured and irritated by Adariel's nursemaiding.

They exited the lifter that fed onto the highest level of Polaris' control spire, the sour tang of tainted vitae clinging to their armour's crevices. It was strongest around the severed head he had chained to his waist. The scent filled his nostrils, nausea churning his stomach as his thirst pooled saliva in his mouth. It served a purpose beyond an olfactory irritant, serving as an effective deterrent to a retaliatory assault from the surviving cultists.

The kelermorph's unmasked, severed head helped.

Barachiel picked his way between the piled dead, noting the varied skin tones and the military-issue wargear they had stolen or been granted. The only thing that united them was the gaunt hue of their infection, and the wrinkled nose inherited from their xenos masters.

'Lord Dante must be informed,' he muttered. Every world would need to be assessed and those that bore the cult infection purged, any ships that docked at Polaris tracked and destroyed.

Teman and Micah stood halfway along the corridor. Their armour was pitted and cracked, thin lines of grey cement running through fields of crimson and ash. Teman wore no helm, his face marked by tribal scarification. He smiled with sharpened pegs in place of teeth, while Micah's visor was partially obscured by a veil of mottled flesh the colour of sour milk. A wyrm tattoo was a minuscule imperfection beneath his left lens.

'Apothecary,' they said, and bowed their heads in unison.

'It is good to see you alive, my brothers.'

Teman clasped Barachiel wrist to wrist in a warrior's greeting. Micah repeated the gesture and they turned towards the bridge. The heaped dead grew thicker. Twice, he stopped them to extract gene-seed from the fallen. He sealed the progenoids in the last cryo-canisters built into the reductor and holstered the pistol. They passed two of Micah's warriors standing guard at the bridge entrance, swords and pistols flecked with blood.

'Have your forces withdrawn from the generatorum?'

'Tumelo supervises their withdrawal, and the transportation of our honoured dead,' Barachiel said. 'I bear their legacy with me, and I shall see their bones interred when we reach Cretacia. They died with honour, and deserve...'

The words snagged in his throat.

Tanthius was slumped against a control console, his throat slashed to the bone and his ruined cuirass sheened by dried blood. His abdomen was torn, offal spilled onto his thighs. It glistened beneath the sickening light of the Rift and local stars, further illuminated by the brief flares of the *Cretacian Justice* and its escort squadron executing commandeered vessels with close-range macro-cannon broadsides and lance strikes.

'What happened?' Barachiel's voice was a strangled whisper.

Micah knelt beside him, taking a xenos-metal rod from the corpse of a robed hybrid. A beaten-brass coiled wyrm haloed its head, and its other hand clutched a curved tulwar of darkest jade. Dark blood soaked the oath papers affixed to imperial purple robes by red wax seals.

'I cannot say for certain, lord,' the sergeant said.

'Try.'

'The captain appeared to lose himself, lord.' The words tumbled from Micah's mouth, weighed down by uncertainty. He pointed to the body he had taken the sword from, its twin, and then a rail-thin creature wearing red goggles and a grey respirator. It clutched a thin staff topped by a large voxmitter in one dead hand. 'When the battle reached its height, the captain struck at the predicant and its life-wards with Lieutenant Teman.'

'Trickery, then cowardice spared them at first,' Teman said, nudging a monstrous hybrid with his boot. 'Then they tried to flee and the captain, already wrathful, began to howl like a man lost to madness. He abandoned me to fight this beast and pressed on alone...'

Barachiel's saw whirred to life, drowning out Teman's words. It ground through the pitiful scraps of plate around Tanthius' throat, and his surgical blade sliced into the meat. He sank his fingers into the incision, removing the progenoid and sealing it in a cryo-canister at his waist. Counterseptic misted the canister, and Barachiel vowed to see it bestowed upon the Cretacian aspirant that proved most worthy of Tanthius' honoured legacy.

'Then?'

'The xenos struck him, though their weapons had little effect,' Teman said. 'The predicant channelled an unholy fusion of sonic and psychic power into its hailer-staff, and lashed out with it.' He pressed his hand to his head. 'Throne, brother, but it felt like my brain was ready to boil from my skull. Blood streamed from my eyes and ears alike. It killed Seveus, though he was scarcely any farther from the degenerate than Tanthius.'

'Tanthius was unaffected?' Barachiel asked, his tone reflecting a sickening suspicion that darkened his mind. The Apothecary deployed a data-probe from his narthecium, connecting it to the neural plugs gouged into Tanthius' flesh. He initiated a neurological scan, hoping that Tanthius' brain was not too damaged to yield useful results. A small wheel spun from red to orange, then slowed as it approached green.

'He was staggered,' Teman admitted. 'It should have killed him outright, as the blast was aimed at him. He managed to slay the fiend before he finally succumbed to death.'

The wheel flashed green.

Barachiel's frown deepened as his eyes scrolled down the litany of severe cerebral haemorrhages, scorched neurological pathways and aneurysms the device had detected. Tanthius' brain was little more than lumpen gruel, its structural integrity almost entirely obliterated by the clamavus' proclamation hailer. It could offer little in the way of answers, the absence of any alternate theories all but confirming his own. Tanthius had survived the sonic assault, the devastation wrought on his mind, long enough for him to slay the clamavus.

It should have been impossible.

'Remove him from this place,' Barachiel said, straightening up. There were no more answers to be gleaned here. 'Return him to the *Justice*, with the rest of our fallen.'

Barachiel watched Kairus writhe and roar as Thuriel fought to save his life.

The wounded Flesh Tearer moaned pleas for blood through gritted teeth, his abdomen opened to the cold air of the apothecarion, his left arm a mangled ruin. Barachiel took a moment of respite to watch his initiate perform surgery, aided only by medicae-thralls. The litany of wounds and procedures scrolled down his right eye. It was a surgery that would take many hours to complete. The hot scent of blood tore at him.

It taunted Thuriel too, a flicker of red that danced in his eyes.

'Apothecary.' Aesha's voice cut through his distraction. 'You are needed in the primus ward. There are matters that require your attention and approval.'

Barachiel nodded and turned from the viewport towards Aesha. Her eyes were ringed by exhaustion, and drying blood stained her surgical robes. Sweat ripened the vile odour of recaff and lho-sticks that shrouded her. A surgical mask hung limp from one ear, and her mouth was a crease worn thin by frustration. Her heart beat a war drum's tattoo, a seductive rhythm that swallowed all other noise. Barachiel's fangs slid from his gums, slicing into his lip.

'Blood.' The word escaped as a strangled moan.

Aesha took a step back, eyes wide in alarm.

'Barachiel?'

The Apothecary took slow ponderous steps forwards, each accompanied by the dry snarl of damaged servos. Her heartbeat quickened, and she took several steps back, short, sharp breaths snapping from her mouth in rapid succession. Barachiel's eyes were fixed on her throat, on the enticing pulse of her carotid artery. The quiet promise of hot, fresh blood was a physical sensation that pressed against his flesh, drawing him closer.

He had not taken blood in days. It would be child's play to take it now.

'Barachiel!'

Her voice cleaved through the crimson fog that clouded his mind, ripe with impotent rage and fearful indignation. Barachiel grunted as he fought his way free from the call of his thirst. He counted the paired beats of his twin hearts, finding a measure of calm and control in the expanding moments between them. He channelled that calm through muscles tense with denied desire and looked upon Aesha with eyes unstained by the Thirst.

She watched him with naked suspicion, a short surgical blade clutched in each shaking hand. Her scalpels were sized for mortal hands, and mortal surgery. They would snap on his armour and do very little damage even were he without it. It was all he could do not to laugh. Barachiel swallowed hard, his amusement at her foolish bravery unable to entirely banish his thirst. Several long moments passed before she put up her blades, gesturing for him to lead the way.

The primus ward was pandemonium.

Wounded Flesh Tearers hissed and snarled as tired medicae orderlies attended their wounds. The Space Marines hacked gobbets of acid-infused spittle on the deck, pleading for blood though it stained their cheeks already. There were twice as many wounded mortals, all high-ranked crew granted admittance by dint of rank or severity of injury. They groaned through the fugue of a chemical haze, or screamed as saws were taken to their limbs. The scent of roasted meat, soporifics and bodily excretions hung thickly over the primus ward, threatening to close his throat with each breath he took. It forced his thirst to recede.

Surgical thralls and senior medicae technicians moved between the mortal wounded, performing triage, even as they continued to flood in. The wounded were divided into three categories. The first were non-critical, requiring minor surgery or medicaments. The second required major surgery within days or hours to prevent death. Aesha and her surgical team would deal with the majority, though the most serious would be sent to his table. The third were those for whom death was unavoidable, and only a matter of time.

The latter was the largest category.

'This is what you brought me to supervise?'

'No, Barachiel,' Aesha said, casting her eye over her dying kind, and their attendants. She guided him towards an isolated cell. 'Though it does present an opportunity.'

'Opportunity?'

'Our blood stocks are draining more rapidly than expected,' she said, her words almost lost to the slamming doors, high-pitched shrieks and animalistic snarls. 'Much of our existing supply has been used to aid in your wounded brothers' recovery. Those category-three patients may be part of the answer to replenishing the stock, and doing so in the quickest, most efficient manner.'

His eyes narrowed. 'Are you suggesting a cull?'

Aesha's eyes flicked away, and she swallowed hard.

'In a manner,' she said. A querulous note entered her voice, her expression souring slightly. He could not tell whether it was shame or simply a moment of physiological distress. 'Nothing can be done for them, and they would have donated their blood to your brothers in the coming weeks. This gives them the chance to serve the Chapter one last time.'

Barachiel pondered the notion for a moment. A thought summoned the apothecarion's logisticae data, including the present state of the blood stocks. Depleted was a generous word. Much had been fed to the wounded Flesh Tearers. What remained would last the company a handful of days if that. Aesha's suggestion was practical, logical. It would ensure the mission continued and save the souls of several battle-brothers if the voyage was a long one.

There was only one flaw in the plan.

'I will not waste medicaments on what is inevitable,' Barachiel said. 'We are not so blessed that we can afford to indulge in such frivolity for a few deck-swabs.'

'There are many ways to end suffering, Barachiel.' Aesha hesitated, fidgeting in her discomfort. 'Not all of them require the intervention of chemical compounds.'

Offence and rage were heated knives that twisted in his gut.

'If you wish them executed, find a blade and do it yourself!' Barachiel snarled, anger sharpening his tone. Who was he to deny the dying their struggle, even if their chance to live was spent? Such was not their Chapter's way. 'I am a Flesh Tearer, and while violence is the song of my blood, that does not mean I, or my brothers, will murder the dying in their beds.'

She bowed her head, contrition forced by fear.

'Yes, Barachiel.'

'We are not that far lost to our wrath.' He towered over her, spittle flicking through his teeth. He exhaled, lowering his voice. 'That is not all you wanted to show me, was it?'

'It is not a matter I would discuss in the open, Apothecary.'

Something in her voice implied the need for secrecy, and Barachiel retained enough awareness of human conventions to not press further as she keyed in her access code. The panel buzzed, its triple lock clicking open. They entered the observation room adjoined to the cell.

It was a small, spartan room with two chairs and a two-way mirror made from a pane of reinforced armaglass. The cell the pane looked into was a room not spoken of, a place of pain and inquisition. It had been used many times, to break subjects and extract useful information necessary to the prosecution of the Emperor's foes.

It was not a chamber he cherished the existence of.

'What is this?' he asked, pushing past her to the window.

The interrogation room's equipment had been overturned or broken, its floor strewn with corpses. Most were servitors, strangled and torn apart. Dismembered limbs jerked as the cybernetics attempted to force life into dead flesh. There were medicae-thralls, too, their skin as white as snow, their surgical robes soiled in death and stained with blood.

One occupant still lived.

A lone Flesh Tearer in Phobos-pattern armour, his face streaked with crimson, walked into view. His armour bore chips and dents, the markings of Thanatos' squad almost lost to a plasma burn. That was of little interest to Barachiel.

His eyes were locked on what the Reiver carried.

He held a junior medicae-thrall in his embrace, his mouth clamped around her throat. She was chalk white with exsanguination, groaning groggily, her blood welling through the narrow gap between his mouth and her neck. He sensed Aesha beside him, trembling – with anger or fear, Barachiel could not decide. It was unimportant in the grand scheme.

'We did not know where to put him, Barachiel.' She offered the words as the silence stretched into minutes, punctuated only by the muted sound of the serf being drained. 'It cost many lives just to lure him in here. We could not allow him free roam of the ward.'

'You were right to do so.' The words were acid in his throat. 'How did this happen?'

'The blood could not satisfy him. No matter how much we offered him, he demanded more. There was an… *incident* with one of the orderlies that led to his incarceration.'

A bestial roar cut through the silence that followed.

Barachiel watched his brother cast aside the woman's drained corpse, bones snapping on the bulkhead. He cast about him like a wild animal, huffing the air, screaming for blood with every breath drawn. The Reiver pounded the walls with bare palm and balled fist, turned to knock aside a tray of sterilised knives. Their delicate chimes were as rain promised by the thunder's peal of his blows on the wall. Barachiel's eyes followed the Reiver's rampage, until he paused, and their gazes met. Despair was a closed fist about his heart.

The Reiver's eyes flickered bloody red.

PART TWO

'Say what you will of the Flesh Tearers, brother, for you carry the Angel's light in your veins, where they bear only his darkness. Their strength is no accident arising from weakness, as you perceive it to be, but a virtue born of their resistance to damnation.'

– Dante, Lord of the Blood Angels

NINE

The *Cretacian Justice* ploughed through the Great Rift.

Its tempest's tides pummelled the strike cruiser, undulating eddies lashing the Geller field with such vehemence that the bulkheads and decks quaked. It skirted screaming vortices of raw emotion, kaleidoscopes of acidic colour that dissolved flesh and metal at the merest touch. Daemons dwelled in those depths, their hunger incited by the scent of human souls in close proximity. They hurled themselves against the Geller field, desperate to crack it open and feast upon the bright, burning soul-morsels of Sanguinius' second sons.

Dumah braced himself against a bulkhead, waiting for the most recent quake to abate, moving only when it had. While his armour underwent repairs in the Technicarum, he wore a monkish surplice and deck boots. Hooded Reclusiam serfs bowed deeply or signed a range of deferential greetings as he passed them. They could not speak, the oaths of silence taken upon their assignment to twelve-aleph enforced by surgery. He enjoyed the silence the tongue removals brought, the lack of inane questions and mewling prostrations.

Dumah reached a cell and unlocked it, stepping inside.

Isaiah thrashed, roaring and raging. He was stripped of armour, the suit damaged far beyond any repair. It needed to be reforged. Restraints glinted at his waist, wrists and ankles, secured to three plasteel posts set at cardinal compass points by heavy chains. Dumah took the seat that occupied the fourth point, far beyond the maddened Flesh Tearer's reach. Pain ribboned his chest, shoulders and jaw, his injuries not yet entirely recovered. Welded bones clicked in his jaw, and his tongue ran over steel pegs freshly grafted to his gums.

'You are healing well, brother,' he said, examining the stump and the lesser wounds Isaiah had sustained aboard the *Herald of Virtue*. Plastek pipes dangled from the ceiling, tipped with thick, sterilised needles. A small trolley was set to one side, filled with medicae supplies and equipment to tend any injuries sustained by the Rage-stricken warrior. Barachiel had yet to see Isaiah as he now was, and it was an encounter Dumah did not look forward to.

'I had hoped you would not succumb to your injuries.'

'Treacherous cur!' Isaiah frothed, angel's teeth snagging on his lips. Blood welled in the fresh tears. 'You dare address me as a brother? You, who set my sons' curse against them at Signus, who dishonours poor Ferrus even in death by retaining his skull as… as *what?* A keepsake of your slaughter at Isstvan? A touchstone to remind you of those you betrayed?'

'I am not Horus, and you are not Sanguinius.'

'You are a betrayer of brothers, a breaker of oaths.'

The Chaplain leaned forwards in his chair. This was far from the first time he had sat with Isaiah since they had entered the Rift. Though he repeated himself many times, Dumah held onto every word that passed his lips. He knew better than to trust the damned, but it was also impossible to not listen. To him, each word was a valuable insight into a time little more than myth to much of the Imperium. To him, these were the Angel's final hours given voice by his sons, and something that brought the Flesh Tearers closer to their father than any artefact they had in their possession, for their Blood Angels cousins hoarded the Great Angel's relics. This was all they had to know him by.

A wet snarl bubbled through Isaiah's lips.

'Your selfishness has damned our brothers! It will damn our sons, and the Imperium,' Isaiah spat. He thrashed again, muscles bunched tight, skin sheened with sweat. The chains' clinks echoed in the small chamber as Isaiah raged at a primarch ten millennia dead. 'Did you even consider the cost before you made your pacts with the warp?'

'There will be no cost to our brothers, or you.'

Dumah spilled the words without thinking, more to himself than to Isaiah. Paschar's instinct to kill Isaiah had been foremost on his mind since they had departed the Imperium Nihilus. At first, he feared the Librarian may have been right. As a Chaplain-initiate of the Indomitus Crusade, he had heard only rumours of brothers disappearing during battle, or in its wake. Rumours of names stricken from the roles of honour, and the orders of battle, of hidden circles among the senior of their order, and the secret instruction given to them. The demands of Dante's own crusade, combined with Cawl's self-aggrandised crowing, had been such that Appollus had little time or perceived need to instruct the Primaris Marines in dealing with the Rage-stricken. Several times he came with his Absolvor pistol, ready to bless his brother with the Emperor's Peace. But each time that changed when he looked upon Isaiah.

The sclerae of his eyes burned blood-bright, any trace of their white long banished by the onset of the Black Rage. The former sergeant forced snarling breaths through teeth strung with acidic saliva, canines at full extension. It trickled down his chin, dripping onto the deck between his feet. Smoke curlicued from the cavity carved there. Distended veins pressed hard against the flesh of his neck and forehead, his muscles swelled and bulged with every clink of the chains as Isaiah struggled to see himself free from bondage.

Dumah marvelled at his fury.

Here was the Angel's truest legacy to his divided, orphaned sons. The Flesh Tearers, the most cursed and savage Chapter of the Sanguinary Brotherhood, were the embodiment of this legacy, both in their resistance to the Flaw and their final embracing of it.

'You have made us into monsters, brother.' Blind rage melted into sorrow, its depth and sincerity surprising Dumah. 'None more so than those you led into damnation. I have seen their suffering, Horus. I felt it as though it were my own, and it brought tears to my eyes. They were *our brothers*, Horus, and you sold them into slavery on the promise of an empty crown and the chance to sit on Father's throne. *What happened to the man I knew?*'

He remained silent while his brother gave voice to their father's words.

'Even after all they have done, it is a fate too cruel.'

'We are Flesh Tearers, Isaiah,' Dumah said quietly. 'Shunned as savages by warriors who share our father's wrath. Fate has never been kind to our brotherhood.'

'Lord Chaplain.' Sergeant Thanatos' voice buzzed in his ear. Dumah tilted his head away from Isaiah. *'You are needed in the strategium. The issue of company command needs to be resolved. It can wait no longer.'*

Dumah breathed through gritted teeth.

'I will be there.'

'Thank you, lord.' Thanatos closed the link.

Dumah stood, stretching the blood back into his limbs. Isaiah gnashed his teeth, as though attempting to bite the throat of an attacker. Streams of incoherent invective spilled from his lips, curses in a multitude of archaic languages. The Chaplain turned away from him, striding towards the cell door. His mind went to the thorny issue of the new company commander. Teman and Hanibal would both seek the command as their right, but Teman lacked experience and Hanibal was reckless, even by Flesh Tearers standards. The sergeants could not bypass the lieutenants to become captain, which left one option.

Dumah was near the door when coherent speech resumed.

'Damn you, Horus! If you are going to kill me, then do it!'

'Horus is not here, Isaiah, and I will not kill you.' He opened the cell door and turned to face Isaiah again. 'You will not die in silence and shadow, but in honour and glory.'

He sealed the cell behind him.

Tension thickened the strategium's air when Dumah entered.

Barachiel and Paschar stood in conference with Techmarine Hariel, while Hanibal and Teman argued with the nine surviving sergeants. Kairus was there too, silent at the farthest edge of the strategium table. His flesh was deathly pale and an iron augmetic had replaced his left forearm. His new rank sat poorly on his shoulders, like an ill-fitting bodyglove. Dumah had no doubt he would grow into it, though it would take time.

Étain was honoured with a place at the council, a testament to their respect for her abilities in the void. She was almost lost in Thanatos' lean shadow, her military discipline the scaffolding that concealed her unease. Dumah saw it blooming in her eyes, not quite fear but certainly discomfort. He could not blame her.

Most mortals would have struggled to maintain their composure at the sight and sound of arguing Space Marines, their voices like thunder inflected by emotion, instead of it merely threatening to undermine their façade.

Dumah's fist hammered into the strategium table.

'This prattle serves none but the enemy.' A low snarl edged his words, the echo of his blow still clinging to the chamber's corners. His gaze roved across the two lieutenants, then the specialist officers, and finally the sergeants. 'Each moment spent in disunity is a moment wasted, a moment this vessel could suffer attack by the slaves of the Ruinous Powers.'

He leaned on the table, the metal groaning under his weight. Dumah's silence held their attention, as he chose his next words carefully. It would be foolish to propose himself as Tanthius' successor outright. It was unorthodox for a Chaplain to assume company command. He needed others to suggest their candidacy first, the overly ambitious and deeply deluded. Only then could he present himself as the alternative. It sickened him to engage in the grimy politicking that hamstrung the Indomitus Crusade in its first years. He was a warrior, not a weasel, though many things depended on his election, the Death Company's creation and the recovery of the Chapter relics resting on Cretacia highest among them.

The others would see the Death Company as an affront, instead of a necessity.

'Our captain is dead,' he continued, allowing sorrow to weigh his voice. 'His body is sealed in our barrow, with the other honoured dead. He will be mourned as a hero, the first of a new generation to be cremated upon the home world, with all the honours due. However, we must look to choosing his successor, and put sorrow aside until the moment is right.'

Dumah looked around them.

'Suggestions.'

'We should settle this as warriors, with bared blades and blood.' Micah stroked the ork-hide haft of his chainaxe, cords of wound human hair strung with xenos teeth and finger-bones curved around his vambraces. 'We are not Unnumbered Sons, our decisions governed by politics. Let our strength determine our suitability.'

The other sergeants murmured to each other, none appearing to agree with the idea. Hanibal grinned and Teman looked uncomfortably surprised. Barachiel, Paschar and Hariel watched, their expressions impassive. Their votes were the ones he needed most.

'Do you take us for World Eaters, brother?' Teman asked. 'Strength and savagery are the qualities Angron's mongrels use to choose their leaders. Not since Amit has a single Flesh Tearer been granted office based solely on combat prowess. Even the savage lord was chosen for his seniority within the Ninth Legion, and for his value to the Great Angel.'

Dumah was certain some of that was untrue but cared little.

'We need every warrior and officer at their finest,' Barachiel added. 'Far worse than Traitor Astartes lurk in the Rift, and the Imperium has lost countless vessels that dared the crossing. Would you leave us undermanned simply to tip the scales in your and Hanibal's favour?'

Micah flushed deep red, his teeth grinding together.

'This conclave is for battle-leaders, Apothecary.' Hanibal bared his filed teeth in a savage leer. Penal tattoos coloured his skin, blue ink faded green and almost lost to the burn scars that marked him. 'You are unworthy, untrained in the nuances of command.'

'I beg to differ, whelp,' Barachiel said. 'I have spilled more blood and seen more war than any soul within this chamber.

I walked the soil of Terra when the Beast made its attempt on the Imperium. I led warriors in defence of the Palace against the Blood God's minions, and in liberating Rynn's World from Rhaxor of the Word Bearers. Is that untrained?'

Hanibal looked aside, face flushed with anger and shame.

'That you believe yourself fit to lead us to Cretacia marks the extent of your delusion, lieutenant.' Pity edged Barachiel's voice, making it unpleasant to hear. 'I would not trust you to lead a squad into battle, never mind a battle company.'

Hanibal's snarl bit through the Flesh Tearers' laughter, his trophies of carven bone and flayed xenos flesh clapping against his armour. Even Étain dared a smile. Micah made to intervene, his blade drawn in challenge. Castiel cut him off before he could.

'The Apothecary is right in at least one respect, brother,' Castiel said. 'A choosing cannot be based on martial skill alone. Who would defend this vessel were we indisposed by injuries obtained in such a foolish contest?' He gestured to Étain with an augmetic arm, his voice rich with sneering amusement. 'The captain's armsmen? Their defence would be token, at best.'

Snide laughter met his jest.

'My armsmen would fight to their last breath,' Étain said, meeting Castiel's glare with her own. 'As will every member of my crew.' Dumah smiled at the fury smouldering in the Hellblaster's eyes. 'We are sworn to serve the Chapter and the blessed Emperor. We may be limited by our mortality, but we take pride in our service, just like you.'

Grunts of amusement and affirmation met her statement.

'You dare speak to your betters in such a manner?'

Dumah moved to stand beside her, unsubtly blocking Castiel's path as the Hellblaster sergeant started towards her. Dumah met Castiel's glare, a mirthless grin twisting his death's-head features. The Flesh Tearer hesitated, his flensing blade partially drawn, then retook his place at the far end of the table, his blade returned to its scabbard.

'Now Hanibal and Micah have shown themselves unworthy of consideration,' Dumah said, ignoring the withering stares of the two Flesh Tearers, 'what of Teman?'

'He is too young,' Toivo said, his objection raising agreement from several sergeants. Dumah counted Thanatos, Castiel and Azariel of the Ninth Company amongst them. Teman deflated like a punctured lung and Dumah suppressed a thin smile. 'He was a sergeant only five years ago.'

'Ten years less command experience than I,' Hanibal snarled.

'Though far less enamoured of bloodshed than you,' Barachiel jibed.

'What else is a Flesh Tearer supposed to be?'

Black misted Hanibal's eyes. Tension coiled through Dumah's body, his hand falling to the crozius mag-locked at his waist. He shifted his balance and footing slightly, ready in case his suspicions were once more proven true. He hoped they were not.

'Wrath must be tempered with wisdom,' Barachiel said. Dumah heard the sorrow in his voice and remembered the Rynnite campaign, and the disaster that had compelled Barachiel towards the healer's path when he had once been on the command track. 'One cannot carry battle to its end through impetus alone, not without horrendous casualties. Our Chapter has been undermanned for centuries, our reputation yet to recover from the infamy that has plagued it for millennia. Seth himself has decreed that there will be no return to either state.'

Hanibal nodded, resigned to defeat.

'What of you, Barachiel?' Toivo said. 'Would you take command?'

Dumah suppressed a snarl, the bottom falling from his stomach. Cold coiled his spine, like the legendary ice-drakes of Fenris sinking their frozen fangs into his bones. Barachiel was certain to block his re-establishment of the Death Company, so desperate to atone for his *mistake* at the Siege of New Rynn City. His damned puritanism would see Isaiah euthanised in a manner unbefitting a warrior. Dumah would not see his brother dishonoured so.

'I cannot take command,' Barachiel said. 'Except in dire circumstances.'

'Not so,' Paschar said. 'It is a well-established tradition of the Sanguinary Brotherhood that captains can be temporarily succeeded by an Apothecary or Chaplain until the incumbent Master can assign a replacement, or one is elected by a conclave of captains and senior officers.'

The sergeants nodded, and the cold coiled tighter on Dumah's spine.

'Allow me to rephrase,' the Apothecary said drily. 'I have no interest in taking command. I wish only to see Cretacia and begin rebuilding our presence there.'

'Election does not require consent,' Hariel said. 'Only compliance.'

'He should not hold command alone,' Dumah said a little too quickly. He ignored the questioning looks and muttered curses, his eye-lenses fixed on Barachiel. 'Another should share it with him, a redundancy in case of death or… *incapacity*.'

Barachiel met his stare, his jaw tightening and fury threading his eyes. Silence held the strategium in a vice-like grip. Dumah did not break his stare. Their brothers knew nothing of truths Barachiel had chosen to omit. The Siege of New Rynn City was among the bleakest days of the early crusade, a slaughter that brought neither honour nor glory to its survivors.

'I suggest Dumah share the command with Barachiel,' Paschar said. Dumah looked at him, suspicious. Paschar was a brother, but not a friend. After their disagreement aboard the *Herald*, he was surprised to hear any support from the Librarian. 'He is a capable, composed commander, and his devotion to the Great Angel's legacy is second to none.'

Hariel nodded, as did Teman. Hanibal shrugged, indifferent.

'Agreed,' the sergeants chorused.

'Then it is settled,' Dumah said, inwardly breathing his relief. Barachiel fixed him with a hooded stare, then left without a word. Dumah chose to let him stew. He would bring the Apothecary to Isaiah once he had cooled down. 'To your duties, brothers. Difficult straits lie before us, and we cannot afford another moment of laxity.'

TEN

Barachiel strode past the empty cells of twelve-aleph, his lips folded in a tight crease. The sound of slammed doors echoed through the cramped confines, and the acrid stench of fear clogged his nostrils, its potency enhanced each time he passed a hunched mute in Reclusiam robes. He ignored their low bows and signed obeisances, uninterested in their respect, or the wet gleam of their salt-rimed eyes and the last embers of hope burning there.

Barachiel's fingers were curled into fists, his blood set to boiling.

Dumah had humiliated him before the council, his low intimation enough to ensure they shared command of the Fourth. Barachiel told the truth when he said that he had no interest in the command, but Dumah's threat stirred his fury. It was Dumah's recklessness in pushing for the attack on Polaris that had cost Tanthius his life and delayed their mission. Servos whined in Barachiel's knuckle-joints, his fist tightening. Dumah swore to never speak of Rynn's World, and yet obliquely threatened to do so the moment it suited his purpose. Now, he dared summon Barachiel with nothing more than vagaries?

The Apothecary's fist slammed into the bulkhead, denting it.

Serfs looked at him, thoughts they could not whisper expressed in wide eyes. He ignored them, spying Dumah in the shadows several yards away.

Dumah was armoured and armed, his repulsive death's head concealed behind the Emperor's grinning skull mask. Barachiel was thankful for that, at least.

'You summoned me?' Barachiel said bluntly. A tortured roar shook the heavy iron of the cell door. Barachiel glanced at it, curiosity piqued, memories of the Thirst-stricken Reiver rising unbidden from his subconscious. 'What do you need, *brother?*'

Dumah unlocked the cell door. Barachiel followed him in.

Shock stole his breath, and wrath scorched his voice raw.

'Isaiah,' he breathed, turning to Dumah. 'He lives?'

'After a fashion,' the Chaplain nodded. 'To everyone save us, he is dead.'

Barachiel moved closer, careful to remain beyond reach. Isaiah thrashed against his restraints, howling in impotent rage. The Apothecary stared into Isaiah's eyes, feeling the fevered madness and endless sorrow of a murdered demigod clawing at his mind, demanding admittance.

'I heard the rumours, but I dared not believe them,' Barachiel said, backing away, breathless and numb with horror. Cold sweat sheened his forehead, his nightmare now writ in flesh. 'This cannot be happening. Not now. *No.* Cawl... He ended the Rage.'

'Clearly, brother, he did not,' Dumah said.

Barachiel's eyes fell to Isaiah's reforged power armour, the ceramite burnished black. Bloody saltires adorned Isaiah's pauldron and poleyn. Its plastron was decorated with rare Baalite bloodstones set in a trim of gilded steel. Barachiel's stomach knotted.

He knew what manner of warrior used such wargear.

Berserkers. Monsters. Warriors consumed by the genetic memory of Sanguinius' death, and the blistering rage that fuelled their father as he faced his once-brother aboard the *Vengeful Spirit*. The Flesh Tearers' history gushed red with the oceans of blood spilled by such beasts. He turned back to Dumah, the blood draining from his face, horror blended with disbelief and complete, utter revulsion.

'You resurrect the Death Company?' he whispered. 'Are you insane?'

Dumah's skull mask grinned, ruby eye-lenses glittering.

'It is a part of who we are, our heritage and identity. There has not been a war that our Chapter has waged without a Death Company at its heart.' Barachiel was sickened to hear a dark, twisted reverence in Dumah's voice. 'It proves we are the Great Angel's sons as much as any Firstborn son of Cretacia, as worthy of his holy wrath as any other.'

Barachiel shook his head, his voice pleading. Dumah could not be this blind.

'It is what our Chapter *was*, not what we should seek to be again.'

Dumah batted the words away, a violent twitch little different to Isaiah's maddened thrashing. Anger ripened his voice. 'What would you have me do?'

'Kill him,' Barachiel said, quashing his regret. 'Lest the old curse infect us all.'

'As I should have killed you?'

'You swore to never speak of that,' Barachiel snapped. Wrath roared in the blood that pounded through his skull. 'I was not lost to the Rage.' He paused, disgust clotting his voice, and his blade rasped free from its scabbard. 'This *beast* is nothing more than a tortured echo of our father and brother. We should put him down, before his madness claims us all.'

'Isaiah is our brother, not a dog. I will not allow him to suffer dishonour.'

'He channels the madness that will doom our bloodline.'

'He channels the spirit of our lord, the strength of his blood that resides within us all. This *madness* is a sacred gift from Sanguinius. It touched his life, and will touch ours, as is proper. No amount of Martian genomancy can change that, and it plagues us far less than the Thirst, my brother. Perhaps you should focus more on your own remit, and less on mine.'

Barachiel bit back an angry retort, wrestling his rage into submission.

'Why summon me if not to seek counsel?' he asked, ignoring his desire to crush Dumah's skull. 'You did not bring me here just to tell me our brother endures, or of your plans to corrupt our chance at a clean legacy with the Death Company's rebirth.'

'Isaiah is our brother, and he deserves better than the Executioner's Axe. He should die in honour and glory.' Dumah watched him, his skull helm's leer mocking Barachiel's silence. 'Who are we to deprive him of that? He may also be the key to retaking Cretacia. Where we may falter, the Death Company will not. They know no hesitancy. They are relentless, and blessed with Sanguinius' might and holy fury. They are the hammer that will break Cretacia if it shows any sign of rejecting us.'

Barachiel snorted. 'Cretacia is the cradle of our Chapter. It will not require retaking, or reject us, and we will not fail. Now, speak plainly, brother. What do you want of me?'

'Isaiah will require your ministrations if he is to maintain his strength for our return to Cretacia.' The confidence in Dumah's voice teased Barachiel's rage to the fore. The Apothecary vented it in heavy breaths, resisting the desire to drive his chainblade into Dumah's throat. 'He must be fit and ready so he can die in glory and earn his place at the Angel's side.'

Barachiel cast the data-slate aside, ignoring the dull clang as it struck the bulkhead, and the crinkle of broken glass that followed. His personal sanctum was stacked with reports from Thuriel and Aesha, the surgical teams and exsanguination slaves. Bureaucracy buried him beneath tedious demands, and his research into the Rage formed his gravestone.

He scowled, glancing over the pile of librarium scrolls, cogitator disks, info-crystals and data-slates that Paschar had delivered. The Librarian was good to his word, delivering every record: detailed treatises on the Rage's nature as a spiritual or psychological affliction; comparative neurological reports and autopsies on warriors who fell to the Rage in the span of solar months and years versus entire centuries, between brothers from a dozen Sanguinian Chapters; and detailed research on the Flesh Tearers' particular gene-seed mutations.

He reclined in his chair, digesting the contents of the last slate, a treatise on the Death Company's effectiveness, calling for it to be a standing force under direct command of the Reclusiam. It was hardly a persuasive argument, doing little to ameliorate his own concerns about their reformation. He feared its return was simply the first step back towards the days of infamy, and that the Flesh Tearers would remain synonymous with unrestrained violence and warriors lost to frenzy and madness. As he had almost been lost on Rynn's World.

The mere thought filled him with desperate vigour.

He racked his brain for an alternate source of information, desperate to avoid the fate that beckoned him with skeletal fingers and a rictus grin, cursing as an idea hit home. There was one he could go to, one with a knowledge of Cretacia that no other aboard the *Cretacian Justice*, or their escort vessels, could possibly possess. The only one born on Cretacia.

Seth's emissary, Venerable Brother Daeron.

Barachiel stepped back from the sarcophagus, offering his thanks to Hariel as he departed the Hall of the Honoured Dead. Cretacian runes detailed battle-honours accrued across centuries of service: Agata, Acralem, Lucid Prime, Cryptus and Baal Primus. A lump bulged in his throat; their import was not lost on him. Daeron had fought beside the Grey Knights and Blood Angels against the Archenemy, and slaughtered civilians and Space Wolves at Honour's End.

'I cannot move.' The Dreadnought's voice crackled through its speaker-grille, timbre tainted by burgeoning wrath and artificial modulation. 'Why can I not move?'

'Your sarcophagus is not linked to your chassis, Daeron.' Barachiel moved to stand before the Dreadnought's optical sensor, stylised like a Space Marine's helm, hands clasped behind his back. Daeron snorted, a short burr of static, but said nothing. Barachiel continued. 'Cretacia remains distant, and there is no enemy worthy of your attention.'

'Why rouse me when there is no home to greet, or blood to shed?'

'One of our brothers has fallen to the curse of our father's fury. Another drags himself from the wilderness of the Thirst, his craving increased a hundredfold. I need your counsel.'

Another burr, though sharper, like a Land Raider stripping its gears, scraped from his vox-caster. It took Barachiel several moments to realise it was the veteran's laughter.

'The Butcher's Primaris Marines are as flawed as we! How proud he must be!'

Barachiel's eyes flashed behind his lenses, and he forced himself above the jibe.

'I need to know more of Cretacia, the potential for our salvation that Amit spoke of. You were an Apothecary before your interment, Daeron. What do you know of this?'

'Return to the apothecarion, brother. You will not like the answer.'

Wrath burned bright in Barachiel's heart, his hand falling to the krak grenades at his waist. Equal breaths slowed his heart rate, counts of four centring him in the moment. He had a purpose, one far greater than the rage roiling within him. Wrath would not rule him.

'Hear me, old one. The Flaw cannot be allowed to dictate our fate.' A low snarl edged his voice, that of a caged beast yearning for the wilds. It did nothing to quash the fear sinking icy fangs into his heart, flooding him with the same crawling cold. 'Our Chapter was caught between death and excommunication for millennia. Would you see us so shamed once more, even as we drag ourselves into a place of pride and honour under the Angel's gaze?'

'We *have* our place under the Angel's gaze!' the Dreadnought blared. 'His fury burns brightest within us, and we honour him with every thought and breath.'

'The Rage must be cured, else we risk failing in our duty to the Imperium when it needs every loyal servant. Such a stain would forever dishonour the Angel, and his sacrifice,' Barachiel said, wrath thickening his voice. Cawl had failed to ameliorate the curse, as had Daeron and his predecessors. He would not fail, nor would he succumb. 'There must be a way to defeat it.'

'You are not naïve enough to believe that. Wrath is part of who we are, as it was for our father and forebears. It was the struggle against it that defined the Great Angel in his own lifetime, his resistance a show of his strength and his purity, even in his darkest moments. The Rage is all we have of our lord, the only thing keeping us close to him.'

Barachiel paused, taken aback by the sudden softness in the Dreadnought's timbre. He thought of the Blood Angels, blessed with the relics Sanguinius had borne in life, the Angel's life story inextricably woven into the very culture of their home world. Not a day could pass where they were not close to the Angel, either to his artefacts or the halls and desert dunes that had once known his tread. It was less so for the Flesh Tearers.

They had only the memory of his wrath to hold close.

'No,' he said, hearing the lie even as he gave it tremulous voice. 'The Angel was pure, numinous, a being of nobility that surpassed all others. He defeated the Rage within himself, as must we. You will tell me of Cretacia, Daeron, or I will bury you here. You will succumb to madness, alone and forgotten, forever denied the honourable death you crave.'

He hated himself for the threat, but he needed the truth.

Daeron laughed. 'I advise you for the final time, for your good and that of our kin. Let Cretacia's secrets lie, for they offer no salvation. The Rage always wins – we can only fight it.'

Barachiel said nothing, and the Dreadnought's bio-signs slid towards somnolence.

'Please, lord! No! No! Please!'

Barachiel ignored the thrall's piteous cries, his focus reserved for Daeron's warning.

Let Cretacia's secrets lie, for they offer no salvation.

The thrall loosed another frightened yowl, squirming in his restraints. He shrieked in pain, tearing tendons in his desperation to free himself. Barachiel ignored his whines, forcing a grox-leather strip between his teeth. The acrid tang of machine oils and lubricants blended with sweat clung to the thrall's tunic and breeches, and his eyes screamed pure, absolute terror.

Let Cretacia's secrets lie, for they offer no salvation.

Barachiel had spent days pondering those words between mass exsanguinations, surgeries and training. It had to be a lie, or a lapse of memory. Such things were not uncommon with the venerable war machines. He reapportioned his focus to the task at hand. The Red Thirst was growing among his brothers. It had to be satisfied. Scores had already died for that end.

'Lord,' a small voice said, its feminine tone shaky. 'He is ready.'

Barachiel pulsed a thought to the auto-chirurgeon, and watched with detached curiosity as its needles penetrated the thrall's wrists and ankles. The Apothecary's pulse quickened as blood oozed through the clear plastek tubes towards the collection tank in the corner, his own Thirst pooling in his mouth. The temptation scratched his throat like sandpaper – it was almost unbearable.

'How many remain to be done?' he asked Aesha, distracting himself.

The adjutant stood in the far corner, clutching her data-slate close to her chest. Green tinged her cheeks and tears trickled from her swollen eyes down the tight lines of her face. She consulted the slate, her voice shaking, and she retched several times.

'Three hundred and fifty-six mortis drains.'

Barachiel nodded and crossed the cell, pressing the release rune. He stepped through, Aesha dogging his shadow, as he moved to the next cell, and the next screaming serf.

Let Cretacia's secrets lie, for they offer no salvation.

That could not possibly be true.

Barachiel swirled a vial of blood into his wine.

Its scent filled his nose, blending with the wine's fragrant bouquet. He knew brothers that drank it straight, relishing its heady, salt-iron tang. Others added it to their nutrient gruel or daily wine ration in the same manner as the Blood Angels, a thin layer of civility to shroud the ritual barbarism of the act. The wine spiced the blood, enhancing its flavour.

Let Cretacia's secrets lie, for they offer no salvation.

The words pressed themselves into his mind, forcing him to stop mid-swirl. The scent of blood-infused wine sharpened his hunger, feeding the flicker of wrath Daeron's warning inspired in him. His continued research had revealed nothing beyond the ancient belief that Cretacia was the Chapter's purported salvation and several telling gaps in the archival data where it concerned the Rage. It was in those gaps the secret dwelled; he was certain.

He drained the goblet in a single draught, its effect immediate.

Galleries of stolen memories reeled across his eyes, private moments of servitude and selfishness, intimacy and isolation he could never relate to. The intensity of the emotions sickened him, and he was glad he was no longer entirely human. They were self-centred and vain, their brief lives weighted with fear, anguish and pain. He could never be like them.

He leaned back in his chair, extracting his identity from the donor's. Warmth spread slowly through his body, his hearts beating faster as he felt the man's strength alloy with his own, an electric tingle that sparked fresh sensations in every molecule of his body.

Barachiel smiled, his Thirst sated for the moment.

The combat-servitor collapsed in a sparking heap, its head torn clear.

'Next,' Barachiel said. He grinned, his feral smile filled with disdain, as another cybernetic gladiator stepped forwards. Hazard stripes marked the exhaust nozzles of its multi-fuel reactor. Plasteel shells protected its high-response fibre bundles and oiled pistons. One arm ended in a spiked cudgel, the other an energised blade. Its life-leeched voice cut the silence of the arena.

'Program Beta-Three-Two. Fail-safes disengaged. Maximum lethality.'

The servitor lurched forwards, the ungainly lumbering that typified its breed absent. It moved with a fluidity that reminded Barachiel of the acolytes aboard Polaris. There was no hesitation, nor trace of fear. Aggression burned in its flat, murder-red gaze.

Its torso pivoted, cudgel hefted to strike.

Barachiel pivoted aside the blow, blocking the decapitating swipe that followed. He lashed out with a thunderous jab that cracked its cheek. Viscous blood sprayed his visor, the servitor's nose reduced to a misshapen lump. He sliced for its throat, chest and arms. Chainteeth skittered across plasteel armour or snagged and tore free.

It blocked his blows where it could, its style more brute force than speed. Blood jetted from cut veins and arteries, though the damage did nothing to slow it. Its biological system was proofed against such easy death by its augmetics and the combat narcotics pumped into its body from a subcutaneous pharmacopeia.

It blended defence into attack with superlative skill.

Barachiel ducked decapitation strikes and weaved aside overarm blows, the disruptor fields blistering his skin. Its cudgel crashed into his chestplate, cratering it and fracturing his ribs. Barachiel quashed the pain, parrying another two blows, driving his chainsword into its shoulder. Teeth chewed through flesh and cabling, and its cudgel arm clanged to the floor. Its sword punched through his abdomen and agony shrieked along his nerves.

Blood seeped from the wound, sizzling on the blade.

Barachiel grabbed the blade, ignoring the thunderclap of shattering ceramite and fatty sizzle of roasting flesh. Servo-muscles snarled as he wrestled the servitor's strength, forcing the blade to remain embedded in his abdomen. Fury dragged his lips into a rictus grin. Pain widened it, and he drove his knuckle-guard into the fuller, shattered ceramite shards burying themselves in his visor. The second blow snapped the blade halfway along its length, and he buried his chainsword in the servitor's neck. He dragged the blade across, its head bouncing free.

Let Cretacia's secrets lie, for they offer no salvation.

'Next,' Barachiel snarled, his vision framed with black mist.

ELEVEN

Dumah stared blankly at the shuttered oculus. The azure light of active cogitator screens cast shadows on the dark metal that cavorted with a hellish life entirely their own. They reminded him of fire-worshipping feral-worlders, voices raised in primitive expressions of praise to the Emperor in His aspect as a lord of light and fire as they cavorted around a pyre.

He thought of the Cretacian tribes, the relics left in their care and the vile desecrations the ignorant savages were no doubt perpetrating. Spears of pure pain lanced through his skull, and sharp pulses were concentrated around his temples. His vision blurred; the roar of distant gunfire and the chemical scent of weapons discharge swam under his nose. He wanted to kill, needed it, craved it more than air and breath. But his incarceration in the worthless tin can of a vessel that tossed and tumbled on the roiling tides denied him the opportunity.

A tocsin sounded, its dolorous clang ripping through his pain.

Étain moved to the edge of the dais, her junior officers gathering at its foot. Dumah tried to focus on them, smelling the vile reek of their fear, and the subtle shifts in their stance that spoke of discomfort beneath even this minimal regard. They spoke, reading from data-slates clutched in sweating hands. The pain ground through his skull like millstones, blurring their voices. Blood trickled from his nose. He tongued stray droplets into his mouth, the Thirst's dry itch and incessant pain fading for several precious, peaceful moments.

'Noted,' Étain said, turning to the next thrall-officer. 'Helm?'

'Our course continues, despite the punishment of the Rift,' replied the helmsman, a young man with a close-cropped beard and blond hair. He licked his lips nervously. 'The Navigator recommends we turn back, before we become lost in the immateri...'

Dumah pushed himself from the throne, crossing the bridge in a heartbeat. The man failed to stifle a whimper as the Flesh Tearer's glittering eye-lenses met his gaze, the musky tang of animal fear filling the Chaplain's nostrils. Tension set every muscle in Dumah's body thrumming. Adrenaline scorched his veins, and his mind swam on a sea of violence, visions of blood and death a terrible siren call to the beast chained in his soul. He had felt it grow in recent days, its touch infused with the sunfire wrath of a murdered angel.

It took every scrap of his will to resist the impulse to kill.

'You dare show cowardice to the Angel's chosen sons?' He leaned closer, his voice a carnodon's threatening purr, made more menacing by the static that crackled from his war-helm's vox-caster. 'You dare question the mission given to us by Lord Seth?'

The serf said nothing, the scent of his fear ripening.

'Worthless wretch. You shame the Chapter with your weakness and your cowardice.' Dumah stood upright, tuning his vox-caster to the maximum. He let his gaze rove across the bridge thralls. They had ceased their toil, and watched him with guarded expressions.

'There will be no retreat!' Dumah bellowed, and several serfs cringed at the sudden, sharp roar. 'The Flesh Tearers do not shirk from this task because it is difficult, and nor will you! The Great Angel watches us all. He weighs our worth through each moment of bravery and cowardice. I will not allow cowardice to bring shame to the name of Sanguinius, or Nassir Amit, who was the greatest of us.' Silence enveloped the bridge, and Dumah let it fill their minds with shame. 'Will any here defy the Chapter's will?'

Seconds ticked into minutes. None dared speak, not even Étain.

The silence held until Dumah left the bridge. Sergeant Toivo stalked past him in the main arterial passage, ready to assume watch over the bridge. Dumah ignored the salute the sergeant offered him, exhaling his wrath in even, regulated breaths that did nothing to clear the scent of sulphur and corpse-flesh still lodged in his nose.

The serf lay dead on the dark flagstones of the Reclusiam floor, his neck broken and his flesh chalk white. Twin puncture marks concealed themselves in the purple bruising over his carotid artery. Dried blood described a glossy reddish-brown pool around the body, yet there was not a single drop of liquid vitae. Only dust, and the lingering scent of blood.

Dumah stepped over the thrall, ignoring the dry, persistent itch in his throat. Five days had passed since he last took blood, and the Thirst threatened to spiral beyond his control. He walked the length of the nave, approaching the kneeling form of a Flesh Tearer in full battleplate, kneeling in the shadow of Sanguinius' effigy set in the starboard transept.

The Angel looked down upon his sons, his noble visage carved in a moment of wrath. One hand rested on the pommel of the Blade Encarmine, while the other was held out, open in an offer of mercy to a defeated foe. This representation defied convention among all other representations of Sanguinius in that it did not capture him in a moment of soulful reflection, nor focus solely on his angelic grace and beauty. It caught him in his truest self, at a moment of struggle between his virtuous heart and furious soul, the struggle that had defined his second sons for ten millennia. It was Dumah's favoured representation of his beloved father.

Dumah's voice cut through the silence like a chainsword. 'Castus.'

The Flesh Tearer rose and turned to face him.

Dents and scorch marks patterned Castus' plastron, each no larger than his thumbnail. Slivers of copper glinted in the firelight of nearby flambeaux, the teasing edge of bullets still lodged in his ceramite. Blood stained his lips and cheeks; its coppery scent thickened the air. Dumah salivated. Something howled in his chest, demanding satisfaction.

Castus fell to one knee. 'My Lord Chaplain.'

'You succumbed to the Thirst,' Dumah said, standing over the other warrior, crozius loose in one hand. The Rage tormented him, seeding his mind with visions of Castus' broken skull, blood and bone staining the disruptor-sheathed head of his maul. He forced them back down, mag-locking the weapon to his thigh. He did not trust himself enough to hold it.

'I did. I profess my guilt before the Angel and accept his judgement.'

'You profaned this place with death, and blood spilled outside the practices of the Chapter for communion with our fallen, our father and the Emperor. This is a grave offence.'

Castus nodded, and bared his throat, as though ready for a blade.

'Explain,' Dumah said, measuring his breaths. The scent of blood was agonising.

'I could not control myself,' Castus whispered, his face screwed by confusion. Dumah said nothing, allowing him to search for the right words to frame his experience. 'The fury, it took me as I trained in the sparring cages. Everything was blood and screams.'

'You slew others?' Dumah asked, indicating his plastron.

'I cannot be sure,' Castus said. Dumah was certain he had. 'I remember little else beyond the blood coating my throat, its scent in my nostrils, and the thralls' screams.'

'You will cleanse your flesh, then divest your armour for a penitent's robes,' Dumah said, suppressing the hot pulse of Sanguinius' rage. It brushed his vision with black, but the Chaplain held firm to himself. The Great Angel was wrathful, but also merciful. 'Return here in three hours. I will pray to Sanguinius for guidance on the measure of your penance.'

Castus bowed his head and departed, the door slamming behind him.

Dumah activated his vox-bead. 'Barachiel, your plan is failing.'

Dumah examined Carnarvon's crozius through the stasis field's haze. It was far from the first time he had visited the weapon since it was transferred from the *Victus*, and each time he left with the same hollow certainty. This weapon called to him, to that part of his spirit that was forged entirely of the Angel's wrath. That crozius was meant for *him*, and no other.

Hesitantly, Dumah deactivated the field, and removed the crozius.

His fingers curved effortlessly around its haft, the scent of sacred oils and unguents clinging to the metal. Kamiel and Israfil had performed its consecration perfectly, though he had redone it to be certain. The Flesh Tearers sigil at its heart glittered silver and carnelian, and the fanged executioner that formed its body seemed to draw the light to it, almost non-reflective despite the flickering glow of the fire-bowls and flambeaux.

After several moments, he replaced the weapon and reactivated the field. Though he tended his flock of one with diligence and patience, he was not yet worthy of the weapon's legacy. It was not only the weapon of Carnarvon, but every High Chaplain that had come before him. Each one had been a Watcher of the Lost, and he had not yet earned that title.

He had not yet led the Death Company into battle.

Screams clotted the fleet-wide vox.

The cries squalled from vox-horns carved in the semblance of hooded, skeletal angels, the interference doing nothing to mute the madness and pain bloating the wails. Serfs ceased their labours and cast fearful looks at Dumah, who stood immobile on his command dais. The screams sent fresh pain knifing through his mind. He clenched his teeth, breathing hard.

'Vox-mistress,' Étain barked. 'Isolate and terminate that signal.'

'Attempting.' The former tech-priest exchanged rapid burbles of binharic cant with a coterie of specialist servitors in her tiny queendom. 'Failed. Reattempting.' Her warbling rose in pitch, a sign Dumah interpreted as frustration as her nerve-deadened face betrayed no such cue. 'Failed. The signal is coded priority aleph-one and must be terminated from source.'

'Reattempt,' Dumah snarled, kneading the side of his head.

'It will do no good, my lord,' the vox-mistress warbled, her inhumanity removing any trace of fear. 'The signal will continue until the afflicted vessel is destroyed.'

He cursed, agony grinding against the reinforced bone of his skull, the rage born from it more than the simple fury of a berserker. It was the cries of the beast shackled in his soul. It moved behind his eyes: red retinal slits filled with the mingled fury and sorrow of a murdered demigod. He kneaded his temple with his fist, waving Paschar over with the other hand. The Librarian's jaw was locked tight by tension, and his flesh clung tight to his cheekbones.

'Brother, can you identify the source of this... *irritant?*'

'The *Wrathful Angel*,' Paschar snarled, wiping blood from his nose. Tics wracked his facial muscles, his eyes swollen with a pain that only psychic souls could know. 'Its Geller field has failed, its decks are flooded with raw warp energy. Its crew's pain saturates the warp's tides, the agony of thousands compressed into a single chorus.'

Dumah grunted, unimpressed by the Librarian's florid description.

'Should we not try to aid them, my lord?' Dumah turned bloodshot eyes on the man who had spoken, the insignia of the Master Scutum on his collar. Desperation and fear clotted his voice. Dumah watched him, irritated the way a human might be with a gnat. 'We can extend our Geller field to encompass them, and send armsman teams to evacuate the survivors.'

'That is too great a risk,' Dumah said, irritated by the man's naïveté, allowing anger to sharpen his tone. 'A fact, as Master Scutum, you should already know. One misalignment in the shield projectors, a single second of weakness in the shield matrices, and we are lost. The warp will swamp this vessel. Its beasts will slaughter all aboard and devour the souls of the damned for their own amusement. I will not allow human sentiment to delay our mission.'

'But there might be survivors,' he said weakly, shaken by Dumah's bluntness.

'There are no survivors,' Paschar said leadenly. 'Return to your station, mortal.'

'Is it so easy for you to condemn twenty-five thousand souls?'

the man shouted, anger rising in a hot flash to cover his shame. It swelled his reed-thin voice. 'Do we mean so little to you that you can brush aside our deaths like dust from a cloak? The Navigators warned we should have turned back days past. Answer us honestly, Flesh Tearer, are you so desperate for home that you will condemn us all to death and damnation simply because you are too stubborn to take heed of reason?'

Dumah closed on the lieutenant, the beast born of Sanguinius' wrath screaming for blood. The man trembled, but stayed firm, even when Dumah stayed his hand a hair's breadth from his throat. Hate flooded his limbs with a furnace's heat. Dumah forced breaths through clenched teeth, taunting the beast with every second of inaction. He would not make this fool into a martyr for malcontents to rally behind. They could not afford to waste the vitae.

'You have your command, human,' Dumah snarled. 'Take it and be silent.'

'I cannot,' the whelp sneered, bravado failing to conceal the tremor in his voice. 'We have lost too many on this voyage already. Friends. Family. Slain out of hand by your kind, or stolen by the dread reapers of the empyrean, their blood drained. We are forsaken, Flesh Tearer, because of your accursed–'

With a roar that would have shamed a bull carnodon, Dumah tore the man's head from his shoulders. Blood spurted on his visor, and the beast roared through his mouth, demanding more. He slammed his fist through a console operated by a woman in enginarium robes, then ripped it from its mounting. His muscles ached with the need to shed blood, but he fought to maintain control, clenching and unclenching his fists with increasing rapidity, frustrating the beast that howled in his veins by refusing to lose himself entirely.

The flat, circular pressure of a muzzle clinked against his helm.

'Control yourself, brother,' Paschar warned. The beast retreated, circling at the edge of his mind like a wolf frightened by fire. Dumah's awareness returned, gossamer strings of logic and recognition reintroducing his mind to the reality around him. Almost a dozen lay on the deck, torn apart with wanton savagery. Breaths sawed between the stylised teeth of his death mask.

'I am myself, brother,' he said, biting down his anger and forcing his voice to flatten. Ice cold trickled down his spine, his brush with the Rage too close for comfort. Chaplains did not fall to the Rage, their mental and spiritual purity was greater than that of the line warriors. 'I will not shame myself with further weakness, by the blood of Sanguinius, I swear it.'

'Ensure that it remains so, or I shall end you myself.'

Dumah sat alone in his cell, helm gripped tight in his hands.

Blood streamed from his nose and ears, breaths escaping between teeth clenched by a locked jaw as wet, rasping snarls. Pain wracked his body, his muscles bunched tight, and his expression twisted by involuntary tics and spasms. Ceramite buckled under the sheer pressure exerted by his fingers. A scream swelled in his throat, but he refused to give it voice.

He was the master of his wrath, not its slave.

'Sanguinius, armour me against the weakness of my blood,' he whispered, working to unclench his jaw. 'Let your light shield me against the darkness of my soul.'

Something stirred behind the skull-faced mask, a spectre of smoky corposant and angular red eyes that burned with raging soulfire. Its humourless chuckles echoed in Dumah's skull, a call to slaughter that sent arcing tendrils of pain spearing through his cranium. The Chaplain ground his teeth like millstones, the mounting pressure carving his vision with streaks of red and black. Dumah armoured his mind and soul, refusing to bow before the pain.

'By your Blood was I made,' the Chaplain intoned, blood beading around his lips. Its taste exacerbated the beast's fury, stirred its cries for slaughter. 'By your Blood was I blessed to become a Flesh Tearer, the brightest of your sons, the avatars of your purest wrath.'

The beast shrieked, pouring its own furious scorn on his devotions. It fought harder to gain its release, pounding against his mental defences, each blow enveloping his mind in fire. It raked its claws across the soft, yielding flesh of his mind, pain screaming in their wake. He leaned into the pain, using it to bolster his resolve, and hurl the beast back into its cell.

'By your Blood shall I triumph over your rage.'

The beast laughed, its armour slashed by red saltires.

Days passed with aching slowness, and weeks passed in scant seconds. It became impossible to determine exactly how long they had spent in the warp through traditional means, so they were reduced to measuring it in lives taken and in moments of lost control.

Deck thirteen's fourth arterial transitory was one such moment, the scene caught between an abattoir and a slaughterer's paradise. Blood stained every surface, a thick film forming on the marble deck. Limbs were scattered across the deck. Red-sheened offal formed thick mounds of pulped organic matter where it had been ripped free from the bodies. Dumah surveyed the carnage with a skilled eye, and he could not decide which category more clearly defined it.

A Flesh Tearer ripped through unarmoured serfs, his armour stained the gleaming red of Baal's Angels. His chainsword was partially defanged, its track and workings clogged with scraps of torn flesh and blood. He wielded it as a club, cracking skulls and shattering ribs with every blow. He growled pleas for blood and promises of death. His eyes were wide and bloodshot, fangs at full extrusion, his flesh flushed deep, arterial red by the Thirst.

Castus was stencilled on his plastron.

'I warned you,' Dumah said, envisioning himself pulverising the Apothecary's skull, tearing his spinal cord and skull free from his body. The beast chortled, delighted by the imagined carnage, imploring him to enact it. 'Your foolish scheme has failed.'

'It amuses me that you can place blame in this other than on yourself, brother,' Barachiel said, standing beside him before the vid-screen. 'It remained under control until we engaged the genestealers – at your suggestion, as I seem to recall. It would have remained so.'

'We could not abandon our duty to engage the Emperor's enemies,' Dumah snapped, ignoring the beast's incessant pounding against his mental defences. Blood trickled from his nose. 'It is cowards and weaklings that flee their mandate in the name of convenience. Had you stuck with the original scheme, Tamael and Castus would not have succumbed to the Thirst.'

They stared at each other for long minutes. The only sounds were the thrum of active battleplate, the measured pulse of the engines, and Castus' blood-crazed howls. Dumah felt the beast stir in his soul, thrashing against the chains that leashed it to his soul.

'This is a disaster,' Barachiel sighed, turning back to the screen. 'An entire section sealed off to contain a battle-brother lost to the madness of our curse. I imagine that pleases you. More proof that we are sons of Sanguinius, as much as our First-born brothers.'

'It does not please me, brother,' Dumah said, and he meant it. He watched as a serf was torn in two by the berserk Astartes, ignoring how Barachiel had cast his own words back at him. 'This one incident carries residual effects for all our brothers. More may succumb to the Thirst because Castus' affliction was not dealt with earlier. We failed in that.'

'What then do we do? Send a squad to isolate and subdue him?'

'No,' Dumah said. 'We all feel the Thirst, and sending brothers into an area drenched in vitae may cause higher incident rates. The section must remain sealed, and the Thirst must run its course. Servitors can collect the blood, and cleanse it for consumption.'

Barachiel nodded, though his distaste for the plan was clear. 'And if the Thirst opens him to the Rage?' he asked, his voice inflected by a panic Dumah never thought to hear from him. 'What then? Should we not execute him, to prevent the contagion spreading deeper through our ranks? The Rage cannot take a foothold.'

'That is not our way,' Dumah said, perturbed by the Apothecary's alarm. There was something behind it, something personal Barachiel was reluctant to spare. The Chaplain thought of his own growing control issues, the scent of sulphur and sounds of gunfire.

Dumah closed the feed. 'If he falls, he will belong to the Death Company.'

TWELVE

Barachiel's pulse quickened as blood sprayed his cheek, the strangled gurgle of the dying serf fading into the adrenal roar rushing through his ears. Blood sheeted into the channel set under the wriggling corpse, its death spasms spurting blood across the deck. Barachiel grinned, moving on to the next thrall, the second of five suspended from the crossbeam. His fingers twitched around the serrated combat blade, eagerness exacerbating the dry itch in his throat.

Your foolish scheme has failed.

Barachiel ripped the throat from the next thrall, anger boiling his blood as Dumah's words echoed in his skull. The itch grew, becoming a searing fire, and Barachiel resisted the urge to howl his pain through the exsanguination cell. It had been days since his last ration, but they felt like centuries. Prayers ran through his mind as he fought to calm himself.

Dumah could not accuse him of failure in this.

Barachiel moved to the third serf, his crimson-tinged flesh

and extruded angel's teeth reflected in the thrall's trembling eyes. He read fear in the excited pulse of his carotid artery and pheromonal changes in his sweat. Blood rouged his cheeks, the flesh swollen with purple bruises and cuts that promised rampaging infections. His right arm ended above the elbow, a sawn mess of muscle and bone, and his chest was marked with fresh brands decrying him as a traitor to the Chapter. The fire gnawed at his resistance.

'Mercy, lord,' the serf whimpered. 'We wanted only to survive!'

Barachiel laughed, a cruel thunderclap sending petrified shivers down the spines of the three remaining humans. They cringed with every step, the scent of blood clogging their nostrils. They shivered at his smile, his teeth like pearlescent tombstones and elongated canines strung with saliva. His pulse thundered in his brain, each beat a fresh peal of agony, and deep within his blood a creature formed of pure wrath stirred, excited by the promise of death.

'There is no mercy for traitors, mortal,' he said, his voice an intoxicated slur.

He dragged his blade across the serf's throat, relishing the hot spatter of blood on his lips. He tongued it into his mouth, savouring every droplet, fighting the urge to sink his fangs into the dying human's throat. Fear was written in the eyes of the remaining two, the acrid tang of sweat souring the blood-stink that clung to his weapon and armour.

Barachiel slashed the fourth's throat to the bone, shock fixing her expression into one of idiot surprise. She thrashed against her restraints, her fingers reaching towards her throat, the bonds denying that instinctual reaction to stem the flow of blood. Her channel was filled in a handful of minutes, the itch in his throat raised to the white-hot fury of a newborn sun.

He spat excess saliva onto the deck, ignoring Aesha's frightened whimper as she hid behind her data-slate. Childhood prayers were seeded into every panicked breath forced from her lungs, punctuated by the hiss of dissolving steel as he approached the final serf.

The man wrenched his entire body against the chains, seeking to dislodge the hook that held him in place. Barachiel watched him, amused by the vain effort, his stomach muscles tightening. Each lungful of dry, recycled air exacerbated his thirst, the beast in his blood howling its frustration with the apoplectic fury of an enraged angel. His head throbbed, his concentration vanishing beneath a sea of red, until all he could taste was the blood.

He could resist no longer. The Thirst demanded satisfaction.

Barachiel sank his fangs into the serf's throat, and blood filled his mouth.

Chainteeth chewed the air, slick with the blood of slain Navis guards.

Barachiel forced the blow aside, its whirring teeth a finger's breadth from opening his throat. Sweat beaded his forehead, his overworked muscles bathed with lactic acids and fresh, desperate energy. His opponent howled in frustration, laying into him with a rapid succession of blows that Barachiel barely blocked. He gave ground with every parry, driven towards the hatch at his back, the sigil of the Navis Nobilite inscribed above its locking mechanism.

'Dumah! Adariel!' he barked into the vox, deflecting a carving slash and launching his own counter that the Flesh Tearer easily blocked. 'Hanibal has succumbed to the Rage. He is trying to access the Navigator's sanctorum. I need reinforcements in the Tower, now!'

Static hissed across the vox-channel, eliciting a curse from Barachiel.

Barachiel traded blows with the stricken Flesh Tearer. He pivoted under a blow aimed for his neck, deflecting a second and third, blending his defence into a counter-riposte with a slight twist of his hand. Blood scorched his veins, his twin pulses beating a rapid tattoo on his skin. His hearts roared over the thrumming snarls of his power armour as their blades sparked against each other, Hanibal attempting to break his guard with two-handed slashes.

'Horus!' Hanibal howled, his black eyes bloodshot. 'Face me, traitor!'

Broken chainteeth stabbed in every direction as Barachiel smashed Hanibal's attacks aside. The lieutenant never stopped moving, his blade a blur chased by ribbons of blood and meat. Sparks sprayed from a rent torn in Barachiel's thigh, his retinal feed bathed by crimson warning klaxons. Sharp, sudden pain shrieked along his nerves, vanishing quickly into the warm haze of suppressors pumped into his system. His dismissed the unsteady biometrics and tactical data that shuddered across his retinal feed, reserving his focus for Hanibal's blade.

'You cannot cower forever, *brother*,' Hanibal howled. 'You will face me!'

The blade screamed downwards, from the high right. Barachiel deflected it left with a hair's breadth to spare and lunged forwards. His blade tore a rent in Hanibal's side, crimson droplets seeping from the wound. Hanibal's fist slammed into Barachiel's cheek, cracking the ceramite and crumpling the helm into his flesh. Barachiel spat broken teeth, ignoring the dry click as they gathered in his neck seal, throwing his brother back with all his might.

Hanibal roared, hurling himself at the Apothecary, fighting with a savagery that would have made a World Eater baulk. He hacked and hammered, chainteeth flying into the bulkhead or lodging themselves in Barachiel's warplate. Their blades locked, the few chainteeth of Hanibal's weapon inching closer to Barachiel's helm. Sweat greased his flesh, a disgusting layer forming beneath his bodyglove. Armour servos whined in protest, and the weapon's teeth sparked against his visor, which fizzed as its systems shrieked with alarms.

The heavy crack of a bolt rifle broke the deadlock.

Hanibal staggered, a crater punched in his side. Blood sprayed across the bulkhead, and the Flesh Tearer howled in pain. Grapnels punched through Hanibal's limbs, their barbs springing outwards to lodge against his armour. Four Reivers piled onto the stricken officer, forcing him to the ground. Barachiel drew his pistol, pressing it to the lieutenant's temple. He stopped twitching, fixing Barachiel with bloodshot eyes filled with pure rage and hatred.

Wrath pulsed in his blood, a whisper urging him to end Hanibal's life.

Black spots strobed his vision. Snippets of a deck formed from human skulls, and the runic markings of a gang culture long purged from the Imperium burned themselves into his memory. His pistol twitched in his hand, the desire to execute his fallen brother swelling with the scent of sulphur rising in his blood. He grunted, lowering the pistol.

'Transport the mortals to the mortuary for reprocessing,' he snarled to Angelo, as the sergeant's squad tightened the chains binding Hanibal. His augmetic clunked on the deck, his rehabilitation time long since passed. 'Seal every access hatch, primary through quinary. Set a fresh guard from the surviving Navis cohort, then triple it, and reinforce it with your own squad. We cannot afford another threat to the Navigators, or the sanctum.'

'What of the lieutenant?' Angelo asked, his voice a guttural snarl.

'Take him to Dumah. If he proves troublesome, execute him.'

* * *

Barachiel's bolt pistol roared, mass-reactive rounds shredding a human to bloody mist.

He shifted his aim, squeezing a burst towards the red glow of muzzle flashes that burst from behind the coiling smoke of a ruined battle tank. A shadow crumpled, its blood spilling from a ruptured abdomen. Return fire pitted his chestplate with fresh impacts, his retinal feed stained with crimson alert runes. He wrenched the helm free, tasting scorched meat and burning promethium. Barachiel cast it aside and surged forwards, blade angled for the kill.

Humans broke before him, hopeless, wailing pleas to their new gods for deliverance. He snarled, delivering death with the brute economy that had long defined his company. His bolt pistol kicked, speaking death in flashes of monotone gold, and the men of his company sowed their own fire amongst the traitors. Humans burst. Legionaries staggered, maimed or killed by the explosive rounds. Dozens lurched forwards, frenzied butchers in clotted crimson and arterial red, bellowing oaths to the Warmaster and their fell gods.

He fought with a fury unbound, his fist demolishing a bestial face crowned by cortical implants. His chainsword tore through a traitor's chest and throat. His pulse quickened, a roar ripping from his throat. A chainaxe skittered across his pauldron, lubricants and blood jetting from the abrasion. His chainblade speared the portcullis visor of its owner, the spraying blood teasing his thirst to new heights, and he deflected the furious swipes of twin falx.

He thundered his forehead into the World Eater's, relishing the dull splinter of bone. Blood spattered his face, and he parried a thunderous succession of strikes from the powered short swords, their weapons locking as tendrils of disruptor lightning scorched their faces.

'Flesh Tearer,' the World Eater snarled, grinning savagely. 'Well met, Amit.'

Barachiel's eyes snapped open. Sweat slicked his brow and his hands were trembling. He forced his breathing into even patterns, rising from his cot bed, the meaning of this inherited memory insinuating itself onto his waking thoughts.

The Rage was coming for them all.

'Dumah.' Barachiel batted aside the thin wisps of incense drifting from the nearby censer, his thirst stirred from a tickle to a nagging urge by traces of evaporated blood in the smoke. He had fed mere hours earlier, but the desire was with him always now. 'You must put an end to this accursed practice. The Death Company's existence is a threat to our brothers' sanity.'

Dumah ignored him, continuing to circle the relic table set between them. Hymnals of ending lilted from Dumah's tongue, words of praise and sorrow for Sanguinius and the fallen battle-brother bound to the table. They echoed in the penitential cell, lulling the stricken Flesh Tearer to silence, and granting his mind a measure of peace from its madness.

Barachiel waited in silence, his mind assailed by thoughts of New Rynn City.

Fingers clawed at him through an ocean of blood, bare flesh and armour plate. Thin screams and inhuman roars pierced the thunderous pounding of his hearts. He swallowed, burying the shame the memories being around one afflicted by the Rage stirred within him. Dumah alone knew of the massacre and had helped guide him back from the brink of madness.

It was why Barachiel had recommended him to the Chaplaincy.

'They should be granted the Emperor's Peace, not kept alive in torment.'

'That is not your decision to make, brother.' Dumah scooped

a handful of ashes from the fire-bowl at his side. He smeared it across the warrior's plastron, blanketing its battlefield of bullet holes and bolt craters. 'I am the Chaplain of the Fourth Company, the guardian of its warriors' souls, and the Death Company falls under the purview of my office.'

'Their existence is one of torment, brother,' Barachiel said, denying the sympathy that threatened to inflect his voice. He considered drawing his pistol, ending the facial spasms and tics twisting the Flesh Tearer's face with a single squeeze of the trigger. He knew all too well the visions that tormented his stricken kin. 'Is it not the greater gift to end their pain?'

Dumah fixed him with a fierce stare, his lips curled in a wrathful expression.

'Do not confuse your weakness with that of our brothers. You teetered on the brink of the Rage, but did not fall. They suffer communion with our lord, channelling the purity and might of his spirit. They deserve an honourable end, not to be slaughtered like cattle.'

'If you will not end Helios,' Barachiel said as he drew and cocked his pistol, 'I will.'

Dumah moved like lightning, interposing himself between the Apothecary and Helios. His crozius crackled to life, its skull-shaped head trailing arcs of killing lightning. Tendrils snapping hungrily at the narrow gap that separated the two Flesh Tearers, and Barachiel's free hand fell reflexively towards his blade. Dumah's crozius stayed at his side, held loosely in one fist. Amusement sparked behind the black mist that poisoned the Chaplain's eyes, and tension set every muscle in his body thrumming. Fratricide lingered one poor choice away.

Barachiel's hand moved slowly, grudgingly, away from his blade, and he let his bolt pistol fall to his side.

'You will do your duty, and keep them alive. If any of them

fall before their time, you will be held responsible,' Dumah snarled, deactivating his crozius. He moved back to Helios' side, resuming his duties to the damned warrior. *'Brother.'*

Barachiel said nothing, his vision sliced by crackling silver talons.

Barachiel sat in Luciferus' cell, watching the former Intercessor as the sedatives wore off and exsanguinated blood trickled into his veins through an intravenous drip. Being so close to one of the fallen teased his own monster to the fore, the beast in his soul seeding his vision with images of a burning sky and Amit's scarred visage. It was the eyes that haunted him the most, black and bloated by the feral hunger of a starved angel, the fury of a nascent god.

He saw their mirror in Luciferus' eyes, and Isaiah's. They were mirrored in his eyes, and Dumah's, and the eyes of every Flesh Tearer when the Rage rose to the fore. Amit truly was the greatest of them, his wrath a thing of terrible beauty that none could match.

They were petulant children compared to the first Flesh Tearer.

Luciferus thrashed against his restraints, his roar muffled by the gag locking his jaw shut. The saliva drooling onto his chest was infused with hydraklorik acid and left horrendous burns in the flesh, tendon and bone peeking through in several places. Skin grafts and growth stimulants repaired the damage, and the gag was set in place to prevent further scarification.

'We walk a precarious path, brother,' Barachiel whispered. 'Your existence threatens our brothers' sanity. Yet Dumah refuses to execute you, though it could save us all.'

Luciferus snarled, his jaws locked shut. His eyes were thunderous black.

Barachiel drew his bolt pistol, racking the slide.

'I am sworn to shield our brothers from any malady. I cannot let them fall.'

Shame twisted his gut at the personal stake he could not bring himself to admit. He aimed at Luciferus' temple, intoning the hymnals he heard Dumah voice over Brother Helios. Though he stumbled several times, he recognised the hypnotic effect of the words, pressing the muzzle to Luciferus' temple as the last bars trailed from his tongue.

Luciferus responded only with a snarl.

Barachiel pressed his gun to Luciferus' temple. It trembled in his grip, the Apothecary steeling his mind and soul to squeeze the trigger. He looked to the stained-glass pane above them. It was illuminated by a pair of electro-sconces, the shutters sealed while they sailed the immaterial tides. Sanguinius looked down upon them both from the window, his expression of paternal love mingled with sorrow. Barachiel gritted his teeth, finger trembling on the trigger, biting back the grief that threatened to undo him. Tears welled in the corners of his eyes, then trickled down his cheeks.

Barachiel lowered the gun.

He could not do it. He could not slay his brother, no matter the stakes or the risk to his sanity. Sanguinius would spit on him for such an act, for the Great Angel loved his sons more than any of his brother-primarchs and smiled upon them all without favour or bias. Barachiel holstered his pistol, meeting the Angel's gaze once again. He felt Sanguinius' approval stir in his breast, a shadow of the primarch's spirit that lived in each of his sons moving within him. The Great Angel had been testing him, teaching him the truth of his place in the company.

He was his brothers' healer, not their executioner.

Barachiel's finger traced the ridged spines of leather-bound tomes. He bypassed phytological and anthropological treatises penned during the early explorations of Cretacia, the knowledge already committed to memory and his power armour's mnemonic coils. He paused briefly on the section pertaining to the Rage, the desire to continue his research clashing with his duty to prepare for deployment on Cretacia. He selected a text moments later.

It thunked on his lacquered wooden desk, upsetting the stack of volumes and scrolls already there. It was a compendium that detailed the fortress-monastery's layout in copious and exhaustive detail, written by Logisticiam acolytes a millennium earlier. He lit the candle on the right corner of the desk, the crude method of illumination preferred to a lifeless lumen-strip. Tuning out the omnipresent thrum of the warp engines, Barachiel began to read.

Seconds eked into hours, and hours ached with the weight of aeons. Barachiel broke from the text several times to pace, review surgical reports and data on the damned, or to tend to his wargear. Twice he checked the inner workings of his chainsword, polishing each tooth to a glossy silver. He stripped, scoured and cleaned his bolt pistol the same number of times, correcting a fractional misalignment in its iron sights on the second reassembly. Each time he returned to the book, sealing his unguent pots, he longed to be done with the volume. Mortal writings were dull, focused on the trivial and mundane.

Scarcely an hour later, he was forced to revise his opinion, his interest piqued.

His finger traced the words as he read them, the crude scrawl barely legible.

...my master did bid me descend with him into the lower halls. There we recorded the current state of the Chapter's ossuaries for High Chaplain Harath.

Their architecture is little disturbed from the records of Lord

Gathis three millennia past. My master guided us through a secondary barrow, its entrance marked with sigils only used around the Black Tower, and we discovered a passage sealed by an iron door, its sigils of unknown provenance. My master determined these marks were the heraldry of ancient angels, and reported their existence to Furico, Guardian of Rage.

Within days, Furico ordered the record sequestered and my isolation…

Barachiel read on with renewed interest, recognising the sigils drawn on the last page. The Flesh Tearers High Chaplain and Sanguinary High Priest, set beneath the icon of the Blood Angels High Chaplain. Hope bloomed bright in his breast, invigorating him. The presence of the Blood Angels High Chaplain surely tied this chamber to the Black Rage, and the crest of the Sanguinary Priesthood implied a genetic component to whatever lay beyond it.

Let Cretacia's secrets lie. Daeron's words throbbed in his skull.

Questions shot like lightning through his mind. Was this one of the secrets Daeron had warned him about? Had they, in secret and shame, attempted to cure the Rage that had defined the Chapter since Amit? If they found a cure, had it been banned by the Angels, or had they merely come close before the same fate was foisted upon them by the Angel's Firstborn sons?

He would discover the truth in the crypts beneath the fortress-monastery.

Cretacia may yet prove to be their salvation.

THIRTEEN

The astropath's silent scream was like boiling acid poured onto Dumah's mind, and he knew that the mind of every soul still enduring aboard the *Justice* suffered the same.

+The savage world will bathe in the blood of fallen angels.+

The psyker's words were rank madness reforged as syllables. Dumah winced, his hand clutched to his helm as the words speared through his skull, each syllable made rancid by the psyker's pain. Dumah batted aside a strike from Adariel, and Thanatos and Paschar fell to their knees, holding their heads in their hands, blood-wet blades slapping against the training arena's sand.

Through eyes forced to slits by pain, Dumah watched the Librarian vomit blood, and thick trails trickle from his ears. His eyes wept crimson fire, fingers clawing deep gouges into his face. Vitae spilled from the torn flesh and muscles. The air snapped and shimmered, pregnant with unstable psychic energy. Dumah breathed in the charged air, listening to the burbles and screeches of training servitors as their neural cortexes overloaded.

+Storms shall rage across its surface, eight to the power of eight, and blood shall fall from the heavens. Beasts will drown in their bowers, and it shall stain the soul of the world with its vileness. The savage will know the temptation of the Skulled One, the disciples of the dark rage, and death shall stalk abandoned halls in plate of black and red.+

'Can you do nothing to silence this, brother?' Thanatos grunted, the fist clutching his combat knife pressed against his temple. '*Hnnnh*… I feel my brain boiling in my skull.'

'She is First Voice of the Choir,' Paschar said, struggling to his feet, his flesh deathly pale, heaving dry coughs between short, sharp breaths. 'She marshals their power and weds it to her own.' Another stream of blood accompanied by facial spasms. 'I cannot block her while she directs them all.'

Pain blurred Dumah's vision, islands of red like drops of blood in the pleural effusion of the rad-sick. He vomited a foul cocktail of blood and stomach lining, toggling his vox-bead to open frequency before he vomited again. He forced agonised breaths in the spaces between each expulsion, dragging himself arm over arm towards the exit.

'Flesh Tearers… Reach the astropathic chamber… Kill her… now!'

'I am… hnnnh… I am nearby, brother,' Barachiel snarled, his voice strangled by pain. Dumah barely heard, his mind running red. *'I will… deal… with her.'*

Static washed across the vox, broken by his brothers' snarls.

The astropath's voice knifed the meat of his mind, unrelenting and savage.

+Bastions of bone and brass will rise to unseat those of iron, obsidian and stone, and the brightest sons will know despair–+

A bolter cracked across their vox-network, accompanied by a chorus of screams.

'Astropath terminated,' Barachiel growled over the vox. *'Nothing will deny our return to the cradle of our Chapter, nor the salvation of our brotherhood.'*

Dumah laughed, mirth born of relief. Barachiel's words did not fully register with him in that moment, residual pain smearing his senses, and he was still drooling blood.

Dumah watched the sergeants duel from the pulvinus, the incident with the astropath many days past, and forgotten. They hacked at each other, bared blades and blood quickening his pulse. It irked him that he was barred from their contest himself, assigned the dubious honour of awarding the relic blade that squatted on the plinth beside him to the victor, the new Champion of the Fourth Company. The clash of blades drew him away from introspection.

Adariel hammered his knuckle-guard into Micah's cheek. It shattered the bone, blood and teeth spraying from the sergeant's mouth. Micah roared, driving Adariel back with a flurry of savage cuts and thrusts. Chainteeth snapped free, digging into the rockcrete of the arena wall. Crimson spurts marked the sand, drawn from Adariel's torso and arms. Micah slipped a blow meant to cave in his skull, carving a deeper rent in the other Flesh Tearer's torso.

'Adariel will not last much longer,' Kairus said. He stood at Dumah's side, his armour freshly marked with a sergeant's insignia. 'He does not possess Micah's relentlessness.'

Dumah laughed. 'You are only sore because Adariel beat you.'

'Where is the shame in being biased, lord?' Kairus grinned.

Dumah nodded, conceding the point. He watched Micah deliver a rib-shattering kick, driving Adariel to his knees. Adariel deflected the mutilating strike threatening to remove his sword arm, chainteeth throwing up sprays of sand. Adariel tackled Micah to the ground, his fists flying. Blood flecked the settling sand. Micah's nose was a bulb of ruined cartilage, his blade flashing into Adariel's side. A pained roar split the chants of the other sergeants.

'My lord.' A lieutenant approached from a shadowed alcove, bowing three times. The pistons of a crude chromite augmetic arm clicked and hissed. 'The Navigators report we have almost crossed the Rift, though we have lost all contact with the *Son of Blood* and the *Spear of Baal*. We cannot be certain whether they will emerge with us, or whether they are lost.'

'Very well.' The relics were closer now. 'Dismissed, lieutenant.'

The mortal lingered, eyes flitting nervously.

'You have further tidings to deliver, human?'

The man licked his lips, his augmetic clanking in time with his shift in posture. 'The crew suffers, my lord. The astropath's ranting seeded doubt amongst them, and conditions on the habitation decks continue to deteriorate at rapid pace. Something must be done.'

Dumah growled. Rumours of death cults and doomsayers spreading recidivist poison on the serf decks had long reached his ears, demagogues using the astropath's madness to stir the crew towards insurrection. Dumah had ordered Astartes patrols on the habitation decks to maintain crew discipline, and remind them of their oaths to the Chapter. They were too close now. He blinked, realising the serf was still blathering about trivial matters.

'...and the hydroponics bays and water purifiers on hab-sectors aleph through kappa have failed, Lord Chaplain. Lord Hariel has been petitioned by the quartermaster, but he has not attempted their repair, nor have any of his Technicarum thralls or servitors.'

Dumah scowled. 'Hariel's attention remains where it should

be. Sustaining the Geller field's integrity in crossing the Rift has placed a strain on the generator. It requires much time and effort on the Technicarum's part to maintain, but Hariel will make these repairs when he can ensure the generator will not fail. That is all. You are dismissed.'

The mortal remained at his side, hate budding in his eyes. Dumah recognised hunger and malnutrition in his greying flesh, in the infrequent shivers that wracked his body and the sunken valleys of his eye sockets, but his focus never strayed from the man's carotid artery. It pulsed weakly against his throat, a tempting flutter.

'My lord, starvation slays our kin in droves, while others disappear in the company of medicae-serfs, summoned by Lord Barachiel for genetic testing, and are never seen again.'

Micah battered Adariel to the ground with a savage uppercut and two thunderous jabs. The other crashed to the ground, drifting into unconsciousness. Medicae-thralls darted from their alcove, taking care to avoid Micah, who eyed them with a predator's raw hunger.

Dumah turned to the mortal, red sparking in his eyes. His teeth were clenched, and he stood from the throne. The man wilted, hands raised in a futile warding effort. Dumah forced himself to be calm, fists clenching and unclenching as the roar in his blood dissipated.

'Leave now! And take care not to speak of issues you know nothing about.'

The man stared at him strangely, eyes heavy with an emotion that Dumah struggled to quantify. He dismissed it and turned his gaze back to Micah, the Fourth's new Champion.

Corpses, and pieces of corpses, littered the corridor.

Lifeless eyes stared at the gore-streaked ceiling, entrails garlanding the lumen fittings like macabre bunting, or flailing in the dry, desert breath of the aeration units like the heraldic pennants of an Imperial Knight. Survivors watched in mute horror as crimson angels stalked through the ruined bodies, their blades and bolt rifles ending any thought of another servile rebellion. Dumah's gore-encrusted cheeks stretched in pride at his brothers' work.

The sound of laboured breathing kindled dark joy in his heart. A survivor.

Dumah followed the sound, finding the traitor pinned beneath a fallen stanchion, his ribs shattered, and his ghoulish death mask cracked. The Chaplain ripped it away, the hooks that pierced the man's flesh tearing ragged strips free. Blood greased the ashen flesh clinging tight to cheekbone and eye socket. The serf coughed more of the precious fluid through broken teeth.

'Why?' Dumah snarled, applying the thinnest pressure to the man's abdominal wound. The agonised screams drowned the bark of bolt rifles and chainswords. 'Why did you betray your oath to the Chapter and the Emperor?' He pressed harder. 'Tell me, wretch!'

'We refused to be... to be cattle.' Pain suffused each syllable that crawled from the traitor's mouth. Dumah's fingers tightened around his throat, and the dry crackle of tearing sinew cut through the low whir of aeration units. 'You have slaughtered us in... in fits of distemper and left us to die in ships overrun with monsters. You culled us to feed your own deviant appetites. You are nothing more than daemons, wearing the guise of angels.'

Dumah laughed. 'You turned your back on the Imperium because service is hard?' He leaned closer, the tang of blood rich in his mouth. He unlocked his helm, exposing his crimson-tinged flesh and fangs at full extrusion. The serf wilted. 'You think you are a fit judge of our souls, traitor? You know only what the myths tell you of our kind, and that is all laughable.'

'Then grant me the truth, Flesh Tearer.'

'The truth, wretch, is that we kill because we must. We are children of war, baptised in the ashes of victory.' He recited Amit's words from memory, their weight appropriate for the moment. 'We cage our father's fury in our flesh, allowing it to ravage our souls each day we draw breath, resisting its inducement to slaughter. His Thirst hounds us night and day, a scourge we can never be free from, but one that lends us strength to defend humanity. Many think us berserkers, without conscience or thought. We simply choose to live the truth our kin deny. Our father was not perfect, but it is his struggle and his wrath that made him pure.'

'Is tha-that... that th-th-the excuse y-you hide behind?' the wretch gurgled, and the Chaplain saw pity flicker beneath the fear in his eyes. Dumah's fingers tightened. One quick squeeze, and the traitor's life would end, his soul forever damned in the Emperor's eyes. The beast roared, its fury like a flurry of hot daggers plunged into his mind.

Dumah resisted the impulse to kill. Barely.

'Y-you... You believe that your crimes are a matter of p-pragmatism? Ones that en-enable you to serve the Emperor with greater distinction?'

'That is the truth, and here is another. Hundreds die so that millions may live. That is the way of empire, and the reason He wrought the Adeptus Astartes as mankind's guardians.'

A sharp twist snapped the traitor's neck.

Relief painted the wretch's face, infuriating Dumah further. His pathetic delusion and mortal self-interest endangered Dumah's flock, their chance at redemption, and the chance to secure the relics. There was not enough suffering in the universe to match such a crime.

Dumah replaced his helm as Thuriel appeared beside him.

The young Apothecary's armour was stained with the impacts of small-arms fire, his breath heavy with the scent of fresh blood.

'Lord Chaplain, we should dispose of the bodies immediately.'

'No,' Dumah snarled. Penance was needed, even from the dead. 'Drain the blood that remains and grind their flesh to protein paste. Feed what cannot be repurposed to the plasma drives. Let them serve faithfully in death as they failed to in life.'

In a cell on twelve-aleph, Dumah stood beside Castus' convulsing form.

Dried blood streaked the Intercessor's cheeks, his lips moving in a crude mimicry of snarling speech. The stench of blood and raw meat wafted through teeth broken by the repeated blows of an armoured fist. His body reeked of stale sweat and armour lubricant, and his eyes darted back and forth behind blood-encrusted lids in a cruel mockery of natural sleep. Battle had stained his ceramite, the crimson and ash cracked by power weapons and boltguns.

Castus convulsed, his restraints groaning under the pressure.

Dumah smoothly adapted his prayer, the calming choral music and sorrowful lilt of the orchestral servitors blending with his own basso-profundo register. Sanguinius' memories waxed strong in Dumah's mind as he recited the prayers. The sky darkened by the hulls of traitor warships. The earth quaking beneath the tread of traitor Titans. The blood of kin wet upon his blade, and the dream of his father forever slain by his brother's jealousy.

Dumah shook free the maudlin introspection, centring himself in the present. Reciting the hymnals induced quiescence in the fallen Flesh Tearer, the tension coiling his muscles at last beginning to ease. Castus' eyes snapped open and glazed over as he slipped into a trance, activated by the Chapter's psycho-conditioning.

Dumah circled the table, applying unguents to the warrior's limbs. For weeks, he had looked upon the damned with pride, blinding himself to the truth, and the possibility of the heinous act he was now forced to commit.

Gently, he lifted an antique bolt pistol from a lacquered wooden box, checked its feed and chambered a round. He pressed it to Castus' temple, forcing it flat against the flesh as the Flesh Tearer resumed his convulsions. Howls echoed in the corridor beyond, his flock's cries as they begged for war, for blood and for death. They were six strong, barely a fraction of the company's remaining strength. The relic bolt pistol shook in Dumah's hands, and he steeled himself, reciting the litany of fortitude even as he flicked the safety off.

'Long you have suffered in the wilderness, brother,' Dumah said. 'Cast upon the path of rage, your body and soul sacrificed in service of Sanguinius and the Emperor.'

Castus snarled. He was the first to slip too far into the Rage, becoming a rabid animal, to whom only blood and slaughter mattered. Dumah knew of such creatures, and the onerous duty the Chaplains bore towards them. Where the rest could still be used, could be plunged into the enemy's heart like blades forged of Sanguinius' pure wrath, Castus was a liability, more a danger than an asset. He would kill them all, given half a chance. Dumah could not allow that, even at the cost of his battle-brother's redemption. The others had to be given their chance to fight for Sanguinius, and to die in honour and glory. He squeezed the trigger.

Castus bucked violently and fell still.

Dumah knelt beside his brother's body like a penitent before an altar and let the pistol tumble from his fingers. He reached for the rosarius coiled at his waist, eyes glistening with the promise of tears. He coiled the rosarius tighter, adamantine wire slicing into his skin, his blood greasing the obsidian beads. He closed his eyes and let his chin slump to his chest.

'Sanguinius keep you, my brother, and may he forgive me for my failure.'

He remained there, the long hours spent in sorrowful silence and prayer.

Dumah had returned to his chamber and his serfs had divested him of armour.

Alone, and dressed in a simple black robe, he walked over to the wooden desk on the far side of his chamber. It was the only item of furniture beside his cot and arming racks. He sat at the desk, then opened a secret compartment, and withdrew a scroll. He unfurled it and took a moment to study the names of those fallen to the Black Rage under his watch.

Isaiah Akhmani – Assault Sergeant, Fourth Company, born of Terra, 654.M35

Hanibal Adamarani – Lieutenant, Fourth Company, born of Mars, 832.M33

Aleksei Tamael – Reiver, Fourth Company, born of Necromunda, 621.M38

Gael Luciferus – Assault Intercessor, Fourth Company, born of Calth, 159.M33

Helios Varro – Assault Intercessor, Fourth Company, void-born, 137.M36

There was a list for every Chapter of the Blood, a secret roll of honour known only to the Chaplains that guarded the damned. Each compiled their own list and added the names to the Rolls of Memory in the Reclusiam. The list was burned with the Chaplain's death.

Dumah picked up his quill, dipped its nib into the inkwell set at his side. He scratched one more name on the vellum before setting the quill down and casting sand across the sheet to dry the ink. He paused, murmuring another prayer for this newest entry.

Nero Castus – Intercessor, Fourth Company of the Flesh Tearers, born of Neogeddon, 547.M36

He paused for a moment, then picked up his quill again, inscribing a dedication under the name. Grief sickened Dumah's heart as he read the words and cursed himself for his failure.

Mortuus sine Redemptio.

Setting the quill down again, he wondered how many more of his brothers would be put on this list, sacrifice their sanity and souls for a world that would see them expelled from their brotherhood for the perceived sin of not being born on its surface. Of those, he thought of how many might also die denied the chance for their redemption.

Cretacia was not worth even one.

The shrill bray of alert klaxons tore Dumah from his mandated sleep cycle. Slices of crimson light slashed through the bars of his cell door at measured intervals. Low voices pierced the clamour, tinny and mortal. Dumah rolled from his cot, his pistol and combat blade drawn in the space of a single heartbeat. The cell door creaked. Dumah cocked the pistol.

Serfs shuffled in, each clad only in black hessian robes. Dumah lowered his weapons, his sigh one of annoyance. The mortals bowed and moved to the trestles, removing from their robes the assortment of drills, hammers and machine tools used in his armouring. The eldest passed them, mouthing blessings and sprinkling sacred unguents from his aspergillum. A serf bowed and indicated for Dumah to assume position beside his armour rack. He did so.

'For what reason do you armour me, serf?' he asked the elder.

We approach Cretacia, my lord, the elder signed, his gnarled fingers forming the complex hand signals of Astartes battle-sign. *The shipmistress is confident we will exit the immaterium in a matter of hours. Lord Barachiel also requests your presence.*

'What of the penitents?' He could not keep the disgust at the lie necessity drew from his lips in check. It demeaned his brothers to decry them as penitents. 'How do they fare?'

They are well, my lord. Lord Thuriel has been seen on the deck, with new penitents in tow.

He scowled. 'Inform Lord Barachiel I will be with them.'

The serf bowed as the others continued to apply his armour.

PART THREE

'Amit looked upon a galaxy bereft of the Great Angel, a universe without our father's love and light, and his soul was mad with grief. In the stars we set out from Terra to reconquer, he saw only a barren wilderness to be filled with wrath and blood.'

– Azkaellon, commander of the Sanguinary Guard

FOURTEEN

Space rippled, the stars dragging out like the ocean before a tidal wave.

The warp detonated into the Corythos System. Psychedelic particle storms leaked raw madness and radiation through the suppurating wound, granting brief life to beasts that could not dwell outside that nightmarish realm. Undulating tendrils of etheric lightning lashed the aseptic stillness of reality; the throbbing clouds of twisted light framing the tear were infected haematomas pressing against reality's skin, its membrane rippling like water on plastek.

The *Cretacian Justice* limped through the fissure alone.

She was a far cry from the gleaming strike cruiser that had parted with the *Victus* months earlier. Entire districts of spinal minarets and battlements were ripped from her dorsal and aft. Mile-long gouges raked her flanks, claw wounds in a prey beast. Her starboard weapon-carriages were shuttered, her prow lance hooked like an arthritic finger, the power couplings retracted.

Engine stacks coughed blue plasma, liquid promethium crystallising in the void.

Battered and badly mauled, almost all aboard her sighed in quiet relief.

They were safe. They were home.

Barachiel reclined in his command throne, weary of the ceaseless chatter.

Hundreds of voices overlapped, male, female and mechanical augment, a ceaseless cacophony that pressed hard against his skull. Shield strength and enginarium reports clashed with gunnery appraisals and repair updates, the ring of swords without the adrenal rush of the kill. They were repeated over and over, thrall to supervisor to officer, each a fresh link in the chain that led from the lowliest deck-thrall to him upon the command throne.

Or rather, to Étain and Toivo, his chosen representatives in void matters.

Barachiel watched the mortal crew bustle between instrumentation banks and tactical stations, kneading his temple with one hand. Pain clotted the sound of blood rushing through his skull, of officers mirroring reports from their cogitators to Toivo and Étain. The clacking consoles and rolling thud of their heartbeats drowned some of their meaningless bleating. He focused his mind on the one joyous fact the endless chatter brought about.

Cretacia was closer now than it had ever been.

The shutters lifted from the oculus, revealing a vista of stars so perfect they appeared freshly brushed by an artistic savant. Something akin to calm settled on him, his eyes finding the mote of throbbing red light that was the Corython star. Cretacia yet remained uncounted millions of miles distant, a mote of shimmering red sand, yet it exerted a strange magnetism on his soul, more than mere purpose or hunger for knowledge. Awe, and a sense of belonging he had not felt from Baal and Terra, leeched away his pain. That was part of the feeling, but far from the whole. For the first time he felt true hope for their salvation.

'It is hard to believe we are so close,' he said to Paschar, shifting his attention towards the Librarian, away from the discordant percussions of hundreds of hearts beating in close proximity. His angel teeth slipped free from his gums, his mouth flushed with saliva. 'So much has been given to reach Cretacia, even I doubted we would see it. Truly, the Angel has blessed us to be here.'

'The voyage was difficult, even with what we expected crossing the Rift,' Paschar rasped. His skin was drawn and waxen, as though he had suffered a terrible malaise. His teeth had yellowed, and his armour seemed loose on his frame. 'It may be our difficulties are not yet overcome.'

'What do you mean?' Barachiel's eyes narrowed. He had no patience for riddles.

'Cretacia is the Birth of Wrath,' Paschar rasped. 'It is not her nature to welcome any outsiders or be forgiving to those that walk her surface. The tribes have dwelled in freedom for many years. They may not welcome us back, just as the world herself may not.'

'Do not become like Dumah, brother, believing only prophecies of doom.'

Paschar snorted, shaking his head. 'Our void-born brother is well-intentioned, even in his errors. You taught him that particular trait, even if you refuse to acknowledge it.'

Barachiel's lips folded into a tight crease, slow wrath boiling his blood. The Chaplain had eschewed his invitation to the bridge, preferring to remain with his relics and his charges. Three more had fallen to the Rage, bringing the Death Company's strength to eight warriors in total, while Thuriel monitored the four gripped by the Red Thirst. Barachiel prayed to the Angel that they would not fall to the Rage. Dumah's selfishness had cost them enough.

Anger inflected the slow rumble that slipped between his clenched teeth.

'I sought to preserve the lives of our crew, where our brother has indulged an ancient, outmoded tradition that has shamed our bloodline for generations. It serves only to speed our decline into the muck that once mired our Chapter. We should be searching for our salvation, the salvation Cretacia holds for us, not accepting madness as our brotherhood's fate.'

Paschar looked at him, and Barachiel read uncertainty in his expression.

They spent several minutes in silence as Barachiel sifted the mortals' chatter, sorting the sensory barrage into data streams that unravelled in his mind, ignoring the resurgent pain pulsing through his skull. Eventually, he noted an absence in the concerto of vox-horns and voices that echoed in the bridge, one that troubled him on a distinctly human level. He shook it off, as best he could, and summoned Étain to his side.

'Your orders, my lord?' Étain asked, bowing slightly.

The shipmistress was gaunt, her skin grey, stained by grime, lips a thin fold pressed tight by tension. Thick black rings circled her eyes and the vile odour of lho-sticks and recaff clung to her waxen flesh. Her uniform was pristine, her medals gleaming beneath the bridge lumens as though freshly polished, the creases of her jacket and trousers still crisp.

'Have we received any astropathic hails from the fortress-monastery?'

Étain consulted her screen, then disappeared into the communications pit. Barachiel's eyes followed her, digesting the changes wrought on the former vox-mistress. Thick bundles of cables subsumed her, and fresh surgical scars marked the little flesh remaining around the grilles that breathed for her, the chem-shunts and implanted nutrient intakes replacing much of her natural bodily functions. Étain returned a few minutes later, her expression solemn.

'There have been no inbound communications, my lord.' She sent a coded data-burst to his screen. He reviewed it, his own expression darkening. 'There do not appear to be any live signals in the entire system, not even augur-pings from border telemetry beacons.'

'Is auspex running passive scans?'

She stiffened, insulted. 'Since our arrival, my lord,' she stated, matter-of-factly. 'It is standard practice when entering a new system, or one cut off for any length of time.'

'Thank you, shipmistress. Inform me of any further developments.'

'It is strange our arrival has triggered no warning,' Paschar said. The Librarian drew back his hood to reveal a scarred, shaven scalp. A jet-black beard framed his thin mouth, and a scar reached along his jaw. 'The astropathic station on Niraya should have detected us.'

Barachiel keyed a command into the throne arm's haptic control pad.

Deck projectors stuttered to grainy life, the soft purr blending into the bridge's noise. A compressed hololithic representation of the Corythos System's seven worlds resolved in spheres of multi-hued light, their surface appearance and macro-agglomeration datascreed unravelling beside them, drawn from the *Justice*'s archives. Imperial settlements and military installations were points of forest-green light on the surface of five worlds.

Another command narrowed it onto Niraya, the seventh world.

Niraya was a frigid ball of ice, its astropathic way station the sole sign of settlement on its surface. The relay had recently returned to service, one of Seth's efforts to restore the Flesh Tearers' functionality and reputation among the Chapters of the Blood. He wondered whether it had been fully manned and resupplied before the Chapter sailed for Baal.

'Can you detect anything of them, brother?' he asked. 'Or astropaths from the other worlds? The Mechanicus outpost, or the Chapter's orbital defences? Anything?'

The Librarian shook his head and Barachiel suppressed a scowl. He keyed in a string of commands, surveying archival data of each world that lay on their path to Cretacia.

He bypassed the sixth world, Cereus. It was a sparsely populated agri world, with a technology level similar to ancient Terra, when ships of wood and sail were key to forging an empire and war was a thing of nations. Cereus had no astropathic stations or vox-relays, and notions of void-capable craft were the remit of the insane. Production rates screeded beside genetic purity records and details of the Chapter's *pabulum* tithe.

He paused at the fifth world, a gas giant marked by the Adeptus Mechanicus' Opus Machina, with a large mining complex locked in geo-synchronous orbit. It was a source of rare ores and minerals valued by the Mechanicus, and Barachiel scanned details of harvesting rights and local criminal labour tithes in return for frequent tithes of materiel and munitions that the Chapter's own, more limited forges could not produce on Cretacia. He moved on a minute later, irritated that the Mechanicus had not shown the proper respect for their arrival. The priests of Mars usually clung to protocol and stricture like it was a saviour pod.

His lips pulled into a tight smile as his eyes rested on the fourth world, the Chapter's icon rendered in crimson and steel above the data that scrolled beside it.

Cretacia was circled by extensive minefields and an orbital-defence array that would have made any son of Dorn proud. A trio of star fortresses formed the lynchpins of her orbital defences, and there was a small shipyard orbiting her lone moon. Training facilities dotted its barren surface, networks of bunkered fastnesses designed to expose the neophytes and Tenth Company Scouts to combat in new, and more hostile, environments.

'Are you certain?' he asked the Librarian, a cold shiver suspended at the base of his neck. 'Could it not be that the warp storm has fouled their psykers' ability to detect us?'

Paschar shook his head, and the cold trickled down Barachiel's spine. He turned to the vox-mistress. 'Scan for Imperial vox-traffic, maximum range and scanning depth. Now!'

Minutes passed in tense silence, none on the bridge daring to speak.

'No communications detected in-system, lord. Imperial or otherwise.'

'We should hold in the system's outer reaches,' the Librarian suggested, indicating a position several hours from their current location. 'We can deploy telemetry beacons to guard our approach and send Stormraven squadrons on scouting runs over the outer worlds.'

Barachiel shook his head. Cretacia could wait no longer.

'It would give us valuable time to see the *Justice* repaired.'

'No,' he snapped, concern unable to override his eagerness. Salvation was days and a single planetfall away. He was too close for caution now. Any delay would allow whatever had devastated the other worlds a chance to inflict the same horrors upon Cretacia, stealing the Chapter's chance for salvation. More time aboard the *Justice* with their depleted resources increased the chance that he, or his brothers, might fall to the curse. 'Deploy the beacons, and servitor-manned probes, but do not break from our course. We can afford no more delays.'

The conclave met in the hours before the *Cretacian Justice* achieved orbit.

Barachiel hammered his fist into the table, calling the gathering to order. Seventeen Flesh Tearers ceased their pacing, their hands curled around sword hilts and axe throats. He was reminded of caged lions, straining to be released, a feeling mirrored in his own enforced inaction. They could not descend without a plan, and the agreement of Brother Daeron.

He watched Cretacia through the strategium's lone armaglass pane, rotating on her axis. Her skies were a painter's palette of black and grey, summer storms ravaging archipelago chains and continental land masses. Cloud breaks were slivers of colour in the grey and black, sapphire seas and emerald islands granted greater illumination by the tendrils of blue-white lightning slicing the skies. Ochre-orange bruises of volcanic eruptions throbbed in violent imitation of life, tendrils of lava carving fresh paths across the northern reaches.

Cretacia was a world locked in its birth pains, beautiful and primal.

But it did not stir his soul. The news from the dispatched capture-drones had weighed heavy on his mind in the hours between the data's decryption and the conclave.

'Brothers.' Barachiel endured a moment of painful severance, their view obscured by dark iron shutters. 'We have achieved what some believed was impossible. We have crossed the Rift and broken through the Annihilus warp storm. Today, our every sacrifice is made worthwhile.' He paused for a moment, suppressing the eagerness and impatience threatening to bubble through as he turned thought into speech. 'We have reached Cretacia.'

Dumah snorted, an ugly leer splitting his death's-head visage.

'However, not all is good tidings. Our efforts to hail Chapter installations continue to go unanswered, and the capture-drones have revealed that much has changed in the two decades since the Flesh Tearers last sailed Cretacia's skies.'

'What has happened to vex you so, brother?' Dumah asked. 'Is this not what you wanted? The world is still here, whole, unburned. If it is not what you expected to find, or what you had hoped to find, you may remember I told you it would not be when we first set out.'

Several sergeants laughed. Even Teman cracked a slight smile.

Barachiel crushed his irritation, suffocating the snarl threatening to rip from his throat. Lucid visions of Dumah's skull crushed between his hands pulsed painfully through his mind. Dumah may not respect Cretacia, or believe in their mission to reclaim it, but the choice was not his to make. Cretacia was their world. They were going to take it back. Breathing hard, he uncurled his fingers from killer's claws, and they scuttled over the haptic control pad.

The hololith activated, the Corythos System rendered as a trembling tapestry of stars, the glowing system map expanded by ribbon projectors cunningly concealed in the chamber's stanchions and girders until it dominated the entire chamber. His fingers danced over the keys again, overlaying the system with an assemblage of hololithic images, quick-cap picts, augur-scan data and vid-feeds from the worlds passed on the approach to Cretacia. Barachiel buried a smirk as Dumah's smug grin disappeared.

The Flesh Tearers gathered closer, parsing the assembled data and imagery.

'Niraya's astropathic relay has been destroyed,' Barachiel said, indicating the toppled tower partially buried by the snows on the outermost world. Girders and support stanchions twisted skywards like an elder's gnarled fingers, with hunks of broken metal scattered like handfuls of iron coins around its base. There were no life readings across the planet, though the notion that human life could survive in the sub-zero temperatures and highly pressured atmosphere was laughably academic.

'Generatorum overload,' Dumah said, highlighting several of the overhead picts. 'The blast patterns evidence as much. This installation was erected eight millennia ago, and unused for two. The plasma core could have sustained damage, and the Technicarum thralls assigned laboured in ignorance of the compromised technologies. Regrettable, but not concerning.'

Barachiel adjusted the image with the haptic controls, highlighting another set of picts. Niraya's frozen surface was exchanged for the swirling bruise-yellow of the gas giant.

'And the Mechanicus refinery?'

Dumah said nothing, studying the trails of icy wreckage locked in orbit around the planet in sullen silence. Barachiel's eyes drifted over the picts, the refinery's guts spilling into the dark in a stream of shrapnel and void-hardened slag that reached slowly around the world. Fuel reservoirs and processing plants leaked liquid promethium and other, rarer minerals into the void. There were no bodies, even the most flesh-spare of the crew complement were either torn asunder in the facility's death throes or had burst due to exposure to the void.

'What of the other worlds?' Teman asked. 'Aristaeus and Cereus?'

Barachiel shifted the hololith's focus.

In its prime, Aristaeus had been similar to Cretacia, a savage world inhabited by monsters and primitive men, though its inhabitants possessed genetic abnormalities that made them ill-suited for ascension as Adeptus Astartes. Now, fires spread slowly across her major continents, islands and archipelagos drops of grey in black knots of poisoned water that formed the world's seas.

Cereus had weathered similar misfortune. Blight slew its crops and livestock, sludge and skeletons left to complete the cycle of decay. Plains of dust-dry earth packed tight by the lack of moisture stretched across each pict, marked by thin lines of stone delineating separate farms and estates. Its woods were graveyards of evergreens and pines, and quaint townships and small, small cities were remade as ossuaries, with bones piled in the streets.

'And Cretacia?' Thanatos asked. 'What of Cretacia?'

'The electromagnetism generated by Cretacia's storms disrupts our augurs,' Barachiel said. He highlighted the three orbital fortresses, and the fortress-monastery on the surface. The maximum range of all weapon batteries layered itself onto the map. The strike cruiser was a sliver of green, anchored in the deep void, far beyond the range of all three installations. 'We have received no hails from the fortress, nor the star fortresses. Scans indicate they are operating under minimal power, likely drawn from the secondary plasma reactors.'

'Then there may yet be survivors aboard the stations?' Castivar asked. The Aggressor sergeant towered over the other Flesh Tearers, his armour clunking and thrumming with each micro-movement. A rebreather concealed his mouth and nose, and his kill tallies were etched onto both flamestorm gauntlets. 'They may be able to explain what befell this system since Lord Seth sailed to Baal and the confrontation with Leviathan.'

'Possibly,' Paschar said. 'Though it is unlikely we would find them coherent, or even sane enough to provide an adequate explanation. More likely this is–'

'More likely the residual power readings are the work of the servitor complement,' Dumah interjected. Paschar shot him a glare, but otherwise fell silent. Barachiel's lip curled. 'If they were not deactivated, and did not lack for subsistence, they would maintain the basic functions of the station until its destruction, or their deactivation.'

'Is this an artefact of the Rift?' Micah asked. He appeared genuinely perturbed by the changes. 'Some strange phenomenon from the warp energy unleashed by its birth?'

'There is negligible evidence of any immaterial bleed-over,' Paschar said. 'It would have more detrimental effects on the planetary biospheres, and agents of the Ruinous Powers never fail to mark their devastation with offerings or unholy runes. There are none.'

Dumah shook his head, unconvinced.

'Cereus is a feudal world, it possessed little advanced medicine and may simply have been the victim of a major pandemic. Aristaeus has seventy-five per cent jungle on each major land mass. Fires are a hazard during droughts and severe storms. It could be human error, or a conflict between the clans that moved beyond their control. You imagine foes where there are none, desperate for us to stay here and re-establish our dominion over this worthless rock.'

'Those were Seth's orders,' Barachiel said coldly.

'Damn Seth's orders,' Dumah snarled. 'He has exiled us here! We should not stay on a worthless hunk of rock, forever denied honour and glory. We should sever our ties to this damned world, harvest a generation of recruits and take what relics remain. We could sail to Seth's side and wage war upon the xenos and the heretic, as we were forged to.'

'That violates every tenet of Seth's order,' snapped Barachiel, alarmed by the number of sergeants that seemed open to the prospect. 'He did not send us here to raid Cretacia, but to reaffirm our oaths to it. One generation harvested is nothing compared to a continuous source of hardened recruits. It is our world, our responsibility, and our privilege to have. You would be wise to remember that you are not empowered to dictate Chapter policy, and nor am I. Only the Chapter Master can make that decision, and he made his will clear to us both.'

Dumah scoffed, playing to the other Flesh Tearers as much as he was on Barachiel's nerves. Barachiel fixed him with a hard glare, imagining ripping his entrails free.

'Barachiel would have us waste our lives here, playing nursemaid to ill-bred savages, and forging their spawn into sons of the Great Angel.' The Chaplain paused, letting the Flesh Tearers mull his words over. Barachiel's violent urges grew. 'brothers, this system has fallen foul of circumstances Seth could not foresee. The Mechanicus refinery is gone, with it all the materiel needed to forge armour and weapons, and it is likely Cretacia has suffered a similar incidence. We should not tether ourselves to the past, but look forward to the future. It will not make us any less Flesh Tearers to accept Dante's fiat and recruit elsewhere.'

One or two of the sergeants nodded. The rest looked conflicted.

'There will be no talk of abandonment!' Daeron boomed, striding into the chamber with Hariel and Thuriel behind him. The deck shook under the war machine's tread, and every warrior in the room lapsed into respectful silence. Even Dumah sank into a shallow bow. Barachiel and the rest of his brothers bowed deeper as the mighty war engine paused at the head of the planning table. 'Cretacia is the future of the Flesh Tearers, as it has been since the days of Amit. It is a worthless world to most, but it is the source of our strength, the purifier of our wrath, a resource that will not be surrendered at the whim of a stripling Chaplain!'

'Not one of us is Cretacian, dead one,' Dumah snapped, refusing to recoil from the Dreadnought's fury, his crozius sparking in defiance. He drew it across the assembled Space Marines. 'A fact that does not make us any less Flesh Tearers than any son of that wretched rock. Our wrath is the same as yours, the pure fury of Sanguinius, his pain and sorrow forever tearing at our souls, and it is the strength to risk madness channelling his holy wrath into leal service that defines us, far more than any notion of home worlds and crucibles.'

Barachiel suddenly understood the source of Dumah's enmity.

Fear. Dumah *feared* Cretacia.

Not its dangers, or the daily threat of death, but the future it promised. He feared their exclusion from the Chapter's brotherhood, the loss of the acceptance and respect it took them seven long and bloody years to earn. Barachiel sympathised. It was a concern that niggled at them all, at one point or another. He had wrestled with it himself more than once.

'Not one of us was born on Baal,' Daeron said, seeming to recognise the same hidden fear. 'Yet we are still sons of Sanguinius and the Blood. Some forget our founders were also born on worlds liberated on the path to Cretacia, as well as Sacred Baal. Amit counted each of them Flesh Tearers, as we have since. Cretacia made them stronger, as it will you.'

Dumah said nothing, stunned to silence by Daeron's speech.

'We must now decide the apportionment of our forces. I would have squads boarding all three star fortresses and sending an advance guard to the Chapter fortress.'

Barachiel nodded, and murmurs of agreement passed through the other Flesh Tearers. The Apothecary stepped forwards, excitement flooding his muscles with searing adrenaline. He envisioned himself on Cretacia, mining the secrets buried in the fortress-monastery for the good of his Chapter, his bloodline and his Emperor.

'It will take the better part of a day for the *Justice* to be in position to launch gunships to all three star fortresses,' Dumah said, indicating the dotted line that detailed their projected route on the star map. 'If we can prioritise the surface launch, the chosen squads could be in the fortress-monastery hours before the first boarding party launches, and the orbital batteries can provide cover to the *Justice* or scuttle the star fortresses should they prove hostile.'

Barachiel blinked, surprised by the sudden shift in Dumah's attitude.

He measured the Chaplain with a hard gaze, as though by sheer force of will alone he could determine whether Dumah was making a genuine effort towards contrition, or a clever ploy to secure the relics that had first earned his consent to accompany the mission.

'Who would lead the surface assault?' Micah asked.

'I will,' Barachiel and Dumah said simultaneously. They looked at each other, and Barachiel felt the enmity swell between them both. Silence reigned for several seconds.

'I should lead the expedition,' Barachiel said, hot anger building in his chest. His fists clenched and unclenched as he struggled to keep his anger leashed. 'I have proven command experience in jungle terrain, and I have studied the Cretacian biosphere and geography as part of my preparation for this expedition. I know its bounties, and its dangers.'

'Knowledge your initiate shares,' Dumah said, eyes sparkling with amusement. They taunted Barachiel with the same denial Daeron and Barachiel had dealt Dumah. 'You are the warden of our genetic legacy and the Chapter's future. It would be the height of foolishness to place you in our vanguard. If you are killed, our hope for survival becomes that much slimmer.'

The sergeants nodded, and Barachiel's heart began to sink.

'I will not be corralled on this tin can with a gang of deck-swabs and your pack of the damned for company,' he snarled, anger's white heat threatening in his voice. 'I *will* walk the surface of Cretacia, and I will know what salvation this world has to offer the Chapter.'

The other Flesh Tearers looked at him as if he had suddenly gone mad.

'You will remain here, Apothecary,' Daeron said. The Dreadnought loomed over Barachiel. 'The Chaplain has the matter right. You are far too valuable to risk in a vanguard action. Without you, our mission cannot succeed. You will have command of the strike cruiser while we launch our expedition to Cretacia.'

Barachiel slumped back, rage smouldering in his hearts.

FIFTEEN

The Overlord gunship *Second Scion* shuddered as she descended towards Cretacia, the flames of atmospheric entry receding from her cockpit blister. Torrential rain lashed the armaglass, and her fuselage groaned under the vicious slam of crosswinds. Dumah mag-locked his boots to the deck, his left hand enveloping the pilot's headrest as she wrestled with the controls, cursing colourfully under her breath. A Stormhawk Interceptor, one of the four fighters set in a loose diamond around the Overlord, wobbled dangerously. Its plasma drives bathed the cockpit in a soft blue glow. Proximity warnings flared on the pilot's display screen. She cursed again, forcing her craft into a sharper descent, beneath the interceptor.

Dumah's grip tightened as it passed overhead, and his cartolith tracked it as it slipped behind them. The wailing pulse of the interceptor's drives cut through the storm, as tireless as the beat of his own hearts. The Overlord's engines loosed a grinding cough, their flight path leading them through a tail of caustic ash rising from the flank of a mountain. Dumah saw the pulsing glow of the volcanic vent clearly enough, and felt the power conduction falter as the crew fought to purge the gunship's turbines. The co-pilot's voice bordered on panic.

'We have not even set down and already this world is trying to murder us.'

'Quiet, *human*, or Cretacia will not have its chance to kill you.'

The man gave neither answer nor acknowledgment, his focus locked on flushing the plasma drives and conduction coils. His third attempt restored full conduction and Dumah watched the flight crew weave the gunship between the tangled ribbons of cloud and ash, and the coruscating arcs of lightning that speared past the cockpit like the particle beams of necron gauss weaponry. They navigated canyons and threaded mountain ranges that raked the heavens like ebon claws, guided by the measured bleeps of the fortress-monastery's telemetry beacon. Shadows shifted on their flanks: broods of quad-winged reptilian beasts, snapping at each other in their jostle for shelter, denied flight by the threat the rain posed to their delicate wing membranes. His sensorium classified them as *ranodon.*

Dumah's eyes locked on the lush canopy that stretched far beyond the horizon, like the desert dunes of sacred Baal. Beasts moved through the trees, predators and prey untroubled by the storm. Dumah caught lightning-lit impressions of muscled reptilian carnivores larger than Warhound Titans, and arthropods with chitinous plates thicker than a Land Raider's hull. Blades of muted moonlight slipped between the clouds, and Dumah felt the first stirrings of respect for the native humans. It was not a feeling he welcomed.

'It is quite something, is it not?' Micah said, his voice unsullied by the vox.

The assault sergeant had joined him in the cockpit, captivated by the savage world. His Assault Intercessors waited in the left troop compartment, while Angelo's Reivers occupied the right. Dumah watched them minister to their battle-gear through pict-feeds mounted in both compartments, making final obeisance and pre-deployment checks before they touched down. He made a mental note to recheck his own weapons. Cretacia's dangers were many, and he was not fool enough to underestimate them, even for a moment.

Arrogance was the fastest way to die on Cretacia.

'I have seen few worlds like it,' Dumah admitted, despising each syllable. That truth made him sound weak. It undermined his stance on abandoning Cretacia when they had collected the Chapter's ancient relics. Still, he could not bring himself to deceive his brother. 'Even Fenris' bleak majesty does not compare.'

Micah nodded, utterly entranced by the terrible, primal beauty.

The Overlord skirted an ocean shoreline, its waters blacker than a child's nightmares and troubled by the high winds. Dumah's sensorium outlined suggestions of immense aquatic life, monstrous beasts several times larger than a destroyer, thickly scaled, with spines longer than a boarding harpoon. The gunship's flight path broke from the ocean before he completed his scan, leading them over acres of open plains and festering swampland. Rivers of bubbling lava cut fresh paths through the land, and grazing beasts drank from lakes and small streams. His sensorium displayed their shifting flight path, and their distance to the beacon.

Miles ticked down, from five digits to four in a matter of minutes.

Several more passed in silence before the distance shrank to three digits. Excitement squirmed through his abdomen. After months of waiting, he was minutes from the true prize. His blood quickened at the prospect of returning the relics to his Chapter, and, for a single joyous moment, he forgot that his plan had been vetoed by Daeron and Barachiel.

'We have entered the fortress' exclusion zone, Lord Chaplain,' the pilot said. Minutes slipped past as seconds before the mortal spoke again. 'Entering visual range now.'

Dumah said nothing, reverence stealing the breath from his lungs.

The fortress-monastery of the Flesh Tearers was a shadow staining the darkness, hard, angular lines slicing the softer, yielding night like a knife through pliant flesh. Built on a mountain flank, the façades of its largest towers were sculpted into the semblance of hooded, skeletal angels. Reaper blades and Executioner's Axes were held across their chests, stained with chips of ruby light, like spilled blood beading moments before its fall. Dumah examined the droplets closer, correctly deducing their purpose as observation blisters, gunship hangars, and solars for the highest-ranking battle-brothers and honoured Imperial ambassadors.

He snorted, doubting *those* cells saw much use. The Flesh Tearers were not a Chapter that received *ambassadors* from the other Imperial organisations, honoured or otherwise.

His eyes moved beyond the central keep, over the inner wall, taking in the vast array of macro cannons, fusion beamers and plasma annihilators that watched the heavens through the blank, shark-like stare of their muzzles. A sprawling complex of bunkers, landing fields, iron-plated towers and hydroponics domes spread between the inner walls, surrounded by the ramshackle dwellings of the indentured workforce. Artillery emplacements and anti-aircraft batteries drifted lazily across their assigned engagement arcs, their intricate targeting matrices guided by servitor brains in suspensor-fluid cradles, synchronised to the command network.

The fortress-monastery's curtain wall was the most impressive. Constructed from rockcrete and granite, the two-thousand-foot plunge from its upper crenellations to the grasslands surrounding the fortress was marked by a series of tiered firing galleries, ravelins and reinforced casemates. Thick iron spikes were set between each firing gallery, thrusting into the darkness like the spears of a Grekan phalanx. Creeper vines coiled around them, a natural defence as much as the jungle's attempt to dislodge the Chapter.

Dumah assumed they were poisonous. His armour's cogitators confirmed it.

He quashed an excited breath, his pulse quickening at the prospect of reaching the fortress. He could not keep the smile from his face, reading signs of habitation in the clean lines the creepers were cut to, and the flickering lights within the crimson observatoriums and the hanger bays. It did not faze him when a tocsin blared, tracking a sudden realignment of the defence batteries, or when similar warnings flagged on the pilot's display panel.

'Transmit clearance request,' he instructed.

'Chapter command nexus,' she said, a mechadendrite snaking from her augmetic arm, linking with the control console. The pilot tilted her wrists slightly, the gunship banking right, continuing its slow descent. 'This is Overlord gunship *Second Scion*, assigned to the Fourth Company, requesting clearance to land in hangar bay two-gamma. We bring the emissary of Gabriel Seth, Chapter Master and Lord of Cretacia, Guardian of Wrath.'

The vox squawked static, like the dull scrape of sandpaper.

Minutes ticked by without a reply.

The pilot opened the vox again.

'Repeat, this is Overlord gunship *Second Scion*.' She flicked a switch on her console, initiating an augur scan. 'We are on approach bearing the emissary of Gabriel Seth, Chapter Master of the Flesh Tearers. Requesting clearance to land in hangar two-gamma.'

Another flush of static, the silence afterwards deafening.

'Is it possible they do not recognise us?' Micah asked, examining a plexi-screen that detailed the Overlord's signum chain-code after the fourth repetition. 'The Overlord was not deployed until the early Indomitus Crusade. They may not recognise it as Imperial.'

Dumah entertained the thought, then shook his head.

'I do not think recognition is the issue, brother. If they did not recognise the Overlord as an Imperial gunship, they would interrogate us, not ignore us. This is something else.'

'Anti-air defences are acquiring us,' the co-pilot said. He flicked several switches, priming the countermeasures. Sweat lined his cheeks, his voice trembling slightly as he read the augur report. 'Short- and mid-range batteries. Plasma, missile and las.'

'Automated defences?'

'No,' the pilot said, forcing the gunship controls down a little further. Their angle of descent sharpened. 'We have been within their range for almost seven minutes, and they did not try to acquire us until *after* our identification signum chain began its broadcast.'

The Chaplain's fingers curled into fists, irritation bunching his jaw.

Calming himself, Dumah removed a data chip from his waist pouch, turning to face the serf seated at the console to his right. She was younger than her fellows, a Technicarum sigil emblazoned above her heart. She reached for the chip, and blanched when he refused to hand it over. The memory of Seth's scarred visage twisted by the promise of violence sent a shiver down Dumah's spine. That moment of weakness shamed him now as it had then.

'Seth's personal code.' Fear was a pungent sweetness on her

breath, her heart beating faster, blood flowing quicker, drawing his angel's teeth from his gums. 'Transmit, then erase it from all databanks and mem-coils.'

She nodded, her expression one of pure terror.

Visibly trembling, her fingers danced across her keypad, layering Seth's command cipher with sophisticated chimeric encryptions before they coded it into a shielded data-pulse. Dumah's eyes never left her, even as the klaxons' trilling grew louder and more insistent with every elapsing second. Sweat beaded her brow, staining her crimson tunic.

'Encrypted channel prepared. Transmitting command ciphers now.'

She had barely sent them when the night sky burst into dreadful life.

Crimson beams knifed towards the Overlord, the chem-enhanced reaction times of the mortal crew sparing them from destruction. The gunship banked and dived beneath the lasers' firing arcs, shuddering as air-burst shells seeded a fresh layer of cloud into the night sky with dull, explosive crumps. The lead Stormhawk suffered a hit, its fuselage consumed by flame. The piercing whine of an uncontrolled descent cut through the cockpit. Dumah did not watch the fighter fall, though the vox-operator reported ground impact several seconds later.

Off-white contrails streaked through the skies towards them.

'Missiles!' the pilot bellowed, banking sharply right.

'Deploying countermeasures!' the co-pilot snapped.

The rippling snaps of flares jolted the undercarriage, and the gunnery thrall activated the servitor-slaved heavy bolters. They spat explosive rounds at the incoming projectiles, and Dumah watched them detonate in brief bursts of flame. His fingers burrowed deep into the protective gels that cushioned the pilot's head, another wave of missiles rocketing past their canopy. Another Stormhawk was ripped from the skies, the screams of its pilot playing across the vox. Dumah switched it off, the sound aggravating and entirely pointless.

This time, he saw the brief flicker of ground impact.

'My lord, we need an alternate landing zone.'

Dumah nodded, mildly amused by the pilot's deliberate understatement.

He blink-clicked his cartolith rune, scanning archival charts and orbital imagery for a viable landing zone near the fortress-monastery. The Overlord cleared the maximum range of the missile silos and defence lasers, the pilots throttling back the engines as they settled into the orbital track. The night sky lapsed back to its dull midnight blue moments later.

Dumah scowled, unable to identify a safe landing zone in range of the fortress.

A coded data-pulse flashed onto Dumah's sensorium, and another voice spoke, its booming machine-tone redolent with ancient authority.

'Transport us to these co-ordinates, mortal. We travel on foot from there.'

The Overlord set down in the landing zone Daeron recommended, a small clearing near the mouth of a river. Her engines cycled down, and Dumah led his brothers out, their chainblades active and their bolt pistols trained on the treeline. Mud dragged at his boots, squelching with every step on sodden twigs and foliage. The others spread out, an interval of several yards between each warrior, the line curving in a half-circle around *Second Scion*.

Dumah tore off his helm, breathing his first lungful of Cretacian air.

It was rich in oxygen, balanced by carbon dioxide, analogous of Terra's atmospheric composition during its prehistory. Dumah tasted nothing of the pollutants that fouled dozens of Imperial worlds, though the air was thick with minor toxins and poisons. The rain pattered cool against his skin, washing the dried sweat away, its taste fresh and clean.

The clunk of uncoupling mag-locks drew his attention.

Mechanised joints groaned and there was the thud of heavy footfalls. The Overlord's plasma drives built to a banshee's wail as the pilots took the gunship back into orbit. The Dreadnought stomped forwards to face the river and the empty clearing. He was silent and still for several minutes, his chassis lashed by the heavy rain. The other Flesh Tearers said nothing, did nothing. They watched for threats, allowing Daeron his moment of quiet reflection.

Dumah was not so respectful.

The Chaplain strode directly over to the silent war machine, drawing and activating his crozius in a single fluid motion. Sanguinius' wrath burned white-hot in his chest, urging him to hammer his maul into the Dreadnought's clunking knee joint. He tormented the idea with his inaction, and his lips pulled taut in a cruel leer. Part of him *wanted* to test himself against the Dreadnought in battle, though he knew such a contest could only end one way.

'Your mindless slaves fired on us!' Dumah snarled, wrath clotting his voice. It ground against his skull like millstones, promising satisfaction if he would simply relent. 'They dared strike against the sons of Sanguinius! Why would they do that? Are they so stunted they do not recognise their masters' return, or were you such poor lords they now resist it?'

The Dreadnought turned to face him, rain sheeting from its sarcophagus.

'Few among them had the skills to operate the defence

batteries, and none could penetrate the control system without the codes. It is likely the weapons' machine-spirits could not recognise the Overlord, or your pilot's voice-print, and opened fire.'

'We transmitted the codes Seth gave us through noospheric data-bridge as well as the vocal transmission. You confirmed the codes, so either the sleep cycles have damaged your mind, or perhaps you have been sent to lead us into a trap on this thrice-cursed world?'

A peal of mechanised thunder rolled from the Dreadnought's vocoder, shaming those of the storm scudding slowly overhead. One of Angelo's Reivers turned. Micah's Assault Intercessors grunted in amusement, and avians perched nearby took panicked wing. Animal calls drifted from the treeline, the rolling clicks of insectoid mandibles and the starved roars of carnivores echoed in the trees. The Flesh Tearers' fingers curled tighter on their triggers.

Dumah lowered his pistol, having trained it on the vision-slit. The Dreadnought had not moved, nor considered him a threat.

'Mind your tone, void-born,' Daeron said, taking a thunderous step towards the Chaplain. Dumah shifted his balance, ready to move aside should the Furioso charge. Two colossal eviscerators chewed the air, their teeth larger than Dumah's head. 'Were I to slay you for your impudence, I doubt the Chapter Master would mourn your death.'

Dumah sneered. He did not care about Seth's opinion.

'Those savages fired upon us!' he said again, jabbing his crozius in the direction of the fortress-monastery. Rain evaporated on its disruptor field. 'I would know why.'

'I do not know,' the Dreadnought said icily. 'Something has changed on Cretacia. It feels *different*, though that cannot be considered a surprise. The Rift has unleashed insanity across the galaxy, seeding Imperial worlds with the blackest madness and vile heresy. Could you blame them for firing on an unfamiliar craft in their airspace?'

'Isolation and suspicion are no excuse. Hundreds of worlds have endured alone and endured *worse*. *They* did not fire on us!' He paused, reciting the litany of fortitude to master the wrath that edged his voice with a beast's snarl. 'If they have fallen to madness, we must first determine its extent. If the entire garrison has fallen, we must learn their weaknesses, their disposition, and then fashion our assault accordingly. Cretacia will not defy us.'

Another peal of mechanised thunder. The Dreadnought stepped forwards.

'You presume Cretacia is like any other world,' Daeron said. 'That is your first mistake.' Dumah felt the urge to strike the veteran swell at his haughty tone. 'It is like no other Imperial world. You would be wise to consider that fact before–'

'Movement in the treeline!' Micah barked, activating his chainaxe.

Dumah spun to face it, the argument with Daeron all but forgotten.

His helm cycled through its visual feeds: ultraviolet, sonic, auspex-enhanced. Thermal silhouettes flashed between the trees, smears of migrainous colour that chittered and barked. His sensorium tagged each beast with a glowing red indicator, outlining their clawed forearms and long, sinuous barbed tails. Their needle-like teeth glinted with secreted venoms. The pack's strength exceeded thirty beasts, all subjects in their physical prime.

'Movement on the left flank,' Angelo called, and Dumah saw a second pack darting through the trees, larger than the group in front of him. 'Native creatures massing.'

They burst through the treeline, a horde of bipedal monsters with snapping jaws and chameleonic scales that shimmered greasily in the rain. They were taller by a head than the Flesh Tearers, their bodies thick with muscle and sinew. Dumah slotted his iron sights on a beast's plated forehead, bolts blasting it apart. The Flesh Tearers' guns lit up the night, the volleys of mass-reactive bolts slaughtering the creatures in droves. They poured towards the Space Marines, loping over their own dead, eyes alive with hunger and bestial fury.

'By Sanguinius, you will hold your positions!' Dumah roared, gunning another down. 'Disgrace not the Great Angel, he who granted you life! We are wrath! We are death!'

Dumah squeezed a salvo into the chest of a larger beast, its head crowned by a small crest of multicoloured spines. The bolts ripped it to crimson mist. He switched his aim, obliterating another creature's skull with a single shot. A third fell, then a fourth, finished by the same spray of bolts. One came too close, claws carving deep gouges into his ceramite. A single blow from his crozius finished it, separating its head from its body.

He ground the head to paste, just to be certain.

'Oviraktors,' the Dreadnought boomed, its autoloaders cycling ammunition into the underslung storm bolters. A hail of blood-shard rounds tore two of the loping beasts to strips of raw, bloody meat. Dumah parried another's grasping claws, filling its gut with a burst of mass-reactive rounds. 'Their tail barbs are coated in potent neurotoxins.'

One of the Reivers, Sendek, fell, his throat slashed by a tail barb.

'Your sense of timing is second to none, brother,' Micah said drily, decapitating one of the beasts. An Intercessor fell, his chest and plastron shredded by the creatures' diamond-hard claws.

Dumah pivoted to avoid the lashing tail of an oviraktor. He put it down with a headshot, his crozius obliterating a second as three rapidly aimed bursts blew apart another two. His pulse quickened as he settled into the rhythm of the fight, lashing out with crozius and pistol alike. His fingers tightened around the crozius' haft, fighting the urge to give into the roar of Sanguinius' rage scorching his blood.

'I am wrath!' Dumah roared, oviraktor blood spraying his visor. He let the Thirst slip free, obliterating the two predators feasting on Sendek's corpse. 'I am death!'

He squeezed a final burst, felling an oviraktor that tried to outflank Micah. The assault sergeant nodded in thanks, slicing the tail from a beast grappling with one of his Intercessors. Dumah eviscerated another, blood spraying his visor. It stained his vision red and black, and the Chaplain howled, channelling the beast in his blood. The world descended into an endless smear of red, the scent of copper and the wet rip of violated flesh flooding his senses.

He killed until there were none left for him to slaughter.

Dumah panted, sweat riming his brow. He let his crozius *thunk* against the mud, its head deactivated. The world was slow to slide back into focus, the red haze reluctant to fade from his vision. Corpses littered the ground, the blood seeping from the torn flesh fouled by the mud. His blood stung with the need to kill, but there were none left. He muttered a prayer to Sanguinius, forcing his breathing to slow, and his pulse to do the same.

His brothers twitched and snarled, each one fighting the killer's instinct encoded into their blood. Seventeen remained, several straining against the desire to charge headlong into the jungle in search of more to kill. Those quickest to restore their equilibrium took munitions and replacement warplate from the dead, while Thuriel had the grim honour of harvesting the fallen Flesh Tearers' progenoids. All three organs were recovered without issue.

'Cretacia does not tolerate the weak.'

Daeron stomped over, speaking the words as though they were axiomatic.

'My brothers were not weak,' Dumah growled, reloading his bolt pistol. He indulged a squirt of adrenaline from his pharmacopoeia, letting it tease wrath back to the fore, allowing it to strangle his grief. He signed an order to Micah, to gather wood for a pyre. Now was not the time to mourn. 'They fell in battle, honouring Amit and the Great Angel.'

'If that brings you comfort, then believe it.'

'You said that I do not know Cretacia.' Dumah bit the words through clenched teeth, resisting the reborn urge to strike the Dreadnought. 'You are right in that. Now, do you have some useful counsel, or simply more childish insults and baseless deprecations?'

'There is an encampment,' Daeron said, and Dumah was uncertain whether he heard a slight smile in the Dreadnought's voice. 'A place of great pilgrimage for both the tribes and the Chapter. It is several hours north, towards the mountains, but it may offer clues on what has transpired in our absence, or people who can tell us.'

Dumah considered it, then stepped aside.

'Lead the way, *brother*.'

SIXTEEN

Barachiel drew a deep breath, then opened his eyes.

His scarred, cedar-skinned visage glared back at him from the bloodstone-and-plasteel Chapter sigil emblazoned on the wall, shorn of the beard and silver-gold hair that had softened its angular lines. Cold bit at his bare flesh, slithering along his limbs to sink its icy fangs into his chest. Frost rimed the glow-globes that were the sole source of illumination in the meditation cell, flickering in tandem with the gentle pulse of the *Cretacian Justice*'s plasma drives. The effect was intended to be soothing, but Barachiel found it deeply irritating.

He took another deep breath and sought to centre himself again.

The white heat of the Great Angel's wrath refused to sit quiet in his veins. Dumah had humiliated him. Again. The Chaplain had supplanted his authority, made him a laughing stock in the Fourth's eyes. Now Seth's emissary freely gave his blessing to it, forced him to remain aboard the strike cruiser, tantalisingly close, and yet achingly distant from answers that could save him – save *them* – from the Rage. The Apothecary's fingers curled into fists, and his teeth ground together. Their inane belief that the Rage was part of them would only lead them closer to damnation. It was sick, twisted, bordering on delusional. He could not understand it.

The vox-plate on the bulkhead bleeped, interrupting his meditations.

'Lord Barachiel.' A minute stretched by in silence. *'Lord Barachiel?'*

Barachiel rose from his seated position, deeming his effort futile, and gently massaged his muscles, restoring his circulation. He had not moved in several hours, though he felt no deeper sense of calm or awareness, just the biting cold of the meditation cell and the thermonuclear furnace of the Angel's wrath. The vox-plate continued its high-pitched chirrup, and he glimpsed the ident-tag that marked it as a priority signal sent from the bridge.

He thumbed the button beside the speaker-grille, and it crackled live.

'Sergeant Tumelo,' Barachiel said. 'I hope this interruption has cause.'

'It does, brother.' Barachiel caught snatches of chatter beneath the young sergeant's voice, and felt the deck's vibrations shift frequency. A course correction, he surmised. *'You are requested on the penitents' deck.'* Barachiel felt, rather than heard, the grim distaste that greased Tumelo's voice. *'One of Dumah's charges requires your ministrations.'*

A wet growl rippled in the Apothecary's throat. He had wasted enough time on pointless exercises. He needed to continue his research. 'Is his status urgent?'

'I have been reliably informed that it is, brother.'

Acidic spittle bubbled in the back of Barachiel's throat, scorching the flesh. It forced him to swallow hard, neutralising it in his stomach. Though he was unable to slay Luciferus, his animosity towards the Death Company remained unchanged. They were a curse, a blight on the Flesh Tearers' resurgent reputation, an intolerable threat to their souls and sanity. But that truth did nothing to detract from his duty to the Angel, and to his afflicted brothers.

'Understood,' Barachiel said, the growl edging his voice. 'I will be there.'

Tumelo severed the link, leaving Barachiel in silence.

Barachiel exited the meditation cell, the taste of incense replaced by the salt tang of human fear-sweat. He passed the wooden desk, still piled with research materials, the lumens above it replaced with a charge-roost for a servo-skull. The device squatted there, a red light blinking periodically on its temple as it charged. Its eyes had been replaced with a tight-beam scanner, its calliper-limbs replaced with additional data-storage devices and a vox-horn. He had committed much of his research to its memory, and he longed to continue his work.

This venture to twelve-aleph served only as a distraction from that.

Serfs stood in a small knot of crimson robes, the space above their hearts marked by the sigils of the Fourth Company and the Technicarum. They twitched and shivered at his approach, and Barachiel felt their furtive glances crawl between his flesh and the floor. He possessed none of his gene-father's psychic potential, but nonetheless he felt their thoughts like searing brands, acid-vile and treacherous. He read them in subtle twitches of their jaws, the quivering dilations of their pupils, and the soft sparkle of perspiration. They were thoughts the mortals would not dare give voice to, even in their cups or the privacy of their billets.

Butcher. Monster. Fiend. Savage. Cutthroat. Murderer.

They picked apart the scars left on his soul from crossing the Rift.

Barachiel reached the centre of the room, where his power armour waited on a trestle to be machined and drill-locked into place by his thralls. Each section was freshly lacquered, the scars earned facing the xenos collaborators and the insurrectionist thralls repaired, with fresh honours on the pauldrons. The serfs waited, tools clutched in sweating, shaking hands. They bowed with remarkable synchronicity and awaited the coming command.

'Armour me.'

The serfs bowed, moving forwards to anoint his flesh with sacred oils and powders, chanting imprecations in High Gothic tortured by the slum accents of a dozen worlds. They slipped his bodyglove into place, careful to fasten it to the neural sockets scraped into his flesh, bowing and murmuring apologies between each benediction when fingers slipped and brushed his flesh, or struggled to secure a clasp. Barachiel barely noticed them, his attention reserved for the servo-skull squatting in its roost, and the research that awaited him.

The industrial sound of the armouring process soon enveloped the cell.

'My Lord Barachiel.'

Another figure stepped forwards as the armour thralls drill-locked the under-layer of fibre-muscles and ablative adamantium mounting frame to his left shin and calf, testing the interface relays. Barachiel's lips twitched, a slight wince as the electrical signal bit hard on his nerves. The figure, a mortal female, bowed as she approached, clutching a data-slate to her chest, her blood-flecked medicae whites a stark contrast to Technicarum red.

Aesha bowed again. 'Forgive my intrusion, lord.'

The insult was unintentional, but it still rankled. His frustration escaped as a seething sigh. 'I am not your lord, adjutant, nor anyone's. I grow tired reminding you of that.'

'Apologies, Apothecary.' She bowed low, and her voice was contrite.

Barachiel accepted the apology with a dismissive wave of his hand. He understood the reasons she had resumed the use of the title. Titles bred distance, creating a layer of insulation between people in different hierarchical roles. After the horrors she had witnessed, and been a party to during the crossing – their attempts to curtail the Thirst and the uprising that followed – it mystified the Flesh Tearer that she had not succumbed to some form of mania.

'Why do you come before me, adjutant? More logistical reports?'

'In part,' she said, stepping further into the light.

Almost instantly, Barachiel saw the dark rings around her eyes, the yellowed tinge to her teeth and the distinct lack of personal hygiene. He smelled the chemical cocktail coursing through her blood, stimulating her mind and body. It was a harsh blend of recaff, lho-sticks and the combat stimms used by the Astra Militarum and Chapter armsmen. His fingers curled into fists, eliciting the barest flicker from Aesha. Several arming thralls swallowed hard.

'There has been an issue with your requisitions for the surface expedition.'

Barachiel grunted. This was the third such *issue*. 'Explain.'

'The chem-foundries have been rendered inoperable by rebellion,' she said, keying something into her data-pad before turning it to face him. He quickly scanned the damage report as she continued. 'The Technicarum's efforts to repair them have proved futile. The replacement parts were used to remedy a sabotage action on the plasma drives.'

Barachiel cursed. Several thralls trembled at the sound.

'How much can be made available for the surface drop? A rough estimate.'

She checked her slate. 'A third, *if* the God-Emperor smiles upon us.'

'A *third?*' The serfs drilling the carapace mounting frames into position at his thigh flinched, and were quickly reprimanded by their superior. 'My requisitions were already far below the minimum. We *must* have those supplies, adjutant, or testing of the local populace will not be thorough.' He winced as another spasm passed through his shin. 'The Chapter can afford no hint of treachery or scandal in this new Imperium. The Inquisition watches.'

His disgust rose at the sharp spike in the fear-scent rising from the serfs.

Aesha nodded, indifferent, meeting his gaze. 'What would you have me do?'

Barachiel considered the question a moment, then smiled. He knew one place aboard the *Justice* where supplies were plentiful. He had approved the order himself, weeks ago.

'Task the cargo servitors to transfer the supplies from the penitents' deck. They have a fully stocked medicae facility, and several smaller suites with additional supplies.' He did not particularly care that Dumah would complain, or that the supplies were earmarked for the damned at the Chaplain's own request. The Cretacians' gene-purity tests took precedence.

Aesha looked as though she were about to say something in disagreement, but thought better of it. 'As you wish, Apothecary. I will order additional storage and transportation prepared.'

Barachiel nodded, grimacing slightly as the neural connectors on his left sabaton linked with the sockets carved into his ankle. 'What other issues do you bring for my attention?'

Aesha tapped at her slate, then produced a handheld hololithic projector. Clicking the activation button, grainy hololithic images illuminated the small cell. They were surgical schemata, the three-dimensional scans overlaid with data-points that were meticulous in cataloguing the damage and the various methods of repair, sequenced in order of inhibiting factors, percentages of risk, and the varying periods of rehabilitation. Barachiel digested the annotated scans in a single glance, a scowl spreading across his face.

Another distraction from his research and the salvation of his Chapter.

'Lord Adnacio suffered severe nerve damage in training,' Aesha said, and short bursts of animation demonstrated Adnacio's limited neural conduction. Barachiel's scowl deepened. 'I have already withdrawn him from the battle line, under your authority, but we need your assistance in replacing damaged nerves.' She released a long, shuddering breath. 'It is beyond our skill.'

Barachiel said nothing for a time, his silence filled with the scrape and whine of tools.

'You overcomplicate the procedure,' he said finally, watching a pair of serfs bless, then bear over, the under-plating for his chest. The polished plasteel was wet with sacred oils blessed by the Martian priesthood. 'Preserving too much of his existent flesh is not a practical method of restoring his combat capability. It also increases the risk of causing further damage during the procedure. A full augmetic replacement is more efficient, and within your skill set.'

He resisted the urge to glance towards the servo-skull.

'My lord,' Aesha began, and Barachiel growled at the use of the title. She seemed not to notice, instead speaking slowly, as if each word required the utmost concentration. 'Such a procedure may be quicker, and simpler, but it is not always as efficient. It can result in longer convalescence and adaptation periods, thereby delaying his return to the battlefield, meaning the company is weaker at a crucial time. I would urge you to reconsider your judgement.'

She consulted the slate, clacking her tongue. He found that *deeply* irritating.

'We already have suitable replacements available, and you have ceded command of the vessel to Mistress Étain. Once the matter in the penitents' deck is dealt with, you have no pressing duties to attend to, and this exsanguination cycle has been completed.'

Barachiel once again resisted the urge to glance at the servo-skull.

'Sundry duties require my attention. Mission-specific, above your clearance.'

Aesha's eyes flicked to the skull, and Barachiel's fingers reflexively curled.

'Sir, I ask you again to reconsider this course of action. Your prime duty is the well-being of the battle-brothers assigned to this expedition.' Her tone was almost imploring, and Barachiel felt a sudden chill slither along his spine. 'Do not give Lord Dumah further ammunition.'

Silence swelled between them, filled with the scrape and whine of machine tools.

'I have given you an instruction, adjutant.' Threat filtered into Barachiel's voice, with all the subtlety of an opened pressure valve. Wrath set his veins to a slow simmer, and Aesha met his eyes with a glazed expression. Her sympathy revolted him. 'Now, *follow it!*'

Aesha bowed and left him to his armouring, her disagreement plain.

Barachiel watched her leave, the industrial sound of his armouring slowly swelling to fill the silence she left behind. He tried to put her from his mind, but the implications behind her words pulled at him like a child tugging its parent's arm. *Was she right to question him? Did he act in his own interests, and not those of his brothers and his Chapter?*

He dismissed the thought the moment it formed.

Of course he acted in their interests.

Barachiel strode along the corridor that led to the penitential cells, the servo-skull bobbing in his wake. There were no mortals to bar his path, only the scent of fresh death and the miasma of anguish pressing from the cold iron bulkheads. He was unsurprised to see a body hanging from the rafters, its eyes glassy and neck twisted at an unnatural angle. Rumours of suicides among the Reclusiam serfs had become increasingly common during the crossing. Prolonged exposure to the Death Company could break even the strongest of mortal minds.

Barachiel passed the body, confident that Dumah's remaining helots would remove it before decay became a problem. He entered the cell, noting the scent of blood and the assortment of servitor parts strewn across the deck. His servo-skull drifted to its charging roost, settling there with the dull *clink* of metal against bone. It warbled a readiness update, its voice almost lost in the low, inhuman growl that rose from the corner like a wolf startled by flame.

'Drone,' Barachiel said, calmly drawing his blade as the cell's other occupant skirted the shadows, reluctant to reveal himself, 'initiate playback on file omega two-three.'

'Compliance,' it warbled. 'Preparing file.'

Barachiel ignored the measured clicks as it cycled through its virtual librarium, his attention reserved for the shadow that lingered atop the darkness. The wet *thunk* of fresh blood striking the deck itched his throat. Barachiel shifted his stance slightly, adopting a defensive posture as he drew the apothecarion needler from his waist. It was absurdly small in his large, gauntleted hands. A simple flex of his fingers would see it crushed like a spent ration canister. An ursine growl rippled from the darkness, the shadow shifting again.

He raised the needler, thumbing the safety off and taking aim.

'I have no time to indulge in games,' he said, as much to himself as the cell's other occupant. A targeting rune flared green on his retinal display. 'Forgive this dishonour.'

Barachiel squeezed the trigger, a small dart zipping from its muzzle. There was the sharp, wet thud of a dart striking skin, and an irritated grunt. A footstep, then another.

The Apothecary cast the needler aside, angling his blade.

Tamael split the darkness with a thunderous roar and charged.

Blood crusted the Flesh Tearer's breastplate and pauldron, coming from the rent torn across his throat that had missed his jugular by mere millimetres. Nubs of exposed bone blinked bright amid the complex mess of compound fractures framing his face, and his eyes were pits of blackest rage. The Death Company warrior lunged for Barachiel, his angel's teeth at full extrusion and his skin tinged red by the Thirst. Fingers curled into killer's claws reached for the Apothecary's throat. Barachiel had the span of a single heartbeat to react.

He weaved aside the first blow, smashing a second away with the flat of his blade. He caught the dry, distinctive snap of breaking bone beneath the crack of ceramite, but that did nothing to slow the black blur of Tamael's arm. He shifted balance, moving his sword in the tight, concentric arcs he had learned as a novice, blocking the series of bullet-quick blows the enraged Flesh Tearer aimed at his torso and throat. Barachiel slipped under the crude swipes, hammering his blade's pommel into the Death Company warrior's breastplate.

Tamael staggered, cracks veining his Imperialis. Barachiel broke from the other Flesh Tearer, watching him lurch like a drunkard after an indulgent evening. The soporific he used was reserved especially for the damned, and was strong enough to render even the strongest warrior unconscious in minutes. Tamael resisted with every iota of his Angel-given fury, screaming slurred calls for vengeance and blood from a traitor dead ten millennia. When he fell, it was with the clatter of ceramite, the grinding whine of armour servos, and the pained whisper of a brother betrayed by the one he had loved above all others.

'I die… I die at my brother's hand.'

His eyes fluttered, and he fell into fitful somnolence.

Barachiel let several seconds pass before he dragged him onto the surgical slab set in the chamber's corner. He removed the breastplate and pauldron for repair, wiped the blood from Tamael's hard, patrician features and chestnut-brown flesh. He longed to sample its genetic holiness, to feel the strength and vitality of his lord coursing through his veins. The smell filled his nostrils, exciting his senses. His Thirst nagged at him, an incessant need that demanded its satisfaction.

Barachiel ignored it. There were other needs – *greater* needs.

He checked Tamael's pulse. It was there, though faint and erratic. He selected a small surgical instrument from his tool tray and leaned closer to examine the tear in Tamael's throat. It would take him several hours to repair, and he had to work quickly to stem the bleeding. He administered a second dose of soporifics, connecting an intravenous line to Tamael's wrist to ensure continued flow. He was not concerned with thoughts of overdose. The damned's enhanced metabolic rates burned through them quickly. He set a clamp on the major bleeder and set to work repairing the smaller ones. The servo-skull's recitation washed over him, and he made a vow to himself.

He would discover what had befallen his Chapter world and uncover its secrets.

Nothing would distract him from his real work.

The *Cretacian Justice* shuddered, the rolling thunder of its distant batteries realigning to lock onto the second star fortress breeding ship-quakes. The gesture was little more than petulant defiance, but it made Barachiel smile. If the star fortresses held hostile intent, then the *Justice* would die quickly. The first barrage would crack their shields. The second would reduce the strike cruiser to a flame-gutted hulk, perfect prey for Mechanicus scrappers and pirates.

The deck shivered beneath his feet, rippling the battle flags and the victory pennants suspended from the ceiling. The banner of the Fourth Company hung at the centre and two score other banners detailed its victories since the days of Amit. The company banner showed a hooded angel bearing a long-bladed axe, four droplets of green vitae falling from its blade into a golden chalice at the angel's feet. The banner rippled and swayed in the dry breaths of the air-scrubbers, the warriors of Squads Tumelo, Burloc and Kairus kneeling at its base, offering their final oaths of fealty to the Emperor and Sanguinius before they deployed aboard the star fortress.

Two squadrons of Stormhawks and an Overlord idled on launch cradles set just inside the atmospheric retention barrier. Teams of servitors and Technicarum thralls engaged in the intricate ballet of readying the flyers for void operations. Gunnery technicians examined their lascannon charge-cells and belt feeds for the wing-mounted heavy bolters, while gene-bulked servitors slotted krak missiles into their pods. Pilots performed their preflight checks, testing ailerons as plasma drives cycled between a banshee's keening wail and a shade's tongueless silence. White-blue energy shimmered in the turbines with each shrieking test-fire.

Barachiel tuned out the relentless chatter of the deck-serfs coordinating the resupply process, watching Teman brief the sergeants in his boarding team. Adariel and Castiel were at his side, both veteran sergeants tasked with boarding the third star fortress alongside Azariel, an Eradicator sergeant seconded to the Cretacian expedition from the Ninth Company.

Barachiel folded his arms across his chest, his blood simmering.

'Status,' he demanded. 'Begin with Paschar's strike force.'

'They have found little save rats and rust,' Adariel said, his face twitching as spurts of sharp pain cut across the inflamed scar tissue ridging his face. 'There is no sign of small-arms fire, or damage to its life-support functions, and the salvation pods are all accounted for.'

Barachiel's lips twitched, his anger at being left aboard the *Justice* resurfacing.

He could not remain here, without purpose. He needed to do something, anything that worked towards setting foot on Cretacia, and unlocking the salvation it had long promised.

'What of Dumah?' he growled. 'Is there word of his expedition?'

'He was fired on,' Castiel said, a smile splitting the latticework of scars criss-crossing his pale flesh. 'They were forced to set down in the jungle, far from the fortress. At Daeron's behest, they march towards a site of local significance, seeking intelligence from the tribes.'

Barachiel's eyes narrowed. 'An enemy holds our fortress, and you smile?'

He looked to Azariel and Castiel, seeing the same amusement in their eyes. All three wilted beneath his gaze, and Barachiel squashed his desire to cut them down. 'They disgrace our ancestral home with their presence, fire upon our brothers, and this amuses you?'

'My lord,' Adariel began, 'we simply relish the opportunity to do battle–'

'I care nothing for your reasons, sergeant!' Barachiel roared, startling a gaggle of serfs working to unload a pneu-train cart filled with additional munitions for Teman's strike force. They dropped several canisters, apologising profusely as they hurried to clean their mess.

'We all long for battle, the chance to slay the Angel's enemies and sate the Thirst, but we do not disgrace ourselves in such a manner!' He took a breath. 'Were there losses?'

'There were some,' Castiel said, handing him a data-slate.

The Apothecary scanned the contents, noting the names of the honoured dead, and the green runes beside them that signified the recovered progenoids. Three Flesh Tearers, along with two mortal Stormhawk pilots. He passed the slate back to Castiel, who tucked it into a bandolier. Seconds ticked past. A flat, toneless voice ordered all non-essential personnel from the flight deck. They flocked past the Space Marines, who watched their brothers board their gunships. Plasma turbines cycled to a piercing whine, and the countdown started.

'It will be another day before we are in position to launch,' Azariel grumbled. They had the third fortress, the largest of the three, sited closest to the fortress-monastery.

Castiel and Adariel murmured their agreement.

'I share your frustration, brother,' Barachiel said, ignoring their questioning looks. 'I find it no easier to remain aboard than you do. That is why I will accompany your boarding mission.' He forestalled their interruption with a raised hand. 'You may need medical support on that station, and I am the only trained Apothecary remaining aboard the *Justice*.'

'My lord,' Azariel said, 'this search is likely a waste of time and effort. It makes little sense to place you at risk on such a trivial mission, especially if the damned may require your care. If battle does await us on the planet, then we will need you, and your skill–'

Barachiel cut him off with a raised hand.

'If I remain here, is the risk not greater?' he said, more harshly than he intended. 'If the fortress opens fire, I would be killed outright, with little chance for survival. Aboard the star fortress, with loyal warriors about me, my chances would be far greater, no?'

'Not if we are shot down by its point-defence turrets,' Castiel pointed out. Barachiel turned a withering glance upon the Hellblaster sergeant, and he fell quiet immediately.

'What of the damned?' Azariel asked, disgust plain in his voice. Barachiel let it slide, mindful of his own aversion to their existence. 'They cannot be left unattended.'

'They are not children, brother,' Barachiel said. 'And I am no nursemaid.'

'It matters not,' Adariel said flatly. 'Dumah ordered that you remain here.'

'I am not subject to Dumah's commands, sergeant,' Barachiel said. 'You labour under the delusion that I offer you a choice. You are not an officer and hold no authority over this company and its assets. I *am* joining you on this expedition, and this is not a debate.'

They looked at each other, and Barachiel knew that he had them.

'Yes, my lord,' they replied in unison.

Barachiel exited the hangar, offering his thanks to Sanguinius. He would discover what had become of Cretacia in their absence, and he would save his Chapter.

The Rage would not claim him, nor would it claim any other Flesh Tearer ever again.

SEVENTEEN

Sweat rolled from Dumah's brow, stinging his eyes. It soaked his cheeks, forming a thin rime around his gorget-seal. The rain had abated shortly after sunrise, the Corython star dappling the jungle floor with spots of shimmering carnelian light. A predator's roar sliced through the trees to their right, wrathful excitement stirring in Dumah's breast. He yearned to slay another beast, to take vengeance for the battle-brothers he had already lost to this accursed world.

He had carved their names into his vambrace, after their bodies had burned.

Sendek. Tamas. Namatar. Ose. Sylol.

Sorrow tainted his wrath, a fresh curse blossoming on his lips.

They should not have set foot on Cretacia. Allowing the Dreadnought's foolish sentiment to guide them here was a mistake, one that cost his brothers their lives and one he would beg the Great Angel's forgiveness for until the day he died. They should have returned to the *Justice* and attacked the fortress-monastery with the full force of the company. His fallen brothers would yet draw breath, or would have fallen in glorious battle. Instead they had burned for his weakness. Something prickled the hairs on his neck. He cursed again, twisting his crozius about himself in an arc of lightning-chased steel. A large carnivorous plant flopped to the earth, its stem broken, needle-toothed jaws stretching open, shivering as it drooled potent necro-toxins into the dirt. It had been inches from killing him, the attempt hardening his conviction and his disgust.

They should take only what they need, then burn this world to ashes.

The Chaplain sniffed the air, his implanted neuroglottis filtering the forest's aromas to individual scents. Strongest was the smell of moist earth and dead vegetation rising from the gelatinous smears staining his breastplate and pauldrons. They camouflaged him in this new and hostile world, a necessity enforced by the ambush that had claimed Ose and Sylol. Thuriel's examination of the beast responsible revealed a highly refined olfactory cavity, its keenness suggestive of bioengineering rather than evolution. At his command, the Flesh Tearers coated their armour with the noxious grime, muting the scents of lapping powders and unguents.

They could ill afford to stand out on a world so inhospitable, so alien.

Beneath the odour coating their power armour, he could smell moisture soaking into the vegetation. The toxins and mild hallucinogens they breathed spiced the hot, dry air, their effects neutered by his advanced physiology. He moved on, tasting the pheromonal-spoor of an alpha-class predator marking the splintered bough of a razorleaf tree, the rotting flesh of a three-day-old kill fouled by the same scent. He quickened his pace, pursuing the shadow of a smell almost drowned in the cycle of life and death that thickened the jungle's air.

He raised a clenched fist, curiosity crinkling his eyes.

'What is it?' Thuriel asked, moving to stand at his side. One pauldron of his crimson battleplate had been badly damaged in their fight with the oviraktors. Five cryo-canisters dangled at his waist, their lumens green. 'Another 'raktor pack? A spynoracx?'

Dumah drew another lungful of air to confirm.

'No. Woodsmoke, five hundred yards north. Mixed with blood. Old. Rotting.'

A vox click summoned Micah and Angelo to the front of the column.

Grime and off-white armour sealant patched the worst damage, and Angelo's poleyn was marked with Ose's name-rune, the plate salvaged from his corpse before their pyre was lit. Micah moved with a hitch in his stride, parallel scabbing wounds visible through a claw-gash in his thigh. They tightened as he crouched beside them, eliciting a subtle wince.

Dumah drew his combat knife, tracing a diagram into the earth.

'The distance and direction correspond with our venerable brother's coordinates for the encampment,' he said, drawing a basic diagram from Daeron's description. 'We can ill afford to assume they are allies, and we cannot afford to spread ourselves too thinly in this hostile environment.' He glanced up and around, his ears alive to the sound of a distant predator's hunting call. 'We must maximise our tactical advantage by dividing our forces and extending the line.'

He marked four points on the crude diagram that described a 'U' shape.

'Angelo, lead your squad to the left and divide into two teams. Micah and I will flank right and do the same. Do nothing until I give the signal to advance into the encampment.'

They nodded and spread out, Angelo's squad moving away to the left flank.

Dumah moved with Micah's demi-squad towards the edge of the treeline, his armour cogitators tagging poisonous flora with amber icons. Red threat indicators pulsed over those with a taste for human flesh, and Micah's chainaxe cut the stem of another such plant. It flopped to the jungle floor, its death rattle releasing a blast of noxious fumes that set his respiratory system aflame. It took Dumah's armour several minutes to purge the toxins.

The squad spread out along a twenty-yard section of the treeline, Dumah and Micah at the centre. Dumah crouched beside the assault sergeant in the long grasses, surveying the encampment across the narrow stretch of grassland that separated it from the jungle.

The encampment was a large, but simple, affair. Its perimeter was ditched and staked, with a second trench dug around the circumference of a small curtain wall of stone, mud and mortar. Wooden posts were evenly spaced between the perimeter wall and the trench, and a number of small torches were secured to each one. His retinal feed tightened on the bonding material, and his lip curled as he recognised dried, age-browned human sinews.

He scanned deeper, counting more than one hundred tents of varying styles and sizes built from wooden stakes and tanned animal hides. The smallest tents were near the edge of the encampment. He surmised they were for latecomers and those of lower wealth or social status, while the larger tents and pavilions closer to the centre marked tribal leaders and other people of influence. They gathered in clusters around evenly placed standards, though he was uncertain whether they denoted a multitude of clans or familial lines. The images could have no deeper meaning whatsoever. The Cretacians were not known for logic or intelligence.

Dumah was forced to revise his assessment, and not without

a scowl, when his retinal feed identified the central structure. It was a pyramid constructed from quarried stone, though not like the ones built for the mythic faros of once-great Gyptia to memorialise their greatest triumphs and to consolidate their power over the populace. It had a stair-stepped design, with staircases sized for mortals that led to the summit. There were a number of windows and entrances to the lower levels sized for both humans and Space Marines.

At its summit was a central, planed platform upon which a small dedicatory had been erected. Statues marked each of the four corners of the pyramid, capturing Cretacian warriors in moments of triumph, humility, wrath and reflection. These statues were mirrored on the dedicatory at the centre of the pyramid, the sigil of the Flesh Tearers visible in marble and bloodstone. Dumah saw no torchlight inside, nor could he see smoke rising from the morning fires or cooking pits they were certain to have. The camp appeared abandoned, the scent of rotting blood strong.

'Life signs?' Dumah voxed Micah, checking his pistol.

'Auspex readings are inconclusive,' the sergeant growled, striking the auspex unit on a nearby tree. The unit squalled angrily but offered no clearer reading. 'The residual effect of the storm is interfering with its function, and the volume of local fauna and biological matter is no help in getting clear readings. We may have to rely on visual confirmation alone.'

Dumah scowled, rising from his crouch and signalling via vox for the other teams to move in. Micah's squad moved with him.

The Flesh Tearers sprinted across the grasslands, crossing the narrow causeway that bridged the fire-trench. Crude oil and animal fat covered the turned earth in a thick sludge, the scent cloying and entirely unpleasant. Dumah strode into the encampment, his Absolvor bolt pistol raised and set to automatic fire, his finger exerting the slightest pressure on the trigger, ensuring he was ready to shoot at a moment's notice. Micah and his squad followed close behind, chainblades chewing the air and pistols raised as they marched between the clusters of tents. Primitive trinkets and bundled herbs were set on tables beside cuts of meat left to spoil and reagents fermenting in small clay pots.

'Lord,' Angelo voxed, and Dumah saw on his cartolith that the Reiver sergeant was at the base of the pyramid already, *'you and Brother Daeron will want to see this.'*

Dumah jogged towards the pyramid, Micah and his demi-squad close behind. There was not a corpse in sight, yet the scent of death lingered everywhere they passed through. He led them past the larger tents and pavilions, noting the increasing number of pennants and tribal fetishes hanging on cords of woven hair and dried tendon. Dumah's jaw locked tight, disgusted by the primitivism and savagery he saw in every tent and pavilion.

They found the dead scattered around the pyramid.

Dumah stepped over the broken, brutalised corpses of men and women, their clothing as disparate as their brands and tattoos. Decomposition was setting in, discolouring their flesh with a greenish tinge and septic yellow, like bruises midway through healing. Their bellies were distended in a vile mockery of pregnancy, the increased girth forced by gases accumulating in the abdominal tract and insect larvae burrowing fresh homes in the fleshy folds. Maggots wriggled through festering wounds and kill-strokes, devouring fatty tissues. Flies filled the air with their droning susurrus, feasting on the flesh that had given them life.

He felt no sorrow, merely irritation.

There would be no answers given by these wretches.

Dumah stepped closer to the pyramid, circling it, ignoring the wet crunch of bone and dead flesh beneath his boots.

Pictographs and cuneiform were carved into every façade, some faded by age and decades of inclement weather. They depicted angels assembled, descending on pinions of holy fire to deliver the righteous fury of the Angel and the Emperor with blade and boltgun. Coiled, serpentine sslyth were butchered beside the reptilian mercenaries of Tarellia, and hooded constructs of the slaugth fell beside the muscled simian forms of orks.

In each scene, the angels were victorious, and drank blood from the dead.

Blood channels were carved into the stone trim of each staircase following the layers of the pyramid. They ended abruptly over deep basins and troughs set at a height convenient for human hands, the outlets carved in crude mimicry of Sanguinius' noble visage, his angel teeth extruded in a bestial snarl. Blood trickled between the teeth, congealing in the basins, darkened by age. Though ripe with the onset of decay, its scent was distinctly animal, and the same odour and discolouration marked the hands and cheeks of the dead Cretacians.

They are us, Dumah thought, the revelation leaving his blood cold and sluggish. He scanned the fire-bowls surrounding the pyramid, the smell of scorched earth and ash mingling with the scent of spilled blood. *The Chapter reshaped the savage to mimic us.*

'There are no children,' Brother Gathrix of Micah's squad remarked, distracting the Chaplain from his nausea. The Intercessor turned over a corpse with his boot, examining the man's face. What remained was slowly being consumed by maggots and flies, bone peeking through in several places. 'There are whole bloodlines present, from elders ready for the pyre to adults scarcely beyond their juvenile years. But there is not a single child here.'

Dumah looked around, and saw the Intercessor was right.

'There should be,' Daeron said, clanking towards the small

knot of Flesh Tearers. It vexed Dumah to see three of his warriors bow to the venerable Dreadnought. 'This is the Chapter's Place of Choosing, where male children compete to become aspirants.'

Dumah glanced at Daeron. 'There would be no point, with the Chapter gone.'

'The Chapter's absence changes nothing. Tribes travel here in pilgrimage to pay homage to the fallen sons of Cretacia across ten millennia, and to witness the Choosing. Amit declared Right of Conquest in this spot and accepted the first Cretacian aspirants into the Chapter. It is a site of significance for any child of this world.'

Dumah said nothing, casting his eyes over the ancient pyramid, studying the histories carved into its stones. The pyramid was more than a shrine to ancient heroes and their days of glory. It was a monument to a moment that had forever changed his Chapter, a quiet reminder that each triumph since may not have come to pass without the blood given by Cretacia and her clans. It was a symbol of the bond that existed between the Chapter and its people, a bond forged in blood and flame. His wrath at the desecration of such an important site in the Flesh Tearers' history was derailed when his Lyman's Ear snagged on an unexpected sound – the sound of chanting.

The others fell silent, heads turned towards the dedicatory.

Dumah signed an order to Micah and Angelo, their squads spreading out around the pyramid, one section to each of the four staircases. They swept upwards, weapons panning across the open expanse. The chanting grew louder, more defined, the scent of herbs and woodsmoke more potent. He tasted opioids and hallucinogens as he entered the dedicatory, his enhanced constitution instantly filtering the toxins from his bloodstream.

Inside the dedicatory he stopped, his breath stolen.

The statue of a Firstborn Space Marine clad in an ancient

suit of Terminator armour dominated the centre, his aura of ruthless, wrathful energy and restrained violence perfectly captured. Underbite chainblades accented the lethality of his power fists, complemented by two storm bolters worked into their surface. Dumah needed no lesson in Chapter history to know that figure. His likeness existed in every reliquary and archive aboard the *Victus*.

Nassir Amit, the savage lord.

At Amit's feet, the corpse of a beast lay broken on an offering plinth. It was far larger than the oviraktors, with flanks layered in thick, shimmering scales and three spiny sails that stretched from the nape of its neck to its tailbone. Its jaws were crocodilian, with razor teeth the length of a Space Marine's arm. Spears of yellowing bone held its stomach open, its offal spilled on the smaller plinth set beneath the main altar. Blood congealed in the channels at its feet, and in smaller passages cut into the walls that led to the lower levels of the pyramid.

Two dozen Cretacian youths knelt before the altar, cheeks streaked with dried blood. They were male, each of appropriate age for gene-seed implantation, the scent of opioids and lingering infections strong on their breaths and in their blood. Deeds were inked and branded into their arms and chests, and Dumah was forced to admit that, beneath the tribalistic veneer, they were fine candidates for implantation. Iron-hard muscle coiled beneath flesh made tough by a lifetime dedicated to survival, and they even carried themselves as warriors.

Micah barked what sounded like a greeting in a Cretacian tongue.

As one they turned. Several reached for clubs and spears. Others remained transfixed, as though witnessing a ghost. They clustered together, showing no sign of the transhuman dread so common among mortals. Instead, they seemed energised, as though Dumah and his warriors were heroes returned from the most ancient fables.

One edged towards Dumah, his skin the coal-dark of the equatorial clans, scarred and branded. Dumah forced himself to remain still, ignoring his discomfort as the youth gingerly brushed mud from his right poleyn. His breath caught in his throat when he saw the Chapter icon. He fell to his knees, chest hiking as he met Dumah's gaze again.

The youth's eyes were wet with tears of joy.

Dumah squatted on a rocky outcropping overlooking a Cretacian clan fastness.

It had taken the better part of a day to discourage the youths from their worship and extract some useful information on those responsible for the massacre. They knew little of it, having been sequestered in the pyramid for days since they killed the beast. Dumah smelled taboo and superstition in their survival. Whoever had devastated the encampment had been unwilling to risk the angels' wrath by desecrating the pyramid itself. His cartolith blinked with green icons, each a Flesh Tearer taking their position around the 'stronghold', a paltry collection of tents surrounded by a heavy wood palisade, its outskirts patrolled by six pairs of humans with wood torches and heavy bone clubs or knapped flint spears.

'In position,' Angelo voxed. *'Awaiting your order.'*

Dumah held for a moment, suppressing surprise that Angelo could resist his bloodlust. He watched figures meander through the camp, hefting hollowed shells and tanned bladders no doubt filled with some vile intoxicant. The smell of cooked meat and burned wood carried on the light breeze, the sound of chatter and laughter stirring his wrath to fresh heights. Black smeared his vision, darker than the night itself. His fingers tightened around his crozius' haft, the joints squealing in protest. These fools desecrated a site sacred to the Flesh Tearers, and they would pay for that insult with their lives. Dumah scanned his path and spoke.

'Eliminate the perimeter guard, and hold. Micah and I are moving in.'

The Chaplain shifted from his position, signalling Micah's squad with a succession of coded vox clicks. A shadow moved at his side, lithe and supple, densely muscled. The youth that had knelt before him in the dedicatory, Hakkad, kept pace with him, his skin slick with mud to defy the eyes of predators or watchmen. Scars lined his limbs and his torso, and he held a flint spear and crude iron dagger in his hands. The dagger had the air of an inherited artefact about it, its fuller cobwebbed with rust and old, unclean blood.

Dumah was reluctantly impressed with the Cretacian tribesman's fortitude, and that of his kin. They had maintained the Flesh Tearers' punishing pace without complaint, though he was discomforted by the worshipful stares the Cretacians cast in the Flesh Tearers' direction. It was hardly uncommon for primitive cultures to worship Space Marines as gods, or avatars of gods, but Dumah recognised something more in the Cretacians' stares. It felt like promise, hope and awe, emotions born from a prophesied return, though he was not sure.

He was no closer to human emotion than he was to an ork's.

'Perimeter guard eliminated,' Angelo said, his voice tinged with eagerness. *'We can handle this alone. We do not need Micah's warriors to break this nest of traitors.'*

'Hold, sergeant,' Dumah snapped, joining Micah's squad at the gate. Hakkad was still at his side. 'I want these fools to know *who* has come for them. I want them to feel the full weight of the Angel's wrath.'

'Understood,' Angelo growled. *'Placing breaching charges.'*

Hakkad tapped his vambrace and uttered something in his guttural proto-tongue.

'He demands to be a part of the assault,' Micah said, directing his remaining warriors into a loose fan around the breaching area. Several had slathered blood across their helms, and the Thirst rose in Dumah, a brief itch in his throat. 'He wants to kill their leader in single combat.'

Dumah snarled. Impressively, the mortal barely flinched.

'Inform him this became Flesh Tearers' work when they attacked our monument,' the Chaplain growled. 'He will stand aside now, or I will kill him myself.'

Micah translated. Hakkad's shoulders slumped. The tribesman nodded and withdrew. Dumah watched the countdown unfurl, anticipation flooding his muscles with hot, adrenal rage. The beast in his blood stirred, its claws caressing his mind with slices of sharp pain. Dumah growled, activating his crozius as the counter hit zero.

The charges detonated, splinters of wood scything through the night air.

Dumah was moving before the smoke had faded, vaulting the shredded stubs of the palisade, his bolt pistol flaring. Bolts carved conical trails through the black smoke, and wet detonations marked their endings. Kill-sign clarions flared on his retinal feed. Muzzles flashed at his side, dull red, Micah and Angelo's squads spreading out around him. Enemy tribespeople detonated in sprays of meat and bone. Cries of alarm went up, babbling streams of language Dumah could not understand, and his sensorium could not track.

The enemy charged forwards, their spears raised.

He smashed a tribesman aside with his crozius, destroying his ribcage, hammering his fist through the skull of another. A bone club shattered on his plastron, and he drove a kick into the offending tribesman's torso. His bolt pistol kicked hard, bodies detonating in welters of blood and bone, and served as a bludgeon when the magazine ran dry. His crozius obliterated another tribesman, and he tore the heart from a woman that shouldered her kin aside to charge at him. A third vaulted the corpses of her fellows, her bone club crashing into his skull helm. It veined a tiny crack through his eye-lens. Dumah headbutted her, atomising her skull and shoulders. Gore spattered his armour, secreting itself in the crevices, teasing his Thirst. He roared, the beast in his blood howling for its release. The slaughter lasted only three minutes.

It took longer to steady his pulse and drive the Rage from his veins.

Dumah pulled his skull-topped crozius from the chest of a Cretacian female, holstered his pistol, and moved towards the rear of the encampment. Cages of wood and bone secured with tight loops of cord formed of human hair predominated. Children clustered to the bars, shouting in adulation and alarm. They bore signs of minor privation, but none of external harm, and certainly nothing that could not be reversed with the correct nutritional intakes.

Dumah signed an order to Angelo, tearing the first cage's door free with the dry snap of breaking bone. The children looked up at him, their terror filling him with something that approached nausea. They edged past him in ones and twos, the groups growing in size when they realised that he meant them no harm. The children babbled in the crude tongue of their clan, pointing at the Flesh Tearers. Dumah felt some minor discomfort at their regard. Even as a boy, he had never much liked the other children. They always unsettled him.

'They are all female,' Angelo said, helm grinding across the flock.

Dumah's scanned the biological markers in each child, the results flickering on his retinal feed. Angelo was correct. Each child was female.

'Find out where the males are,' he instructed Micah.

Micah removed his helm slowly and knelt to meet their gaze. They watched him with naked suspicion, the older girls shielding their younger kin. Micah placed his helm and blades on the ground, repeating the question in several dialects. At first, the children were bemused by his accent, but comprehension soon dawned and they answered with enthusiasm. Colour drained from Micah's face. He repeated the last word in their babble, then looked to Daeron for confirmation when they nodded, his expression one of incomprehension and dread.

'What do they say?' Dumah asked. He was rapidly losing patience.

'That the males were taken,' Daeron said, stomping through the ruin of the palisade, his mechanised voice thick with horror. Several children blanched at his approach. Some cried out. 'They were offered as recruits for the "angels".'

EIGHTEEN

The Overlord nosed through the atmospheric retention field, squeezing its massive frame into the primary hangar. Barachiel surveyed it through the external pict-feeds, a cavernous space lit only by the wing-mounted lumens. A handful of Arvus and Aquila shuttles squatted in launch cradles, crowding its mouth. Corroding pressure hoses trailed from fuel ports to rows of tankers and silos. Plasteel hulls gathered rust. Bright flickers fringed the feed, timed to precise bursts of ionised plasma vapour as the craft steadied itself to land.

A countdown flickered live on Barachiel's retinal feed, and he felt his pulse quicken in both anger and pleasure. He stood at the head of the assault column, his armour bathed in the blood-red glow of the overhead lumens. His frustration at being left behind on the strike cruiser was only slightly ameliorated by the opportunity to search the star fortress. In the absence of a chance to grasp their salvation with his own hands, he wanted to work towards it.

Once the star fortress was cleared, nothing could keep him from Cretacia.

The Overlord settled into the primus hangar, her engines cycling down and her assault ramps descending before the landing claws touched the deck. Barachiel thundered down the assault ramp, his armour servos absorbing the shock with a sharp squall as he dropped the last five feet. Castiel's six Hellblasters and the three Eradicators of Squad Azariel dropped behind him. They fanned out into a broad arrowhead formation, weapons trained on every approach. Adariel's Assault Intercessors swept from the second compartment to join him.

'This station has not been functional for twenty years, at least,' Adariel said, indicating the Militarum-issue ration crates stacked to their right. Dates were stamped in off-white paint, and dust formed a thick layer atop them. Scaffolding and sheets of industrial plastek extended along one wall, machine tools and varied lengths of pipe left next to sections of plasteel with scuffed white paint and directional markers. 'Are we certain of the augur data? The station does not seem under power. It does not even appear that servitors have been active here.'

'Hariel himself confirmed it,' Barachiel said, his helm's cartolith identifying the hatch that led to the command deck. He blink-clicked the rune, the cartolith's projection shifting to show an overhead view of their route, a gold line between thin blue lines.

At Barachiel's signal they exited the hangar, helm stablights active and guns panning across every hatch and firing position. Shimmering heat spills curled from their reactor packs. The air was thin, void-cold and sluggish, yet scrubbed clean of contaminants. It was the only life-support function operational in the outer layers of the star fortress. The rest of the critical systems read as minimum, or null, on his retinal feed, the power siphoned away to other areas of the installation. Only the command-deck cogitators could provide more details.

The hairs on Barachiel's arms prickled in response to the cold, anticipation tightening his abdominal muscles. Torn cables trailed overhead like forest creepers, puddles of frozen coolant and armaglass glittering like gemstones, an eerie grey beneath the star-white stablights. Ochre patches of rust cobwebbed the corners of several bulkhead plates, and hatches to the inner sanctums were sealed shut or jammed open. The lights snapped over the dark walkways, the ruptured piping and strewn crates providing ample ambush points.

They ventured deeper into the star fortress, passing training facilities and gymnasia adjoined to armouries and medicae facilities. Abandonment had its claws in everything, equipment rusting and supplies left to expire. Barachiel glanced into a tertiary mess hall as they passed, mouldy food and brackish water still lying on plates and in mugs as if the crew had merely been interrupted mid-meal. His power armour's limited auspex function pulsed at measured intervals. He watched their squads' unit signifiers split and re-form as they cleared chambers for threats. Not that anything here *could* threaten them.

They reached the end of a corridor that crossed from the outer sanctum to the inner. It was scarcely a few hundred yards from the command deck. A large hexagonal hatch sealed the corridor. Its control panel had been smashed and the interface socket crumpled. Azariel and his squad stepped forwards, towering over the others in their heavy Gravis plate. Their melta rifles roared, thick streams of ionised gas reducing the hatch to a shimmering pile of radioactive sludge, like the spill from a breached reactor. The Eradicators stepped through first, their weapons whining as they charged for a second blast.

'This is a waste of time,' Azariel said, as Barachiel joined him.

The corridor split in two ahead of them, one fork sloping down to the primary generatorum, while the other curled up to the command deck. 'The mortals are dead, or else fled to the surface in salvation pods.'

Barachiel led them upwards, stairs creaking beneath his armoured bulk. The staircase connected the star fortress' lower reaches to its uppermost spires, one of several hundred set at intervals across the gargantuan structure. Armaglass panes were secured to stanchions by skull-stamped rivets, offering a view of the entire fortress. Towers and squat, bunkered fastnesses that should have been illuminated by pinprick lights were instead dark.

'There is no indication of ejected life-pods, brother,' Castiel said, indicating the banks of salvation pods visible through an upper pane. 'And there were no missing gunships.'

Azariel waved his hand dismissively. 'Does that prevent them being dead?'

'No,' Castiel admitted. 'It simply makes it unlikely, as does the absence of bones.'

Three Hellblasters jogged ahead of Barachiel, taking point from Azariel's Eradicators, whilst the other three and Adariel's Intercessors followed close behind. The assault sergeant clung to him like a shadow, his squad like the retinue or honour guard of a feudal monarch. It vexed Barachiel more than he could willingly admit. Such cosseting was unworthy of a Flesh Tearer, though he was perfectly aware of the reason for it. His status as the sole fully trained Flesh Tearers Apothecary in the Fourth Company and Imperium Sanctus made him almost invaluable to his brothers.

'We should give this up as an exercise in futility,' Azariel snapped. 'There are no survivors, and we can learn nothing here. We should be on the surface.'

'Survivors or not, we must ensure nothing dwells on this

station. They could present a threat to any ground forces, or an attempt to retake the fortress,' Castiel countered.

Barachiel scowled.

'Your concerns have been noted, Brother Azariel,' he said. 'Do not feel the need to keep voicing them, as I tire of telling you to be silent. We continue until I am satisfied, and the events that befell these installations are revealed. The bridge's cogitator banks may contain critical information that we simply cannot afford to lose. We must know what evil befell these worlds, and see it destroyed.'

Barachiel bit back the inference that they might reveal something of Cretacia's fate. It was unnecessary. They all knew it, even if they did not share his motivations.

Azariel grumbled but said nothing more.

They reached the landing, the measure of distance to the command bridge set beneath their unit signifiers dropping rapidly. They disposed of the top hatch as they did with the hatch at the bottom. A threat rune squawked on his retinal feed, highlighting the twin heavy bolters set a short distance from the hatch. His auto-senses layered a magnified image across the right corner of his vision. The emplacements' gimbal and motive units were damaged, their ammunition feeds long starved of shells. He dismissed the rune and continued along the corridor, noting the scattered bolt-shell impacts that cratered the bulkheads.

They passed artificer and maintenance airlocks – external hatches jammed open while the inners were sealed shut. Claw marks carved deep gouges into the metal. Crystallised blood described the telltale patterns of arterial spray, and several interface panels had been ripped away to expose the wiring. The sheaths had been pulled back, the metal filaments twisted together in an effort to spark life in the doors. They drifted lazily in the null gravity, and his pulse quickened slightly, stirrings of sympathy for the unfortunates that died gasping for breath. He shook the sickening feeling off, as Azariel's squad breached the bridge.

As was the tradition with Imperial construction, gothic architecture and artifice waged a ceaseless war with function for dominance over their shared space. The star fortress' bridge was a fine example of that war shifting in favour of function. Serried ranks of cogitator units dominated the lower tiers of the bridge, crowned by an observation gallery that ran the length and width of the chamber. Simple stanchions suspended the gallery and the ceiling, the wiring concealed behind simple metal plating rather than the elaborate friezes and mosaics so favoured by the Blood Angels, and aeration ducts were hidden by slatted grates. Barachiel enjoyed its simplicity, finding it in keeping with his own sensibilities.

'Castiel, trace the source of the power readings. Azariel, access the cogitator logs and determine what happened here. Adariel, your squad will set and hold the perimeter.'

The squads spread out, and relentless tapping once more haunted the chamber.

'My lord,' one of Castiel's Hellblasters called, 'auxiliary power has been rerouted to weapon carriage theta-four-one.' He examined the screen before him, its pale blue light darkening the ash of his helm and pauldrons. 'Life support has been redirected into the area around that section.' The Space Marine's voice rose an octave. Barachiel's stomach dropped at his alarm. 'Four lance cannons also register as under residual power.'

'Their configuration indicates alignment towards the surface,' another warrior shouted from the weapons bank. He checked again and cursed. 'The inputted firing solution matches coordinates for the fortress-monastery. Maximum range is... sixty-five minutes away.'

'Estimated time to firing?' Barachiel barked, his desire to kill like a warm, prickling pressure in his chest. He squeezed his chainblade's activation bar, the weapon giving voice to the roar caged in his heart. He was too close now. This threat could not be allowed to stand.

'Approximately one hour. Power levels are insufficient to fire.'

'Summon Brother Hariel. Brief him on the situation by coded data-burst.'

Barachiel exited the command deck, hearts hammering in his chest, his brothers' pleas pawing at his ears. He paid them no mind, his focus reserved only for the threat.

Barachiel stalked the corridors alone, the counter on his retinal feed slowly unfurling. Almost forty minutes had elapsed since he had departed the bridge, his orders for the squads to remain in place reluctantly followed. The route revealed its own suite of madness and horrors. As with the bridge approach, the airlocks' external hatches were locked open, and the inner ones stuck fast. Traces of blade-scarring and small-arms fire marked the metal. Sympathy stirred once more, but Barachiel crushed the irritating emotion. Cretacia was threatened, and the fortress-monastery that held their salvation. His fist curled tight on his chainblade, its teeth chewing the cold, empty air. No threat to salvation would stand while he drew breath.

'My lord,' Castiel voxed, his tone edged by vexing urgency, *'the lances will have sufficient power to fire in less than ten minutes. You must hurry, else our mission here has been for naught.'*

More than you know, the Apothecary thought darkly.

'I am well aware, sergeant,' he said, scorn cutting into his tone like a chainsword. An abrupt intake of breath answered his retort. Barachiel grinned. 'Have you attempted to hinder or disrupt the power transference. If not that, then perhaps derail the targeting matrix?'

'We cannot access the central mainframe, nor any of the subordinate systems. Access is restricted by vermilion-grade protocols. A gene sample, retinal scan and full voice-pattern match is required to access it, and all three are coded to the last commander. If we attempt to breach without the proper access, one-time emetics will purge every shred of data.'

Barachiel cursed long and loud in the Terran dialect of his birth, a guttural stream of invective unbefitting of an angel. 'What of Hariel? Where is he?'

'Hariel is soon to arrive from the Justice,*'* Castiel said. *'I have dispatched Adariel and his squad to escort him here, but I do not believe he will be able to deactivate the data-wards before the lances are able to fire. Deactivation at the source remains our best option.'*

Barachiel scowled, closing the link without offering a response.

He forced open a rectangular hatch, emerging into a small intersection. Faded white paint marked directions to gun carriages theta-38 through theta-42, and to the barrack-pens used to cage their enslaved crews. The barracks were nearest, the doors to several still open. Barachiel spied row upon row of sheet-metal bunks sized for between three and five mortals. There was a long refectory table at the centre of each barracks, rusty mugs and bloody rags still left on the table. Barachiel pressed on, following signs towards carriage theta-41.

Darkness yielded to flashes of intermittent light from glow-globes and lumen-strips as he passed theta-40. The dry patter of booted feet on metal echoed through the bulkheads, and the air soured, turning bitter to the taste. His rad-counter began to spike, its clicks increasing to a thunderous barrage as it climbed into orange. Words were scratched into the bulkheads in a multitude of languages, some of which he did not recognise, all written in the same hand.

Summoned by Cretacian blood, did the angels bring damnation.

Barachiel did not stop to ponder their meaning, forcing open the hatch to the gunnery control room. The low thrum of energised machinery and inane binharic chatter of cogitator units washed over him. Servo-skulls squatted in their charge-roots, auto-sanctifiers squirting bursts of dry, tasteless air from aspergillums that had long expended their supplies of incense and oils. Squat cylindrical generators wheezed on the deck, venting shimmering trails of radioactive air. Their armaglass containment shells were flushed red by volatile energies, and the cabling that connected them to dusty tactical stations generated an electrical field that made his teeth itch. His rad-counter climbed higher as he advanced into the room.

There were two banks of tactical stations set before an officer's console on a raised dais. They faced the gun carriage, and the four lances that dominated the cavernous chamber. The batteries' power capacitors were all exposed, and thousands of squat generators were crudely wired into two of the lances. Hundreds had shorted out, curls of grey steam still twisting from their ventilation grilles. The remainder glowed red, as unstable as those in the control room, seeding his retinal display with crackling interference. A quick scan showed radiation building towards lethal levels, even for a Space Marine. Barachiel sealed his armour, noting the collection of spent anti-rad stimm cartridges on the supervisor's workstation.

'Power transferring to starboard lances, carriage theta-four-one,' a voice murmured.

The Apothecary shifted his gaze towards the officer's cubicle.

A single human emerged, a stimm injector clutched in one hand. He moved between tactical stations, muttering unintelligibly. His cerise tunic and breeches were ragged and badly stained. A junior gunnery officer's rank insignia marked the collar, partially obscured by layers of accreted grime. His rad-scarred features were drawn and dirty, his jawline, finger and wrist bones clearly defined through his parchment-thin flesh. Burst blood vessels seeded his eyes, his lips were cracked and the teeth remaining to him were rotten in his skull. A collection of bones were scattered in one corner, their gnawed appearance telling a tale that had become far too familiar to Barachiel.

'Mortal,' Barachiel said, stepping closer, pistol trained on him. 'Cease.'

'Channel reserve power to lance batteries,' the man muttered, keying a command into the tactical station. He appeared not to have heard the Flesh Tearer, moving between the different consoles, drawing down levers and pushing buttons. 'Drawing from life support and auxiliary. Reconfirm firing solution and time remaining until maximum range reached.'

Barachiel watched him drag at the levers with two hands. There was no movement in the lever, in the nine-hundred-strong servitor teams chained to the colossal lance batteries. He saw their flesh components were swollen with infected sores that wept pus, whilst others had reddened or darkened skin. The cannons were already at their lowest elevation, and further adjustment was impossible. Barachiel moved closer, but the human took no notice.

'I have identified the source,' he voxed to Castiel, as the human officer moved back towards the control banks. 'A survivor, a thrall-officer from the gunnery crews. He has siphoned power to the second and fourth lances from a network of portable generators. He appears delirious and to be suffering from radiation poisoning. I do not think he even knows that I am here.'

'Lord,' Castiel said, *'the lances will fire in under five minutes.'*

'I am aware of that fact, sergeant,' Barachiel said, moving closer to the mortal, who offered him a dead-eyed stare, then continued to flick switches. He seemed to be mouthing something else, something squeezed between the slow narration of each action. Barachiel studied the motion of his lips, determining the words they described by their third repetition. He moved closer to the mortal, his blood running suddenly cold and sluggish.

Summoned by Cretacian blood, did the angels bring damnation.

'We cannot pass up this opportunity to discover what has happened in our home, and to the worlds we are sworn to defend.' Barachiel recalled his humour when he found out Dumah had been forced down, and anger turned his stomach to hot iron. His need to discover the truth warred with his need to defend their salvation. He checked his retinal feed's chron. Less than four minutes remained before the lances were powered enough to fire.

He closed the vox-link, snatching the emaciated thrall from his feet. The man gasped, scrabbling at Barachiel's armour until his fingertips were blooded and torn. Pus oozed from ruptured sores, the stench of old sweat and blood strong on his ragged uniform. Barachiel's throat clogged, his stomach turned by the vile aroma. The man wailed nonsensically, salty tears tracking down his rad-reddened cheeks. Barachiel checked his chron. Three minutes and fifteen seconds.

'Thrall, listen well! I am Barachiel, Apothecary of the Flesh Tearers. You have trained weapons on my fortress-monastery. Cease this madness at once and explain your actions, or in the Great Angel's name, I will kill you.'

The thrall met his gaze, and grinned. Barachiel's fingers tightened around his throat. Tendons crackled and bones scraped. Blood misted every cancerous wheeze snatched through the mortal's flaking lips, the stench of tainted blood and decaying organs flooding Barachiel's nose, tightening his throat. Madness burned in the dying thrall's eyes.

'Cretacia's corruption must be cleansed in fire and fury.'

'Corruption?' he snarled, a priority vox-request blinking on his retinal feed. Barachiel ignored it. Castiel could wait. Answers could not. 'What corruption? Explain yourself.'

The serf prised at his grip, gasping for air. Barachiel loosened it a fraction.

'The voices in the dark, they whisper of it.' He was twitching, the sharp movements sloughing skin from wasted muscle. 'The ripple becomes the flood… and the flood… drowns the stars in a sea of red!' He fought the Flesh Tearer's grip, an infant squirming in its parent's embrace, desperate for release. 'Cretacia is the stone that casts the first ripple.'

Two minutes, nine seconds. The thrum of the generators grew strained.

'That is not an answer!' Barachiel snapped. 'Speak!'

'Cretacia *must* burn, ere its crimson lords drown the galaxy in blood.'

'Cr*imson lords?*' He paused. 'You mean the Flesh Tearers?'

The man nodded. 'I have seen them on their knees, broken before the Lord of Skulls, bound to his throne by word and deed. I saw the God-Emperor's subjects defenceless before Cretacian blades, and the oceans of blood spilled to slake the thirst of the Great Angel's most savage sons.' He struggled again, a futile effort to break free from Barachiel's vice-like grip. 'The voices, they told me it would be so. It *cannot* be so.'

'Lies!' His grip tightened, and the man's breaths emerged as strangled gasps. Blood trickled from thin tears in his throat, tempting Barachiel's thirst. 'Heretical delusions!'

The mortal coughed another fine spray of cancerous blood across his visor.

'What about the rest of the orbital's crew, *mortal?* What became of them?'

'The others, they… They *killed* each other! It took them…

twisted their minds… turned them on each other! They… They had to be dealt with! The voices said so… They… They had to be dealt with… dealt with *decisively*… It needed to be done…'

Barachiel's eyes narrowed as the mortal trailed off. 'What needed to be done?'

The mortal tapped a grubby finger against his temple, the nail long and yellowing. 'It took them… in here,' the man said, an insane grin suddenly lighting his face. 'They fought each other… killed each other… *I* killed them. They could not hear… They did not know… The fortress below… The source… The madness… They wanted to protect it… They had to die, you see?'

Barachiel dared not imagine which agent of Chaos was behind the 'voices'. The whims and whys of the Dark Powers were beyond the comprehension of mortal minds, and each one of their endless facets was as cunning and deceptive as its fellows. In truth, he knew that it did not matter now. He hauled the serf closer, the scent of rot strong on the man's breath.

'The fortress-monastery?'

The man nodded frantically, blood welling around Barachiel's fingers.

Thirty seconds.

'*Why* must it burn? Tell me now, *what happened?*'

'It must be burned, lest the crimson lords' corruption infect the entire world.'

His fingers closed with the wet snap of breaking bone. The thrall spasmed, and the Flesh Tearer cast him aside like a rag doll. He deactivated the power transfer sequence, his armoured fingers cumbersome on the small keys. Power vented in shimmering waves from the lances' capacitors, and the squat generators hardwired into them. A chime sounded on the supervisor's cogitator as he worked to erase the firing solution. A targeting window opened, and, for several seconds, Barachiel saw his fortress-monastery – his salvation – framed by targeting locks and warning runes. He stared at it for long seconds after the targeting locks fizzled. He should have been entranced by it, the home of his Chapter since its earliest years, but all he could think of was the madman's warning.

Could the garrison truly have fallen to Chaos? Were they rebuilding the Flesh Tearers into a force loyal only to the Blood God and the call of slaughter?

Questions. Too many questions. Barachiel activated his vox-bead.

'Threat eliminated.'

NINETEEN

Dumah shrugged aside the grimy, grasping fingers of the Cretacian savages. He cast his gaze over them, pressed together like sheep in a fold, their body language a curious blend of awe and caution at the presence of the Flesh Tearers. Hands strayed close to spears and sheathed axes, or reached out to brush lightly against their sacred ceramite. Elders whispered to children and younger adults, lowering themselves to their knees with pained gasps and the crackle of old, seizing joints. None had expected to see the Flesh Tearers again.

The children the Flesh Tearers had freed sprinted ahead of them to the waiting arms and joyous tears of their kindred. Parents and grandparents were as common as siblings and friends, and only a handful remained unclaimed by a member of their tribe, drifting beside those they had forged a close bond with, hoping to be taken in. Dumah let his attention drift to the pennants that snapped in the hot, dry wind, recognising the sigils of almost a dozen clans present at the massacre outside the pyramid. It was readily apparent to him that, while many tribes were represented, only the select few would be allowed make the pilgrimage to honour Amit and watch their kin compete for the honour of becoming a Flesh Tearer.

Dumah marched his warriors past many joyous scenes, entirely unmoved. The quiet awe that framed their first minutes among the tribes had faded, replaced by something more in keeping with the fawning displays he had seen on a dozen worlds. Narrow, tear-streaked faces gazed up at his armour with worship in their eyes, offering benedictions or their infant children for the sons of the Angel to bless. Some offered hand-carved trinkets or petty riches, items meaningful to a human's existence but worthless to an Astartes. The Flesh Tearers ignored them all, pushing aside the rising swell of human flesh to reach the settlement's centre.

Dumah scanned the settlement, the crude dwellings hewn into the sides of a crevasse and joined by bridges of wood and rope that swayed dangerously in the rising wind. Warriors patrolled the bridges and maintained the fires that cast illumination over the cityscape of tents that dominated the lowest level, where the poorest or the most unwanted dwelled. Far above, the jungle reared, dark and threatening. Hunting calls and cries carried on the wind, but the Cretacians refused to look up, their eyes focused on the ground, or the angels that now walked in their midst. Dumah scowled to see them so cowed. The martial promise of the Cretacian warrior-castes and her hunter-clans was legendary across the civilised Imperium, yet they huddled together here like children frightened by the dark.

It was pathetic.

What has become of these savages I feared would corrupt our bloodline? What could have weakened them so? And what threat could see a dozen clans cowed by one? Have the vile squatters in the fortress-monastery some bearing on this, or is that mere coincidence?

At the heart of the encampment, the tribal chieftains were gathered.

None was a day younger than dotage. Cloaked in scaled hide and tanned leather, they each bore an assortment of scars and macabre trophies. Muscular physiques were undermined by liver spots and skin wattles, their flesh decorated with tribal benedictions in as many hues as there were shades of skin. Dumah read the tension between them as easily as he might verses from a chapbook, or a Chapter rite. Their unity was forced, a thin veneer that coated generations of distrust. A weakness to eliminate or exploit.

Dumah filed it away for later.

They looked upon the Flesh Tearers with naked surprise, and many fell to their knees in awe. Dumah spotted several girl-children from the liberated camp amongst them, flanked by guardians heavy with muscle and scars. One girl dared to smile at him, a sudden flash of yellowing teeth not yet worn down by use and decay.

Dumah grunted, and the smile fell away.

'Your children are returned, safe,' Dumah said. Micah stepped forwards to translate, and many flinched at their grating machine-snarls. 'We are the Flesh Tearers, the sons of Sanguinius and the lords of Cretacia. We have returned to our home world and would know what has befallen it during our absence.'

Dumah faced the chieftains across a blazing fire.

Beyond the chieftains, their tribes hunched around their cooking fires, the crisp sizzle of flesh and fat like raindrops striking water. Children clung to their parents, every Cretacian watching the Space Marines with a mixture of adulation and terror. Rapid bursts of language snapped between tribespeople like bullets from a stubber. Dumah identified a dozen dialectal variants, straining his

Lyman's Ear to separate them, as surely as the variety of cooking spices and damp, earthen smells plunged into his nostrils like white-hot, sharpened daggers.

'They cannot be trusted,' Angelo hissed. 'This could be a trap, brothers.'

'I doubt these people are stupid enough to set a trap for fifteen Space Marines,' Micah said, patting his chainaxe. 'If they were, I doubt they would survive to see the sun rise.'

'They could be in league with whomever fired on us,' Angelo insisted.

'You whine like a petulant child,' Dumah said, even as he considered the validity of Angelo's point. They knew nothing of these tribes beyond the fact that their children were taken, but it seemed unlikely that one coalition would attack this number of tribes without support from an unseen hand, likely whoever dwelled in the fortress-monastery now. 'The truth is we do not need to trust them, my brother, but we do need our questions answered.'

'This is foolishness,' Angelo growled. 'I cannot allow–'

'Be silent,' Dumah snapped, a thunderous drumbeat bringing him to full alertness. It echoed in the cavern, and all about the chieftains' fire suddenly fell silent. There was only the snarl of Astartes armour. 'You allow nothing, brother – I command it. Remember that.'

A crone shuffled towards the Flesh Tearers.

Rheumatism hunched her shoulders and curved her spine, just as age had wasted her to parchment-thin flesh and bone. Interlinked esoteric designs formed a shrivelled tapestry on her flesh, though each design had nothing in common with the clans' markings. Her scarred lips framed a battlefield of decaying teeth as she muttered invocations in an archaic Cretacian dialect. In hands wracked by palsy she carried a human skull, yellowed by age, its cranium sawn open. She stirred its contents with a grimy, crooked finger, then handed it to the first chieftain.

His mouth watered as the chieftains dipped two fingers into the opened skull and traced hard-edged glyphs onto each cheek. The scent of its contents sliced through the spices and body-stink that shrouded the cave. Its flavour was distinctive, dry yet sweet, the metallic taste fouled by the damp earth and fusty smell of unburied bone. They uttered short strings of syllables, as he often observed the Imperial Cult's faithful do when they accepted their divine sacrament, before they returned the skull to the priestess. He could smell the witchery on her, a foul gutter-psyker held in high regard by the clans, yet too weak to serve the Chapter.

A proximate translation of each utterance was scraped onto his retinal display, and the analytical part of his mind observed the handful of similarities that spoke of a root language that had deviated from Gothic long generations ago. It had lost much of its grammatical structure and its nuance to time and its speakers' cultural regression. His armour translated it into Low Gothic, matching this trait perfectly. Bile seared his throat as he reread the same words.

'By blood, we speak honesty.'

Dumah caught Angelo's arm, meeting the acid-green glare of his optics. Though he shared the Reiver's outrage at their aping of Chapter rites, he understood that it was a facet of the cultural graft that bound the Flesh Tearers to the memory of the Cretacian tribes. This was not a time appropriate to express his fury. That would come, of that he was certain.

The contest broke only when the crone offered the skull to Micah and brushed a thick yellow fingernail along the swirling script carved into his left pauldron. The sergeant shifted, uneasy at the attention, dipping an armoured finger into the blood. He traced the same runes onto his helm, and hissed the same vow. Dumah bit back the bare flutter of amusement at the primitives' attempt to suppress their fear. The eldest amongst them would have been a callow youth when Flesh Tearers Chaplains last descended on the tribes in the search for recruits.

Most would have never seen a Space Marine before.

Dumah took the skull, the ambrosial tang of the offered blood baiting the angel's teeth from his gums. His muscles ached, bathed in lactic fire, the silent promise of renewal through the consumption of stolen life whispering from the dark corners of his mind. His thoughts ran red as he sensed the blood of the mortals around him, the sweetness of their marrow scintillating on his tongue. Dumah wrestled the Thirst down, caging it for the day it would be needed in battle. He marked his skull helm with the same jagged runes. The vow scratched from his vox-caster.

'By the Blood, I vow to speak honestly.'

Angelo, though reluctant, swore the same, and the circle was complete.

'We grateful angels return clan daughters.' His armour's cogitators scraped the translation onto his retinal feed in time with the woman's words. 'We feared other clans make them into offering to earn angels' favour.' She glanced affectionately at a young girl seated behind her. 'Is good they returned home.' She met Dumah's stare with her own, suspicion plain. 'Angels never refuse offering since time beginning, nor visit tribes save take offerings, shamans say. Why angels come here now?'

Dumah snorted, amused by the woman's bluntness. It was refreshing.

'The Chapter has returned from its great battles in the heavens,' he said, careful with each word he spoke. It irritated him to pander, but they needed to choose terms the Cretacians understood. 'We took many trophies from the dread creatures, and earned much glory in the Emperor's eyes. We seek now to restore our bonds with Cretacia and her people.'

Micah translated, his Cretacian flavoured by his heavy Terran underhive accent. The primitives blinked, taken aback by the unusual modulation. The woman nodded slowly, her eyes losing none of their suspicion. Her kin shared the reaction, several murmuring to each other. Dumah let it wash over him, passively scanning their translations. There was little of interest in their conversations, and he erased them as quickly as he assimilated them.

'Angels' iron birds flew stone temple, a great exodus many summers past,' another elder said, a heavily scarred man with dusky skin and a withered arm. Dumah was surprised that such a being had survived, let alone risen to such distinction within the clan. 'Since, we see few iron birds, few angels. We think they die in heaven-war, and here angels die too.'

'As you can see,' Angelo growled, 'we are not dead.'

Micah snorted, though he duly translated Angelo's words, and Dumah sneered.

'Neither angels in temple,' the elder said, his face scars pulled tight as disgust twisted his expression into a grimace. 'Instead, demand offerings, meat and blood. Have many tribes under thrall, give power for offerings. Tribes lose many children this way.'

Dumah leaned forwards, his voice lowered to a whisper.

'Our brothers remain in the fortress-monastery?' Dumah felt rage boiling from him with every breath forced through gritted teeth. His eyes narrowed to slits, and the prospect of deceit warred with the potential for veracity. Questions clashed like a ring of swords, and veins in his temple pulsed as he strove to sort them. 'This is true? Know that if you lie, I will kill you all before you can blink.'

Micah translated. The chieftains nodded, fear blossoming in their eyes.

A wet growl ripped from Dumah's throat. 'Will you take us to them?'

The chieftains looked to each other, and Dumah read the answer in their consternation mere seconds before the scarred woman shook her head and gave a rueful smile. She was one of the few that expressed no fear, as their answer imprinted itself onto his retinal display. It was a weak, timid scraping, as fragile as the word that bubbled between her lips.

'No.'

Dumah bit back the roar that swelled in his throat, the servos in his knuckles whirring furiously as his fingers curled into fists. Grinning skulls capped his knuckles, and he pictured them splashed with fresh blood. It was all he could do not to tear them apart.

'Why?' he snarled, forcing his hands to unclench.

'Angel light storm reject you,' the old man said. 'We see, as ever see those rejected by light of angels. Angels not know you. Tribes not know. We not take you angels' temple.'

At this, the woman took over, her voice trembling slightly.

'Prove you true angels of Cretacia.'

Dumah took them both by the throat, a sudden snarl of armour joints and servos cut by human squeals. Angelo and Micah stood, swiftly dissuading the other chieftains from any foolishness. Their warriors did the same, cowing the Cretacians with the simple virtue of their immense physicality. Quiet settled like a smog, the reek of fear pungent and strong.

'You *dare* to deny us?' Fury set Dumah's jaw with a tight line. He forced the words between gritted teeth, releasing the tension that corded his muscles with heavy breaths. It was becoming increasingly difficult to mask the Rage inside him, the white-hot purity of the Great Angel's final hours. 'Do you not see the crest upon our shoulders?'

The Chapter's serrated saw blade glinted in the firelight.

'We are the rightful lords of this world,' the Chaplain growled, fingers tightening on the Cretacians' throats. Sinew crackled and breath escaped as crinkled exhalations. Someone, somewhere, cursed, and the wet wrench of a bolt tearing flesh soon followed. 'You will obey, or you will die.'

Impossibly, the woman bared her yellowed, blackening teeth in a tight smile. Dumah almost killed her for that alone, reading the words that scraped from her throat in gasps.

'One test. Prove you true angels of Cretacia. Do so, we take you.'

'We do not answer to you,' Dumah snarled, even as the insult of the mortal's demand warred with the necessity of reaching the fortress-monastery. The relics, along with the answers they sought, awaited them. An ursine growl slipped through gritted teeth. 'We are the sons of Sanguinius, his holy fury writ in flesh. You will not deny us, *human*.'

'Yet you denied. Take test. Prove you true angels of Cretacia.'

'Kill her, Brother-Chaplain,' Angelo snarled. Tension weighed heavy on the air, and Dumah felt the adrenal promise of battle fire his veins. 'They must learn obedience.'

The woman's smile widened, even as blood vessels burst in her eyes. Dumah thought only of crushing her throat, his armour's servos whining as his grip began to tighten. It did not faze the woman in the slightest. She grinned at him, her nerve stronger than steel.

'Kill us, you choose. But never return temple.'

Dumah snarled, then released her.

'What would you have us do?' he asked, biting each word between a sharp breath. It sickened him to speak them, and he forestalled the protests of his brothers with the murder-red stare of his optics. They had little choice, if they wanted to succeed.

'North here, beast hunts. Killed many hunters. Angels kill it, and tribe follows.'

'You would have us play at hunting monsters now?' Angelo scoffed.

'First angels did, so legends say.' Dumah scowled, knowing well the tale she referred to. 'Crimson Lord killed raktoryx, made angels' bond with tribes strong.'

'It matters not what Amit did then,' Angelo growled, his fingers fixed firmly around his blade's hilt. 'We are the lords of this world, and our will is their duty. If they will not honour the pledge made to our forebears willingly, we can force their compliance.'

'That is not your decision, sergeant,' Dumah said, his heart and words leadened by bile. He signed an order for his Flesh Tearers to stand down. They did, with reluctance and breathy curses. 'It is mine, and mine alone to make.'

He turned to the mortals, hating his decision.

'Where can we find this... "beast"?'

Even without the Cretacians' aid, locating the beast's trail was little trouble.

Dumah trudged through the shadows of bent and broken trees, their split trunks and splintered boughs hollowed out and blackened by rampant disease. Bloated corpse-flies and parasites of less-identifiable genera dined on the carcasses of gargantuan creatures left to rot by the beast. His boots crushed the ossified husks and pulped, dismembered remains of vermin to powder, and crunched on dried bark and broken stone. The scent of blood lingered, its corroded-iron taste spiced by toxins and organic decay that reduced iron-hard muscle and sinew to spongy slurry. Angelo strode to the nearest creature, squatting beside its kill-wound.

'We cannot be far now,' the sergeant said. 'This carnage is recent.'

Dumah nodded, reading very little evidence of feeding on the bodies, and far less of struggle, only the ragged tears in thick belly meat and throats that spilled entrails and blood. He paused, detecting a richer note in the dried blood at his feet. His brothers stiffened, and he knew without asking that they could sense it too. They looked to each other, the unease clear in their every movement. 'We must move on and see this beast slain.'

'We should burn the forest,' a Reiver, Brother Kosmos, said. 'No beast could survive magma rounds. This foolish endeavour could be finished in a matter of moments, lord.'

Grunts of acknowledgment crackled over the vox. Though the idea appeared solid on the surface, the use of such munitions would see the dispersal of intense radiation that might mutate the Cretacians' genome. Dumah almost considered doing it for that fact alone. But he could not, much as he might want to – it clashed with their mission on this damned world.

'Have you become tired of your life, Kosmos?' Dumah asked, a thin smile pulling at his lips. 'Or are the noted tracking skills of the Reivers merely Ecclesiarchal tales?'

'Since when did you take instruction from mortals, *Chaplain?*'

Many of his brothers chuckled, their contempt coloured clearly in their voices. They thought as little of this hunt as Kosmos did, as Dumah also did if he was truly honest with himself. It was a lowly distraction, an unworthy diversion from their objectives. Yet it was necessary, a chance to rebind the tribes to the Chapter, and the best way into their fortress-monastery.

'I take instruction only from Seth and Appollus, brother. They instructed us to retake the world of our Chapter, to secure our legacy here, and to recommence recruitment. If that means we must kill a beast for the tribes, then I will learn to hunt as the savage does.'

'As you say, Chaplain. I will not disabuse you of a chance to ape the savage lord. It is not often we are afforded the opportunity of walking in Amit's footsteps.'

More laughter, followed by ear-splitting silence.

Dumah ignored the mockery and led the Flesh Tearers onwards. Carnage described a long and winding path through the jungle, traces of dried blood and random spurts of hyper-violent destruction guiding them to the base of a lone mountain, towards a narrow track wide enough only for a mortal to pass along with ease. The coppery scent of blood grew stronger as Dumah edged along its length, his body pressed against the mountain face, while his black gauntlets smoked as heated rock crunched and crumbled in his grip. The path soon reached its end, opening to a sheer drop into a seething pool of lava.

Dumah sighed and scanned the cliff face above him,

He reached up, moving arm over arm as he hauled himself higher up the mountain, drawn on by instinct and the scent of blood. The dull scrape of ceramite on stone beneath him signalled Angelo's squad commencing their ascent. A chunk of rock crumbled under his feet, and he tightened his grip, hauling himself upwards. Scalding winds lashed him as he climbed higher, black-and-bone lacquer blistering under the intense heat. He avoided a rockfall, holding his place with one arm as his power plant pressed him forwards, threatening to unmoor him. A boulder struck one of the Reivers and he fell away without a sound.

A rune flickered on Dumah's retinal feed, the Reiver's body broken on the valley floor.

The Chaplain found his footing and continued his climb, the surviving Reivers following close behind. Avian caws cut through the whistling wind and Dumah spied the distant forms of the quad-winged beasts he had seen upon first descent. They flew closer in scattered flocks, harsh screeches splitting the air. Mass-reactive rounds speared towards the flocks, the wrench of violated flesh rolling into the thunder of heavy bolt pistols. The fusillade did nothing to dissuade the approach, and the creatures swooped towards the Flesh Tearers, beaks and claws glinting in the low light.

'Climb, Chaplain,' Angelo roared. 'Squad, secure yourselves and open fire.'

Dumah continued to climb, even as the harsh crack of his Reivers' heavy bolt pistols joined those of Micah's. Blood spattered the rock, and his battle armour. Dumah drooled at the heady scent filling his nostrils. A pained roar tore the vox, and a signum rune sizzled to grey non-existence. His heart became leaden when he saw that it was Angelo, and he looked downwards to see his brother picked at by two beasts, even as bolts tore their wings apart.

Dumah continued to climb, cursing the Chapter world with all his heart.

The sounds of battle faded as he reached the top, and he sighted a small cave in the mountain's flank. Bones were littered outside, picked clean of meat and gnawed upon. He moved into the cave, following the rich note he had detected on the corpses below. Dumah kept his pistol trained on the darkness, his auto-senses struggling to penetrate beyond a few yards. His crozius crackled at his side, casting jagged shadows along the cave walls. There were claw marks sunk deep into the rock, with shards of black ceramite jutting out.

He caught a beast's low growl. He came upon the creature

mid-meal, surrounded by the skeletons of slaughtered men and small beasts alike. It hunched over a hunk of meat, tearing at it with teeth lengthened to needle-sharp fangs. Scraps of black ceramite clung to muscled flesh strained by swollen veins and dyed cerise by the need for blood. Dirt clung to the skin, and scars criss-crossed it, years of murder writ in pale lines. The Chapter's serrated saw blade was visible at belt and shoulder.

The Flesh Tearer hurled himself at Dumah with a bestial roar.

Dumah leaned back, avoiding the pile-driving punch the beast levelled at him. It was definitely a Flesh Tearer – Dumah could see traces of the Angel in his countenance and smell the purity of his gene-seed perverted by the Rage. Blood matted his flesh and cracked armour plates. Dumah slipped and blocked more of the punches, though one caught his pauldron and overbalanced him, and he drew his combat blade in a reverse grip.

With crozius and blade, he worked to bring the beast down.

He struck at knee joints and elbows, each blow landed drawing spurts of lubricant and cascades of sparks from damaged fibre bundles and armour servos. The Flesh Tearer howled and roared, his eyes gore red from burst blood vessels, his teeth strung with saliva that pitted Dumah's battleplate. The Chaplain turned aside fast, furious blows, each capable of splitting his helm and the skull beneath it. Several broke his guard as he struck at his brother, warping and shattering the ceramite. Pain sang anew with each connection, and the technical readout on his retinal feed became a riotous display of orange and red armour sections.

Dumah fought to control his fury as he continued to trade blows with the fallen Flesh Tearer, the blood pounding in his skull as the warrior's demented howls blended with the roar of the beast caged within his own soul. He parried attempts aimed at his throat and chest, his assaults dwindling to rapid strikes and counter-lunges. Sweat slicked his brow and layered the salty rime already formed around his neck seal. Breath flushed between his gritted teeth, hot and coppery. It was a rare thing that a Firstborn could beat a Primaris Marine in battle, but the Rage shifted any contest in favour of those in its thrall. Suddenly, Dumah saw an opening in the relentless assault, burying his knife into the Flesh Tearer's primary heart.

The warrior roared, a swift right cross splintering his cheek. Bone scraped on bone, and Dumah hammered his crozius into the warrior's chin, his skull snapping back with a force that would have sent a mortal's head spinning hundreds of yards. He drew his pistol, levelling it at the Flesh Tearer's blood-slick forehead. The warrior snarled and tried to rise, the dull scrape of broken bones grinding against his hearing. Dumah saw no fear in his eyes, no trace of anything that might indicate a human soul. There was only wrath.

'Know rest at the Great Angel's side, brother.'

His pistol barked, and the twitching warrior fell still.

How had he come so far from the fortress-monastery? What had driven him out? Had he escaped, drawn by the scent of blood and violence? Or had something else transpired?

Questions. It always, always came to questions, but never answers.

Dumah freed his combat knife and, for a single moment, considered carving open the legionary's cranium and tasting the grey meat within. One bite, and he would metabolise the warrior's memories from the moment of his awakening to his death. This metabolisation was unsettling, even to those used to the process, but this was not the reason for his hesitancy. Despite the fact that it was the fastest route to his answers, he knew well the stories of those who had sampled the brain-meat of the Rage-stricken and fallen into madness.

He watched the corpse slowly cool, before he put up his blade.

Such grim feasts were of the ancient past, when the sons of Sanguinius were yet the blood-streaked Revenants and not the Angels of the IX Legion. The oaths sworn to their primarch also forbade such feasts except in the direst circumstances. Dumah made to stand, then stopped to close his brother's eyes with a tenderness that belied his frame.

Dumah lifted up the Flesh Tearer's body, and headed towards the daylight.

TWENTY

Barachiel rewatched the static-sliced feed of the star fortress' final moments.

Relativistic physics separated the moment of actual death from the timestamp by long minutes, but such incongruities made little difference. It was still dead. Tongues of fusion fire unfurled from its plasma drives, flames blinked through the open gun ports and hangar bays. Armaglass windows shattered outwards, momentary flashes of diamonds in the pure-white starlight, before they too were incinerated. Minutes passed. The fires reached into the tallest towers, then it vanished in a plasmic fireball, bright like the birth of a sun.

Barachiel folded the plexi-slate and stowed it into its container, his brothers sharing the left troop compartment of the Overlord, silent as they too watched it burn. Barachiel knew that for some the silence was one of regret, of their wrath at being forced to weaken their adoptive home world's defences. Barachiel regretted its destruction, though he knew it was entirely necessary. Corruption rode in its iron bones, enough to taint even the most devout or lobotomised of crews. He pushed the thoughts from his mind. The Chapter could rebuild. It would rebuild. The star fortress would be replaced by one equally as powerful, and the Flesh Tearers would grow strong again. They would rise from the infamy that had plagued them in recent centuries, matching the glories of Nassir Amit and the Blood Angels themselves.

Cretacia would never be left vulnerable again.

Barachiel prowled the corridors of the *Cretacian Justice*, relieved to be back aboard. He breathed its recycled air through lips curved into a thin smile, his servo-skull once more bobbing at his shoulder like a witch's familiar, its tinny warble filtered through the vox-bead implanted in his left ear. He passive-scanned tone-dry recitations for useful information, ignoring the obeisances of the Reclusiam serfs and medicae-thralls. The accounts he had listened to thus far were of little to no help, but Barachiel refused to be discouraged. Salvation rested on the world that turned beneath his feet. Resistance and madness were nothing, a fresh set of bumps in an already-ragged road. Whether they would call it fate, destiny or foolishness, the distinctions were little and made no difference to him.

He would not be denied.

His smile widened as he thought once more of Cretacia, and the fact that he would be boarding an Overlord in the coming hours, and it would bear him to the planet's surface. The vanguard had established a safe landing site for the remainder of the company, and Dumah had given the order for them to land. This knowledge helped to settle him as the data-slate clutched in his gauntleted hand pinged. The sound was a knife blade in his ear, a reminder of the whispers he had heard more than once that he was more scholar than a warrior, more an Ultramarine than a Flesh Tearer. He cut the thought away before it could develop further, and stir the wrath that forever simmered just beneath his skin. It was closer now, his father's dark legacy, gnashing at his heels as he trod salvation's road.

Barachiel consulted the data-slate, ignoring the howls echoing in his mind.

He bypassed the folder containing summarised reports of the various purity tests that each battle-brother had undergone on their return from the star fortress. It had taken him three days to complete them, painstakingly combing each helical strand of their gene-code for unnatural aberrance with every medicae-serf working non-stop to expedite their results and prove them pure. As he probed their flesh, so did Paschar scour their minds and souls for any trace of the seditious thoughts and heretical sympathies that would indicate their corruption.

Barachiel suppressed a shudder, remembering Paschar's brutish intrusion into his own psyche. It had left him hollow, violated, like his mind had been carved apart by surgical blades to show each thought as it was formed and forgotten. In his long life, he had never known such a pain, even when Cawl's knives had flayed and filleted him, fashioning the child he had once been into the transhuman weapon he now was. Those memories were forever with him.

The Apothecary opened the second file.

Aesha had followed his command to the letter, providing several detailed reports and real-time updates, as well as detailed picts. The subtle petulance of the gesture did not escape his notice. Nor did the fact that she had been right that Adnacio's adaptation period would be slightly longer than the projections for the procedure she had suggested. Shame twisted his gut. He should not have been dismissive of his brother's well-being so readily, yet it was for their well-being that he chose his research and continued his distasteful acquaintance with the Death Company. Competing priorities demanded he compromise, even though compromise was the crucible of regret.

Barachiel shook it off and focused on his current duty.

The damned shrieked, at once united and isolated by the pain of their existence and of their communion with Sanguinius. The cries curdled his blood with the richness of their pain, echoing through the corridor, cut by the clang of ceramite on iron and the scent of fresh death that clung to the robed suicides lying in pools of dried bodily excretions, or dangling from knotted hemp cords tied to the gantries. Barachiel offered them nothing in the way of regard or sympathy. The wretches were weak, and the weak did not merit his attention.

He unlocked the first cell, striding into it with a sense of grim purpose. Its inhabitant, Tamael, was shrouded in the thick, impenetrable gloom, the strained clink of the manacles that secured his ankles, waist and wrists betraying his location. The air was rank with the taste of blood and sweat, its circulation limited by narrow ventilation grilles, the deck beneath his feet pitted by saliva and warped by impacts. Chains clanked and armour servos whirred.

He did not care that Dumah would rage.

The damned needed to be confined.

'Where is he?' roared Tamael, lurching forwards. 'Horus! Come! Face me!'

Barachiel moved aside, out of the Death Company warrior's reach, surprised despite himself by the changes wrought on Tamael. There was little recognisable of his brother in the red-skinned monster chained before him, veins bulging with rampant wrath, his flesh torn and melted by his acidic saliva. Common humanity regarded the Adeptus Astartes as the angels of myth, but were they ever to bear witness to one fallen, they may yet call them daemons.

'Tell me, traitor,' Tamael snarled, 'where is your master?'

'He is not here,' Barachiel said, consulting his data-slate. Tamael's bio-signs appeared as close to normal as any Death Company could be. The affliction ran roughshod over every normative measure to monitor health, and each gave wildly conflicting signs. Two days ago, Tamael's hearts appeared ready to burst, and the day before they had barely registered at all. To some, such may cast his concern as pointless, yet they were still his battle-brothers, and his duty to care for them would endure until the moment he expired on the battlefield.

Barachiel left the cell.

He checked Hanibal next, noting a faint whisper of sulphur woven into the stale ship's air. The former lieutenant was the polar opposite to Tamael, having beaten himself into a barely conscious state, his nose and cheekbones reduced to blackened bulbs of ruined cartilage.

The screams of the damned washed over Barachiel, the sound like nothing that should ever rise from a human throat. The warship's air was alive with the teeth-itching hum of active plasma drives, the scent of sulphur growing stronger as he moved to Luciferus, and he noted with stomach-churning horror the wall of flesh split by grinning maws, their teeth blackened by rot.

'Toivo,' he voxed, his golden fingers scraping against the slimy flesh. It trembled to the touch, and acidic mucus hissed as he pulled away. A tongue, scabrous with sores, reached for his hand. His blade sliced it from the root. 'Corruption has taken root, twelve-aleph.'

The sergeant's response was lost in a wash of static.

'Sergeant,' he said. 'Repeat! Sergeant!'

More static answered him, snatches of voices impossibly distant.

Barachiel marched onwards, resolving to speak with Toivo when he returned to the bridge. His boots clacked against the deck, and he was horrified to see plasteel replaced by interlocked skulls, both human and xenos. Vile god-runes were scorched into their foreheads, burning with the hellish light he had seen in the eyes of Ka'Bandha and Madail, and in the eyes of his brother during his moments of prescience. Daemonic choirs gibbered and laughed, promising grisly death for everything he loved. Barachiel's stomach dropped, fear a cold rush in his blood. He had experienced this before, at the Siege of New Rynn City.

'No,' he mouthed and threw back his head, howling in wordless frustration. His vox-bead crackled with curses in archaic Baalite and rough-edged Cthonic. 'Not now.'

He glanced around him, through the narrow companionways and into the distant halls that fizzled into being, where warriors in red and sea-green butchered each other with bolter and blade, and the righteous fury of sundered brothers. His mind rebelled, threatening to sink into the maelstrom of white-hot pain that would scour it of all identity. Words forced through a knot of anger bulging in his throat, a mantra, keeping him sane, keeping him focused.

'I. Am. Not. Sanguinius.'

The illusion shivered, then strengthened, and he saw only the Avenue of Glory and Lament, goldleaf names scorched beyond legibility. Legionaries in black Terminator plate, or mismatched green and crimson, breathed their last, their blood staining his golden gauntlets. The cloying musk of sulphur and tainted meat filled his nostrils, a depraved incense that twisted his stomach. Horus' Eye, superimposed on the octed of his gods, glared from the doors of the strategium in glittering chips of amber, jet and ruby, daring him to approach.

'I am not Sanguinius,' he whispered over and again. 'I am not Sanguinius.'

Something crackled in his vox-bead, a familiar voice, tinny and distant.

'Toivo?' Hope bloomed in his breast. 'Toivo!'

'Lord Barachiel.' The sergeant's voice was riven with concern, but to Barachiel it was a lance offered by the hand of the Great Angel himself, to pull him from the precipice of the Black Rage. *'Cease your rampage, you are slaughtering the crew!'*

Reality snapped back with spine-chilling clarity.

A mortal lay at his feet. His corpse was an anatomist's diagram made real, organs and veins laid bare. Breaths rattled from his ruined throat, his last words denied by the loss of his tongue. Red life dribbled from the twin puncture marks in his jugular, its scent washing the foulness of the taint away. Whispers snatched at the edge of his hearing, and the musky scent of human fear clogged his nostrils. He felt the deck-thralls' eyes on him, imagined their horror and their morbid fascination with the madness that had gripped their master.

'Toivo.' He forced the sergeant's name through lips thick with blood. His brush with the Rage shamed him, as did his perverse enjoyment of the release it brought. He *wanted* to kill, to experience the release of wrath and indulge the Thirst. His vision shimmered again. Panic, or something as close to it as a Space Marine could experience, settled on him like a mourner's shroud.

'We can wait no longer – we must land on Cretacia now.'

Barachiel marvelled at the Cretacian landscape as he descended from the *Justice*. Miles-wide tributaries carved paths through the dense jungle, filtering into shimmering blue oceans and lakes so impossibly vast that they might be considered seas on other Imperial worlds. Rivers of lava reduced fauna and flora alike to ash and atoms, laying the foundations for new life in the death they left behind. Soaring mountain ranges cut the heavens with peaks of ebon stone that glittered in the thin light, and valley basins were thick with trees and the skeletons of the immense monsters that haunted the wildest depths of Cretacia's dark jungles.

Flocks of quad-winged ranodon circled the peaks, tearing at each other in their battles for dominance and mating rights. Smaller avians circled them and were ripped from the skies, offerings from the males to attract a female. Ranodon mobbed the Overlords and their escorts, claws and beaks scraping thick trails of ceramite from dorsal and flank. A Stormhawk fell, torn in two by a pair of competing males. Wing-mounted heavy bolters shredded several beasts for their temerity, though several more died before they abandoned their attack.

The Overlords touched down in the tribes' gathering site mere minutes later.

The Apothecary debarked first, followed by the warriors of Adariel's squad and Aesha's medicae-thralls. They were followed closely by the score of gene-bulked servitors tasked with bearing Barachiel's medicae equipment. The thralls each wore a bulky rebreather that purified the air in a series of harsh clicks and whispering rasps louder than the metronomic ticking of the servitors' cybernetics. The Cretacian air was not immediately lethal, and human life had adjusted to breathe it easier, but it remained toxic enough to cause complex respiratory issues for those not born on the world's harsh surface.

'Set them there,' Barachiel ordered, gesturing towards the portable bunker being deposited by another four Overlords. The earth shook as it struck, and mud stained the closest Cretacian tribespeople. The most curious were unceremoniously moved aside by the warriors of Squads Castiel and Tumelo. 'Ensure the generatorum is live and begin the gene-purity tests.'

'At once, my lord,' Aesha said, and Barachiel noted the strain in her voice.

He dismissed her and continued on.

Flanked by the Hellblasters of Squad Castiel, Barachiel approached the populace. Some watched their approach, idiot expressions of terror and awe plastered on their scarred yet childlike features. Others, the braver souls, those with the supple, muscular physiques of warriors and hunters, let their hands fall to axe-throats and sword hilts. Barachiel scoffed at the unsubtle display. There was little they could do to injure him or his warriors, yet part of him, a quiet part concealed deep beneath years of wrath and discipline, was irritated by the stand-offish welcome. They were the Flesh Tearers, Angels of Wrath, the Sons of Cretacia, yet Cretacia showed little joy at their return.

His rational mind whispered that it was to be expected, while another part whispered of injustice and promised vengeance. Barachiel's heartbeat began to climb, from a canid's growl to a carnodon's roar, his fists bunching around his chainblade. Red clouded his vision, shaded with black at its fringes. These traitors would die, screaming.

Then he heard the drums, an asynchronous shadow to his heartbeat.

The red dissipated quickly, though the shading lingered a while longer. He spied men and women striking beast-hide drums with whittled thighbones, the rhythm like the beating of a human heart after a long period of rigorous exertion. The scents of burning wood and roasting meat rose from firepits and filled his nostrils, a promise of chaste celebrations. Cups of baked clay clanked, cheers and oaths sharing the same moment, and his neuroglottis broke the crude intoxicant they imbibed into its constituent parts. Mildly toxic berries mixed with spring water, several animal venoms and the tears of local flora.

'What do they celebrate?' Castiel asked, his disgust plain.

'I know not,' the Apothecary said, watching two Cretacians battle a beast with shimmering scales and a high red crest, its multi-pronged tail-barb slick with venom. Wrath bayed for him to join the fight, but he refused its counsel, taunting it with inaction.

The creature made the first kill, its barb skewering the chest of one combatant, a male of barely twenty Terran years. He slumped, convulsing, mottled pink foam falling from his jaws as rigor locked them. The beast surged forwards, ripping the flesh from his bones in a storm of claw and teeth, reason and instinct overcome by the insatiable hunger glinting in its eyes. Consternation slithered down Barachiel's spine with glacial slowness.

He had seen it mirrored in the Death Company's eyes.

Mirrored in his own.

The beast backed away from the corpse, scraps of flesh hanging from its teeth. The other Cretacian, a dark-skinned female of dense muscle and supple proportions, ducked a wild swipe of its tail-barb and speared it through the throat. Its blood baptised her, and cheers rose from every reveller. The youth howled in victory, slicing the tongue from its mouth with a knife of sharpened bone. A dozen more were tied to her waist, each one fresh and dripping blood. Some were animal. The rest were human.

'We should not linger,' Castiel said. 'We must find the Chaplain and move on.'

Barachiel turned away, eyes passing over more fights between humans and beasts. He spotted Daeron at the revel's edge, power plant belching black smoke. Firelight played over his frontal glacis, over the multitude of battle-honours sculpted into his sarcophagus and acid-etched onto the reinforced ceramite plating. Barachiel pushed his way through the tribesmen, the Hellblasters following close behind. Fear flickered in the Cretacians' eyes, sharpened by the glow of plasma coils. Despite this moment of weakness, Barachiel saw great pride and strength in the tribespeople. They were a fine and hardy stock, disciplined, despite their outward savagery, enough to contain the Rage and channel it upon the enemies of the Chapter and the Great Angel. Barachiel felt a certain satisfaction as he cast an eye over the assembled warriors and hunters. Truly, the Angel had smiled upon his sons the day Amit had found this world.

'Greetings, ancient one.' He was careful to maintain his neutrality.

'Apothecary,' Daeron boomed, his chassis clunking and snarling as it rotated to face him. His voice scattered the Cretacians that dared stand near him, and his eviscerators chewed the air idly. 'It is good to see you survived your unsanctioned expedition.'

Barachiel snorted. 'I needed no sanction. You forbade my descent to Cretacia before it was first scouted. No mention was made of the star fortresses being off limits.'

'True.' Barachiel detected a note of amusement from the Dreadnought.

'What do they celebrate?' Barachiel's arm swept over the assembled humans.

The Dreadnought made a strange sound, like gears slipping, and Barachiel could not tell whether it was laughter or a snarl. 'Life and honour returned to them by death.'

Barachiel's eyes narrowed at the cryptic words. 'And Dumah?'

'The Chaplain waits with the elders at the centre.'

Barachiel turned, and there saw Dumah surrounded by fire.

Tribal elders formed a circle around Dumah, each bearing

a torch that flickered wildly across the Chaplain's cracked and scarred armour. Much of the damage was superficial, yet there was the unmistakable shimmer of lubricant under the firelight. He was unhelmed, his face cut into an expression of studied neutrality, but Barachiel knew him better than most. Others might have discounted the lips pressed into a thin line, or the slight crease around his eyes, but Barachiel read these signs of displeasure as easily as he might read words written on a page.

His eyes found the warriors behind Dumah, the seven survivors of the first expedition to Cretacia's surface. Barachiel was quietly relieved to see Thuriel among them, though his cheek was disfigured by a fresh scar that sprinted from his eye socket to his jawline. Like Dumah, their armour was scraped and scored by battles against the Cretacian fauna, ragged tears encrusted with dried blood that promised fresh-healed wounds and a litany of damaged servos and torn fibre bundles. Repair and reconsecration would busy Hariel for days.

A crone hobbled towards the kneeling Flesh Tearers, abrading winds lashing the bone talismans suspended from her neck and the age-browned hides that seemed to press her frail, faltering form together. Two younger women aided her, and Barachiel saw the designs inked on their flesh shared similarity only with hers, and none of the clans. He knew this caste and had spent much time in study of their place in the Cretacian social structure. They were clan to themselves alone, weak psykers that took no part in war and feud, above both, yet with the power to uncrown even the most powerful chieftains with a single word.

The ancient woman dipped her hands in the flensed skulls held by her initiates, her fingers emerging slick with heathen reagents. She circled the Flesh Tearers, a gnarled finger tracing Cretacian runes and glyphs onto their armour with bone powders, viscous pastes and bubbling liquids. The odour was beyond objectionable, and Barachiel's nose wrinkled as his gorge rose. They clotted and clashed, reminding him of the foetid corruption that plagued the *Vengeful Spirit*, the taste as alive in his memory as it was at the moment of his father's death. The reek of fermented urine and crude promethium blended with mouldered leaves and herbs reduced to ash. He smelled the blood and bile of Cretacian monsters, the tears of flora, and sulphides and arsenic. These stenches washed across him like a tide of hive-sump sewage.

He read Dumah's distaste, a slight creasing around the eyes. A twitch of the lips that might have been a snarl.

Barachiel's frown deepened. 'For what does he need a shaman?'

The Dreadnought's shoulders clanked in what he interpreted was a shrug. 'Himself? Nothing. It is the tribes that have insisted upon it, and for the alliance he agreed to it.'

'To what? What purpose does this ritual have?'

'Acceptance.'

'Through death, you have proved your worth, mighty angel,' the old woman croaked, anointing his forehead with a bloody thumbprint. She dipped it back into the blood, marking him with a second just above the left eye. 'With their blood, Cretacia accepts you, and her tribes accept you.' Her third thumbprint marked his right eye, and she pulled a bone-knife across her palm, offering Dumah a measure of the blood in her veins. The Chaplain accepted, eyes betraying the merest flicker of the Thirst. 'You rise now as kin to the tribes, and a new son of Cretacia. Stand, Lord Dumah. Stand, Flesh Tearer, and be one with us.'

Barachiel's lip curled, his heart heavy with sudden fury.

TWENTY-ONE

Death prove you true, great angel.

Dumah applied another layer of unguent to his deactivated crozius, buffing chips and scratches from the polished plasteel of its skull-shaped head. He sat in an antechamber, the tools and sacred oils required for weapon maintenance laid out before him. Through the hatch at his back, the scent of woodsmoke and incense reminded him of his final hours aboard the *Victus*, and the lifetime that separated him from that moment. So much had changed since the meeting with Seth and his chosen, and again when they reached Cretacia. Some changes were for good, others for ill. The flimsiest shred of gossamer separated the two categories.

He snorted, wondering which one his brothers might place *him* into.

The Chaplain rotated the crozius, grunting in irritation at the patch of dried brain meat that stubbornly refused to budge. He set aside his metal-mesh cloth and picked up a hooked, half-inch blade to scrape it free. The stain remained defiant, shedding minuscule flakes onto the stone floor. Minutes passed, the only sound the persistent scratch of metal on metal. Irritation soon evolved into frustration, the dry scent cutting his nostrils with temptation, as potent as the memory of the tribe-witch's blood wetting his skin. Her dry, cracked voice rattled in his skull.

With blood taken, Cretacia have you. Tribe have you.

Dumah scrubbed harder, his breaths quickening, the scratching sound grinding at his nerves as much as the memories of the Cretacian rite. He still felt the weak, palsied pressure the witch's thumbs exerted, the echo of her blood greasing his skin like the shadow of a memory made manifest. A growl rippled in his throat. It repulsed him, as much as the memory of the clans' adulation. Their yellow fingernails and grimy hands touching his flesh and armour was utterly repugnant. Yet they cheered themselves hoarse for Dumah and his battle-brothers, bleating the witch's words like a sacred blessing bestowed upon the Angels of Death.

Stand, new son of Cretacia. Stand, kin-brother. Stand, Flesh Tearer.

He snorted, contempt flowering where memory faded. *Son of Cretacia.*

The title was an insult, demeaning every Primaris Flesh Tearer that had served and died in the years since the Devastation. Part of him longed to rip the witch's head from her shoulders and glut his thirst on the tribes that dared believe their approval meant something to him, or that he was more of a Flesh Tearer for the world adopting him as its own. His compliance was a means to an end: learning who had fired on them from the fortress-monastery, and kept the relics from them. He would have killed them all had the circumstances been different.

Keep telling yourself that, a voice whispered inside his head. *Keep telling yourself that the boy born without a home rejects one because he doesn't need it.*

Dumah ignored the rebellious twinge of subconscious, channelling calm through tight and controlled breaths. Outside, he could hear his brothers training under the watchful eyes of their sergeants, while Micah and Tumelo rearmed in the barracks. Their squads were detailed to accompany him to the fortress-monastery, a decision he had to sell Barachiel on. It was not a conversation he looked forward to. Dumah knew he had conflicted with his brother far too many times already, a fact that would taint Barachiel's interpretation of his intent now.

He checked his chron, and cursed. Barachiel would arrive soon. The Apothecary had asked to discuss the gene-purity tests he was set to start on the natives, and their next steps to reclaiming the fortress from whomever held it.

Anticipation swelled in his chest as he left his private cell, emerging in a prefabricated facsimile of the company chapel aboard the *Cretacian Justice.* He paused before the ossuary shrine, where the boiled and disarticulated bones of his fallen brothers were set under a soft cerise light. There were no names, nor any identifying marks, the second sons of Sanguinius made equal before their father and brothers in death. There were more bones than he would have liked, or expected, and a square of plain stone for those he had burned when they had first landed on Cretacia.

It was his duty to inter the bones in the catacombs when the time came.

His eyes lingered on Angelo's bones, easily identifiable despite the lack of markers or signs. The Reiver sergeant's cranium had been shattered by his fall, and deep furrows torn along his reinforced clavicle struts and fused ribs. Regret was a knife cruelly twisted as it punctured Dumah's heart. The memory of Angelo's body on the forest floor, torn apart by the ranodons' razored claws and beaks and pulverised by ground impact, lingered like morning mist over his thoughts. Despite their disagreements, Angelo had been a trusted friend and a valued brother. He deserved better than to be butchered by such beasts.

Beast.

The word turned Dumah's mind from the shrine to the bones hidden beneath his black basalt pulpit, the temporary resting place of the Firstborn Death Company warrior he had killed. There was no better word to encapsulate everything that man had become in his madness. It was what they would all become when they could no longer hold the Angel's wrath in their souls. Ascension moulded them from children into weapons, and the Rage made monsters of them. To see that raw, ruinous potential unleashed was breathtaking and invigorating.

'Greetings, *son of Cretacia*.' Bitterness made a blade of the title.

Dumah turned, greeting the other Flesh Tearer with a nod. 'Brother.'

Barachiel joined him by the shrine, his fist clanging against his breastplate in salute to the fallen. Grief flickered in eyes narrowed to a knife's point, and features hardened by wrath. Dumah saw his jealousy lurking there, his frustration and disdain lingering in the bestial glint, a static charge that passed between them. He suspected they masked something far deeper, a force purely elemental, like ocean swells and thunderstorms heralding a hurricane.

Dumah's balance shifted slightly, perceived threat coiling his muscles tight.

He moved aside, seating himself on the front pew, beside the aisle, allowing the Apothecary to pay his respects undisturbed. Questions flocked to his mind, carrion feeders summoned by the scent of doubt and dying faith. Was it the Rage, or simply stifled aggression? Their Chapter had ever danced on the knife's edge between the two fates. Had he something to do with his brother's wrath? He looked again into his brother's eyes.

It had vanished, as though it had never been there in the first place.

His respects paid, Barachiel sat on the pew at Dumah's left. They sat in awkward silence for several long minutes. Tension thickened the air between them, until they could taste it.

'You have achieved much in the time you have been here, brother,' Barachiel said, his head bowed, hands clasped. 'By bringing these clans together, you have fulfilled part of our purpose here, in securing this world and safeguarding our Chapter's future.'

'Not I alone. *We* have achieved a great deal, and paid heavily for it.'

Barachiel nodded, as silence again held for several minutes.

'Did you see the fortress-monastery?' Dumah asked.

Barachiel shook his head. 'We could not take that risk with the medicae equipment. There are devices of incomparable value, taken from the *Victus* or supplied by Cawl in only limited number. Far better to set down here, away from the monastery and in a secure zone.' He gestured to the chapel door. 'Have they given you any indication of who holds it?'

'They continue to insist that our brothers hold it.' Dumah quelled his irritation at the tribes' vague answer. It was likely genuine, but born from wilful ignorance on their part.

'Is it possible?'

Dumah considered the question. He thought of the Flesh Tearer he had killed on the mountain, and the limited data he had managed to mine from his armour's cogitators. It gave little insight into the last years, and brief snapshots of a massacre in the reliquaria. 'No,' he said eventually. 'It is more likely they succumbed to the Rage when the Rift opened.'

'We will soon know,' Barachiel said, positivity flickering in his tone.

'Not all of us,' Dumah said quietly. The atmosphere thickened in an instant.

Barachiel rounded on Dumah, rage darkening his eyes again. He drew his blade in a single flourish, tipping it in a tight arc to point at Dumah's throat. Its teeth chewed through open air until they were a finger's breadth away. Dumah made no sudden moves, and it took every ounce of his restraint. Tension tightened his leg muscles. His heartbeats quickened, flushing his bloodstream with stinging adrenaline as they matched the relentless howl of the Apothecary's chainsword. Dumah envisaged himself tearing Barachiel limb from limb. The Chaplain teetered on the edge of fury, and he just about held himself back.

'Explain yourself,' the Apothecary snarled.

'We cannot all leave here,' Dumah said, steadying the drumming of his hearts with quiet, shallow breaths. 'A smaller force is likely to move quicker and remain undetected in the undergrowth, and one of us must remain here to supervise the purity tests on the natives.' He paused a moment, weighing his words. 'It is better that you remain, to familiarise yourself with the tribes as I have, and carry out the genetic tests as they take longer to complete.'

'*You* should remain, watch over the equipment and recruits,' Barachiel countered, sheathing his blade. 'My thralls can carry out the basic genetic tests unsupervised. They even now gather samples for testing. The Cretacians also require spiritual examinations, do they not? It matters not, as I will not be denied again. I will discover our Chapter's salvation within those walls.'

Dumah raised an eyebrow. 'There is nothing we need salvation from, brother.'

Barachiel looked at him as though he were mad. 'You know nothing.'

Dumah snorted. 'I am not the fool whining about fables of

salvation, terrified by the memory of innocents and brothers ended by my blade in a single moment of wrath.'

Barachiel's fist hammered into Dumah's nose, and there was the sickening crunch of broken bone. Dumah reflexively threw an uppercut that caught the Apothecary on his chin, snapping his head back. The Chaplain leapt forwards, a palm-strike chambered to break Barachiel's nose in turn. The other Flesh Tearer pivoted, right hand lancing towards Dumah's throat. Tracheal paralysis robbed the Chaplain of breath and he fell, wheezing. Barachiel laid into him with thunderous blows, raining them into his forearms and torso.

Dumah caught his arms, shoving him back. He pushed himself to his feet, breathing heavy, blood seeping from his ruined nose and cheekbone. His hearts thundered in his chest, demanding he retaliate. Barachiel fixed Dumah with a cruel sneer that twisted his angelic visage into that of a murderer. In that light, his expression was far more haunting than the death's-head leer that Dumah fixed him with. It was the image of an angel laid low by vice and cast from the heavens to drown in the sin of the mortal realm.

'Do not mention New Rynn City again, brother, or I *will* kill you.'

Dumah spat. Teeth clattered on the stone floor.

'As you wish, *brother*.' It was through sheer force of will alone that he did not attack the Apothecary. 'However, I will not be held responsible when your delusion crashes down around you.' He spat again, tonguing the blood from his lips, the gaps where his teeth had been stinging sharply. 'That does not change the facts. I am the ordained spiritual leader of this company.' He quieted the drumming beat of his hearts with steady breaths. 'I have earned the respect of the tribes, and it is me they will guide to the fortress. I have already issued the mobilisation orders to Micah and Tumelo's squads. They await me now.'

Barachiel snarled, his eyes flicking to the nearest window. 'I am better prepared,' he said, taking a step forwards. Dumah's fingers curled into fists. 'I have studied every passage and chamber of the fortress-monastery, and I know its layout as I do my own apothecarion. You have not, and only earned the tribes' respect through cursed fratricide.'

Dumah did not point out the hypocrisy of the statement, contenting himself with a far simpler statement. 'I performed the remit of my office, delivering peace to a brother that had fulfilled his oath of service. You must follow your own remit and begin the testing.'

'I will not be set aside again! You do not deserve this chance!'

'Begin your testing,' Dumah said, locking his helm into place and pushing open the chapel doors. His sensorium adjusted his light filters to compensate, and he saw Tumelo and Micah waiting in a cluster. 'Seth will demand a full report, and recruits soon after.'

Dumah smiled, feeling Barachiel's eyes cut ragged holes in his back.

Dumah scowled at the octagonal star carved into the crashed Thunderhawk's fuselage.

Though the flames had long since guttered out, they had left their mark on the craft and the forest surrounding it. Its emerald-and-amethyst heraldry was almost entirely obscured by rust and grime. Creeper vines and thick ferns continued the glacial process of claiming the gunship, the deep furrow it carved into the surface already filled with new life. He scraped a fistful of filth from the hatch, and he saw a multi-headed serpent, the hydra of Terra's ancient myths, emblazoned there. The Chaplain's scowl deepened, and his fingers curled to fists.

'These were Alpha Legion,' he said, the words like bile in his throat.

'Angel light storm bring them low,' Hakkad said, tapping the fuselage with his spear. The youth bore fresh surgical scars on his chest and arms, signs of genetic testing and the first stages of gene-seed implantation. 'Many years past. Survivors not last long here.'

Dumah wrenched the door from its hinges, a feat made easy by their partial corrosion and damage. He stepped inside, the scent of decay lingering over a score of skeletons clad in ancient and baroque suits of power armour. Legion-era bolters, blades and sniper rifles were stowed in a weapons rack near the pilot's compartment, and a broken hololith squatted in the centre. Dumah read the stories of their deaths in the broken bones and scorched ceramite.

He left the Thunderhawk scarcely a minute later, curiosity satisfied.

Micah and Tumelo primed krak grenades, and tossed them in.

'What could have brought the heretics to our door?' Micah asked.

Detonations ripped through the foliage, felling trees and incinerating plants in a wave of petrochemical fire. The explosion sent flocks of featherless avians darting for the skies, and the roars of larger, more monstrous denizens shook the trees. The Flesh Tearers advanced with greater caution, bolt pistols and plasma incinerators trained on their flanks.

'Who can guess the motivations of the traitors?' Dumah said, even as the same query ran through his mind. The Alpha Legion were the most secretive of the Traitor Legions, with no clear goal aside from confusion. 'They are venal and self-serving and should not be known.'

Micah nodded and let the subject die.

The Flesh Tearers cut a path through the jungle, chainblades and combat knives slicing through branch, brush and bough with little effort. They marched for almost two hours and found one of their crashed Stormhawks and two more Legiones Astartes Thunderhawks. The Thunderhawks, their crews picked clean of flesh by decay and scavenger beasts, were checked and destroyed in much the same fashion as the first. As they moved away from the traitor craft, Dumah noted the buckled ceramite plates and rusted bolt casings littering the floor at several points along their advance. It was clear the Alpha Legion's purpose on Cretacia, whatever it may have been, had been frustrated by whatever denizens dwelled in the fortress.

They found the Stormhawk last, its wreckage scattered across several dozen yards, both its wings and tail snapped from its fuselage. Trees had been toppled in its wake, and it had cut a deep groove into the earth. Claw marks framed its cockpit, the armaglass cover ripped away by a predator's claws. There was no trace of the pilot, save his boots and bloody feet.

They had sight of the fortress-monastery after another hour's march. Tumelo and his warriors had not seen it on first insertion, but their awe was matched by Micah and his warriors. Even Dumah was unable to disguise his reaction.

'It is an impressive sight, is it not?' the Chaplain said.

'I have seen few sights like it,' Tumelo admitted.

'Even the *Phalanx* does not compare,' Micah said, and Dumah agreed. He had never seen the space-borne home of the Imperial Fists, but he could not imagine that Dorn's war-masons were able to build something more impressive than this.

'They say Amit himself had a hand in its construction,' Dumah said.

The others murmured their agreement, and they pressed on.

It towered over everything, even the mountains of black and blasted rock that gave it purchase on Cretacia's surface. The falling sun soaked the monastery in shimmering light that reminded the Chaplain of Martian gold. Steeples glinted like sharpened swords in that light, scraping the very heavens, while the stepped firing galleries and drum towers cast their long shadows over the grasslands. They were blunt, brutal affairs even in the daylight, stone shod in iron that promised unremitting violence as much as the hooded, skeletal angels that held vigil over it. A smile touched Dumah's lips, one of humbled awe and great respect.

It took a further hour to cross the field, and with each second that passed, Dumah grew more wary of the silence. The vox-bead was a dead thing in his ear, save infrequent communications from Micah and Tumelo's squads. There were no hails from the fortress, no chimes of augur-sweeps or the rattling echo of aircraft on patrol routes. His fingers tightened around his crozius. He could feel the raven-black eyes of the wall batteries upon him, and the eyes of whoever dwelled in the fortress. They watched his every move, studied them, deciding whether they would fire or let them draw closer.

Consternation was a cold chill that slithered down his spine, his armour's cogitators providing a detailed analysis of its defensive capabilities. A single, well-aimed blast from one of the batteries could obliterate their force. But there were no muzzle flashes, nor did the air crackle with the music of earth-shattering weaponry.

They crossed the field without issue, and Dumah's heart soared as he laid eyes on the great gates that led into the fortress-monastery. They were immense, tapering flawlessly into an arch of black granite and framed by a small outer bailey by which defenders could open fire into the back of an invading force. Cast in adamantium and plated with polished bronze, the Flesh Tearers saw blade and blood drop was rendered in plasteel and Baalite bloodstones and framed by reliefs of angels at war, looked upon by the greatest of their kind.

The sharp rush of released breaths reflected his brothers' awe.

'I have seen few sights finer than that,' Micah said, barely above a whisper.

Dumah nodded, recalling the histories written of Nassir Amit, both when he served as the Blood Angels Fifth Captain and as Master of the Flesh Tearers. Several held that Amit was a great craftsman, as well as a warrior. Dumah wondered briefly whether their savage lord had truly aided in the construction and design of the fortress-monastery, in particular their gates. It was no secret that Amit had disapproved of Guilliman's decision to divide the Legions, and there was something of the Arx Angelicum in its architectural aesthetic, like a dark mirror.

'Spread out,' Dumah said, indicating for Hakkad to wait. The awe he felt at the sight of his Chapter's ancient seat did not dismiss his unease. 'Weapons at the ready.'

His warning was rewarded with bolter fire.

It scythed from the bailey's ramparts, slicing apart a Hellblaster before a single Flesh Tearer could react. Warning runes and reticules splashed red in Dumah's retinal display, tracing angles of fire and the disposition of warriors across the bailey's ramparts. Plasma scoured stone from the ramparts, and bolts detonated against them. A clarion sounded in his helm, a kill made, and he caught a glimpse of a blood-armoured champion directing fire.

'Traitors!' Micah roared, bolts striking his plastron and pauldron.

An Intercessor fell, his chest a mess of ruined plate and ruptured organs. A roar ripped through the battle and Dumah turned to see Micah stumble, restrained by Tumelo and two of his warriors. The Company Champion's eyes were dark with fury, and Dumah felt them resonate in his soul, the beast imprisoned there demanding slaughter with apoplectic howls.

Dumah squeezed his pistol's trigger, and a flurry of mass-reactive rounds kicked free. They sparked against the stone, blasting chunks from the wall. Another kill-clarion sounded – a second traitor killed. Two more Flesh Tearers fell, their visors and chests cratered. One tossed a grenade at the Heretic Astartes, his arm dripping blood and sparks in equal measure. Dumah cast his gaze at the ramparts and the traitors that fired on them, hatred and wrath compelling him to charge.

'We cannot breach the gates, lord,' Tumelo grunted, stumbling as bolts sparked on his pauldron. He indicated a structure to the right of the bailey, and Dumah's cogitators identified it as the gatehouse. 'We will be slaughtered like cattle if we dare attempt it.'

Frustrated anger soured Dumah's breath. Tumelo was right.

'Fall back!' Dumah roared, the words like ash in his mouth. 'Fall back!'

TWENTY-TWO

Traitor Space Marines walk the surface of Cretacia.

Blood boiled like acid in Barachiel's veins as he watched the pict-footage transmitted from Dumah's helm for the third time. The traitors fired from the bailey, their bolts directed by a champion in baroque armour with a monstrous black-iron power axe. Foul runes burned on its blade, visible through the filth and warp-born secretions that encrusted it, while spines of bone and brass curled from his back and shoulders, oozing thick, bubbling liquid.

Traitor Space Marines walk the surface of Cretacia.

The notion was ludicrous and vile, yet it propagated like poison, running acidly rancid with each neuron that fired it onwards. He kneaded his temples, a slow circular pattern to thin the rage infecting him like venom and banish the ache from his skull. Minute knuckle-servos clicked and whirred. Barachiel gritted his teeth, bunching his will like muscles, ready to push the thought from his mind, and prevent him drowning in its venom.

Traitor Space Marines walk the surface of Cretacia.

Barachiel locked eyes with the colourless hololithic ghost opposite him. Even through the poor projection matrix, he felt Dumah's fury like a furnace against his skin. Bolter rounds had fractured the stylised ribs and bone trim of his plastron and pauldron. They were stained with blood. Between them, Cretacia rotated lazily on her axis. Updated cartographic data had been factored into the projection – Thanatos' reconnaissance missions and the scouting sorties performed by gunships had supplied them with the migratory routes of Cretacia's nomadic clans, and the locations of those that resided in fixed encampments. They were splashes of muted colour.

The fortress-monastery was a sharp and bloody red.

'Who are these traitors that dare occupy our ancestral home? Why are they here?' Teman keyed a sequence into the haptic control pad. The projection of Cretacia was replaced by a flat black square, colour scattering onto it in isolated pixels that clumped together to form the traitor champion atop the wall. The projection matrix narrowed to his pauldron. Beside it, outlined in teal, was the warband's heraldic crest, a grinning skull stamped with two crossed chainaxes set beneath a tear of blood.

It meant nothing to Barachiel, and Dumah looked equally blank.

'We do not know. The Heretic Astartes rarely maintain the same sigil, unless they are a warband of some dark reputation or an inheritor of the original Legions,' Hariel said. The Techmarine detached himself from a cogitator unit in the corner, data-input cables retracting to the housings cut into his wrists. His artificial voice grated through the command centre. 'They have been observed to change insignia when new leadership rises to power, or to commemorate a momentous victory. It is difficult to keep track.'

'Companies and Chapters alike fell to Chaos when the Great Rift tore the Imperium asunder,' Paschar continued. 'Several of our most honoured Firstborn cousins suffered with terrible outbreaks of recidivism, and strike forces long lost on crusade re-emerged as Chaos devotees. It is impossible to track them all. I doubt even the Inquisition holds a complete record of every traitor host that now batters itself against the Imperium's shrinking borders.'

'They multiply like maggots on a corpse,' Dumah agreed.

'It matters not whether they are warriors of the Traitor Legions or heretics of a newer pedigree,' Barachiel snapped. Shivers ran through his muscles, his fury and need to kill made manifest. 'They hold our fortress-monastery, and they will die for their temerity.'

Dumah and the others nodded, silent in their approval. The Techmarine adjusted some of the hololith's controls, and several of the larger tribal icons flickered traitors' crimson. Together they formed the eight points of a star, with the fortress-monastery at the convergence. Smaller icons also flickered visceral red, each forming another eight-pointed star around the major encampments. A multilayered meat shield for the traitors.

Barachiel scowled, his pulse drumming harder. 'These are the traitor tribes?'

'The Cretacians have identified these clans as the traitors' protectorates,' Dumah said, his voice mirroring Barachiel's disgust. *'Thanatos has mounted a recon mission to confirm it. They are encamped across every viable ground approach, so we must destroy them first.'*

'We were not sent here to kill the tribes, brother,' Teman said. 'This could be internal strife, or a manipulation by the heretics to force us into spilling the blood of our own people. Some may turn a blind eye to any collateral damage, but Seth is not among them. He would have our heads for such an action, and he would not think twice about it. Would it not serve us better to conquer the fortress-monastery first, then determine whether corruption has taken root among the tribes? We can at least gather evidence to prove it and satisfy Seth.'

'Do you fear the Guardian of Rage now, lieutenant?' Dumah laughed, but Barachiel saw the false bravado behind it. Seth's wrath was not a thing to be courted lightly.

The conversation devolved into a half-heard clash of voices, their tones sharpened by wrath. Barachiel let it wash from notice, focusing his mind on the octagonal arrangements. He held no doubt the obscene pattern had some significance for the traitors, that it was either a statement of their power or the foundation of a ritual to draw their gods' notice. Barachiel was inclined to believe the latter, loath as he was to recall the times he had faced the forces of Chaos as an Unnumbered Son. Their strategies were informed by occult significance, if not entirely predicated on it. Even the irreligious Night Lords made use of it when they had to.

Barachiel studied the hololith closer, identifying a second pattern in each cluster.

Each tribe that formed the inner star had been a powerful influence in their province, with access to Cretacia's surfeit of natural resources, but they were never the most powerful. They were the second, or third, or lower still in the shifting web of matrimonial agreements, blood-pledges and ancient feuds. They were stewards, pretenders to power, with a handful of protectorates and a grudge against their sworn masters. Centuries of anthropological studies screeded through his mind and Barachiel grunted in annoyance, an idea of exactly how the traitors had swayed so many Cretacian clans slotting into his mind.

An unsatisfied ambition for primacy would have made them

amenable to the traitors' offers of alliance, just as their positions in the Cretacian social structure would have made them strong, enticing allies for the traitors. Barachiel believed it very likely they would have traded every scrap of flesh and raw material with little or no thought, enamoured by the chance to be the first in power and gain the favour of the angels. Some may have resisted. He did not know and did not care. Such knowledge would do little to alter their current plight.

He resurfaced to the argument still raging between his brothers.

'We cannot attack the fortress without destroying the major tribes,' Dumah snapped, indicating each central point of the smaller stars. *'We must ensure the traitors can draw no reinforcements or outflank us. Their loss will weaken the traitors' hold on our world, while strengthening our union with the other tribes through the delivery of vengeance.'*

The words hung on a swell of silence, like an unpleasant smell. Barachiel glanced at Dumah, startled by the shadow of affection and respect in his voice. The Chaplain had done little but complain about Cretacia for months, and yet now fought to avenge its people.

'Then we should scour them from Cretacia's surface with orbital fire,' Teman said, hammering his fist into the table. Barachiel glanced to Hariel and Paschar, reading nothing in the Techmarine's visage and a glimmer of disapproval in the Codicier's. Barachiel's double-pulse drummed hard against his wrists and throat. 'We eliminate the treacherous clans and avenge our allies, while also freeing us to assault the fortress-monastery itself.'

'The *Justice* is undergoing repairs to its weapons batteries,' Hariel said, data screeding across his glowing ocular strip. 'While they are still viable, several gun carriages have been damaged and require restoration. My thralls inform me they are proceeding on schedule.'

Barachiel made to speak, but Dumah cut across him.

'Bombardment is a coward's tactic,' Dumah said, and Barachiel heard the amusement in his voice as he twisted the knife in Teman's stomach. *'It is extremely ineffective when it comes to stamping out vermin, as some invariably survive, and it shirks away from the purity of battle.'* Dumah's smile widened as he continued. The Chaplain gestured to the robed figures slinking around the Flesh Tearers. *'Would you rather stay here with the clerks and serfs, brother-lieutenant? Arrangements can be made, if you wish.'*

Hariel chuckled, a raw bark of static. Paschar looked exasperated.

'I believe Brother Teman would rather eliminate the source of Cretacia's corruption, not just its symptoms,' Barachiel said, holding back the enraged lieutenant. He felt his pulse quicken, Teman's fury stirring to his. 'You propose the systematic elimination of corrupted tribes, when a decapitation strike against the fortress-monastery would stop their corruption spreading to other tribes and limit Traitor Astartes resistance to our reconquest of the planet.'

Dumah chuckled, as though amused by a slack-jawed initiate. *'The Astartes hold the high position, and will not expend themselves in great numbers for their slaves. If we attack the fortress-monastery before we eliminate the traitor tribes, they will scatter like chaff on the wind, professing loyalty to conceal corruption. The work of mere weeks would grind across decades, for we are warriors, not witch hunters… Or would you have us call in the Inquisition for assistance rooting out heresy on our own home world? It may even be that Cretacia would never be free from the corruption, and we would have to abandon it.'*

Barachiel bit back a retort. The truth ever had an unpleasant sting.

'Then how long before we can begin the assault?' Teman asked, his voice thick with anger. He leaned on the hololith table, the metal creaking. 'One week? Two?'

'More,' Dumah said, and Barachiel could not miss the conflict in his voice. His relish for the slaughter to come warred with the desire to preserve the relics. *'And then more still to ensure the last traitor clans are eliminated–'*

'We cannot afford to wait!' Barachiel snapped, numbers and calculations sprinting through his mind. Something about them did not add up. 'You would staunch the bleed and not tie the vein. The corruption must be purged before it can spread to more branches.'

'We cannot breach without the full range of the *Justice*'s batteries. Eight weeks is the time needed to restore them to full functionality,' Hariel said.

'I thought bombardment was a coward's tactic,' Teman remarked snidely.

Barachiel laughed, and felt Paschar's eyes burning through him.

'Against foes of flesh and blood, it is,' Dumah said. The Chaplain's smugness was a cold grease on his skin. *'However, we have no Titans or super-heavy tanks to crack the void shields and walls. How else would you propose we break them open, brother?'*

Teman looked crestfallen. Barachiel could find no counter-argument.

'How then shall we strike at them, Brother-Chaplain?' Paschar asked.

Barachiel beat him to the punch, crushing his irritation in a fist formed of iron will. The plan did nothing to further the Chapter's salvation, but there was no arguing that it was necessary to secure Cretacia for the Chapter. 'I recommend simultaneous attacks against the tribes along this flank.' He indicated the relevant icons. 'We can secure our advance and drive them to seek refuge with the larger clans, before we slaughter them. To do the reverse would see them scatter, and the corruption spread. Would you agree, Dumah?'

Silence hung between them as Dumah considered his plan.

'I agree, brother,' Dumah said, and Barachiel blinked, surprised. *'Not only would the elimination of these clans secure our advance, but it would deny the traitors significant sources of materiel and open up multiple avenues through which we can strike into the north and the desert. I will lead these attacks, while Teman and Paschar strike the other southern clans.'*

'What of me, Dumah?' Suspicion coloured his tone.

'You must continue to remain in the encampment,' Dumah said, and Barachiel heard the smile in his voice. *'Hariel will remain also. Your duties are not yet complete, and you are vital to the future of the company, and the Chapter's efforts in Imperium Sanctus.'*

'I am a warrior *before* I am a healer,' Barachiel snapped. 'I *will* fight!'

'Your oath as a healer takes precedence in this situation,' Dumah said, and Barachiel saw Paschar nod. Wrath scorched his veins like boiling oil. *'We can punish the traitors, and their vassals, but only you can replenish our ranks and ensure those tribes that we now fight alongside are untainted. We cannot recruit from a world tainted by Chaos, and we must now prove beyond any doubt that they have not been. This is your responsibility, Barachiel.'*

Barachiel barely heard him, the rush of blood thundering through his ears. His hearts beat violently against his fused ribcage, and rage smeared his vision with an inky black frame. To be denied a chance to seek their salvation was one thing, but to be forced to remain behind yet again was entirely another. He made to speak, but Dumah cut him off.

'Purpose must come before feelings, Apothecary.' Dumah grinned, hand ready to make a throat-cutting gesture. *'Was that not always Tanthius' maxim?'*

Barachiel fell into sullen silence, knowing he was beaten.

* * *

Barachiel forced his hand to remain steady as his surgical blades opened the Cretacian male unconscious on his slab. An incision made along the sternum and upper abdominal tract was carefully pulled open and secured by an array of polished silver steel hooks and clicking auto-clamps.

The Cretacian's face twitched, a subconscious response to the pain firing his nerves as the clamps ratcheted wider. Needles and data-probes bored into his body, administering high-dose sedatives and extracting numerous biopsies for analysis. The Apothecary doubted he would find anything. Seven batteries of gene-testing found nothing to indicate unnatural mutation or genetic deviance in the future neophyte, as it had not in any of his tribal kindred. Repetitive testing had blended hours into days, and days to weeks, a small mercy for him.

Barachiel placed the surgical blade into a gleaming steel bowl, and a thrall-apprenta carried it away for sterilisation. At his command, a surgical servitor stumped forwards, its hands replaced with magna-clamps that grasped a sealed incubation cylinder. Inside, a knot of throbbing tissue was suspended in nutrient-rich fluids. It was no larger than his thumbnail, and those untrained in the internal physiology of the Space Marines, and the process of gene-forging a mortal child into an Angel of Death, would not have recognised the seedling form of the secondary heart, the first of twenty-two additional organs grafted into neophytes.

Muscles glistened wetly under the icy fluorescence of surgical lighting as Barachiel pulled them back and set clamps to hold them. A thought erected a data-bridge between his power armour and the auto-chirurgeon suspended over the table. Its systems meshed with his and a suite of fresh bio-analytics and atmospheric data screeded before his eyes. The male's organs shivered, as though aware of his regard, and a surgical thrall extracted the seed-germ from the artificial capillaries and veins that sustained it, placing it in the chirurgeon's micro-forceps. The calliper-arms descended and, for one moment, Barachiel's mind ran black with thoughts of murder. A grin tugged his lips. One slip, and life would run free and red.

'My lord,' a thrall said, 'the organ will expire if not bonded to the host.'

The words jolted Barachiel back to sanity, and he pulsed a command that positioned the seed-germ beneath where the right pectoral would be. Careful control, combined with the auto-chirurgeon's deft movement and specialised tools, allowed him to open the Cretacian youth's arteries and splice the seed-germ into his circulatory system. Counterseptic squirted from the nozzles mounted on the auto-chirurgeon at regular intervals, cleansing the new heart of any trace contaminants. Its resistance to infections was diminished by its youthfulness and its artificial growth. It needed to be, to properly blend with the neophyte's immune system.

At his command, two small steel paddles descended from the auto-chirurgeon. They pressed gently against the implanted organ, slowly massaging it to sharp, ticking life before it fell into the rhythm set by its larger twin. It would follow that pattern for many days, until the organ had fully meshed with the body's rhythms and the intense regimen of nutrient feeds and hormone stimulants had force-matured it to match its natural-grown twin.

Barachiel deactivated the auto-chirurgeon.

His vision returned to normal.

'Close him up,' Barachiel said. A sharp twitch from the neophyte caused a flush of alarm. 'Monitor him for signs of arrhythmia, or any signs of organ rejection.' They were uncommon, but not unheard of. 'Ensure that he receives the proper nutrient feeds to stimulate the new heart's growth and that his adaptation to the organ is successful.'

The surgical thralls bowed and took over, talking in hushed tones.

Divesting himself of his surgical robes, Barachiel headed towards his private sanctum. Passing through the infirmary, the Apothecary threw nods to the warriors of the Fourth Company convalescing on treatment slabs, mobbed by mortals in white smocks that attended their injuries and aided in their adaptation to the new augmetic limbs and organs. Most would return to combat within a few days, though Dumah's campaign against the clans was nearing its inevitable conclusion. Beneath his calm façade, Barachiel burned with jealousy.

At Dumah's order, he had not left the facility.

He had not killed in days.

The knowledge chafed Barachiel as he passed through the complex web of corridors that separated the infirmary from the other apothecarion facilities. He was a Flesh Tearer, and he belonged in the vanguard of an assault, vambrace deep in blood. It was not in him to sit at the rear, *in safety*, patching his brothers' wounds and cosseting mortals like a son of Dorn.

He passed a tertiary surgical suite, where Thuriel worked with a small team of thralls to graft augmetics to the stumps of a Flesh Tearer's legs. The warrior twitched, a response to the tissue-fusers bonding natural and artificial nerves. A pair of Reivers waited outside the suite. They offered him respectful nods before resuming their conversation about one thorny moment during their last reconnaissance mission, and his envy swelled. Denied the chance to kill anything save local fauna and training servitors, he was tormented by an addict's feverish hunger. Once again, his thoughts churned black with murder.

He passed the observation cells next, where the youths he had begun gene-forging into Flesh Tearers suffered in the aseptic cold. He watched them shiver and twitch, breath misting from their mouths in short bursts, distracting himself from his impulses. Several had died already today, killed by the cold or the organs their bodies rejected. The latest statistics flickered orange on his sensorium display, summoned into being by his thoughts.

One hundred and fifteen aspirants had died in the last few weeks, and sixty-eight yet drew breath. They were highly favourable numbers, considering the quality of the facilities he was forced to work in. Footsteps drew near. He grunted, recognising the skin-scent and rattle of repairing bones. Aesha offered him a shallow bow, and stood straight-backed.

'Adjutant. Do you bear news of my brothers, and my freedom from this base?'

She snorted humourlessly. 'The Chaplain advances into the desert, and the lieutenant returns covered in glory from the coastal clans' pacification.' Barachiel suppressed a flicker of irritation. 'But it is the death toll among the aspirants that I would discuss with you.'

'The numbers are excellent. We are fortunate to possess such hardy stock.'

Her breath caught in her throat, and Barachiel turned to face her. She was ashen and drawn, her eyes bloodshot from lack of sleep and repetitive stimulant use.

'They are not what they could be, Barachiel.' She stopped for a moment, eyes flicking as though she was about to make a choice. 'You charged me to speak plainly to you, and that I shall. The mortality rate is unnecessarily high because your attention is divided between the aspirants and your own desires. It cannot continue, or we risk failing Master Seth.'

'You answer to me. The Chapter Master's happiness is not your concern.'

'It is not just about him,' she said, wrath stirring in her voice. Her hand trembled over her holstered laspistol. Barachiel watched her. 'They are children who dream only of being your brothers, and think nothing of the risks therein. You ignore them in favour of the dusty tomes and the Chapter's ancient past. You dishonour their sacrifice in your apathy.'

He snorted. 'You, who once suggested a cull, now care for others' lives?'

'They were crew,' she said sharply. 'And they were dying anyway. It was triage, not indifference. I suggested the cull to replenish our stocks because I feared what your brothers would become without it.' She shuddered, as though gripped by a painful memory. 'I never imagined that such a beast lurked in your soul, that you were capable of such horror.'

'What do you know of my soul, *human*? What do you know of *anything?*'

'I know fear when I see it. I have seen it drive you since we set sail.'

He stepped towards her, fingers curling to fists. 'You dare speak to me in this way? You dare name me a coward? I am Astartes, a son of the Angel. *I know no fear.*'

'Fear is a poison that takes many forms, and even the mighty Angels of Death are not immune to them all. The prospect of failure is enough to chill your brethren's blood, just as the threat of dishonour drives you to suicidal acts of valour. Both reactions are born from fear because you have been taught that such are anathema to the Adeptus Astartes. You may not fear guns, or swords, or even death as humans do, but your kind has their fears.'

Barachiel said nothing, seething behind his helm visor. *Who did this mortal believe she was, to speak to him so?* Clearly, he had been too indulgent of her.

Aesha interpreted his silence as acquiescence, and continued. 'I have seen you at your research, lord, and I know what went undone whilst you were engaged in it. You worked with the feverish drive of one driven by desperation. It can only be that you seek to purge this monstrousness from your blood, and be as your lord intended.'

He almost killed her then and there. Discipline barely held his arms by his side.

'You presume to speak for the Angel, human, and accuse *me* of self-interest in the same breath? What arrogance has grown within you! I do this for *all*, not just myself!'

She started to back away, fear glistening in her eyes.

He advanced on her, fury scorching his vision black.

'I meant no offence, lord. I only meant that–'

Her skull fractured before she could finish the sentence, her last word terminating in a surprised grunt as her body struck the wall and she fell, dead. Barachiel watched as blood and brain matter leaked from her head and dripped from his hand, uncertain of how he should feel.

He exited the facility several minutes later, leaving the body where it was.

Barachiel crossed the small courtyard towards the company barracks, passing a duelling arena demarcated by a circle of stones and upended blades, the dirt scorched smooth and void black. Two Flesh Tearers fought in its centre to the cheers and jeers of half a dozen more. Their blades sparked against each other, the chainblade's guttural roars tortured as its teeth skittered along the crackling length of a power sword. Barachiel smiled darkly, recognising Micah and Raziel at the centre of the circle. Raziel pressed the Champion hard, but even a cursory glance told Barachiel that Micah was merely toying with the assault sergeant.

For a moment his frustration eased, the pulsing pain in his head lifting.

Barachiel entered the barracks and headed directly to his own cell.

The sound of his brothers at their prayers or making ritual observances to weapons and armour echoed in the corridors. The sounds were alien, even after years in this new Imperium, and the pain returned as the blade-clamour faded. He pressed his hand against his forehead, forcing the pain back. Entering his cell, he deactivated the lumens, for even their low setting was like hot daggers driven into his eyes. He summoned a hololithic rendition of the fortress-monastery and its surrounding mountains, twisting dials to show new angles.

'I will *not* be denied,' he muttered. 'I will find their salvation.'

He scanned the hololith for a way that would achieve both ends, and make the campaign bend to his will. His brothers may not understand, but they would thank him in the end.

Aesha's blood and skull fragments still dripped from his gauntlets.

TWENTY-THREE

Dumah trod carefully across the shifting sands, ears and auspex attuned to their sibilant song. The desert wind threatened to abrade the lacquer from his armour. It swirled across the soft dunes, raising ghosts formed of sand and shimmering light. They beckoned him with fingers that lingered on reality's edge, drawing him deeper into the desert, to be claimed by thirst or starvation. Conflicting temperatures set the air trembling, daylight refracting into wondrous mirages that promised mountain ranges and rivers, relief yet many miles distant, or that may not exist at all. He shook his mind free from their lure, focusing on the path ahead.

His auspex pinged, and he stopped, his fist raised. Behind him, the twenty-six Flesh Tearers selected for his mission also stopped, weapons trained on the dunes. Seconds elapsed like hours, hearts thudding a steady rhythm against his breastbone. The midday sun's heat beat hard against his shoulders, sweat drying mere moments after it exited his pores. A thick layer of salt formed in his neck seal. It scraped his skin red raw, the smell an olfactory irritant.

'Is it much further, mortal?' he asked.

Their guide was a Cretacian, though of a different breed to those he had first encountered. He was a wanderer, an outcast exiled into the Cretacian wilds, to live or die as the Emperor decreed. The brand curved around his right eye, a serpent's tail of blackened skin that marked him as one apart from the clans. Few survived long in the wilds. Those who did quickly became superlative hunters, and would sell their services to feuding tribes. The nomad's voice carried the touch of the desert in its rough edge. Dumah hated him, his venality and mercenary nature utterly repugnant.

It was an insult to the Chapter that such wretches existed on their world.

'It is over that rise, angel,' the wanderer said. 'It is an area the skorpidus cannot reach, as they cannot burrow through the rock. We will be safe there, and you can parley.'

Dumah grunted and signalled their advance.

The Flesh Tearers resumed their march, though a wary eye was kept on the sands. The skorpidus had proved extremely troublesome to deal with. Beasts of chitin, claw and poisoned spines, they were formidable ambush predators, crippling their prey with brute force or venom and vanishing into the sand. The largest beast they had encountered was the size of a Predator battle tank, and he had lost two warriors bringing it down. The guide maintained that they hunted by sound and the subtle pressure of foot against sand, forcing the Flesh Tearers to move carefully between rocky areas. It dragged out their march by several hours.

They crested the rise without trouble, and Dumah killed the guide quickly, a savage twist of his wrists that broke the man's neck before he could even wheeze. The effort brought him no joy. It was a necessity, to protect their purpose and prevent him betraying them.

The traitor clan's war-camp spread out beneath them, small knots of hide tents set along the remains of a cobbled stone path. Mortal warriors moved between firepits and tents, or huddled together in small groups and squads, bearing an assortment of clubs, sharpened bones and spears, wrapped in heavy furs, tanned leathers and chitin plates ripped from the subterranean monsters and the surface-dwelling prey. A Heretic Astartes warrior moved among them, his armour cracked and burn-scarred, ignoring the benedictions offered by the mortal slaves. Even from this distance Dumah could smell their sweat, the animal fat and burned roots of their cooking, and the manure that fuelled their fires in place of dried wood.

His nose wrinkled.

'This is the last, my lord?' Castiel asked, eyeing the camp with feral lust. It was his warriors who had been lost fighting the skorpidus, and the sergeant wanted vengeance for their deaths.

'The rabble seem hardly worth the effort,' Adariel observed, the dour assault sergeant gripping his chainaxe tight. 'We have broken the clans – there is no fighting force left with them to join our enemy, only these dregs. Surely we have succeeded.'

'All who side with the traitor must be put to death,' Dumah snapped. 'We do not leave treachery unpunished. There can be no trace of this filth left, no one to reinforce the traitor position, or provide them succour when the fortress falls.'

'It does seem a waste of our time and talents, lord,' Burloc offered.

Murmurs of agreement rippled over the vox.

'I am not interested in your opinions, sergeants,' Dumah said, pulsing the most recent cartographic data to their sensoria. Every clan and tribe set within the octagonal defences was gone, save this. The ground avenues of approach and escape were closed, and the *Justice* watched the skies for traitor fleet assets, or fleeing gunships. 'Their deaths free us to take the fortress-monastery and expel the heretic bastards that have taken root within.'

He grinned savagely and began tracing his battle-plan in the sand.

'Adariel's squad will join me in the vanguard. Burloc, your Intercessors will advance with us, laying down suppressing fire. Castiel's Hellblasters will provide mid-range support.'

'You believe them that dangerous?' Castiel laughed.

'I believe they will do anything to survive,' Dumah said flatly. 'We cannot allow any to escape and spread their taint to those still faithful to the Emperor and blessed Sanguinius. Target their tents and stone hovels. Drive them out, into the open and onto our blades. Leave nothing unburned, and let not a soul live to draw breath and tell of this day.'

They nodded, grinning savagely, and returned to their squads.

A green rune flickered on Dumah's display as Burloc's squad reached their nominated position. Combat narcotics flushed from his pharmacopeia, his veins singing of fire and sacred fury as he stretched blood back into his muscles, readying himself for the fight ahead. Another blinked green, Castiel's squad reaching their own position. The Assault Intercessors at Dumah's side strained with the need to spill blood, muscles pressing against their armour until it creaked. It was a need Dumah shared, and it filled his throat with a wet growl.

'Execute! For Sanguinius and the Emperor!'

'We are wrath!' they howled, and the day burned bright with ionised plasma and bolt-rifle flashes. Panicked cries carried on the air, paired with the crackle of flame and flesh. He broke into a thunderous run, his crozius buzzing with lethal energies.

Warriors at the heart of the camp grabbed weapons and heavy shields, reacting with admirable discipline.

'We are vengeance!' the Chaplain answered with a roar. 'We are death!'

His first blow took a muscled warrior in the chest, separating his torso from his legs. Bolt-rifle fire reduced another to thin crimson mist, while a plasma detonation set a clutch of men garbed as traders aflame. Dumah slaughtered another with a swift upswing, his skull and torso imploding. Another ran at him, the skin sloughing from his body, pulling Dumah into an embrace. The Chaplain snarled and ripped the man in two, cratering another's face with an elbow strike. Dumah ignored the flames blistering the lacquer from his armour and roared in ecstatic fury. He butchered with the same, the Angel's wrath singing loud in his blood.

The foe buckled before them like a paper shield before a broadsword.

Warriors shepherded their kin away in tight packs, while others purchased time with their lives. Some fled alone, shoving aside their fellows in their haste to escape. They were slain first, their cowardice repellent to the Flesh Tearers. They dragged relatives or carried trinkets they deemed worthy of risk. Bolts blew their backs open. Plasma immolated them. Chainaxes and combat knives sliced them to ribbons. Tents of age-browned flesh and scaly hide burned, and stone huts were toppled and scorched to dust by plasma and grenades.

The air was electrified with pain and fearful screams.

Anger fuelled every strike, spilling from every blow in blood spray and broken bone. Dumah sprinted towards the leader of their resistance, the Heretic Astartes, noting the welded steel-and-iron ring mail grafted onto his armour. The warrior ripped a curved chainsword from the chest of an Intercessor, and pointed the blade at the Chaplain. Dumah felt his anger mount in the face of such a challenge, bludgeoning his way towards the Chaos Space Marine.

They traded blows, each a match for the other in strength and fury, and Dumah's eyes drank in the hard, angular runes that pledged the traitor to the Blood God. The scent of rotten gore clung to the crevices of his power armour. Scalps hung from delicate chains bonded to his shoulders. Dumah's mouth watered at their nearness, the echo of lives lost clinging to the scraps of skin and sinew. The heretic struck for his throat with a serpent's liquid speed, and Dumah smashed the blow aside, ignoring the teeth that buried themselves in his armour.

'Why did you come here, to our world?'

A laugh ground from the fanged vox-grille. 'The same reason as you! Blood! Blood for the Blood God! Disciples, eager for his blessing. You will join with us, for you walk the same path, Flesh Tearer. Join us! Bathe in blood, and savour glorious battle!'

Dumah launched himself at the traitor. His crozius smashed the Astartes' chainblade to slivers of ceramite and plasteel. Shards buried themselves in his armour, biting into flesh. Pain flared and the traitor cast the ruined blade aside, fingers curling to fists. Dumah ignored his punches, and the alerts that blared angrily on his feed. His crozius caved in the traitor's plastron, splintering ribs, and he slammed the pommel into the heretic's head, cracking his skull. He pressed his knee on the traitor's throat.

'Who are you?' the Chaplain snarled.

'We are your future, Flesh Tearer,' the dying warrior rasped. A smile touched his lips, one of both admiration and contempt. Dumah's fingers tore at the traitor's flesh, drawing runnels of black ichor. He wanted to crush the warrior's skull there and then. 'Khorne covets your breed, Angel's son, and he cares not from whence the blood flows, only that it does.' He chuckled, coughing up blood. *'Welcome home, little Flesh Tearer.'*

All else devolved into twitching, maddened laughter.

Dumah obliterated his head with a thunderous downswing, skull fragments spiralling. Seconds passed like wayward hours, the import of the traitor's words weighed against the question of their veracity. Lives drained along his brothers' blades or ended on the discharges of their guns. Nothing was left standing, and eerie silence settled across the killing ground, broken only by the executions made with chainblade and boot. Yet Dumah made not a move, the meaning he divined from the traitor flushing his eyes with inky black.

'They are eliminated, my lord,' Burloc said, a deep groove in his plastron.

Dumah grunted, his jaw and muscles locked tight by fury, listening once again to the songs of the sand. The wind whispered across the grains, whistling between the stones. The sheer calmness grated on him, as did the stillness. A whining growl swelled in his throat. He strained to contain the darkness, the urge to abandon sense and slaughter all within reach. It roused his hearts to a thunderous cacophony, seductive in its promise of slaughter.

He white-knuckled his helm, resisting the call building slowly inside him.

Storm clouds churned overhead, black and threatening. They rumbled with the fury of a violent god, battering Dumah and his Flesh Tearers with scalding winds. Droplets of arterial fluid slashed sidewards, staining his bone trim a muted, mottled pink, rising from a patter to a monsoon in the span of six heartbeats. The sanguine tempest stirred his thirst, summoning the memories of the First Voice's keening wails, grinding against his skull like millstones.

He looked heavenwards, to where the *Cretacian Justice* lurked, hidden behind the storm clouds, waiting for his arrival and the implementation of his contingency. His lip curled in a snarl. This was not the first such unnatural storm to occur during his campaign and, though he could not understand its significance, he recognised ritual when he saw it. They could wait no longer. The fortress-monastery had to fall, and it had to fall now.

'Pilot. Ready for extraction.'

The mortal's reedy response was lost to the roar in his veins.

Xarthus Gaedan had served the Disciples of Rage for over seven hundred years. He recalled little of his time before then, his service as an Imperial Space Marine, his home world, or the primarch to whom he claimed kinship. He was grateful for that. They were weaknesses shed the moment he set foot upon his true path as a servant of Khorne and a disciple of his most divine rage. Since then, he had slaughtered every foe the galaxy had sent to end him, the pile of skulls he had gathered for Khorne's throne greater than that of every other champion he had fought beside.

That did not prepare him for his task today: delivering ill tidings to his master.

He strode along the processional hall that led to the Flesh Tearers throne room, his sword sheathed at his side, his bolter mag-locked at his hip. Slaves scampered past him, their shrill voices offering benedictions and blessings from the god of war, as if they could give such to him. It had mystified him why his master had ordered the cessation of their slaughter, and why he allowed the loyalist clans to remain alive, worshipping the corpse-god in their crevasse and fighting those the Disciples had illuminated. He resolved that he did not actually care what the First Disciple's reasoning was. It wasn't for him to know the petty details of his master's plans, only to relish in the glorious battle that would inevitably follow.

He pushed open the doors to the throne room and entered.

The First Disciple, Chosen of Khorne, lounged in the Chapter Master's throne, a seat of rough-hewn granite. Xarthus' lip curled. The throne appeared more in keeping with a tribal monarch's dingy hall than a Space Marine lord's audience chamber. The First Disciple had divested his power armour, wearing only simple robes, though his broad-bladed axe rested against one arm of the throne. Xarthus dared a glance at his master's visage, at the creases of age and war that had ravaged his aquiline countenance, the strength of his ancient muscles and the strange red eyes through which he saw the world, and which were the source of many myths amongst the Disciples of Rage and their mortal slaves.

He felt their regard like a diamond drill boring into his skull.

Xarthus knelt eight paces from the throne, averting his gaze.

'Rise.' The First Disciple's voice was colder than wilderness space.

Xarthus rose, though his gaze remained far from his master's.

'You bear ill tidings, champion,' the Chaos lord said smoothly, and Xarthus barely caught the sly amusement in his master's tone. The First Disciple had reigned supreme for long centuries before Xarthus' birth, and the Disciple knew well the stories of how he dealt with failures. The torments of the warp were nothing by comparison. 'Is that the case?'

'It is, my lord. They were brought to my attention less than one hour ago.'

'Speak.' A purr edged his voice, laced with threat. 'See your burden lifted.'

Xarthus drew a deep breath, and felt a cold trickle slide down his spine.

'The False Emperor's slaves have dealt with the last of our defences. They rally the clans that refused your offers of allegiance and march upon us even now. They will be here within a matter of days.' His voice tightened. 'These warriors appear different to the Throne-loyal dogs we have faced previously, my lord, yet they bleed and die just as easily.'

'Their strength?' His master's purr grew more pronounced. A bad sign, surely.

'Less than a single company, my lord. They have a strike cruiser in orbit.'

Silence, save the sound of dry respiration and a building leonine growl.

Xarthus braced himself for his master's displeasure. His hearts raced, waiting for the command that would see him consigned to the oubliettes in the fortress' undercroft, and the centuries of ceaseless torment that would follow for daring to fail his lord.

It never came, and Xarthus dared a look at his enthroned lord.

'Everything proceeds according to my design,' the Chaos lord said, and Xarthus felt the weight slide from him to hear the genuine amusement in his master's voice. He even smiled, though the sight was enough to send another shiver down the champion's spine. 'Monitor the Imperial advance, my champion, and prepare my forces for the siege.' He paused, and the smile grew wider. 'Have my armour slaves report to me before the day's end.'

Xarthus bowed and retreated. 'At once, my lord.'

His master's laughter chased him from the hall.

PART FOUR

'I stood at Amit's side on the day our father passed from this world, his life given to halt the Warmaster's insurrection. He stood strong against the Rage in Terra's halls, as he has each day since. He fought the dissolution of our Legion when Azkaellon and Raldoron bowed to the Butcher's demands. Of all Sanguinius' sons, I believe he alone has the strength to save us, if he can but find the will to save himself.'

– Zophal, Chaplain of the Flesh Tearers

TWENTY-FOUR

Barachiel met Dumah in the command pavilion, far from the watchful eyes of the other Flesh Tearers. The pavilion lacked the luxurious appointments and artistry others of the Sanguinian Chapters invested their war-tents with. Such was not the Flesh Tearers' way, and had not been his, even before his draft into the Chapter. A tactical hololith dominated its centre, framed by three rows of vox-banks and augurs operated by serfs in sweat-soaked tunics of crimson and ash. They bowed when the Flesh Tearers entered, and they fled at the first instruction.

'All stands in readiness?' Dumah asked, once the last serf had left.

Barachiel ground his teeth, irritated by Dumah's commanding tone. 'It does, though the shipmistress has yet to report on the status of the batteries and Hariel works to placate *Spear of Sanguinius'* war-spirit. Our brothers tend to the battle-gear and their souls.'

'The shipmistress will be ready to do her part. What befell the *Spear*?'

Barachiel grimaced. Dumah acted too much like an officer, and too little like a Chaplain. It was his sworn duty to oversee their brothers' spiritual needs before battle, not the minutiae of logistics and command. 'An alignment issue in its targeting matrix, our brother says.'

If Dumah realised his discomfort, his scarred visage offered no sign.

'All will be ready for tomorrow,' Dumah said, as though by sheer force of will he could make it so. 'We will smash the traitors aside and claim what is rightfully ours.'

Barachiel snorted. 'If this plan of yours works, that is.'

'You doubt me, brother?' Dumah smiled, a taper-thin crease that reminded Barachiel of the expression a devious diplomat might wear with a knife held behind their back.

'As a warrior, never,' Barachiel answered smoothly, adopting the same false smile the Chaplain wore. Tension crackled between them, thoughts of murder churning through both of their minds. 'Your instincts have been good, though now you abandon them for haste.'

'Then enlighten me with your tactical brilliance, brother.'

Barachiel activated the hololith, studying the grainy representation of the fortress, its fortifications, herbal cultivation and hydroponics bays, as well as the civilian structures. It was difficult to separate them as they all served as defensive structures. Dumah's tactical plan ran its course, numerically tagged blocks of proxy warriors assaulting the walls through the breaches torn by the *Cretacian Justice*. Barachiel executed his own variants in his mind and ran his own estimated attrition rates against those the cogitators forecast for Dumah's.

'We should infiltrate the lower vaults through the aspirant tunnels,' Barachiel said, his finger jabbing towards the mountains that framed the fortress-monastery, and the narrow path that climbed three-quarters of the way towards the peak. 'One squad enters here, through the tertiary apothecarion facility, and cripples the generatorum, disabling the void shields and the wall batteries in a single strike. They can then exfiltrate and join the advance when our main strength breaches the outer walls.'

Barachiel watched Dumah's expression twitch, as though he was working it through.

'An audacious plan,' Dumah said. 'Well thought out.'

'Then you agree?'

'No.'

Barachiel flinched. *'No?'*

'Do you grow hard of hearing, brother?' Dumah snorted, amused by his own jest. 'I do not agree. I will not divide our forces. When the Angel's blade falls, it must sever the head in a single blow. The *Justice* will break the void shields and strip away the defensive batteries, but we will fail if we do not maintain our momentum, and we can best do that together.'

'This will ensure they are disabled without risking the *Justice*, or our brothers' lives,' the Apothecary snarled. 'This will guarantee the traitors' defeat.'

'Therein lies the difference,' Dumah said, adjusting the hololith. 'I do not seek the heretics' defeat, but their annihilation. The Cretacians must learn to respect our rule again, and the spirits of those who have sided with the traitors must be utterly crushed so they will never again dare draw a blade against the Emperor's rule. Our brothers understand this, as does the *Justice*'s crew, and both are willing to pay the cost demanded of them. Do not think me blind to your true agenda in this.'

Barachiel's eyes narrowed. 'What agenda?'

'You have been seeking a cure to the Rage since it first started to manifest among our brothers,' Dumah said. 'Do not deny it, or seek to shroud it in noble ideals and greater meaning. You seek to avoid that fate yourself, fearful of that future since you first tasted our father's rage. You believe there may be something in the fortress-monastery that can help you. There is nothing.'

'You know nothing, even in your exalted position as Chaplain. You believe the Rage is a gift, a final boon granted by our lord. You do not see it for the curse that it is!'

'I do not see it?' Dumah advanced on the Apothecary, hand striking the knife at his waist. 'I see well enough, Apothecary! I see it in our brothers who suffer aboard the *Justice*. I saw its fullest measure in Castus when I granted him the Emperor's Peace. I see far more than you realise, my brother, including your little adjutant's untimely demise.'

Barachiel scowled, his blood beginning to boil. 'You seek to chastise me for her death now? That is the rankest hypocrisy, brother. You killed dozens of rebellious serfs.'

'I care nothing for her death. She pushed beyond the boundaries of her station and she paid the price for it. But that does not change the fact that fear and foolish hope rule your heart.'

'You have never suffered the Rage's grip yourself! I saw what our brothers suffer, and what awaits each member of our bloodline, and I was horrified. I would ensure that not one of our brothers ever suffers that again, that it becomes a thing of hateful memory and we honour the Angel's name as it deserves to be. I do not embrace it as inevitable like you.'

'There is no cure to the Rage,' Dumah said slowly, as though he addressed a simpleton. 'It has been attempted by our cousins across the millennia, and by Cawl in our creation, but not once has it met with success, because the Rage is *not something to be cured*. That it could be is a fable embraced by the Chapters who cannot bear to face cold reality. The lure is programmed into our genetic code, awakened by our father's death. The Rage is a shriving our souls must endure to prove our worth. It is our chance to know him as no bloodline knows its father, not even Guilliman's – to commune with him and to bear his sacred legacy against his foes.'

Barachiel hated the look of wondrous rapture in Dumah's eyes.

'It is all we have to know him, and you would cast it away?'

Barachiel bit back a retort and bowed his head in mock acquiescence. He would find the cure for the Black Rage, no matter what his fool brother tried to dictate. The Rage was an affliction, not a blessing, and death would find any that dared block him from his goal.

Outside the private war council, the battle's eve passed differently for each survivor of the Fourth Company, and the clans that followed them to war. Many gathered in squads, in their family units, sharing food and drink, tales of old times and prideful boasts of a tomorrow that carried certainties for none. Others checked their weapons, sharpening them with flint and whetstone or smearing them with night soil and other potent toxins by firelight and lumenator. Few slept soundly in the trenches, mortals holding close the relatives that may well die tomorrow.

In the morning, Cretacia and the Flesh Tearers would wake and march to war.

Hakkad rolled onto his back, discomforted by the cold iron bunk the angels demanded that he sleep on. It lacked the soft warmth of Cretacia's earth, and the gentle caress of a hide cover or winter furs. His breath misted as it left his mouth, and the hairs on his arms and chest rose in sympathy with the cold. The bare metal walls carried an odd chemical taste, like the *kolabim* extract the healers used to cleanse wounds of venom and infection. Pain twitched his muscles, the sutured pink scars lining his chest and arms still swollen with inflammation.

He looked at them for several moments, a slight smile twisting his lips.

Already he could feel his body changing, evolving him from a boy into an angel. He saw sharper than before, and strange colours washed across his vision. When he breathed, he could identify the individual chemical tastes used to clean the walls, though he could not yet name them. His muscles swelled with strength. His mind ran quicker than it had before. He sprinted longer, tired slower, and fought harder than even the greatest hunter could.

But it was in his blood that he felt the greatest change.

It ran like lava, aflame with the desire for unfettered violence and the promise of pure, holy rage. It tainted his thoughts in moments of peace and privation, that burgeoning fury and the need to wreak wrath and death upon whoever was in reach. In it echoed the death-shriek of a father he would soon know and mourn, and in whose name he would bring ruin to the enemies of the Emperor. Both angel-lords in black and white had promised him that.

Hakkad shifted back onto his side and indulged in dreams of murder.

Shipmistress Kara Étain glanced disapprovingly over the reports presented to her by Hariel's chief acolyte. Fury and fear filled her chest at the thought of a promise undelivered to Lords Barachiel and Dumah. She looked at the creature before her, its augments so extensive that she could not determine whether it was male or female. In truth it did not matter. She longed to strike it all the same, to inflict pain for its gross failure in its prescribed duties.

Squashing the urge, for the simple fact that she would more

likely break her hand than harm the tech-priest, Étain's gaze snapped back to her console and her fingers danced across the insubstantial buttons. Data moved from the tech-priest's data-slate to her cogitator screen, and she ran it through an algorithm to measure the efficacy of the starboard batteries against the estimated strength of the void shields. Her lip curled into a bestial snarl.

The shields might not be breakable with their current strength.

Étain dismissed the acolyte with a curt hand gesture her father would have deemed unbecoming. She could hear it now, if she listened hard enough, the echoes of the admiral's sanctimony scraping against the bone walls of her skull, chastising her for manners befitting a lower crewman instead of an officer. She had hated him, and her glee was all but private when the bastard assigned her to the Flesh Tearers' reconstituted fleet. Serving the Adeptus Astartes promised adventure and glory, or so she had thought.

Even though her hatred remained, she realised what an utter fool she had been.

Étain tapped at her screen, crew rosters and equipment manifests scrolling before her eyes. Her fingers danced across it, a flux of fresh data adding itself to the algorithm. Calculations shifted, and a series of options were tiered in order of greatest risk. She scanned them all, their likelihoods for success and their consequences, before she decided.

It took her less than a minute to issue orders that doubled endurance enhancers, recaff and booster stimms for the next shift, and she prayed that the tactic met her desired end. She knew some of them would die, that the stimms would force them to burn brighter in exchange for damage to their internal organs, and that not all could survive the added strain. She did not care. She could not care. It was a necessity she had to embrace. Dumah and Barachiel had commanded the batteries be ready, and Kara Étain would not be found wanting.

Her life might depend entirely on her success.

Chainaxe and power sword.

Micah examined both weapons, and the trail of broken servitors and armature blades left in their wake. The machine-helots twitched and spasmed, their artificially sustained lives gushing from wounds to their chests and throats. The floor of the training cage was a mess of orphaned limbs, shattered gimbals and broken gyroscopes. Grey flesh shivered with failing electrical currents, and shattered weapons glittered in the light of overhead lumens.

Soon he would be asked to choose between them, between his honours as a sergeant and as Champion of the Fourth Company. It was a choice he could not make.

The Company Champion mopped sweat from his brow with a fresh cloth offered by a robed thrall. Her heart thundered in her chest, and copper spiced her breath, the promise of blood enriched by fear. His fangs slipped from his gums. Micah fingered the power sword's activation stud, the inexorable call to violence woven into his father's blood demanding new, fresh death. It promised to focus him for the fight that came with the morning's light.

What did one mortal's death matter against the thousands who would die tomorrow?

He stepped forwards, and her scream cut the night air.

Paschar knelt alone in the centre of a ritual circle, his staff driven into the earth at his side. He was hunched forwards, his knuckles pressed into the dirt, sweating profusely inside his power armour. Pain wracked his body with violent spasms; a howl pressed hard against his gritted teeth. Blood ran in thick ropes from his mouth, stringing his lips and chin, pooling on the grass under his body. He forced a mantra through a throat made hoarse by screams, the world's sensations fading in a cascade of white noise.

'Sanguinius, walk with me in struggle and stand with me in death,' he mumbled, each syllable washed in pain. The wards and sigils carved in swirling spirals over his battle-armour flared a bloody red, his eyes streaming tendrils of psychic fire. 'Lend me your strength for the moments between, for by your Blood was I made, and by your Blood shall I triumph.'

When he saw, it was through the sixth sense that separated him from his brethren.

Disembodied souls swirled through the Cretacian skies in shrieking eddies, lamenting the violent deaths that forever ripped them from the mortal coil. They blazed white-hot in his mind's eye, in shimmering halos of anguish, fury and sorrow that circled the smears of dark light sculpted into immense towers and formidable bastions. His physical form shuddered as he brushed the minds of its inhabitants, their corruption by the Ruinous Powers complete. An endless stream of incantations spilled from his lips as his mind ventured deeper.

'Sanguinius, armour my soul against the weaknesses of my flesh, and the darkness of my blood. Let me not succumb to temptation, and fill me with your righteous fire, that it may burn away any impurities and I may know of your grace and fortitude. Walk at my side, lord father, and neither the daemon without nor the darkness within shall hold dominion over me.'

The Librarian fought to remain conscious, venturing through corridors that once knew the tread of Amit and a thousand heroes since. Sorrow, pain and raw aggression pressed from within the walls, a vice that enclosed his soul and crushed the breath from him, a wasting disease that promised to rob him of agency. There was something else, something that drew him on despite the pain. It was ravenous hunger, like that of the hive mind though several orders of magnitude more powerful and more base. It craved flesh and bone, blood and souls. It craved destruction and knew pain not even the Adeptus Astartes could stand. He pursued it towards the reliquaria, the flesh of his immaterial form peeled from bone in ragged strips, and there he found the source, and the warp-anchor. He felt its pain as his own, its torment and terrors.

When his eyes opened, his world was veined with red and black.

A monument that had once been a man shivered.

Blood dripped from its opened palm and re-formed as knuckles of glowing crystal on the cold stone floor. It pulsed as though living, the memory and colour of blood once pumped through veins by the monument's living heart. A corpse once rested at its feet, but it had long since been consumed, little more than the crystalline suggestion of a man's skeleton that the warp-touched gemstone had congealed around. Thousands more had been added to it, their blood spilled to fuel its transformation and the portal that shrieked at its side. The crystal coiled around the monument's calves in jagged swirls, piercing flesh and peeling it back, scorching strong muscle and sinew to blackened wastage as it reached for his midriff.

That was not the source of its pain.

The warp blazed in its veins like quicksilver mixed with madness.

It tormented the monument, seeding the remnants of its mind with visions of what it was destined to become, a figure of stirring sanguine beauty, skin of living crystal and blood like holy flame, a herald of polluted rage. It saw the death of worlds reflected in its eyes, tides of fire unleashed by howling, red-skinned warriors in crimson and ash across the myriad worlds of humanity. War machines like iron-skinned gods toppled in pools of nuclear fire and angels were torn from their heavens. Vitae filled its nose and throat as the Flesh Tearers slaked their thirst on the innocent, slaughtering with frenzied abandon.

Somewhere, a shred of a divested identity whimpered.

+You are weak,+ the voice crooned, cruel laughter caressing what remained of its mind. That same shred of identity wept again. +So afraid that your angels would not return that you gladly welcomed damnation in their stead. How does it feel, little wretch, to know that your cowardice and foolishness has damned your entire world? Does it hurt?+

The monument had no response, save to shed tears of the same red crystal.

+Poor Reyan Abdemi. Cretacia is damned, and it is all down to you.+

What remained of Reyan Abdemi sobbed and bore witness to horror.

Barachiel grimaced as pain flared along his temples. The Apothecary tightened his grip on the servitor's head. The wet crackle of bone broke the unusual tranquillity of the training arena, and Barachiel roared as he ripped it free from the machine-slave's shoulders. He cast the head aside and used his forearm to parry the spear-strike from a second combat-servitor. Barachiel fought without a weapon, using only closed fist and palm to do battle.

Once again, he had tried to do his best, to bring about his brothers' salvation.

Once again, Dumah had dismissed him, like he was nothing.

Barachiel drove his fist through the skull of a servitor with twin cudgels, tearing the mutilated grey matter from its housing of cables and iron. He slammed his palm into the face of another, breaking reinforced bone and augmetic lenses. The Apothecary roared and bunched his fists, advancing on the largest of the three remaining servitors. Its blades lunged towards him and he pivoted aside, snapping one halfway along its length. Disruption fields shattered ceramite and scorched flesh, but he felt no pain. He was beyond such things now, watching his father's Palace burn under the guns of traitor sons and Titans, and he rammed the blade into the heretic's throat, the Luperci's white fire dying in his eyes.

'Barachiel!' The name struck a chord in his rage-fuelled mind.

The Flesh Tearer turned, drawn to the voice by dim recognition.

'Take care not to fall to your Rage, brother,' the voice said. Barachiel turned, his fury venting from him like an opened pressure seal as Paschar, grey-skinned and drawn, propped himself against one of the supports. Barachiel vaulted the bars and sprinted to his brother's side, the last two servitors staring dumbly. They could not leave the arena.

'What ails you, brother?' Barachiel whispered, all trace of anger gone.

'The taint,' Paschar groaned, and Barachiel could see the muscle wastage in his face alone. It appeared as if a ghost inhabited his armour. 'It began in the fortress, spreading to the other worlds when the Great Rift was born. Our Chapter's absence damned this world.'

'Do you know where in the fortress?' he asked.

'The reliquaria,' he wheezed, his tongue tracing his lips in search of moisture. 'The warp-anchor is there, and something else. I can feel its hunger tearing at my soul.'

'Rest now, brother. We will bear the burden from here.'

TWENTY-FIVE

Dumah pulled himself through the cupola of his Repulsor Executioner, the Primaris battle tank waiting beyond the maximum range of the fortress' batteries. The surviving warriors of the Fourth Company, and the tribes pledged to their cause, halted beside his tank, thousands of mortals and seventy-five Astartes with a squadron of Repulsor Executioners as armoured support. They strained at the leash, ready to deliver the Emperor's justice. A feral gleam lit Dumah's eyes, bright and burning red, his lip curling over fangs at full extension.

The air vibrated – a persistent tremor accompanied by a bladed shadow that drew cries of alarm from the mortal auxiliaries. Some shifted back towards the treeline, the millennia of ingrained survival instincts overriding thoughts of shame in the sight of the Emperor's Angels. Chieftains struggled to maintain cohesive battle lines, bellowing orders and threats in jagged Cretacian, bearing weapons of flint, wood, sharpened bone and bronze no finer than those of their people in unsubtle threat.

Most held position. Bolt rifles barked, marking executions and the restoration of order.

Dumah's smile widened, the first rune pulsing green on his retinal feed.

The *Cretacian Justice* descended into low orbit, her movements slow and unhurried, a queen on a stately tour of her domain. Her wounds were dressed in scaffolding rigs and layers of reinforced sheet metal, easily visible even without the visual enhancements offered by his helm's auto-senses. Macro cannons groaned through her starboard gun ports, her dorsal and ventral batteries swivelling to face the Chapter fortress. The crew had had enough time to effect all the necessary repairs, and the shipmistress had proven her every promise true.

The thought of battle to come set adrenaline coursing through his veins.

Dumah relished that feeling with every fibre of his being, fingers closing tight around the haft of his crozius. The grinning skull of its head carried the scent of old blood as much as the unguents used to cleanse and consecrate it. It permeated the crevices of his armour, the cloak that billowed behind him and the air around him. He wore its fragrance like a badge of honour, a promise of the price he would exact from the foe for the temerity of their hateful existence. He imagined them unmanned before the power he commanded, and a smile wound its way across his face as he opened a channel, uttering a single command. 'Fire.'

The heavens sparkled, then gave voice to a shrieking chorus.

Solid shells cascaded from the strike cruiser's batteries, streamers of smoke and flame describing their earthward trajectory. Laser beams stabbed from prow and ventral carronades, the thermal blooming effect widening the beam dispersal and reducing their kinetic power by mere fractions. Such was the bombardment's volume that the very air itself trembled. It cracked, boomed, shrieked, the fury and despair of gods given voice by the strike cruiser's guns. Even with his audio baffles tuned to maximum, it was deafening.

Smears of eye-watering colour rippled across the void shields as the lances struck, the energy absorbed and negated, shunted into the warp by the ancient, arcane technology. The conventional munitions struck moments later, neon-bright blasts that birthed a false dawn and leeched the heavens of their natural colours. Roiling waves of multihued flame lathered the etheric bubble shielding the fortress-monastery, setting ablaze the ground around it. Cretacia shuddered, the tremulations tangible even through the anti-gravitic cushion of his Repulsor.

Minor miscalibrations saw several shells fall short of their mark, striking earth beyond the void shields in billowing plumes of nuclear fire. Acres of field and forest were burned to cinder, scoured clean of life on the molecular level by phosphor warheads and plasma bombs. The air was thick with smog and soot, ash and earth that fell across the Imperial host, coating armour and flesh in mourning grey. Dumah maximised his helm's filters, a spike of annoyance needling his wrath to wakefulness when he saw the shield still endured, tangles of lightning crackling across it, strained a deep puce by the orbital fire.

The beast within his breast howled, demanding release from its prison.

'Second wave,' Dumah ordered, crushing the beast beneath the boot of his iron will. It had almost escaped aboard the *Justice*, but it would not do so today. The shield's endurance was an irritant, made worse by the feeling of Barachiel's sly smile, like daggers in his back. It would fall, and it would be by his design that they retook their home. 'Launch!'

Phalanxes of strike fighters and bombers spilled from the hangars like enraged insect swarms, diving headlong for the fortress-monastery. They weaved through the storm of lasers, plasma and solid shells that rained from the heavens, through air corridors specifically cleared by the gunners to let them pass. Dumah listened to the conflicting mess of squadron leaders and pilots finalising their targets and positioning themselves for attack runs. The interference of the bombardment seeded the vox with static, and he watched them soar towards the target, bomb bays opening and heavy cannons cycling fresh loads of ordnance. The Cretacians that had joined their attack cried in awe and adulation, howling their praises to Amit and Sanguinius, and their Flesh Tearers, as if their display of aerial power proved their divinity.

Then the fortress-monastery spoke.

Weapons roared in unison, lethal patterns of beam and shell stitching across the skies as the ground shook once again to the steady thuds of anti-air fire. Strike fighters and lesser flyers were atomised in plasmic fireballs. Cumbersome bombers blazed from the heavens in tear-trails of petrochemical fire, or vanished in rippling explosions as their ordnance cooked off. More fell with every barrage, ploughing deep grooves into the earth. The Cretacians' cheers melted away, the stunned silence filled only by the rolling thud of anti-air carronades and the keening snarl of flyers falling to the ground. Their own defences made a fool of him.

Hatred swelled Dumah's hearts.

'We need to press the attack,' Kairus snarled, his wrath a welcome note in the chorus of panic that gripped the mortals. Bolt rifles and chainblades kept them in line, and gruesome examples were made of cowards. 'We should not wait. We cannot be weak before the foe.'

A chorus of agreement rose from the other sergeants.

'Do not be a fool, brother,' Barachiel growled, his words

crashing like the volley of bolter fire at a battle's dawn. He watched from the cupola of his own Repulsor, the red heat of Thirst-born fury radiating from him in nauseating waves, yet his words were spoken with tight, measured control. 'If we attempt to breach now, the defences will cut us apart.'

'You counsel cowardice, Apothecary,' Kairus barked.

'I counsel sense,' Barachiel countered, his finger thrust at the sergeant. His other hand brushed his pistol. 'We cannot retake the fortress-monastery if we lie dead at its gates. The shields resist bombardment, and we have no means to breach the walls. Its outer guns alone will tear us apart, and then where will the grand lesson and annihilation be? Nowhere!'

'Launching our assault will force the heretics to divide their attention between the airborne assault and the ground assault,' Kairus spat, gripping tight his chainsword.

'Such a division in their focus will allow us to breach while the air squadrons pick off the wall defences,' Azariel said, and Toivo snarled, made wordless by his battle-lust.

'That is a dangerous plan,' Barachiel said. 'The risks may outweigh the rewards.'

'Coward!' Raziel snapped. 'You disgrace the line of Sanguinius!'

Barachiel snarled a wordless curse, hand straying towards his bolt pistol. Dumah was forced to admit that he admired the Apothecary's restraint, his ability to hold his wrath in check despite intense provocation. He would not have endured it so easily.

'By what right do you dare judge me, or the worth of my service?' Barachiel roared. 'I serve Sanguinius as well as any of you, and none have the right to question it!'

'Silence!' Dumah snarled. 'None have the authority to lay those charges, save me, and you will not hear them again, Barachiel, unless I make them. Am I understood, sergeants?'

'Aye, lord,' they chorused, sullen and wrathful.

'Now, your suggestion?' Dumah snarled, his fingers curling into fists as he imagined them tearing the sergeants' skulls apart. Breath whistled between his clenched teeth.

'It is no different to my plan yesterday. We dispatch a squad into the aspirant tunnels to infiltrate the fortress,' Barachiel said, and Dumah hated the savage joy in the Apothecary's voice. 'That squad disables the generatorum, eliminating the void shields and the wall batteries, allowing us to bring the *Justice* and its squadrons properly to bear on the enemy.'

Dumah's eyes narrowed. He had dismissed the idea at their council the previous night. It was foolish and cowardly, and it exposed the Apothecary to temptations Dumah was not certain he could resist. 'I will not consider that option, brother. The Flesh Tearers will not be synonymous for cowardice before the enemy, as the Raven Guard are, while I draw breath.'

Barachiel laughed, bleak and bitter. 'You believe to exert sense is cowardice?'

'It is cowardice to skulk any longer behind these fortifications,' he snarled, indicating the trenches dug at their rear. 'We should face the foe, and let them taste our wrath.'

A signum rune flickered green, and a reedy mortal voice pawed through his vox-bead. He dimly recognised the ship-mistress' voice. Terror set it shaking. *'Lord, I have ordered the withdrawal of our air assets. They need to regroup and rearm for another assault.'*

The Chaplain stared at the wall and its batteries, his hatred like a lightning rod for his wrath. The walls mocked him in their defiance, and their sheltering of the traitors. Each burst of beam and flame was another insult to the tally, each fallen aircraft another scalpel's slice to his honour. The wrath that scorched his veins burned brighter than the sun, the promise of blood yet to be spilled washing away any thoughts of enduring shame.

Dumah switched to the general vox. 'Attack!'

The first assault failed, and it failed in the most spectacular fashion.

Dumah limped into the command pavilion, Barachiel close behind. His armour servos snicked and wheezed with each step taken, ceramite plates grinding together like millstones. Lubricant dribbled from tears and gold sparks cascaded from torn fibre bundles and cabling. His growl dismissed the tactical serfs, their rebreathers' measured clicks vanishing into the roaring drumbeat of his double pulse, the beast in his blood calling him to wrath. He pressed a hand against his head, a poor balm for the pain that blistered his mind.

'Thirteen of our brothers lie dead,' Barachiel snapped, driving his fist into Dumah's breastplate. Cracks veined wider, and pain flared on scorched nerve endings. The Apothecary's right fist cannoned into his helm, hard enough to split ceramite. It shattered his nose, blood trickling across his lips. A second blow cracked his cheek, the pain fading into a warm wash of soporifics. Barachiel towered over him, his body language bleeding restraint.

'May their blood stain your hands forever, *Chaplain*.'

Dumah said nothing, working his jaw until the bone clicked back. There was no point denying the truth, or the fact that he deserved the Apothecary's denigration. It was fortune and Barachiel's skills as a medicae officer alone that allowed them to preserve the number of progenoids they had. Left to Thuriel alone, he suspected they may have lost half.

'Three from Micah's squad,' Barachiel seethed, placing their cryo-canisters on the hololithic table between them. Guilt twisted Dumah's stomach as he read their names printed on the display in bright green text. 'Four from Tumelo's, including Tumelo himself.' Another four cryo-canisters. 'One warrior from Castiel's squad, and Azariel's entire squad.'

Silence hung over the cryo-canisters and the ovoid organs packed within.

'Are you going to say nothing?' Barachiel hissed.

'What do you want me to say, *brother?*' Fury swelled in his chest.

'I want to see guilt, or contrition!' the Apothecary screamed, driving his fist at Dumah's helm. This time the Chaplain was prepared, blocking with his forearm and driving his palm into Barachiel's nose. 'Your arrogance killed thirteen of our battle-brothers!'

'You do not need to tell me, medicae. I can read, and count to thirteen.'

'Such intelligence from a stripling,' Barachiel said, feigning shock, but there was no amusement, nor the cruel malice of sarcasm. There was only wrath, and the things that were born from it. 'One might think such a genius would listen to reason and good counsel.'

Dumah spat, acidic saliva hissing on grass and earth, and envisioned himself tearing Barachiel's arm from its socket, then his head from his neck. He resisted the impulse, and for a short time there were only the clicks and snarls of their power armour and the hololithic table stuttering to life. Dumah hammered his fist when static promised an impending crash. It surged into activation, goading him with a retelling of their failed assault.

Sorties of Stormhawks and Stormtalons were torn from the heavens, and shells fell on the approaching host like winter sleet. Las-fire and plasma bursts annihilated everything they touched. Casemates exploded and set creeper vines aflame. Stone sheeted from the walls like crumbling ice and siege engines collapsed in flames. Divisions marked in gold and blue were annihilated by thickets of gunfire as they approached, while the red defending regiments only dimmed. It did not take long for the blue to pull back, and those sections marked by the Flesh Tearers sigil were the very last to retreat. It cut for several minutes, then replayed.

'Does that sight not stir your heart, brother? Some measure of guilt?'

'Guilt achieves nothing. Only through victory can we honour our fallen.'

'Then I say to you again, let me infiltrate the fortress-monastery.'

Barachiel froze the battle and adjusted the hololith, magnifying the track that led up one of the mountains. 'One squad, and I can ensure the wall batteries and void shields are disabled before our next attack.'

'Lord,' Micah voxed, *'the enemy marshals a counter-attack. They will be on us in minutes.'*

Dumah activated his armour's sensorium interface, and his retinal feed fractured into two distinct views. Micah's signum rune blinked in the corner of the second view. Thick dust clouds were thrown up by Rhinos and Razorbacks festooned with bloody spikes and withered cadavers, their hulls proudly displaying the axe-stamped skull of the Disciples and the Blood God's rune. Mortals sprinted in their wake, bearing an eclectic array of weapons looted from the fortress-monastery's armoury and their tribal kin. Heretic Astartes kept the mortals in line, herding them towards the Flesh Tearers' lines with blade strikes and bolter fire.

Dumah turned to Barachiel, unsheathing his crozius and checking his pistol.

'Do what you must, brother. My plan has failed. We cannot break the walls while the void shields and wall batteries remain in place. Take Adariel's squad, and may the Great Angel keep you all.'

TWENTY-SIX

Barachiel grimaced as he watched the battle below unfold. The air churned with the war cries of Flesh Tearers and Disciples of Rage, and the mortals warring in their shadow. The hard bangs of detonating grenades and the serpentine hiss of plasma discharge carved deep furrows in the traitor horde. The dry roar of flamers dissolved armour and flesh alike. Ceramite crashed against ceramite, chainblades roared and bolters thundered. Flesh tore. Blood flowed.

Barachiel salivated, hearts racing. How he yearned to be amongst it.

'We need to move, lord,' Adariel said. The assault sergeant crouched at his shoulder, his chainaxe snarling in time with Barachiel's hearts. Barachiel could hear the strain in his voice, the same longing to hurl himself into the carnage. 'Our mission lies before us.'

Barachiel straightened, hand straying from his blade. Adariel was correct.

The Apothecary led Adariel's squad towards the craggy rock face that shielded the rear of the fortress-monastery, along a narrow winding path the aspirants had to tread to be accepted as neophytes. The air thinned, as did the sounds of battle, the Cretacian scouts that had guided them to the plateau already making their way back down.

They would not be missed.

Despite Dumah's petty insistence that the mission was worthless, Barachiel knew they could never break into the monastery until the casemates were disabled, nor bring the *Cretacian Justice*'s batteries to bear while the void shields remained active.

His mission was the key to their success.

It did not take him long to discover the narrow embrasure through which the aspirants had to pass to access the fortress-monastery. It was rough and jagged, cleaved instead of cut, barely wide enough for two mortals to pass through. Barachiel edged inwards, ignoring the dull scrape of rock on ceramite, flakes of white lacquer falling like first winter snow. He activated his pack-mounted lumenator, the star-white beam breaking the gloom for a few yards. There was the scuttle of insectoid limbs as cavern beasts fled into the dark crevices. Barachiel kept his pistol ready. These creatures possessed proboscises that could penetrate Gravis armour and toxins capable of thickening Astartes blood or turning it to a thin, acidic slurry.

Barachiel squeezed his trigger. A spindly proboscis retracted, trailing blood.

They shuffled sidestep for several hundred yards before the passage widened enough for them to walk normally. Hand-cut wooden frames supported the uneven ceiling, and small shark-tooth stalactites protruded between them. The lintels were carved with elaborate swirls of Baalite script, and scratched into their jambs were Cretacian logographs, partially shrouded by the bones carpeting the floor. They were all human, the fallen aspirants of ten thousand years, and numerous generations, left to decay in ignominy. The most ancient formed a thin silt on the floor, while the more recent crunched beneath his tread.

The Flesh Tearers advanced, uncaring for the desecration.

Their path took on a circuitous route, widening and narrowing at random. Barachiel tasted potent toxins and hallucinogens, sweet and sour in the same breath, sticking to his tongue like wet sawdust. The gloom was complete, and would have rendered a human blind. Even his armour's systems could not penetrate it beyond a few yards. Broken red lines highlighted the faint suggestions of skeletons, aspirants abandoned to survive or die.

Where the pathway ended, stone bridges stretched across wide chasms, and creatures that had never known sunlight slithered across each other, thick jaws and curved teeth snapping at the Flesh Tearers. One warrior, Brother Seimos, stumbled, and was dragged down by the monsters.

His screams strangled the vox for several punishing minutes.

'We near the final gateway into the Chapter fortress,' Barachiel said, their pathway long committed to memory. It was scarcely a few hundred yards until they reached the entry to the lowest vaults. The burial site would not be far from the generatorum. 'The fortress will be ours again, my brothers, the enemy forever driven from its halls.'

And salvation brought to our ranks, he added silently.

Las-fire stitched across his plastron.

Barachiel stumbled, collimated bars of searing energy biting into his armour's joint ribbing. The needle-thin beams fell like a flurry from a stone balcony set above the entryway, where a squad of carapace-armoured slaves crouched behind the balustrade, firing and reloading with practised efficiency. Slaves armed with rusting iron sabres and cudgels rushed them from the entryway, firing guns that ranged from well-oiled laspistols to flintlocks and ancient arquebuses. Several misfired, killing their bearers.

Barachiel advanced into the teeth of the enemy fire, his stride breaking into a sprint as his bloodlust overtook him. The Apothecary let the Red Thirst slip free, tearing into the ranks of combat slaves, Adariel's squad at his side. His blade threshed lives the way a farmer's scythe threshes wheat. Kill-clarions echoed in his helm, blending with the sharpened crack of mass-reactive rounds kicking free from his bolt pistol on bright golden trails, detonating against the balustrade's aged stone, or misting blood over its railing. Barachiel sliced through them, his blade wet with gore, laughing and roaring, the rush of battle coursing through him.

The traitors' paltry defence was broken in minutes, to his disappointment.

The Flesh Tearers spared no time to conduct a check for survivors. There were none. Instead, they pressed on, entering the fortress-monastery through a tertiary apothecarion used by thralls to treat wounded aspirants and begin the first stages of ascension. Diagnostic slabs gathered dust, and the spidery limbs of auto-chirurgeons dangled over the empty tables. Their data-looms had been purged, the medicament containers and gene-seed vaults pillaged.

Barachiel's lips pulled into a snarl at the blatant desecration.

They navigated between the slabs towards the apothecarion door.

Barachiel led the Flesh Tearers at a jog, following the pulsing blue dot on his cartolith that denoted the generatorum's location. They encountered little resistance, scattered packs of mewling slaves and mutants that were put down with minimal effort. Kin-bands of beastmen fought with admirable fury, if not skill, and a score of Astra Militarum renegades clad in their regiment's defaced carapace acted as a minor impediment. The Flesh Tearers slaughtered all that dared stand before them with bolt and blade, the effort inspiring little joy in Sanguinius' sons. The lack of Traitor Astartes resistance both surprised and disappointed Barachiel.

'Dumah's counter-attack has done its work,' Adariel said, ripping his combat blade free from a Khorngor's abdomen. Barachiel bared his teeth in a feral smile, the acrid scent of burned fur and blood filling his nostrils. He pressed his boot against a minotaur's chest, pulling his own blade free, squeezing its activation bar to cleanse its teeth of the mutant's tainted flesh, his mind firmly fixed on his own goal.

All that barred him from it was this mission.

'It has,' Barachiel agreed, concealing his eagerness. His brothers could not yet know that he had his own objective, one entirely separate to Dumah's precious battle-plan. That would come later. 'Now we must do ours, and see these traitors forever expunged.'

The Flesh Tearers continued their advance, and were met with storms of hotshot and bolt shell at several key junctions, servitor-slaved defence turrets forcing them to flank through secondary and tertiary access corridors. Chainblades made short work of the ceramite casings, and the Flesh Tearers saw budding growths of brass and bone protruding from them. Krak grenades devastated their internal mechanisms, cooking off their rounds. Only one brother fell, his body savaged and his gene-seed unrecoverable.

Barachiel mourned the loss as they moved deeper, the empty cryo-canisters weighing heavily at his waist. Sorrow was transformed into revulsion as mutation grew rife, and there was the crooning of countless daemons at the edge of his hearing. Plasteel was subsumed by warp-forged brass and bronze. Sheaves of scorched bone were suspended from ceilings like osseous chandeliers, and quivering flesh stretched in vile tapestries across stone walls.

Barachiel's lip curled, disgust swelling his gorge at each new sighting. The sensation was hot, rancid, as vile as the corruption working through his Chapter's fortress-monastery. By bolt rifle and blade, he led his brothers in the destruction of the osseous furnishings, and with a stolen flamer, his brothers immolated the corrupt flesh. The skin crackled as it burned, fat fuelling the firefalls that lit the gloom, pooling on the stone in shimmering puddles, viscous and hissing. The smoke trailed them as they reached the primary generatorum.

Adariel paused, ordering two of his men to secure the door. He indicated the bundles of cabling that snaked across the walls, the Technicarum's mark imprinted on each one. 'Lord, we should plant our charges here, then withdraw to support the Chaplain's advance.'

Barachiel shook his head. 'No, brother. We must take the generatorum, and plant our charges closer to the source. We must be certain that it is offline before we leave.'

'But the risk to the fortress–'

'Is minimal as long as we are careful in our placement,' Barachiel answered. 'There can be no way to restore the defences' power, or our brothers will be lost. For that, we must plant them inside the generatorum, and ensure the machinery is compromised, as well as the cabling. We are close to our goal, my brother, and we can afford no risk now.'

Adariel nodded, ordering his men to stack on either side of the door.

Barachiel strode over to the door, and two Intercessors forced it open.

He was the first inside, the squad fanning out around him.

The generatorum was vast, a natural cavern repurposed when

the Flesh Tearers had first established themselves on Cretacia. Steel gantries and walkways were a spider's web that spread across it, reaching heights and depths beyond even the ability of Barachiel's auto-senses to fully perceive. Thrall workstations were set along one wall, operated by rake-thin dishevelled creatures overseen by a gaggle of black-robed magi. Vile sigils of allegiance to the Dark Mechanicus and the Ruinous Powers marked their robes, and they communicated in multi-cadenced bursts of scrapcode. Their canting battered his armour's cogitators, seeding his vision with static and insanity, but Cawl's blessed info-emetics held firm.

Barachiel's grip tightened around his chainblade.

'We eliminate those wretches first,' he hissed, then indicated the secondary platforms around the generator. Power conduction coils and transmission veins were set on each one, arcs of blue-white power snapping between them. 'Then we set our charges. Their destruction will ensure the generatorum cannot be restored before the fortress is retaken.'

He picked his first target, a corrupted magos with calliper-limbs that reminded him of an arachnid and clockwork organs that pulsed in a vile imitation of life. He gently squeezed the trigger and it pitched backwards, ripped apart by the mass-reactive rounds.

Cries of alarm rose from the slaves, and, as one, they charged him and Adariel's squad. The other Flesh Tearers opened fire, revving their chainblades as they counter-charged. Bolts detonated inside scabrous flesh, spraying tainted blood across dark stone. The heretic magi howled hymnals through fanged vocalisers and lips turned blue by cyanosis. Their hooked blades and crackling electro-staffs were little use against power armour, but it was the wrath with which they were wielded that some might have argued posed the real danger.

But those fools knew nothing of the Flesh Tearers.

Barachiel kicked one aside, his boot shattering the creature's steel ribs; Adariel was at his side, dragging his chainaxe through a hulking mutant's throat. They swarmed him, a press of sweating flesh and tainted bionics, trying to force him back with sheer weight of numbers more than any skill at arms. He hacked them down, each swing of his blade separating limbs from sockets and heads from necks. Sprays of lubricant-thickened blood splashed his visor, the scent and spasm of death fuelling the fury that tore at his soul. The traitors' blows were little more than gnat bites on Barachiel's flesh, the pain singing along his nerves made silent by the touch of Sanguinius' wrath. Alert klaxons whined like petulant children, red warnings flaring on his sensorium. He ignored them, revelling in the chance to kill.

Even these paltry offerings were better than nothing.

'Plant the charges,' he barked, punching the head from a black-robed creature with a trifecta of grease-yellow eyes while his brothers executed those not yet quick enough to die. A light pant inflected his words, more from unsatisfied fury than exhaustion. It was ever the curse of a Flesh Tearer, each instance another paved stone on their route to the Rage.

'Quickly,' he snapped. 'We cannot tarry here.'

Adariel's squad spread out around the generatorum, slaughtering the few maintenance thralls that remained alive. Most were servitors, mono-tasked to various duties, but they were killed anyway. The plan permitted no interference, even from such mindless and debased creatures. The Assault Intercessors sprinted between each platform, setting charges on every power conduction coil, transmission vein and bundle of exposed cabling. Redundancies were set for each charge, to ensure there was no failure in their detonation. His armour sensorium registered each charge as it was set, a swarm of red dots on his magnified cartolith.

Barachiel set his own charges on the thralls' workstations, another measure to ensure the generatorum could not be brought back online. Adariel handled the bank in front of him, kicking aside the ruined corpses of its attendants. Scrapcode screeded along the cogitator screens in endless lines, the meaning of the crude, angular symbols utterly lost on Barachiel. Part of him had been unwilling to destroy the generator, concerned by the months of work and volume of materiel it would take to restore the ancient device to full function. The scrapcode made those concerns meaningless. Destruction was the only cure for this form of corruption.

The squad returned to him in pairs, synchronising their own charges to the detonator. They filed from the generatorum at a light jog, and he data-pulsed a command code to the charges, activating the detonation sequence. A counter flickered on the plexi-slate, unfurling from sixty seconds. Barachiel was the last to leave, sealing the blast doors behind the squad. One of Adariel's men worked to fuse them with a stolen plasma-cutter.

The counter hit fifty as Adariel's squad secured the flanks.

'We should withdraw to a safe distance, my lord,' Adariel said, as the brother with the plasma-cutter reached the halfway point. The countdown reached forty seconds. 'We are too close to the generatorum. We should pull back, and wait to confirm successful detonation.'

Barachiel nodded, and the battle-brother with the plasma-cutter finished his task.

The counter hit thirty seconds.

The Flesh Tearers pulled back towards the catacombs, passing the smoking ruin of defence turrets and the hissing pools of molten flesh and fat. The counter ticked past twenty seconds as they reached the minimum safe distance and waited.

The counter hit ten seconds.

Five seconds.

Zero.

The fortress-monastery trembled like a leaf in a hurricane. Dust clouds billowed from the walls. Crimson lumens flashed, and klaxons cycled up to their tone-deaf whine.

'We have succeeded, my lord,' Adariel said, his blade indicating the passage that led to the apothecarion. 'We should withdraw and rejoin our brothers in the main assault. They will need our support to take the inner gatehouse and to carry the assault forwards.'

'I cannot,' Barachiel said, the force in the words surprising even him.

Adariel looked at him, and Barachiel could almost see the cogs turning in his brother's mind. 'My lord, we *must* rejoin our brothers. To remain here courts unnecessary risk.'

'Nonetheless, I will remain. There is a task I must complete.'

'Then allow us to join you, lord,' another said.

Barachiel smiled sadly, appreciating the warrior's sentiment. 'This task I alone must pursue. You will be needed in the advance, brothers. You cannot abandon your duty to help me fulfil mine. You must leave and do so quickly. The Disciples will send hunters.'

'The very reason we should stay, my lord. You will need our protection.'

'One warrior alone can move unseen where several cannot.'

'What of the wounded?' Adariel asked. 'They will need your attention, lord.'

'They have Thuriel to attend their needs,' Barachiel said flatly, frustration forcing the words from his tongue. 'This task is every bit as important as retaking the fortress. I will not abandon it, nor will I draw any resources away from Dumah in his time of need.'

'As you wish, my lord,' Adariel said grudgingly.

* * *

Elsewhere in the fortress-monastery, the First Disciple watched the red icons ripple across the pict screen suspended before him. He stood rooted to the spot – his legs and abdomen encased in ceramite plates, his arms held out in the very image of an Imperial saint. Cowering slaves darted through his shadow, bearing the necessary tools to bind a Space Marine into his battle armour. Drills squealed, wrenches scraped and serfs sweated as they secured each layer to his black carapace.

The First Disciple paid little attention to the malodorous serfs, his attention reserved for the pict-feeds and vox-reports of the battle outside, and the portal that shimmered and roared at the farthest end of the chamber. The Flesh Tearers advanced into the teeth of his counterstrike, packs of these strange, new Space Marines ripping entire phalanxes of his warriors and human slaves to chunks of bloody meat. His sergeants and champions barked orders and updates, seeking to press the enemy, push them further down the path to rage. Several of his Disciples lost themselves to the god's sacred fury, abandoning all thoughts of cohesion in their desire to slaughter the Imperium's blood-hungry slaves.

The warrior smiled. Everything was exactly as he had ordained.

Phantasms capered at the edge of the portal, echoes of red flesh and ebon horns, their blades burned with god-runes. His retinue awaited him, their ornate Terminator armour clunking and wheezing with every step taken. Like his stolen battleplate, their suits were the pilfered relics of revered heroes, desecrated and restored to functionality by his Warpsmiths and cabal of magi. It made for a delicious insult, and he looked forward to its delivery.

In their shadow, the poor fool that had opened the way for the Disciples of Rage wept over the corpse of his elder, his pain and sorrow meat for the warp portal that howled at the centre of the chamber. Spectres of unborn daemons circled his forehead in an ephemeral halo, whispering their poisons. The warrior watched with only a flicker of amusement. The wretch had long succumbed to madness and tormenting the deranged gave little sport.

The helm slid into place, completing his armouring. Ancient neck servos snicked as they readjusted to movement after long millennia gathering dust. The First Disciple took the first, trembling step from the armourium plinth, the insatiable hunger and raw, wrathful power of the armour's ancient war-spirit suffusing his inked, scarred flesh with new vigour. Immense fingers curled and flexed, and the underbite chainblades revved to a cacophonous roar. Slaves wept and fell to their knees, mouthing supplications to their lord and master, and to Khorne, the Chaos god of war.

The First Disciple strode from the hall, called by the promise of carnage.

Barachiel watched his brothers depart through the door at his left, filled with an icy certainty that he would never see them again. Part of him wanted to call them back, to leave with them and take part in the glorious battle to reconquer the fortress-monastery.

Instead, he turned to the right, and marched through the portal.

He ventured further into the fortress-monastery, ascending towards the surface as he closed to its centre. There was no great warren of tunnels that interconnected every structure, and he knew he would have to fight to reach his destination. A fresh squirt of combat stimms fired his blood, purging the dull ache from his muscles and bones. Light grew and tremors shook the earth, born of ordnance strikes and distant explosions.

Barachiel continued his ascent in complete silence.

TWENTY-SEVEN

'The shield has fallen!' Micah roared, ripping his blade through a traitor's neck.

Dumah tugged his crozius from his foe's chest, tendrils flaring, energy chasing up his arm and his eyes alight with a feral glee. The maul traced a burning arc of death through the air, its skull-shaped head trailing thin ribbons of tainted blood and meat. It atomised flesh and obliterated bone. Muscles frayed and ruined organs spat ichorous effluvia.

The Chaplain leapt into the trenches, his bolt pistol stitching a deadly pattern across a Disciple's plastron. Black tatters of rancid organs slid through the craters as he drove his crozius into a third traitor's horned helm. Gore showered Dumah's helm, shards of bone and ceramite clinking from his power armour. His hearts roared in his chest, a savage need to kill every foe that dared present itself vocalised in every painful, thunderous beat.

'The shield is down!' Micah cried again. 'Lord, command the advance.'

The Chaplain's back slammed into a trench wall, narrowly avoiding a burst of heavy-stubber fire. He leaned out, emptying his bolt pistol into a heretic gun crew. One round struck the magazine box and it detonated, shredding them. Mobs of tribespeople fell on their heretic kindred, tearing them apart, or worked together to bring down Heretic Astartes. They were always in motion, never presenting a stationary target for the traitors, slipping inside their reach to strike at exposed joints and battle-damage. They worked with the unity of a pack, communicating with rapid clicks and hunting calls that reminded Dumah of the creatures of the forest, and the oviraktors that had plagued their landing site. Were he prone to sentiment, Dumah might have been impressed by their bravery.

'Lord, we must seize the initiative!' Micah shouted.

The Champion's plea broke his concentration, and the sound of klaxons bled into his ears. His retinal feed was awash with armour breaches and targeting reticules, the wounded at his feet yet to entirely expire. The Thirst tried to slip free, angel's teeth digging into his gums. He resisted the urge to tear his helm off and sink his teeth into the wounded's pliant flesh.

He would have many chances to indulge Sanguinius' lesser curse.

The traitors were withdrawing, leaving only those that could not separate themselves from their fury. Dumah's crozius obliterated one such heretic, a warrior in spiked armour of several conflicting marks. Another leapt at him, his right arm mutated into a spiked morning star of ceramite and warp-touched bone. Mass-reactive rounds shredded his chest. A bright finger of plasma seared the cheek of Dumah's skull helm, the air flashing blue-white, the taste of scorched ozone foul on his tongue. Around him, every warrior in crimson and ash strained with the need to advance, to savour the rush of killing in close-quarter fighting.

That same longing burned in his chest too, and it would not be denied.

'Fourth Company! We advance on the fortress. Slaughter all in your path, but ensure *Spear of Sanguinius* and its squadron reaches the gate. They will gain us entry to the fortress. Let these traitors taste well the sacred fury of our father,' he snarled, crackling arcs of disruptor lightning scorching skin from a traitor's cheek. Another died, trampled to paste beneath his boots. His pistol ended a third heretic in sprays of blood. 'We are wrath!'

'We are vengeance!' his warriors howled in response. 'We are death!'

The Flesh Tearers hurled themselves after the foe, screaming, killing any they caught or who were stupid enough to turn and face them. They fought with the savage, unrelenting ferocity that had made the Chapter infamous across the length and breadth of the Imperium. Bolt rifles and plasma incinerators fired until their magazines ran dry and containment chambers cracked. Chainblades, pistols and a savagery at last unfettered carried Dumah and the Flesh Tearers forwards, a tide of howling, angel-faced murderers that ended lives in arterial sprays and bolter fire. The Cretacians kept up as best they could, fighting at an increasing distance from the Flesh Tearers, falling behind as the sons of Sanguinius let slip their fury.

Bolter fire hammered down from the fortress walls, and Dumah crouched behind the flame-gutted husk of a Rhino. One of Raziel's men stumbled, his visor reduced to a crater of blood and bone. Others found their own cover, or returned fire, and another two Intercessors were cut down. A dense hum set his teeth itching, his tongue and gums aching, and there was the grinding whir of a gatling cannon cycling up to fire. A casemate exploded in a multi-hued plume of petrochemical flame, and heavy rounds punched chunks of masonry from the battlements and walls. Their three

Executioner-class Repulsors, led by *Spear of Sanguinius*, powered forwards, flattening churned earth and corpses alike under the anti-gravitic cushions. Their machine-spirits grumbled, as eager to spill traitor blood as the warriors themselves.

Two more gatling cannons cycled up, providing suppressive fire.

'Target the gate!' Dumah roared, emptying his clip at the battlements.

'Aye, lord,' the lead driver said, the red-armoured Techmarine-apprenta shifting their fire along the battlements. Bodies pitched over the broken stone. Several were Astartes.

Their cannons opened fire, beams of ruby energy and gouts of blue-white plasma battering a gate first cast at the Imperium's dawn. The bas-relief bubbled, distorting angels into daemons as bronze ran in thick runnels. The bloodstone glittered and cracked, shedding burning fragments across the churned earth.

The reinforced plasteel groaned and started to buckle.

Dumah did not care, the sound of the heavy artillery fading into the roar of his hearts. The sensations of the world fell away until he heard only that sound, felt the growing ache as his muscles remained idle under the reassuring weight of his weapons. The beast shackled in his soul demanded a death, and he taunted it with his refusal to kill his brothers, even as his mind became consumed with the desire to crush their skulls and tear their throats out. He read the same struggle in their tensed muscles and locked jaws. The gate collapsed, and a savage roar rose from the Flesh Tearers as they hurled themselves towards the breach.

'For the Emperor! For Sanguinius!'

Twisted rebar and heat-warped metal jutted outwards like the spears of a phalanx and scraped lacquer from his armour. Smoke obscured everything and targeting reticules tracked the hazy suggestions of armoured giants and mortals alike. Brittle bones crunched under his feet and thin red las-beams sliced past his head as shrieking mass-reactive rounds tore fresh swirls through the grey miasma. Several sparked against his plastron, a pitiful few compared to the storm of fire that greeted Dumah as he emerged onto the central causeway.

Solid shot and las-beams hissed and snapped on his battleplate, scorching dents into his black-and-bone panoply. Reticules resolved onto the chests and heads of mortal gunners and Heretic Astartes. They were entrenched in servile habitation units and munitions storehouses, the cheap plastek of the prefabricated structures as common as stone or black iron, their frames bowed by set heavy weapons or cracked by bolt fire. Several Flesh Tearers were brought down by massed volleys, and Dumah's blood seared like boiling oil.

'In Sanguinius' name, let not the blasphemer and the heretic draw breath. Know that he watches us now, weighing our worth as sons of the Blood. Honour him with death, that he may know only pride for the day he sired the first Flesh Tearer!' Dumah's roar was a thing of strangled fury forced into words. 'We are wrath! We are death! We are vengeance!'

The Flesh Tearers roared and hurled themselves into the traitors' fire.

Dumah led from the front, caring nothing for the las-beams and bullets pattering against his battleplate. Bolts slammed into his chestplate, ceramite debris spraying free. A bullet bit into the joint ribbing between his pauldron and plastron. Bolts shredded a woman in tribal furs, bio-analytics sizzling away as she fell apart like rotten meat. He shifted fire to a Traitor Astartes warrior in the Skulltakers' gore-red battleplate, taking him down in thick sprays of arterial red. Combat stimulants squirted into Dumah's blood, quickening his pulse. The Flesh Tearers unleashed a last blizzard of return fire as they crashed into the traitor ranks.

Dumah killed two warriors in mismatched battleplate looted from loyalist Chapters, their former heraldry obscured by red saltires and the Disciples' heraldic crest. A heretic with bronzed skin and uncontrolled facial tics hurled himself at Dumah, his frenzied strikes slicing for the Chaplain's throat and chest. Dumah parried, hammering his fist into the heretic's face. Blood spurted and bone broke. He crushed the Disciple's skull on the backswing.

The earth trembled beneath his feet, an impact pattern he recognised.

Daeron smashed into the fray, a mechanised howl ripping from his vox-casters, his eviscerators slick with heretic vitae. 'We are wrath! We are death!'

Castivar's Aggressors followed the Dreadnought in, moving as fast as their bulky warplate permitted. Tongues of superheated flame roared from underslung flame projectors, roasting flesh inside carapace and ceramite. Mortals screamed as they died, milling about as their flesh liquefied the instant fire kissed it. Ceramite baked bone-dust dry and crumbled. Disciples were boiled alive inside their armour. One charged at Dumah, his face a wretched horror of waxy, molten flesh and blackened bone. Dumah's crozius smashed into the traitor's chin, and his head tore free in thick crimson spurts.

Dumah howled, smashing aside another burning defender, liquefied flesh spraying the other Flesh Tearers. His bolt pistol kicked, mass-reactive rounds obliterating two mortals in defaced carapace. He powered into a pack of shrieking Imperial Army renegades, their electro-staves cracking his battleplate. Las-bolts fizzed and spanked uselessly. Dumah snarled, his vision washed by red and black.

He was wrath incarnate.

A powerblade bit into his side, charring his flesh and golden armour. Dumah roared, ripping free the arm that dared strike him, decapitating the heretic. Human auxiliaries charged him, shouting the praises of the Warmaster and their gods, their ticking neuroslave implants punishing any unwilling to charge him with nerve-shredding agony. Daggers bit through joint ribbing, ruby droplets seeping from the tears. Warriors in black Cataphractii armour lumbered after them, firing combi-bolters. Their rounds sparked pathetically against his panoply.

'Horus!' Dumah screamed, his blade parting armour and flesh with equal ease.

The Arch-Traitor did not come, and Dumah bludgeoned a path through his sons.

'Focus your mind on the present, Chaplain,' a mechanical voice boomed. Dumah recognised it, and a part of his mind latched onto its words as though the Emperor Himself spoke them. 'Disgrace not the Angel nor your office with a single moment of laxity, for those of your calling are the shield against the curse. You must not fall to it.'

The *Vengeful Spirit* shivered, though not from the fire hurled at it by the Palace's few remaining guns. Dumah trod its iron decks a little further, watching iron ripple to stone as the sulphide smoke blistering his oesophagus and lungs faded into sweet, coppery ambrosian musk. Black and sea-green flaked from the enemy's battleplate, unseated by a deep crimson uncomfortably similar to their own heraldry. Dumah forced his breathing to even patterns, armouring his mind and soul. Blood trickled from his nose, and his skull flushed with pain.

Fresh shells crashed against his armour, slivers biting into his flesh.

The Disciples refused to retreat, hurling fresh waves of traitor militia and squads of Heretic Astartes at the Flesh Tearers. Dumah braced himself against their charge, bolt pistol firing. Mass-reactive rounds obliterated gaunt skulls and torsos, showering him with gore. His brothers were at his side, firing into the advancing host. Traitors fell in a tumbling tide of orphaned limbs and tattered organs, those behind crushing the wounded and the dead.

'I will not fall,' Dumah snarled, as much to Daeron as to himself. He barrelled into a pack of traitor tribesmen, maiming and killing with each sweep and strike of his crozius.

'Good. Seth would not like two officers slain, and one missing.'

Dumah stopped. His voice was honed to a razor edge. *'What?'*

'Sergeant Adariel and his squad have returned, I see their signum chains closing to ours. There is no sign of your Apothecary, and they do not report him killed.'

Dumah emptied his clip, kill-clarions sounding in his helm. 'I do not like your implication, old one. Barachiel is loyal to the Chapter.'

'I imply nothing, Chaplain, save that it would be a great misfortune if he were to be lost,' the Dreadnought boomed, his eviscerators shredding a Terminator. 'He may have questioned your decisions and embarrassed you at the war council, but you made one competent war leader between you. Friction forced the best from you both, and whether he is fallen in battle or lost to the Rage, it would be a bitter blow for the Chapter.'

Daeron cast the legionary aside and plunged headlong into another pack of Heretic Astartes with a rage-fuelled howl, ribbons of tainted blood trailing his blades.

'Seth's emissary seems pleased,' Micah grunted, his blade as wet as Dumah's crozius. He whirled like a dervish, his blade never still, decapitating and dismembering heretics in a crackling blur of lethal motion. 'Even with the Apothecary's flight from battle.'

'I will not discuss Barachiel with you, brother, nor anyone.' Dumah bit off the words harsher than he had intended. Micah's silence spoke more than words ever could.

'Aye, leave such matters to those with rank, Champion,' Toivo chuckled, and Dumah was suddenly filled with the desire to rip the sergeant's spine out. 'Kill until killed, that is all we need be concerned with. Let us hope these weaklings do not break soon.'

Minutes ticked to the clash of blades and kill-clarions.

...these weaklings do not break soon.

It bothered him, though he could not say why.

Dumah fought to regain his calm, to think unfettered by the chains that wrath placed on the mind. Litanies spilled from his lips in a tumbling tide of half-chewed words and animalistic snarls. The blood madness refused to fade, and his soul ached for its return to the fire, for the pure distillation of life and death only found in the cut and thrust of battle.

He plunged back into the fire with a bestial roar.

TWENTY-EIGHT

Barachiel felt the fortress-monastery shake beneath the *Cretacian Justice*'s bombardment, a minor tremor like that of a distant earthquake. He pushed on, higher into the fortress.

Corruption had sunk its claws into the lower levels. Calcified bone and brass slowly spread over walls of damp moss and uneven stone. Stalactites and calthemites scraped the top of his helm, the sound echoing in the tight corridor. He passed rows of small sleeping cells, the twisted stench of animal-human genetics and warp corruption gripping his throat like a vice. The area was once the Chapter-thralls' living quarters, but now housed the lowest dregs of the traitor horde. Beastkin and mutants incapable of fighting instead served their vile masters as armourcraft slaves, engineers and, more commonly, food. He encountered a handful of the misbegotten creatures and executed them with bolt-rounds to the heart and head.

He was almost glad to see them. They quietened his pain, his hunger for death.

The Apothecary's cartolith led him through a small chapel, its masonry of a far superior quality than the living quarters. A pit had been dug at its centre, defined by stone and hewn wood. Its floor was sand, like the primitive arenas of feral worlds and the lyceums of hive worlds, where the rich wagered fortunes on a single death, blood bringing colour to otherwise colourless lives. Barachiel knelt to examine it, casting an eye over the arterial spray and spatter. The freshest stains spoke of ritual combat, the oldest of summary executions.

Decapitated skeletons had been left in piles outside the arena, their skulls stacked into two intersecting pyramids that would tower over even a Dreadnought, carved with runes that turned his stomach. Eight corners and eight faces, the number he had heard in whispers was sacred to their vile god. Something creaked above his head, and he looked to see crucified skeletons riveted to shattered fragments of an Imperial aquila. Vestments and cassocks were stained a ruddy brown. Doubtless they had been alive for the first hours of their crucifixion.

Barachiel moved on, white-knuckling his chainblade.

The tremors increased in intensity, and several times he was forced to steady himself against the walls. They possessed the soft monotony of an expert stonemason, age-worn, yet sturdy. Stone dust shook free, each lungful scraping his throat raw. Pink light poured through cracks in the walls and the ceiling, streaked with gleaming trails of weapons fire, the ion trails of fighter engines and convulsions of purple lightning induced by the bombardment.

He tasted ash and fire, even through the fusty flavour of old stone.

The Apothecary sprinted through an open portal, across a bastion walkway towards the buttressed barracks that had once housed the First Company. Above it, the Black Tower of the Reclusiam scraped the heavens, shod in cratered iron, its ruby-tinted glass sparkling in the light of the bombardment. Two Heretic Astartes spotted him crossing the wall, their surprise granting the split second he needed to raise his pistol. They charged him, their battleplate shimmering crimson and black. His bolt pistol ranged and auto-locked, and he squeezed the trigger. One fell, his visor blown out, his face a smoking crater of blood, bone and scorched meat. The second was staggered, his shoulder destroyed. He returned fire, bolts cratering Barachiel's plastron. Blood seeped from the wounds, shards piercing his chest.

Barachiel's second volley blew the traitor apart.

Barachiel paused to collect ammunition from the slain heretics, then carried on, passing over a firing gallery studded with Icarus stormcannons and towed flak batteries that spat air-burst rounds into the skies. Though scarcely a few hundred feet beneath him, their fire was audible only as a faint patter against the shriek of macro-cannon shells and plasma blasts that rained from the *Justice*'s batteries. Barachiel resisted the impulse to fire into the chained gun-crews and black-cowled supervisors, unwilling to delay himself further. He glimpsed a flight of Stormhawk Interceptors swooping in for an attack run against the gun batteries, emptying their missile packs in trails of fire and feather-white smoke.

In the middle distance, a casemate toppled in a cloud of vaporised stone.

He shouldered the door at the end of the walkway open, shredding a creature of quivering tendrils and greasy iron mechadendrites in a spray of bolts. A black cowl reduced prominent mutations to mere suggestions of disfigurement. Oil and dark blood jetted from its wounds, the stench of spoiled meat clinging to its pallid, unwashed flesh. Its colleagues shrieked in fury and alarm, disconnecting from the cogitator banks that monitored local defence batteries. They flew at him with electro-staves, lashing whips and buzzing saw blades. Barachiel leapt to meet their charge, thumbing his shot-selector to full-automatic. His bolts struck walls of weaponised sound and detonated prematurely, showering the floor with golden shards.

'You will fail, Flesh Tearer,' a cowled magos chirped, its head fashioned into the semblance of a leering daemon skull. 'The war god's chosen await you.'

'I do not care,' the Apothecary said, eviscerating the creature with a second volley.

'You will,' another magos said, its oily voice rising above the scrapcode howling and deranged war cries of its slaves. 'The true gods will soon have their victory, and those still enslaved to the corpse-lord will be damned to an eternity of pain and suffering.'

Barachiel grinned and activated his chainsword. 'You do not know suffering.' He raised the blade. 'Allow me to demonstrate for you.'

Fanged voxmitters blared agonised scrapcode as his blade tore wide arcs across the press of bodies. With every pass, severed limbs tumbled free and glossy black organs spilled in rushes of ichorous fluid. Barachiel was revolted to see several bore lamprey-like maws at the joints between artery and organ, and distended tongues that lashed frantically at the dying magi. The maimed died beneath his boots or were bludgeoned aside. Skulls shattered and bones snapped. Binharic curses bubbled through death rattles.

They offered precious little challenge.

He strode through the dead, ignoring the wet pulp of flesh and the dry snap of bone as he attached magnetic grenades to the main cogitator banks and processor towers. Explosions hammered the door with shrapnel as he sealed it, and Barachiel sprinted onwards. He met no resistance amid the solars and cells of the First Company, any warriors that may have called them home deployed to front-line or defensive positions across the fortress. Standards and trophies marked its walls, the heraldry of legendary champions, sergeants and captains that had led the Flesh Tearers to their greatest glories and slept now in crypts beneath his feet.

The corridors beneath the Black Tower, and the Tower itself, were formed of different stone to the rest of the fortress. Constructed of black basalt and cassiterite instead of granite and iron, its corridors were heavy with the traces of mouldering incense and, when touched, the volcanic heat that birthed it. He sprinted through the corridors, passing the trophies of a thousand wars and the relics of legendary heroes that could never be restored to function. He passed penitential cells furnished with dry stone biers, nine-tailed electro-lashes, and coils of razor wire for flagellation, the golden dot on his cartolith continuing to grow.

Minutes passed, and the fortress-monastery continued to tremble.

He was brought to a sudden stop before an immense arch that framed sealed doors of dark iron, the sentinel posts set at either side long bereft of guardians. The doors themselves were carved with Cretacian runes that detailed the oaths sworn by each brother on his ascension to the Chapter. They were a reminder, Barachiel thought, that slaughter was not the true purpose of their Chapter. It was the defence of the Emperor's people and realm, for which Sanguinius had laid down his life. In their battle-hunger, his brothers sometimes forgot that.

Barachiel attempted to force the doors, his servo-muscles straining against the locking mechanisms, whining in direct competition with the metal as his fingers buried themselves knuckle-deep in the dark iron. Beads of sweat traced the curve of his eye socket, dampening his close-cropped beard. His efforts came to naught, and he fished the last krak grenades from his bandolier, attaching them where his armour deemed the metal vulnerable to breach. He backed away, watching the counter on his retinal feed tick towards zero.

The grenades detonated. Metal shrieked. The doors gave way.

The Basilica of Remembrance was the Reclusiam of the *Victus* writ large, walls of the same black basalt, complemented by cassiterite, and a carved granite floor. The alcoves for the auto-choristers and cyber-cherubim were noticeable in their absence, taken up instead by Chapter relics. Barachiel was thankful for it. He deeply disliked the religious overtones their inclusion brought to Chapter rites. He was a warrior born of a forgotten age, when religiosity was a crime among Astartes, and humanity still held loosely to reason's light.

Silver-steel honour blades jutted upright in a moat of volcanic sand, carved with the names of fallen warriors and legendary heroes in infinitesimal text. The battle standards of the ten companies framed the congregational space, battle-honours dating back to the Great Scouring and the Chapter's birth in faded embroidery of arterial red. They were arranged in order of seniority, First and Second to the front, Ninth and Tenth to the back. He saluted the standard of the Fourth and the Chapter standard that hung above the basalt lectern.

His eyes narrowed, the hairs on the back of his neck suddenly erect. He felt eyes upon him, an insatiable hunger for violence and slaughter. Barachiel bunched his muscles, shifting his stance. His eyes swept the shadows for threats, fingers tightening on his activation bar.

Adeptus Astartes instinct saved his life.

A comet of black armour and snarling chainteeth slammed into him, his throat almost speared by the blade. Instead,

Barachiel was barrelled over, reflexes guiding him into a roll and to his feet. The chainblade slashed for his throat again, and he snatched a glimpse of red streaks on a black field as he parried the blow. Realisation gelled around two words, icy tendrils that coiled fear through his mind and hearts.

Death Company.

Questions swam through Barachiel's mind.

How had the warrior endured all this time so close to the enemy?

Was he a true Flesh Tearer, or an artefact of the Rage sent to test him, his mind weakened by the hallucinogens he had inhaled during the infiltration?

The Death Company warrior's blade hissed through the air towards his skull, the blow powerful enough to shatter tank armour. Barachiel, almost caught unawares, sidestepped, its momentum such that a light touch was enough to redirect it into the granite. Stone shattered under the blow; a crater formed where he had stood. Barachiel thanked Guilliman for his time with the Black Templars' crusade fleets, and for the sword skills the knights of Dorn had taught him in their arenas. Barachiel swayed to dodge a blistering series of strikes, the chainteeth snarling for his throat and arms, turning aside those he could not avoid with the flat of his blade.

Failure frustrated the maddened Flesh Tearer, his attacks growing in recklessness and ferocity. A thunderous jab shattered Barachiel's cheekbone, a thin crack meandering over his left lens. Dislodged teeth clinked against the inside of his visor, and the traitor's chainsword bit deep into his thigh. Pain bleached his nerves white-hot and his Larraman cells rushed to clot the wound as the chainsword was ripped free. His pharmacopeia dispensed a cocktail of analgesics and synthetic stimulants to keep him conscious and fighting.

The creature lunged at him, frothing curses in archaic Baalite.

He stepped inside the blade's arc, a savage headbutt knocking the enemy off balance. He hacked at the other Flesh Tearer, uncaring of the damage done to his weapon or the chainteeth that buried themselves in his plastron. The call of his blood sounded more keenly than it ever had, drowning the toneless blare of warning klaxons in the roar of his hearts and the adrenal tingle that promised a purity of purpose enjoyed only by Sanguinius' most savage sons.

He drove the warrior back in a series of thunderous slashes and strikes, driving a boot into his knee, shattering the bone. Barachiel forged a blade of his fury, leashing it to his will and to the chainsword snarling in his grip. He rammed the blade into the Flesh Tearer's armour and dragged it across his chest. The warrior thrashed, clawing for Barachiel even as his hearts were ground to gelatinous paste by the monomolecular teeth.

The Apothecary drew deep, calming breaths to restore his equilibrium.

Horror squirmed through his veins, and he watched the twitching warrior at the end of his blade, life leaking in an expanding pool of red. This was no illusion of the Rage, nor of a hallucinogen. A Flesh Tearer lay transfixed on his blade, soon to be dead. At his hand. This was not a kill in the grip of Sanguinius' rage, with self-control a rose-tinted memory.

This was a kill, cold and sober and clear.

Blood bubbled and burst from the warrior's mouth, rattling breaths spraying like a malfunctioning water feature as the life slipped forever from his grasp.

Numbed by what he had done, Barachiel searched for the catacombs.

TWENTY-NINE

The heretics were in full retreat.

They flooded between the grenade-gutted ruins of munitions bunkers, past the sheet-metal and plastek overnight quarters of their workers, now little more than bubbling pools of liquid plastek and hillocks of malformed metal. Predators and Razorbacks rolled backwards on caterpillar tracks stained with mud and sacrificial blood. They crushed the cowardly and unwise, who sought to use them as cover to hide from the vengeful Flesh Tearers. Only the Disciples maintained the semblance of an orderly retreat, sections firing and falling back. Their displeasure was evident in their scowls and strained expressions, and in their hesitant movements. They held in place too long, firing their bolters from the hip, their chainblades twitching in armoured hands. They longed to rush back into battle, to lose themselves in the slaughter. Those who did, or who lost their self-control to blood madness, were left to die, and die they did, to the bolts and blades of Sanguinius' wrathful sons.

Dumah held his crozius aloft, taking quick stock of his forces.

To his front, the heretics had retreated and were approaching the extreme range of their bolt rifles and plasma incinerators, leaving behind scatterings of radioactive ash and corpses with their backs split open like macabre flowers in bloom. His warriors did not chase, though they strained against his order to hold position, their desire for bloodshed thickening the air. They vented their frustrations on the wounded. Their screams were drowned out by the roar of his double-pulse, his blood singing with a gene-coded need to kill.

Further afield, the outermost districts of the fortress were falling to the Flesh Tearers, and almost half their tribal allies now cleansed it of life and loot. The landing fields and the innermost districts were under siege, the heretic defenders fighting ferociously for each inch of ground. Flames consumed empty habitation units and barracks, and the blinking flashes of detonations and weapons fire could still be glimpsed through the smoke. Trails of poison ash stretched up high, darkening the skies to a grey twilight, as the wind cast the fumes out over the Cretacian wildlands. They would be contaminated for generations, and Dumah knew the damage to the local ecosystem was potentially irreparable.

Dumah opened the vox, rage clotting his voice. 'Teman, report.'

He waited several seconds, listening to the grunts of effort and the crackle of bolt-rifle fire on the lieutenant's channel. When his reply came, it was breathy and phlegmatic.

'The heretics are crippled, brother. The outer armouries are ours, as are the factorums and refineries. The servile habitation district will soon fall. The landing fields and battery command are next to be retaken.'

'Understood.'

'How fares your assault?'

Dumah cut the lieutenant off without a reply, anger setting his jaw.

The enemy's cowardice irked him.

'We should not grant the heretics another moment's respite,' Micah said, his armour scorched black by flame-wash. What little remained of his reddish-brown hair was matted to his skin by blood and sweat. Gore greased his powerblade, curling from it in crackling motes of crimson steam. It vented from his chainaxe's teeth when he depressed the activation stud. 'They will fortify the inner sanctum, and it will cost us much in blood to dig them out.'

Dumah turned his gaze to the inner wall, and to the gatehouse less than a mile from their position. Cretacians swept towards it in a tide of screaming killers, unconcerned by the prospect of defensive positions or death. They killed because the enemy were before them, and they would not stop until that enemy was dead, or they were. There was a purity in that he could not help but admire, a purity he had seen in Seth and Harahel and Harox when they stalked the battlefields. At first, he assumed it had come from the Great Angel.

Now he knew it as one of Cretacia's gifts to her wrathful sons.

'We waste time here,' Castiel said, even as he flayed the face from a Disciple's skull. It slapped wetly against the others chained to his waist. 'The Champion has the truth of it.'

Dumah hesitated. Something did not feel right. There was something he had missed. It niggled at him, the seedling form of a thought forever stuck on the cusp of realisation.

'Is this cowardice, Chaplain?' Daeron sneered. 'We cannot allow the initiative to slip from our grasp. Give the order, and we shall see this place reclaimed.'

Dumah let his crozius fall, a feral grin forced to his lips.

'Bring them death!'

He leapt from the burned-out hull of a traitor Vindicator, his boots blending into the rolling thunder of the Flesh Tearers' charge as it built momentum. Stragglers and wounded survivors were gunned down or crushed beneath their boots. Gunfire licked out from towers and battlements. It dappled their armour with black scorch marks, slivers of pain biting their nerves where it found weak spots. Dumah felt pain knifing his knee joint, but he did not break stride. Adnacio fell, his visor a hissing crater of blood, bone and plasma.

Thuriel did not stop to aid Adnacio, nor collect his gene-seed. Instead, he stayed at Dumah's side, his sacred duty forgotten in his need to shed blood.

Explosions split the skies with sudden fury. Towers detonated in showers of rock and shale. Mines detonated in sprays of severed limbs. Cretacian warriors were crushed by falling masonry, or entombed in the rockslides. Hands grasped for aid and muffled pleas were carried on wisps of dry air. The Flesh Tearers scrabbled across the ruins, the surviving Cretacians at their side. Neither cared for those doomed to die buried in rubble. The chance to spill blood mattered above all.

They smashed into the defensive line around the inner gate with the force of a cavalry charge. Mortals crumpled like wet sacks of meat. Disciples were bowled over, bolt shots and plasma gouts flying astray, killing their own as often as the Imperials. Dumah felt bones snap beneath his boots, heard oaths and war cries snatched from lips by pulped lungs and larynxes. His crozius moved in a swift upward trajectory. A heretic tribesman came apart at the torso. A second died on the downswing, his skull and shoulder shattered.

The Thirst rose, and Dumah let it come to the fore.

He revelled in the roar of his twin hearts as he crushed a Cretacian tribesman's throat, casting the corpse aside like a rag doll. Pivoting aside a clumsy spear-thrust for his neck seal, Dumah loosed a furious backhand, cracking the offending tribesman's skull like an egg. He dodged backwards as a traitor with a blade-crested helm swung his two-handed chainaxe in a wide arc. Its teeth raked his breastplate, tearing ceramite and flesh. Blood seeped through the gouges. He hammered his crozius into the warrior's skull. Blood and bone fragments sprayed across his lenses, obscuring his vision for precious seconds. A bolt shell exploded against his helm, knocking him down, a thin fissure worming through his right lens.

A muscled male with Cretacian tattoos hurled himself onto Dumah, driving a brass dagger at the Chaplain's cracked lens. Dumah's vision swam, and he half-heartedly blocked the attack. He tasted blood, and felt a section of his skull helm detach, scraping against the whole. Awareness returned with the crunch of the dagger against ceramite, and the light press of the Cretacian desperate to kill him. His sensorium display was a mess of screeching alerts, his armour rendered in conflicting yellows, orange and reds, the battle-damage and breaches filled by grey armour sealant. The Cretacian hammered his fist and blade into the Chaplain's helm, until Dumah's hands wrenched his head clean from his shoulders.

The Chaplain rolled to his feet, reloading his bolt pistol. Rounds snapped through the carnage on golden contrails. He gunned down a Disciple that threatened Micah's flank, and a Cretacian with surgical scarring that spoke of genetic enhancements. He shifted fire, mass-reactive bolts tearing apart a Disciple in rust-caked armour of ancient provenance.

An Intercessor died, decapitated by a Chaos Space Marine who then turned to face the Chaplain.

Dumah ducked the lightning-wreathed jab of the champion's power fist, as he blocked the sharp thrust of the powerblade in his other hand, a gilded Ultima encasing the pommel jewel. He emptied his bolt pistol into a second traitor's face, the pale flesh crusted with growths of bone and brass. Dumah parried each sword strike with his crozius, avoiding the power fist. His helm thundered into the champion's exposed face, his crozius detonating his midriff.

Organs slapped wetly onto rockcrete.

'Sanguinius watches us, brothers!' Dumah roared, sending another mortal arcing back into his kin. They stood their ground, lean and hard-muscled, refusing to flee. These were the finest Cretacia had, men who might have been his brothers under different circumstances. He killed them as he would any other apostate. 'Let your wrath be uncompromising, your focus unrelenting. Offer the heretic no quarter, and honour he who gave you life with each one you take!'

'For the Blood!' his warriors howled. 'We are wrath! We are death!'

They cut into the mass of cultists and Disciples with unrelenting ferocity. Micah shielded his back, his relic blade tearing a bloody furrow in the traitors' ranks. Paschar wielded his psychic powers with a skill and fury Dumah had never seen before. He scattered mortals and Traitor Astartes with blasts of carnelian energy, or set them aflame with gouts of crimson fire. Entire platoons crunched to their knees, their flesh flayed with subtle twitches of the Codicier's fingers.

The enemy pressed back, stubborn and inflexible, where before they had been pliant. Yards were bought with a high price in blood, the deposits sloshing against the Flesh Tearer's boots. His brothers fell, carved apart by the Disciples' chainblades or undone by their slaves' massed fire. It took every ounce of restraint for him to keep his helm in place, to not feed on the crimson fluid lapping against his boots. Sweat beaded his forehead, but he refused to submit to his thirst.

A bloodthirsty howl, flawed by a mechanised snarl, cut through the battle.

The ground shook, though Daeron was still.

A nightmarish fusion of daemonic flesh and warp-tainted ceramite crashed through the press of Heretic Astartes and human slaves, uncaring that each swing of its powered fists and splay-clawed feet spilled its allies' blood. In form, it was an obscene mockery of the Castraferrum-pattern Dreadnought, its angular body cut with god-runes and bedecked with grinning skulls. Its vile, warp-wrought flesh bulged and rippled around joints and pistons, throbbing a light crimson with each kill made. Braying snarls rose from horned, daemonic faces of bio-ceramite leering from its greaves, tasting the blood it spilled. Dumah felt horror coil his spine, the Flesh Tearers sigil just visible beneath the corruption.

With a wordless roar, Daeron drove to meet it.

Dumah switched his attention from the Helbrute, confident in the Firstborn's ability to deal with it. A life-rune failed: an Assault Intercessor decapitated by a chainglaive. Dumah's secondary heart kicked in, las-beams and bullets sparking against his armour. He dragged his crozius across the press of tainted tribespeople, crushing skulls and chests, separating limbs from joints in pained shrieks and spatters of dark blood. A chainaxe gouged a deep furrow in his plate, shearing fibre bundles and servo-muscles. He deflected a killing blow away from Thuriel, hacking the creature apart as the Flesh Tearers continued their slow, bloody push to the courtyard. He paused a moment to haul the other Flesh Tearer to his feet.

Thuriel howled, hurling himself back into the fray.

Another vox-flawed scream cut the air, and Dumah spun, killing a Cretacian with an almost dismissive stroke of his crozius. What he saw stole his momentum.

Daeron's eviscerators slashed a deep furrow in the Helbrute's glacis, biting into the warp-flesh around its thigh-pistons. The movement was slow, hampered by fused durasteel pistons and damaged joints. The Helbrute suffered minimal damage, though lubricant and ichor leaked from several wounds. It drove its fist into the war machine's sarcophagus. Once. Twice. Thrice. Finery fell away like glittering rain, and a sickening crack cut through the clamour of battle. Dumah fired on the Helbrute, his rounds sparking away or absorbed by the foul warp-flesh that cut an accurate echo of an unarmoured Astartes body.

The Helbrute ignored him, tearing away one of the Firstborn Dreadnought's arms, a maddened howl snapping from its vox-mitter. Daeron roared, swinging his remaining eviscerator at the traitor war machine. It caught the blade and broke it, resuming its assault on the sarcophagus until the armoured shell cracked. Amniotic fluid spilled from the wound, but Dumah was too far away to glimpse the ravaged corpse within.

A proximity warning flared on his display. Dumah smiled.

'For Sanguinius!' Daeron roared. 'Sanguinius and Cretacia!'

The Helbrute and Daeron vanished in a starburst of nucleonic fire.

Vows of wrath and vengeance clotted the vox as the Flesh Tearers renewed their attack. Dumah hurled himself into a squad of Disciples, Micah at his side. They chanted the virtues of wrath and the praises of Sanguinius as they slew, complex litanies and poems that thickened to incomprehensibility as their rage grew beyond control. The Disciples' line began to bow again as they pressed into the courtyard, where the Chapter could train and muster as a whole or as a strike force when the occasion called for it. The courtyard was now an armed camp, with prefabricated structures set out beside the large tents, ammunition dumps and training facilities. Pennons of scale and fur flapped in the wind, trailing smoke and flame. Nothing could stand before the Flesh Tearers' fury.

'Dumah,' Micah said, jabbing with his blade. 'The heretic lord.'

Dumah followed Micah's thrust and his blood ran cold.

On the terraces of the citadel, suspended by the carved hand of the hooded angel that faced them, a knot of traitors clad in artificer and Terminator plate watched the battle unfold. Dumah's lip curled into a bestial snarl, recognising the relics of ancient heroes, replete with honours and kill-tallies that would shame several recent-founding Chapters.

But their lord…

'No,' Dumah whispered, horror stealing his fury. 'No… No… No… No!'

He slew another heretic, his head detonating in a shower of crimson.

'It cannot be. They would not dare… Such an offence…'

'You see as I do, Chaplain,' Micah said, his own fury returning to the fore. His power sword carved smoking rents in a heretic's battleplate. 'There is no illusion at work.'

The Disciples' lord dwarfed his retinue. His Terminator armour was of an ancient pattern, thick slabs of crimson-and-ash ceramite layered atop reinforced plasteel and an adamantium exoskeleton. Its immense fists were weapons of terrible beauty and lethality, tendrils of actinic power crackling around each finger as underbite chainblades chewed the air. Storm bolters were worked into their backs, barrels still bearing angel wings.

He knew that armour, as well as any Flesh Tearer, having memorised every detail of it in the picts and drawings stored in the *Victus'* archives and its sacred spaces.

The Crimson Plate. *Amit's armour.*

Dumah roared, the ice-cold sensation crawling up his spine with glacial slowness lost in the surge of something darker, the wrath of a murdered angel embodied by one of his sons. The Black Rage throbbed hard in his breast. Phantom pain lanced his abdomen and legs, and the wings furled at his back were riven by a hundred fresh wounds. He saw with the Angel's eyes, and he murdered with the Angel's fists. He bellowed the Angel's pain to loyal son and heretic alike, even as he forced himself away from the lure of the Black Rage. 'By the sands of Sacred Baal and the blood of our father, I will see that bastard slain for his sacrilege.'

He did not see the gates to the courtyard begin to close behind them.

THIRTY

Barachiel traced the ancient paths of the dead, where Apothecaries and Chaplains had borne the fallen Flesh Tearers of ten thousand years on their final journey. The stone was cut with expert lines concealed by heavy layers of grime. When he wiped it clear, he saw murals and frescoes of Flesh Tearers engaged in acts of heroism long forgotten by the Imperium. The whirlwind of gore that consumed their reputation over the last few millennia had seen to that.

He smiled, and limped into the deeper darkness, towards the crypt.

He moved forwards at a cautious pace, trusting to his instincts and the accuracy of his cartolith. Pain shrieked through the meat of his thigh where the Death Company warrior's blade had shredded skin and muscle. He walked as though lame, like a decrepit elder bereft of their cane. The steps were cut at a sharp angle, and the gloom veiled his helm's auto-senses – even his pack-mounted lumenator only pierced it a few yards. Where the stairs ended a narrow passage continued the path towards the crypt, and his fingers traced the rough stone of a passage hewn by primitives. Bioluminescence appeared as natural light trapped in the dark, on the cusp of being enveloped, a metaphor he deemed apposite for the Flesh Tearers. Their souls burned bright against the Rage that threatened to immerse them in its darkness.

Yet darkness, as was its wont, could snuff out even the brightest sparks.

The tremors of the bombardment had faded to the merest shudder, slithering through the rough stones into his calves. His chainsword's teeth chewed the darkness, a throaty growl that matched the apoplectic snarls of the beast in his soul. That part of him hungered for the release of violence, for him to charge back to the battle and feel the adrenal rush of the kill. He denied it with every fibre of his being, determined to continue his mission. Gravel and rockcrete shards ground dully beneath his feet. Analgesics had scoured the pain from his thigh, but nothing could cleanse the guilt and wrath that simmered in his breath, and in the double pulse that roared in his ears.

A Flesh Tearer, brought low by the Rage, had died at his hand.

At the bottom of the corridor, a pair of electro-sconces illuminated another set of age-faded mosaics and frescoes chipped by falling stone. Amit stood at their heart, newly clad in the Crimson Plate, the sons of Baal and a dozen other worlds at his side. A knot of crimson, they battled the orks and the beasts of Cretacia, claws and fangs matched by chainblades and power weapons. His flesh crawled at the sight of the warriors in black, whom he had first taken to be Chaplains, before he saw red saltires marking pauldron and poleyn. The Death Company had been born in the dark days of the Scouring, but its cursed legacy would end now.

Turning away, he ignored the swell of fear and fury that pressed against his mind and approached the grey arch that marked the barrow's entrance. The sigils of the Reclusiam and the Sanguinary Priesthood were separated by the icon of the Flesh Tearers, and the Cretacian runes for life and death were cut into the pillars at its side. There was the fusty suggestion of ancient death spicing the air as he took the last few steps towards the ossuary. For a single moment, his mind begged him not to enter.

He passed beneath the arch, and shock stole the fury from his veins.

In the wake of the Devastation, when he was first integrated into the Flesh Tearers, Barachiel had walked the catacombs beneath the Arx Angelicum. He had marvelled at the artistry invested into each sarcophagus and the niches they were set into. It had stolen word and breath. Each design was unique, sharing the barest similarities in the use of line or artistic influence, and genius was clear in many. Dumah labelled it a waste of effort and time, but Barachiel immediately recognised it as an attempt to preserve and honour the man in the heart of the Space Marine, a memory for their brothers and their inheritors.

The Flesh Tearers made no such effort.

Empty sockets stared accusingly from both sides of the immense cavern reserved for the dead, envious that he walked and killed when they no longer could. Grinning skulls, dusty and yellowed, delineated squares of flensed and disarticulated bone miles across. The horrendous kiss of war was evident in the broken and re-fused bones, projectile markings and blade-scoring. The Apothecary's tool marks were also much in evidence, in anchor marks for cybernetic organs and shortened limbs where augmetics were attached. Barachiel saw the memory of his Chapter laid bare, an empire of death erected on slaughter and sins.

The bones stretched far beyond the reach of his eyes and his helm's magnification, the small and solid glow of biolumes in the lightless depths and dizzying heights revealing the thin paths that allowed the Chaplains and Reclusiam serfs to honour and inter the newly dead. Its silence was perfect, a stillness undisturbed by the orbital assault. Set fast, not a single bone had been dislodged by the bombardment or by time's passage, not even a slight crack in the ossuary. Barachiel saw no markings to denote the identity of the bones on either skulls or the stones. He wondered why the dead were given no names in death, why the generations of battle-brothers that survived them would be unable to mourn their remains.

Surely they had earned such a simple honour in the Emperor's service?

Barachiel ventured deeper into the cavern, moving carefully through the winding path as small stones spilled from it. There were squares of rockcrete set at seemingly random posts between the bones, islands of grey amid the ivory and cream. They were planed flat, adorned by the Chapter symbol with a thin frame of stylised skulls. They were smaller by far than the walls of stacked bones, and it was only as he advanced that he truly appreciated the scale of these stacks. He pondered the reason, considering whether they were to honour the brothers whose bones they could not recover for interment, second to the bones' anonymity.

He walked for almost half an hour more before clarity struck him.

In death, all Sanguinius' sons were equal, whether they be a Blood Angel or a Flesh Tearer, a Golden Son or an Angel Encarmine. They would meet their lord the same and be embraced by the Great Angel the same. The Flesh Tearers made that sentiment real, making the fallen anonymous so that all were mourned equally by the Chapter, no matter what their triumphs and their failures were. To mourn one Flesh Tearer was to mourn them all.

The simple purity of the practice made him smile.

Barachiel continued his slow walk through the ossuary, time twisting beyond his care. Emotion stole the thought of his purpose here, until he spotted a stone skull set amidst the bone, marked with the Death Company's saltire rendered in maroon above its left orbit. He approached it slowly, searching for an entrance. It was artfully concealed by its angle and by the setting of the bones that framed it.

The passage was entirely of bone, and Barachiel noted rosarius after rosarius placed between the bones in neat lines, the Death Company's grinning skull carved into each one. A strange cold crept down his spine. He was careful not to scrape his armour on the bone, fearful of dishonouring the dead with such a disturbance. There were no lumens here, and the shadows pressed in on him until he reached an iron door that blocked the passage. It was stamped with the sigils of the Sanguinary Priesthood and the Reclusiam, and above them, the Death Company.

None belonged to the Blood Angels, nor their High Chaplain.

He muttered a curse as he offered a gene sample to the ancient bioscanner.

'Flesh Tearers' genome detected,' a voice hissed as the door ground open into an unlit passage of yellowing bone and musty air. 'Countermeasures disabled. Access granted.'

Barachiel strode into the Death Company's vault, and sorrow gripped his hearts like a vice, ice-cold and burning in the same instance. This was the future he fought, writ in broken and calcified bones and embodied by the Firstborn slain in the Basilica of Remembrance. He moved deeper through the unlit crypt, watching the bones ascend far beyond his sight. It was said the Chaplaincy kept a record of every warrior fallen to the Black Rage, both under their watch and across the Flesh Tearers' history. He suddenly doubted the claim's veracity.

The dead and damned numbered far too many to keep an accurate record.

He marched past stacks of bone shards and shattered skulls. They showed even greater damage than the wounds that had brought down their unaffected kin, and it was a stark lesson to Barachiel in what the damned suffered in the Rage's grip. Where he may have read shame and sorrow in the unlit and concealed crypt, he saw fraternal pride and reverence in their placement. In death, they remained brothers, and were accorded the same honours.

He reached the end of the crypt, and a portal marked with three sigils.

His heart leapt at the arrangement from the text, even as his mind repeated Dumah's warning like a servitor that burbled the same audio-fragment over and again. Barachiel brushed a hand over the access panel, noting a gene-scanner like a square of obsidian. He unclasped his gauntlet and slipped his hand inside, waiting for the needle's inevitable bite.

Nothing happened, even after several minutes passed.

Barachiel forced the portal open, its rusted hinges grunting and grating in a symphony of squeals and groans. He channelled his wrath as he had against the Death Company warrior, the hinges screeching and finally tearing loose. The chamber was utterly black, as if even the trapped bioluminescence of the caverns dared not fall within its bounds. Instinct screamed for him to turn back. He hardened his heart with fresh resolve. The Rage would be defeated, and the Flesh Tearers would rise in Sanguinius' estimation again. He activated his lumenator.

The past would not rule its future.

Claw marks spoiled the rough stone walls, overlapping patterns of five that spoke of frenzied violence more than an escape attempt. Calcified bones littered the floor, malformed abortions that bore better resemblance to the experimental overspill of an insane genomancer than the sculpted perfection of an Adeptus Astartes warrior. There was no thought of honour after death here, instead a sense of shame that weighed his muscles like lead. Even Barachiel, hardened to the deformities and distortions that a progenoid implantation failure could wreak on the human form, felt more than a little nauseous to see such complete and catastrophic rejections. Once more his mind urged him to turn back, towards the battle that pulled at his blood. He refused, pressing onwards into the barrow.

He ventured deeper, witnessing the remains of creatures that were lifted from childhood nightmares. They possessed hunched spines and bloated ribcages, swollen craniums and jaws mangled by teeth elongated far beyond description as fangs. They were uneven and needle-thin, more akin to those of the beasts that dwelled in the oceans' darkest depths than anything that should ever be present in a human mouth. Curved talons tipped their fingers, and several of the skeletons showed intense bowing or knuckles of unnatural growth.

If the catacombs beyond were the Chapter's twinned memories, this was a moment of shame and conscience buried beneath accreted layers of fury, sorrow and denial.

Barachiel reached the barrow's end, his count of the mutated skeletons well into the hundreds. Illuminated by his pack-mounted lumenator was a corpse clad in ancient, rusted power armour, dusty and cobwebbed. It was propped up against a wall, surrounded by the aberrant dead like a teacher with a crèche. Barachiel knelt beside it, carefully wiping away the patina on his shoulder guard, revealing the ancient crest of the Sanguinary High Priest.

In calcified fingers, he clutched a brass stasis-cylinder, still functional after uncounted centuries concealed in this tomb. Within the cylinder, held in micro-threads of blue light, there was a neatly folded square of parchment. Barachiel's eyes narrowed at the waste of such valuable technology, searching the corpse until he found the key, a short piece of monofilament wire. He slipped it into the narrow point of the Chapter icon on its surface, extracting the parchment and unfolding it into three distinct sheaves that his eyes scan-read in a matter of seconds.

His legs sagged, and his mind buckled beneath its weight.

THIRTY-ONE

Dumah sprung backwards as a Disciple's twin chainaxes shrieked for his throat, their song one of rust and ruin. Monomolecular teeth skittered on his breastplate, tearing chunks from his plastron. The Disciple lunged forwards, blades raised and ready – Dumah parried each strike. The Disciple's expression was a mask of old blood and fresh hatred. Dumah caught him by the throat, hammering his helm into the reinforced bone of the traitor's forehead. It split with a dull *tock*, and Dumah hammered his crozius into the traitor's chin. His head tore free, spurting gobbets of dark blood.

'Lord,' Micah snarled, cleaving a Disciple throat to pelvis, 'on your left.'

Dumah swung his bolt pistol, squeezing off a volley of explosive rounds that shattered another Disciple's visor, cratering the skull beneath. He shifted aim, atomising packs of men and women clad in brass carapace and crimson tunics. Several men bore scars consistent with various stages of gene-seed implantation. More spilled from the postern gates in the walls and towers, driven on by whip-fisted overseers and scarified fanatics that openly wore the favours of their gods. Twisted pride burned in their eyes, and Dumah grimaced at such overt displays of Chaos-born mutation. He gunned three of the wretches down, ejecting the spent magazine.

Las-bolts spanked against his plastron. Bullets clinked off it like steel rain.

The Chaplain looked up, a curse grinding through his gritted teeth.

Gunfire fell in sheets of sapphire and ruby from battlements welded inside the walls. Bolters coughed peals of metallic thunder in the hands of advancing Disciples, and heavier weapons opened up from prepared positions. Fyceline flavoured the air, as did blood. Flesh Tearers staggered and fell, killing as they were killed themselves by massed fire or the pinpoint accuracy of the Disciples of Rage. Their signifiers faded to grey on his display.

The Chaplain watched rune after rune sizzle to nothingness, like fat on a griddle. His company shrank. Forty-five. Forty-four. Thirty-nine. Thirty-seven. Toivo's entire squad was wiped out by warriors in ancient Cataphractii plate, the sergeant himself torn apart by their champion's wickedly curved lightning claws. Dumah's rage mounted, his mind spiralling further into the haze of red and black that threatened to swallow it. He barely felt the gut-punch of a bolt-round detonating against his plastron, nor shrapnel biting into his chest. Wrath bleached it to insignificance, urging him only to surrender to his need to slaughter. He layered control atop his frenzied strikes, even as his pain slathered his muscles with adrenaline. Wrath would not use him, not until no other option remained.

'Lord,' Adariel snarled, fighting back to back with Micah. His blade misted blood and aerosolised meat through the air, the dead piling at his feet. 'The traitor… He has fled.'

Dumah glanced at the terrace and saw it was true.

Wrath burned anew, and his vision was sliced by warriors in unfamiliar battleplate, of thoroughfares and causeways he had never seen before, piled waist-high with corpses in Imperial Army fatigues and armour of gold, white and red. A howl tore from his lips at the sight of so many dead, drowning the hooting war-horns of corrupted Titans that felled distant walls.

Reality reasserted itself as a bolt-impact, a crack cobwebbing his eye-lens.

'Where is he?' he snarled, ripping out another mortal's throat.

'He flees towards the reliquaria, lord,' Paschar rasped.

Red and black washed Dumah's vision anew, and he felt sudden, painful premonitions of iron bulkheads and emerald flames. He saw a figure shrouded in black, the leering spectre of an impossible foe towering over him. Its face shifted, ever inconstant, between the face of Horus Lupercal and a red-skinned daemon, fanged and furious. Dumah knew nothing of what it meant, whether it was the Rage or a trace of Sanguinius' prophetic foresight.

In truth, he did not care. Only killing mattered now.

Dumah barrelled headlong into a pack of Traitor Guardsmen, the regimental crest on their carapace armour and lasrifles defaced by the eight-pointed star. He slew and slew, raging at them for daring to invade the Emperor's realm, for their temerity in soiling his new Chapter's home world with their presence. A mortal detonated, slain by an errant bolt-round, showering Dumah in gore. Another bolt exploded on his helm. He laughed, blood stringing his lips, and dragged breath back into his lungs, spitting shattered teeth into his helm.

'Why there?' Dumah suspected he knew the answer already.

'It is the seat of the corruption, my lord,' Paschar answered, his voice barely audible over the throaty rumble in the heavens. Storm clouds gathered, and blood sheeted from them like a monsoon. 'The warp portal through which they hope to spread to other worlds.'

Rage spotted his vision with black, roused by the Disciples' twin insults.

'That will not happen. Flesh Tearers, advance. We kill their lord, now!'

'We cannot reach him, my lord,' Adariel said, carving apart a heretic with chiropteran wings and claws. It shuddered as it died, the shade of its daemon-soul shivering its way back to the warp. Micah slew its larger twin. 'We are outflanked and surrounded by the foe.'

'We should withdraw,' Paschar added, his voice little more than a rasp. 'The initiative is lost, and we will soon be too few to carry the assault any further. We should withdraw, and order the *Justice* to obliterate this place from orbit, and the heretics that occupy it.'

Dumah did not respond. A chainsword snarled across his vision, its adamantium teeth gnashing barely a finger's breadth from his visor. The second strike jammed into his forearm, splitting ceramite and flesh. It bleached his nerves with pain. The Disciple's blade ripped free and swung down, cutting diagonally across his body. Blood seeped through the tears. Dumah slammed his crozius into the traitor's plastron, atomising it and the organs beneath.

'Withdraw to where, Librarian?' Micah laughed, indicating the sealed gate. It trembled, loyalist men and tanks trying desperately to break in. 'The gate is sealed behind us, and the enemy is before us, their throats bared to our blades. We cannot flee this, even if we wished to.'

'Not all of us intend to die this day, Champion.'

'More blood to spill, more lives to reap.' Micah's laugh twisted to a rage-strangled howl. He leapt into a squad of Disciples, his blade flashing, trailing misty ribbons of blood and flesh. 'We kill until we are killed, Librarian. That is the truth of our Chapter.'

Dumah looked around, and saw that reality played out everywhere.

Their last Aggressor, Brother-Sergeant Castivar, staggered, his armour breached in a dozen places. His gauntlets unleashed torrents of acidic fire onto the foe, dissolving mortals and Heretic Astartes alike. They fell before his rampage like wheat before a scythe, those who strayed too close pulverised by his immense fists, even as they tore at him with chainblades and power weapons. Bolter fire hammered him from every side and plasma bursts scored deep gouges in his armour. A promethium canister detonated, bathing the Flesh Tearer in liquid fire. He clubbed another heretic down, bellowing curses as the fire devoured his armour seals, his biocodes flatlining as a thunder hammer caved in his helm.

Flesh Tearers fought in small knots, isolated by nooses formed of Disciples and their mortal allies. They fought back to back, butchering with a ruthless efficiency that would have made Seth and Amit proud. They left none alive to sob, or vomit, or vent their bowels as their last breath arrived. Each stroke ended in a kill. Yet they fell, riven by dozens of wounds, the sacred blood of Sanguinius spilled, diluted and desecrated by contact with traitor vitae.

They fed our wrath to lure us here. They drew us to the killing ground.

The reality was an unwelcome one, the truth that he had brought them to this crashing into his mind. Dumah beheaded a traitor with bullish features. A welter of sparks sprayed as a chainaxe skittered along his pauldron. He caved in the owner's visor. A powerblade carved a smoking rent in his chestplate, drawing a sliver of hot pain along his ribs. Their second blow was deflected by a poor angle. Blood matted his black plate. He killed and killed, the name of Sanguinius on his lips, splitting skulls and ribcages, his bolt pistol blowing out throats. Bodies, and parts of bodies, carpeted the ground, threatening to pin him in place.

All the while the Rage pulsed in his blood, demanding more.

Only thirty warriors still stood, plus a smattering of tribespeople that had survived the counter-attack by some twist of fortune. He had no time to be impressed by their fortitude, a chainfist snarling for his helm. A thunderclap of disruptive force severed the arm, and the crozius' backswing atomised the traitor's skull. Heavy las-fire ripped past his cheek, close enough to set its lacquer bubbling. *Spear of Sanguinius* endured, grinding fallen humans and Disciples to cerise paste under its anti-grav plates. Entire swathes of ceramite had been peeled from its hide by the weapons teams on the walls, though many of the positions were shot to pieces. It cut a bloody swathe through approaching heretics with its gatling cannon and Ironhail heavy stubbers.

Even with the tank, he doubted they would last much longer.

'To *Spear of Sanguinius*!' he bellowed, hauling warriors back with his pistol hand. He hated every syllable that left his mouth, the beast in his blood loosing apoplectic roars that echoed in his skull as sharp bursts of pain. He killed another heretic wearing the blade-crested helm favoured by the World Eaters. 'Defensive perimeter around *Spear of Sanguinius*!'

To their credit, the Flesh Tearers obeyed the instant the order was given, fury leashed to the discipline they had possessed as Unnumbered Sons. Firing lines were formed with bolt rifles, heavy pistols and plasma incinerators, the corpses of friend and foe alike piled into barricades. Several fell, cut down covering their brothers' retreat. The Black Rage pulsed hot in his veins, the beast within demanding he bathe in blood and death.

'Lord, we cannot last like this.' Fresh steel girded Paschar's voice.

Dumah saw the truth in the Librarian's words. His crozius decapitated another heretic warrior. Three life-runes sizzled grey. The Chaplain turned his voxmitter to its highest amplification, chanting the praises of blessed Sanguinius, fortifying his soul and the souls of his brothers against rage and the growing likelihood of death. It exhorted the Flesh Tearers to give their greatest efforts, and the rampart of the dead grew in height and depth. The traitors were forced to scrabble across it, slaves to their wrath as the Flesh Tearers were momentary masters of theirs. That control lingered like blood on a knifepoint, ready to slip away.

'Something must be done!' the Librarian pressed, and a chorus of strangled agreement swelled the vox. Even Micah grunted, fighting beside the remains of his squad and Adariel's.

'Duty demands we survive, Chaplain,' Adariel said. 'To die here will leave the heretic in control of this world. Such a stain on the Angel's honour cannot be countenanced.'

A heretic scrabbled towards Dumah, raising an ancient chainaxe thick with scraps of flesh and dried gore. A volley of mass-reactive rounds cut him down, and the Disciple behind him. Dumah gave his thanks to the warrior who had fired the shots.

Dumah knew what needed to be done. He had planned for this exact scenario, his contingency their best chance to break the ambush and emerge victorious.

'Then we must unleash the Death Company.'

Static and gunfire greeted the announcement.

'Dumah, you cannot mean that.' Micah cut the head from

another traitor, his plastron little more than ceramite shards sheeted glossy red. 'Their rage cannot be controlled.'

'It is insane,' Adariel interjected, his words punctuated by bolt-rifle fire.

'They exist for this very purpose, and their rage need only be directed.'

'Lord,' Paschar groaned, 'is it wise to unleash them? We should withdraw–'

'What would you have me do?' he roared, squeezing his trigger. Bolts cut through the air, punching fist-sized craters into a traitor's plastron. 'We cannot withdraw, we are cut off from any path of retreat and even were we not, it would be the act of a coward. Should we surrender and allow them to kill us? Would any of you like to die in such a dishonourable way?' He hefted his pistol meaningfully. 'Present yourselves now if that is the case.'

Silence spoke the answers they refused to give. Dumah switched the vox-channel, his words thickening on his tongue. A strange anticipation filled him, building with each word.

'Shipmistress, hear me! The order is given. Unleash the Death Company!'

THIRTY-TWO

Barachiel limped towards the light of a world on fire.

His mind churned over the parchment taken from the stasis-cylinder, now folded in a bandolier at his waist. It sickened him to have it near, though he could not be entirely certain why he had taken it. He considered destroying it, tearing it to scraps or setting it aflame with one of the sconces lighting his way, wiping clean the forgotten history he had read there. The thought appealed, so much that he drew the sheaf from his bandolier, but he resisted it, some form of masochistic pride compelling him to keep the weapon that murdered his hopes.

There was no cure to the Rage, no salvation to be had on blasted Cretacia.

The dead in the barrow were the result of their one, and only, attempt.

The fusty scent of old blood lingered in his nostrils, spiced by a bouquet of sulphides that he could not source. His fist hammered into the stone wall. The faint clang of iron faded into the roar of the blood thundering through his veins. His vision was slashed by black scars, through which emerald fires burned. The thrum of colossal plasma drives slithered up his calf muscles, and his back ached with the weight of his twitching wings.

'I am not Sanguinius.'

He screwed his eyes shut, the vile scent of sulphides strengthening with each passing moment. Skulls clacked and cracked beneath his feet: the decks of the *Vengeful Spirit* paved in flensed bone. Bolters crashed in distant corridors, chainblades whickering and snarling at each other. His brow knotted, the war cries and battle-oaths hurled between the loyalist and heretic falling strangely on his ears. Pain rinsed every muscle with infernal flames, injuries dealt by the daemon Ka'Bandha yet to fully heal. They would never get the chance to.

'No,' Barachiel said, screwing his eyes tighter. The visions blocked out, the other sensations wavered slightly. 'I am not Sanguinius. I will not fall to his curse.'

He pressed on, the walls now the solid dark basalt of the undercroft. Torches burned with a steady orange glow. He emerged into a long processional hall lined with the statues of ancient heroes cast in marble and granite. Impact craters and stippling grafted a layer of gritty realism atop the effigies, as though they had just stepped from the battlefield into immortal stone. When he looked at the statues again, they were all hunched and twisted parodies of the Astartes, their angelic visages blighted by fangs and depthless fury.

The creatures in the crypt flashed through his mind again.

The shame Daeron had implied, and that was written onto the parchment, was not that the effort to cure the Rage had failed, but that it had been attempted at all. They were angels born of wrath, and the struggle to overcome the Black Rage in themselves was their greatest strength, the prime source of their relationship with their father, one that should not be pruned by genetic manipulation or cast aside on a whim, even if it could be.

Disgust closed his throat like the phantom of Horus' hands.

He limped on to an armaglass colonnade, drawn by the runic identifiers of the Fourth Company. Through the panes, he watched Cretacia burning.

The fortress-monastery was in ruins, with entire wall sections collapsed. Casemates and battery towers had been blown to crude escalades, the stone sticky and red. The remaining air-defence arrays and orbital batteries were silent, and the taste of scorched air had faded when the void shields failed. Armouries and support buildings were mounds of scorched rubble and twisted rebar. Barracks hosted massacres and sites of mutual annihilation. The skies throbbed a luminous orange, lit by blazing fields and forests that were reduced to charcoal sketches.

Bolt rifles roared. Chainblades screeched. Lives seeped onto stone.

The sounds of slaughter resonated with the beast in his blood.

Its siren call promised power and slaughter in exchange for its freedom. He would share the sensation, a fragment of consciousness lodged in the mind that, even now, was no longer entirely his own. Its lure was charismatic and terrifying, encoded into his genome, the insatiable hunger driving him to spill blood. Garbled vox-intercepts lanced through his vox-bead, the howls and war cries of his brothers strangled by the Rage shackled in their souls.

He could feel himself slipping away, giving in to temptation.

The beast thrashed against the chains that bound it within his mind, pleasure entering its roars at finding them slackened. They were chains forged of memory and ideal, of experience and belief, all the base composites of identity. Everything that was Barachiel kept the creature confined in its prison. It whispered to him through its cell bars, seducing him with promises of blood and death, battering him with the pressure of the Arch-Traitor's hands crushing the life from him as the Throneworld burned beneath his ire.

'I cannot fall to my father's curse,' he whispered.

Barachiel turned away from the terrace, tracing his brothers' signum locator runes. He limped up a long flight of stone steps. Footsteps, too small to be those of an Astartes. A pack of mortals crested the top, experiencing a moment of transhuman dread before they opened fire. Bullets clanked on his armour. Las-bolts left stippling and scorch marks on the dusty white plate, blades veined with rust and maroon stains glinting in his optics.

They burned with crimson fires, wrath personified.

Barachiel broke into a run, surprising them with his swiftness. Their fire snapped past his head or clinked off his battleplate. Pain flared where they pierced joint ribbing and bit into his skin. Panicked cries rose from the fools and they started to flee, firing over their shoulders, the bravest refusing to give ground before his charge.

He crashed into their firing line, bones breaking and necks snapping. They grasped at him with emaciated fingers – hunched, mewling creatures in tattered expeditionary uniforms. Their blades snapped on his golden armour. Once he might have felt sympathy for these men and women, piteous and deluded though they were. He might have offered them mercy, or sought to save them from their folly with illumination. But these creatures had chosen to serve Horus, to turn their backs on enlightenment and embrace treachery. His blade was the reward reaped for their heresy. Lives ended in crackling disruptor arcs and the slicing silver blur that was the Blade Encarmine. He would slaughter every heretic dog that separated him from his final destiny. Nothing would stay him from confronting Horus.

The sheer wrongness of the thought jolted him to sanity.

'No,' he muttered, blood trickling from his nose, his skull flashing with waves of hot pain. He forced himself to see the truth, blood-slick stone, scatterings of orphaned limbs and entrails trailing yards behind him, the bodies devastated by blade and fist. Scraps of crimson tunics and brass carapace clung to the meat, not the uniforms of the Imperial Army. 'I am not Sanguinius, nor am I afflicted by his curse. The madness shall not hold dominion.'

The words rang more hollow with each passing heartbeat.

Barachiel left the slaughter behind, passing through training halls and corridors lined with faded mosaics, friezes and frescoes that detailed the Flesh Tearers' early history. Sparks and lubricant trailed his armour, the damage done by the Firstborn Death Company warrior reopened by the mortals. Blood seeped through the cracks in his ceramite, his Larraman cells already working to seal the wounds. Pain throbbed with each step and breath, the weakness that flooded his muscles a distraction from the Rage and the lingering smell of sulphides, like rotten eggs.

The vox-intercepts grew clearer, the voices more distinct.

He moved onto a parapet that overlooked the courtyard, the humans that used it as a firing position turning at the clunk and snarl of his power armour. Heads burst, showering him in a thin, bloody mist. He barely felt the twitch of muscle that depressed the trigger, the hot squirt of serotonin notable in its absence. Barachiel kicked corpses aside, the boiling blood sheeting from black storm clouds blistering his armour and flesh.

The Fourth Company fought in the courtyard scores of feet below him, boxed into a desperate battle for survival. Heretics ground against them in an unceasing horde. Bolts cracked ceramite at point-blank range, detonating in gobbets of flesh and blood mist. Ionised plasma immolated mortals and Astartes. Gouts of flame ignited tunics and tabards of flayed flesh. Bones were broken with stone, fist and pistol grip. Skulls shattered. Men and women were dismembered with armoured hands. Flesh Tearers killed, as they died themselves.

Dumah himself fought with a wrath unbound, as furious and elemental as a hurricane. Death followed wherever his crozius fell, and Barachiel felt a momentary well of pride. The Chaplain was born to be a Flesh Tearer, his hearts and soul forged of their primarch's rage, and, like all Chaplains, he was proving capable of wielding it without succumbing to it.

A percussive boom split the air.

Barachiel glanced heavenwards, the motion accompanied by the snarl of neck servos, into the roiling storm clouds, a glimmer of flame visible against the black. It wreathed a small speck, like the eye of a primordial god, and it swelled with each passing second. The building whine of terminal velocity ground against his gums, making them ache. Anti-air arrays rose to meet it. Air-burst shells smudged the skies with their inky-black mist. The black drop pod rocked under the sustained fire, but nothing could touch it. Nothing came close to it.

Arrestor jets fired, bathing him in peripheral heat wash.

The pod slammed into the courtyard, crushing those mortals not quick enough to flee. Bolts spanked against superheated ceramite. Though he knew not whether it was the rising churn of his own blood or simple imagination, Barachiel could feel the agonised souls of the warriors within, their fury as tangible as the deck beneath his feet. The drop pod's armoured petals slammed open in a burst of explosive depressurisation.

Black-armoured warriors leapt from the converted drop pod, disruption energies sheathing the blunt faces of thunder hammers and honed edges of power swords. Strangled cries choked the vox, curses first voiced ten thousand years ago given new life. Their rage called to him, lances of fresh agony spearing his skull. The air shivered with weapons fire, the snarl of chainblades and the braying cries of daemons as the IX Legion met the XVI in this last, desperate battle. The beast howled in his veins, its chains breaking one link at a time as the future of the Flesh Tearers, unleashed in their terrible glory, unfolded before him. The revelation crashed against his mind. A scream pressed against his lips, fury framing his vision with black.

His gaze found Dumah, fighting to clear the Death Company's path.

'You were right, brother,' he said quietly, his rage lingering for a moment like a wolf cowed by the fire. The young Chaplain smashed his crozius into a frothing berserker, moving to join the Death Company as they carved into the cordon that defended the entrance to the citadel. Stone shimmered to dark iron. The recoil of continent-shattering weapons quaked the deck beneath his feet, the rotten-meat smell clogging his nostrils. 'The Rage will forever be part of us, as will the Death Company. Fear blinded me to that, but it does so no longer.'

The air quivered, re-forming as bulkheads of petrified flesh. Justaerin Terminators and Word Bearers twitched on a deck of interlocked skulls, the rich scent of Astartes blood firing the secret, shameful hunger hidden in his soul. Entrails garlanded his gauntlets, ripped free in moments of blackest fury. He cast them to the deck, retrieving his sword and spear from the hunched forms of two black-clad Luperci, approaching the strategium's double doors. Horus' slitted eye glared at him, as if daring him to enter. Destiny and death awaited beyond.

He forced a sad smile, remembering, for a moment, better times.

'I want you to know, brother, that I forgive you your trespasses.'

The Angel of Baal strode forth to meet his destiny.

THIRTY-THREE

The Death Company carved through human slaves and Heretic Astartes in a whirl of powerblades and thunder hammers. Streamers of fire and tainted blood trailed their weapons' arcs, mass-reactive rounds banging from the muzzles of bolt pistols, embedding themselves in flesh and armour, detonating in sprays of ceramite and crimson fluid. Organic slurry slid greasily from their coal-black armour. Piteous death screams were drowned in savage, bestial snarls.

Dumah watched their rampage, pride and sorrow swelling within him.

They fought like the *erinyes* of ancient myth, recalling naught of defence or doubt, the decades of training overwritten by a demigod's sacred fury. They were Sanguinius' legacy at its purest and most potent, and it was his sacred privilege to guide them to an honourable end. Yet they were still his battle-brothers, and his hearts ached with the certainty that they would not see the next sunrise.

He shook off the maudlin thought, hefting his crozius.

'Witness the wrath of Sanguinius unleashed!' Dumah roared, slamming his maul into a Disciple's helm, the ceramite and skull beneath imploding. Shadows of memories not his own flickered over his eyes, cataracts of smoky black and emerald flame. Growled pleas for blood and saliva-strung snarls choked the vox, his brothers suffering through their proximity to the damned. 'They walk in the shadow of our primarch's trial, their communion with him complete. See the heretics flee! None can withstand the cleansing flame of his anger!'

His warriors roared their assent, volleys of explosive rounds and sizzling gouts of plasma scything the enemy apart. They spat, cursed, roared, straining against the Rage, the urge to abandon sense for slaughter. Most resisted, raking their fire left and right, howling in pain and ecstasy. Some were not strong enough, vaulting the barricade to fight beside their brothers who walked the darkness of the Angel's final trial. Dumah felt his brothers' agony, rage caressing his soul with serrated claws. They could not restrain themselves for long.

He checked the active signum chains on his retinal feed.

Fewer than twenty warriors of the Fourth Company remained.

Dumah stepped onto the rampart formed of the recently slain, his crozius raised high. A bolt crashed into his pauldron, splitting ceramite, threatening to unbalance him. Las-bolts and bullets skittered sparks along his cuirass. 'Take up your blades, brothers, and let your bolters sing! For the honour of Sanguinius, and the restoration of Cretacia, be the sword of righteous vengeance upon the heretic! For the Angel! For the Emperor!'

'For Sanguinius and the Emperor!'

The Flesh Tearers burst from behind their barricade, shoving aside the stacked bodies. Solid rounds and las-bolts struck their armour, nipping flesh exposed by battle-damage. The incoming bolt shells were now few and far between, the Disciples distracted by the Death Company. Alert runes flashed on Dumah's retinal feed, registering damage in minute drops of red ink and screeding data. He emptied his pistol, relishing the serotonin rush that accompanied each squeeze of the trigger. The Thirst scratched his throat. Dumah embraced it, letting it power his limbs for the last few yards.

His boot crushed a wounded mortal's skull to paste, his crozius trailing arcs of killing light, its furious buzz itching his teeth. Blood roared in his ears, his twin pulses pounding in time with the rise and fall of his crozius. It thrust, parried, hammered – thunderous detonations shadowing every impact. Corpses tumbled from his path, death rattles flowering in the bed of pulped, shredded meat beneath his feet. Waves of pure aggression hammered his mind, a part of his soul yearning only to indulge the impulse for indiscriminate slaughter. Dumah ignored the compulsion, recognising the Blood God's taint and drawing on the purer rage within.

He had only one immediate objective: reach the Death Company.

The septet of screaming killers carved a path towards the citadel steps, demarcated in broken bodies. It lapped at the Fourth Company's boots as they battled to keep the path open, swords and axes whirling in adamantine blurs chased with arterial fluids. Dumah fought the hardest, never pausing or hesitating. His crozius smashed aside the clumsy lunge of a warrior in the desecrated battleplate of the Steel Confessors. The traitor's backswing almost tore his throat out, the teeth screaming mere millimetres away.

'Paschar!' Dumah bellowed, deflecting a blistering series of strikes. The traitor raged, his chainsword partially defanged. 'Does the traitor lord remain in the reliquaria?'

The Librarian's voice was as wasted as his flesh, the undercurrent of pain unmissable. 'Aye, Brother-Chaplain... *hnnnh*... The empyreal energies wax strongest there, building towards critical mass... *hnnnh*... The traitor guards it, waiting for that moment.'

Dumah glanced heavenwards, at the sanguine tempest and rage-red skies. A notion slid greasily up his spine, one that veined his gut with fear, the first tentacles of a poison that threatened to undermine him. The air rang with the stench of cordite and fyceline, lubricant and blood. A sharp thrust through the traitor's guard crushed the muscles in his throat.

'You believe they seek to corrupt Cretacia, to make it a daemon world?' Micah asked, and Dumah caught a glimpse of the Champion carving through a squad of Disciples, his warplate matted with gore, the traitors' and his own. Dumah pushed towards his flock, following the path they had opened towards the citadel, a feat his unafflicted brothers were not able to manage. The Death Company fought their way up its steps, butchering the Heretic Astartes guarding the doors with reckless abandon. Only a handful remained to oppose them.

One warrior, Tychos, lay gutted and headless at their feet.

'It is possible, though I believe that incidental, not intentional.'

'Then we can tarry no longer.' Dumah did not relent, pushing himself onto the next Disciple, loading another clip into his pistol. He had only two left. 'Monitor the energy build-up. Inform me when it approaches critical mass. Micah, the Fourth Company is yours to continue the extermination. I will slay the traitor myself, and stop this rite before its completion.'

'You should not go alone,' Micah growled. 'Let me accompany you.'

'Who is left to take charge, if not you, Micah? The company is yours. Lead it.'

Bolts sparked against his pauldron, blasting chunks of ceramite free. He ducked under the wild swipe of a chainaxe, shouldering into the howling Disciple of Rage. They collided with the resonant clang of ceramite, the traitor forced back into the burned-out ruin of a battle tank. Bolts detonated against Dumah's shoulder, shards of liquid pain knifing into his muscle. The Disciple launched forwards and Dumah parried a blistering series of strikes, throwing a savage counter-thrust that left the heretic's visor a crater of charred meat and ceramite.

'You cannot go alone,' Castiel interjected. 'Let my squad accompany you.'

The other sergeants chimed in with similar sentiments and offers.

'The damned will accompany me,' Dumah said flatly, his crozius shattering another Disciple's breastplate, pulping the flesh and organs beneath. He was close now, slaughtering stragglers at the base of the steps. 'They are our best hope of reaching the traitor quickly.'

Silence deadened the vox. Animal snarls lingered in his peripheral hearing.

His hearts hammered in his chest, the realisation that he was already moving among the Death Company sending strange shivers down his spine. Three of the damned circled him like pack hunters, the others venting their fury on twitching masses of ceramite and meat that were once Disciples. Firing pins struck empty chambers. Overheating plasma coils shrieked, itching his gums. The proximity pulled at his rage, the beast within urging surrender.

This was his final trial of worthiness as a Chaplain of the Blood.

One false move and they would tear him apart like rabid jackals.

He drew a breath, marshalling his resolve. 'brothers. Hear me.'

Helmed heads snapped to face him, incessant snarls rumbling

from throats ravaged by fury. Hunger bled from their emerald optics, their fury a wall of pressure that boiled against his skin and stirred the roar in his veins. The impulse for indiscriminate slaughter ravaged his mind, threatening to flense him of sanity. It was every bit as blunt as the Blood God's lure, the white heat of his lord's sacred wrath indecipherable from the unnatural storm that raged overhead, or the rolling crash of his brothers' bolt weapons.

Dumah girded himself against it, the conflict tightening his throat.

'Traitors stalk the Palace, seeking the death of our beloved Emperor.' The lie sat like ash on Dumah's tongue, his words emerging as a choking hiss. 'They cannot succeed in their foul task, or all shall fall to ruin.' His crozius rose, then fell. 'Kill until killed, brothers.'

The Death Company roared, then charged into the citadel.

Phalanxes of mortals met them in screaming tides of sacrificial meat, or stood stupidly in their serried ranks, firing into the relentless advance. Dumah moved among his charges, a nexus of relative calm in the swirling maelstrom of wrath and violence that rampaged through the terrified mortals. Viscera slapped against stone walls and age-faded frescoes. Gore misted the air, sizzling to steam on his crozius' disruption field. Thick ichor congealed in shallow pools in the tiles' natural depressions, oozing, bubbling, hissing as it devoured the stone. Screams faded into bestial snarls and the wet thunderclap of disruptor fields on flesh.

The remaining Death Company slaughtered everything living in their path.

It was only upon reaching the inner sanctum that they began to die.

Hanibal was the first to fall, scythed to bloody mist by the blizzards of bolter fire that poured down the dimly lit corridors, muzzle flashes marking the defensive positions taken by the Disciples of Rage. The Death Company advanced into the teeth of their fire, pain and the promise of blood stirring them to greater feats of fury. Bloodstones shattered and gilt edging cracked. Black armour shards were blasted free, bloody wounds torn across their bodies. The damned endured wounds lethal enough to slay a Space Marine thrice over, yet they fought on, unperturbed. Slaves and Heretic Astartes died by the score.

'Chaplain…' Paschar groaned over the vox. *'The empyreal energies… I can feel them growing. The blood spilled in battle… It feeds them… Ripening the ground for what is to come. The storm intensifies… The ritual rapidly approaches its crescendo.'*

The newest warrior, Aurelius, vanished in a cloud of ionised particles.

Dumah barrelled into a squad of Disciples, squeezing a burst of bolts that felled one traitor and staggered another. His crozius arced upwards, smashing into the staggered heretic's chin, and he spun to deflect the frenzied strikes of a warrior wielding paired cleavers veined with rust. The blades shattered, and Dumah emptied his bolt pistol into the traitor's abdomen, blood and diced meat spraying his armour. He slapped a fresh magazine into place, emptying it in tight, controlled bursts. Explosive rounds vaporised skulls and torsos.

'You are certain?' Dumah shot a traitor through the throat, taking no time to watch the blood spray between grasping fingers. He ducked a decapitation strike, the Librarian's reply lost in the Disciple's howl. Dumah split his skull, cursing. 'Say again your last, brother!'

'You would be certain if you could sense it as I do! The veil grows thin.'

'We are mere minutes from the reliquaria, our progress delayed only by the last of the retinue! The Death Company can do this. We need only a little more time to finish it!'

'You have no time, Dumah,' Paschar argued, agony swelling his voice to a roar. *'The damned have served their purpose. Abandon them, and see yours complete!'*

Shock made Dumah hesitate, mistiming his block.

A chainblade skittered across his plastron, its razored teeth scraping fresh furrows into the stylised ribs, tearing fibre bundles and flesh. Blood seeped from the tears, pooling on the stone at his feet. Dumah barged into the Traitor Astartes responsible, a thunderous headbutt snapping his head back. Dumah pressed the haft of his crozius onto the warrior's throat, frothing denial and hatred through clenched teeth. The traitor's strength was prodigious, far beyond that of a loyalist Firstborn, but Dumah was empowered by Sanguinius' sacred fury, and he would not be denied. Muscles crunched, and he gutted the traitor with point-blank pistol fire.

He looked to each of them.

Tamael, blunting a Terminator's bull-snouted helm with a single blow of his thunder hammer. Helios, his power axe slicing into a Disciple's helm, the skull beneath bifurcated by the strike. He could not see Isaiah, though whether the sergeant had been drawn by the promise of blood, or was simply lost in the melee, he could not be certain.

What was certain was that they were his flock, his responsibility.

He could no more leave them than a shepherd could leave his livestock to be set upon by pack hunters. Dumah bludgeoned another heretic to death, shattering a second traitor's jaw with a savage left hook. His mind raced, searching for an alternative, venting frustration, rage and grief in a bloodthirsty howl that ravaged his throat and sent mortals cowering. His crozius was a crackling blur, soundless for the realisation that crashed against his mind, fuelling his rage.

The Death Company had done their duty. They had brought him this far.

Now he had to do *his* duty, to quell the ritual and see the traitor lord slain.

'Horus,' Tamael growled, his voice ravaged by fury. 'Come face your destiny!'

Cursing the traitors with all his heart, Dumah fought his way clear of the Disciples, sprinting and killing until the sound of battle was little more than recent memory. His double-pulse slowed, his veins beginning to cool. His bloodlust refused to fade, stirred by the silence that persisted in the corridor, and the fact that he had abandoned his Death Company.

Tamael's rune was the last to flicker grey.

THIRTY-FOUR

The reliquaria's doors were open when Dumah reached them.

The Flesh Tearer strode through them, the ruins of two gun-servitors occupying the sentinel positions. Exhaustion nagged him, a dull ache in his forearms and calves. Snippets of vox-chatter teased news of the battle beyond, though too riven by static and data corruption to give him a clear picture of it. His retinal feed suffered the same, offering him senseless translations of the cuneiform carved onto the iron doors. He deactivated both functions. If he failed here, Cretacia would be forever lost to the Chapter, and with it their sacred relics.

Taint soured the air, and Dumah's revulsion almost rooted him to the spot.

Corruption had sunk its claws deep into the reliquaria.

Flesh carpeted the floor, giving beneath his boots. Where it ripped, ichorous blood beaded – viscous, and far too dark to be human. Denuded bone described alcoves and arches, framing diabolical friezes that showed Space Marines clad in gore-red battleplate engaged in wanton slaughter, their skin streaked with innocent blood. Between the vile artworks, skulls formed the plinths that housed the Flesh Tearers relics, the mechanisms that sheathed them in stasis replaced by clanking, smoke-belching obscenities of brass clockwork. Vitae marred each relic, a sacrament to corrupt their noble machine-spirits to the Blood God's service.

Dumah's disgust churned to hot, ready anger as he reached the hall's end.

There, amid the defiled relics of Amit and the first Flesh Tearers, a nauseating vortex of impossible colours stained reality with its presence. Tendrils of crimson power lashed out from its fringes, casting shadows that coalesced into the hazy suggestion of Neverborn. They hissed at the approaching Chaplain, flexing immaterial claws or swinging rune-etched blades in impotent rage. Their infernal whispers scratched at his mind, drawing on memories of pain and loss to stir his wrath, and drive him to spill the blood they needed to fully manifest. Through the haze, Dumah glimpsed something else, something formed of a shimmering red crystal. It throbbed with the measured rhythm of a heartbeat, the glow unhealthy.

'I expected Seth, or at least one of his favoured dogs.'

The voice rasped across his shoulder, like a whetstone dragged across a blade's edge. The throaty snarl of armour joints followed, and then the heavy thud of ceramite boots. Chainblades roared to life, and activating disruption fields slicked his tongue with a greasy, charred ozone taste. The Chaplain spun, raising his crozius to guard. His bolt pistol snapped up in the same instant. His ammunition count was low, and only a single magazine remained at his waist. The Flesh Tearer thumbed the shot-selector to full-automatic.

From a pedestal's shadow, the heretic lord prowled forwards.

Clad in Amit's armour, he dwarfed Dumah, snide amusement burning in his emerald optics. Disruptive power snapped along each digit of the immense fists, and clanking autoloaders slotted fresh shells into the integrated storm bolters, but the heretic made no move to attack Dumah. Instead, he circled the Flesh Tearer, one apex predator assessing another for a weakness that might yield an advantage, each step taken with the smug arrogance of a traitor warrior experienced in the use of Tactical Dreadnought armour. Dumah moved in opposition to the heretic, mirroring his steps to maintain the distance between them.

Dumah bit back his irritation at the traitor lord's casual dismissal, and the flush of acidic cold that raced down his spine. Terminator plate boosted a Space Marine's formidable strength almost beyond measure, and those traitors skilled in its use were amongst the deadliest of the Emperor's foes. 'The Guardian of Rage busies himself with foes far worthier than your pitiful band of heretics and slaves. He serves at the right hand of Commander Dante.'

The First Disciple chuckled, the noise jagged and cruel, like a tank stripping its gears. 'Is that the reason he sent a facsimile to reclaim Cretacia? This poor imitation of a Flesh Tearer?'

Anger sharpened Dumah's tone. 'I care nothing for your petty insults, traitor.'

'Do you not?' the heretic asked, his amusement that of a hunter tormenting its prey. 'I think you do, so-called Flesh Tearer. You seek to prove yourself a worthy inheritor of Amit's legacy.' He paused, the silence ripe with cruel delight. 'So naïve. I have fought your forebears across centuries, and I know them as only a foe could. They were warriors worthy of the title, of the divine rage that forever tears at your bloodline. You are a petulant child by comparison.'

Fury surged in Dumah's veins, though he recovered quickly.

'You wield insults like a craven,' Dumah sneered, his twin hearts beating a savage tattoo on his breastbone. He wanted to butcher this heretic, to tear the skin from his back and cast his corpse from the battlements. But the traitor was baiting him, trying to draw him in, he could see that. His uncontrolled fury would only bring this ritual closer to completion. He restrained the impulse, barely. 'You cower behind them like an aeldari, spending them in the hope they will extend your wretched life by another moment.' He pointed his crozius at the traitor. 'Even if Lord Seth knew of your pitiful incursion, you prove it would not merit his attention.'

The acid-green eye-lenses bored into him like a lascutter. Dumah readied himself for the traitor's inevitable charge, contracting his muscles, adjusting his stance with subtle micro-movements. His double-pulse quickened, adrenaline stinging his veins.

Then, *impossibly*, the traitor hung back… and laughed.

It rumbled from his immense chest, the promise of an avalanche in a distant mountain range, the voxmitter's crackle twisting it to something darker. 'You speak of Seth as though you stand next to him, a brother in battle, honoured and valued. If he is unaware that Cretacia was invaded, why then did he send you across the Rift, so very far from him?' A sick grin twisted the heretic's voice. 'Could it be he deemed you unfit to fight at his side?'

Dumah's knuckles creaked, his grip tightening on his weapons.

The silence stretched, pregnant with mocking judgement.

'Did he name you a *coward*, little Chaplain?'

Dumah's self-control faded into the black thunder of his father's fury. It bubbled from somewhere deep inside his soul, a caustic cloud as dark and infinite as the void that settled on his mind, visions of murder stripping the cogency from his thoughts. Fresh energy flooded his muscles, propelling him forwards. Sweat stung his scabbing wounds and his jaw twitched. A bestial roar drowned out the portal's tortured wails, man and monster speaking as one.

This heretic would end his days eyeless, tongueless, skinless…

Bolts slammed into his plastron, clustering around his hearts, shattering the stylised ribs. Alerts flared in his sensorium, a wash of red icons and armour diagnostics that screeded down the right side of his display. His armour buckled, pain prickling his chest. Larraman cells worked to clot the wounds, and sealant foam plugged the armour breaches. His pistol bucked, explosive rounds blasting chunks of ceramite from Amit's armour. It pained him to damage so storied a relic, and he screamed oaths of vengeance against the traitor lord and his warband. They would pay for the dishonours they had heaped upon his Chapter.

The heretic laughed, breaking into a lumbering run.

Chainfist and crozius met in a thunderous boom, the clashing disruptor fields spearing actinic tendrils in every direction. It burned the flesh beneath their feet to blackened waste, and scorched crevices into both warriors' chestplates. The heretic pushed forwards, his Terminator plate granting him advantages in strength and height. Dumah was forced to rely on agility and speed, ceding ground without true contest, parrying and deflecting those blows he could not dodge. It frustrated him to fall back, but he suppressed the feeling.

The Disciple laughed harder, pressing his attack.

The heretic lord moved with a speed and supple fluidity that the sheer mass of his armour should have made impossible. Dumah dodged aside, barely avoiding a skull-shattering right cross, its underbite chainblade chewing the air a finger's breadth from his lenses. Moments later, Dumah slipped under a decapitation stroke, driving his crozius hard into the traitor's abdomen.

The ceramite plating cracked under the disruption field's detonation, a shallow crater that trailed hairline fractures. Lubricant trickled down the Crimson Plate, the damage mostly superficial.

'Even unleashing your black-clad berserkers, you hesitated,' the Disciple taunted, his fist driving towards Dumah's head. Dumah pivoted under the blow, parrying a second into the wall. Stonework split. 'I wondered whether you had the mettle to go through with it.'

'I know more of mettle than you, *heretic*,' Dumah snarled, deflecting his blow into a nearby column. It shattered, collapsing in a heap of jagged stone. 'I honour my oaths.'

'Oaths of slavery to a wailing corpse enthroned on a soul-engine.'

Dumah ignored the provocation, pushing himself beyond anything he had endured in the decades since he was awakened. Sweat sheened his skin and hot breaths heaved from his overworked lungs. The heretic was a blur of crackling knuckles and snarling saw-teeth, blows falling harder, heavier, faster, like rain transmuted into hail. All thoughts of the conflict that raged beyond the reliquaria, of the Fourth Company and the traitor warband, melted away.

There was nothing save the warlord and his stolen warplate.

He twisted beneath a right cross, his crozius slamming into the left knee joint. It was the first truly solid blow he had struck. Ceramite splintered, servos and fibre bundles spitting golden sparks, but the Crimson Plate was born in an age of wonder, an age of enlightenment and technological advancement undreamed of by the Adeptus Mechanicus. Its mechanisms were proof against all but the most terrible of blows, and the knee joint held. Dumah had no time for a second strike, a chainfist snarling towards his pauldron. It bit through the ceramite into the flesh and muscle beneath.

The Chaplain fell back, hot agony washing through his shoulder, pulsing in time with his racing hearts. His armour whined into higher activity, flooding his body with the last of its soporifics. It barely blunted his pain. He stumbled backwards, forcing movement through his injured shoulder. The armour section flashed crimson, and reams of data screeded beside it. Much of it was meaningless to Dumah, his comprehension fading into the black swell of his fury. What he did recognise was the impaired range of motion and level of protection.

The First Disciple accelerated his attacks, each strike blending effortlessly into the next. Their weapons crashed together, each lightning exchange releasing rippling, thunderous booms that shook the cavernous hall. The warp portal shimmered, its vortices swirling with a feverish intensity, the maddened shrieks twisting from its maw rising in their pitch. Visions assailed Dumah. His brothers on their knees, willing supplicants before a throne of brass and bone, Khorne's hard-edged runes carved into their battleplate. The Angel's Bane, monstrous wings beating gusts of hot air that reeked of old blood, casting him to the ground before the Eternity Gate. Horus Lupercal, lounging on his basalt throne, watching Terra burn.

'Is that what passes for fury amongst Amit's chosen warriors now?' the heretic lord crooned, breaking from the combat for a moment. Dumah caught the dull edge of exhaustion in his breaths, but they were not yet ragged as his were. Weariness made the Chaplain's limbs sluggish, and weighed his muscles like mercury. 'How disappointed he would be.'

Dumah frothed a meaningless string of syllables, his jaw locked by fury.

Chainteeth sliced across the Chaplain's right thigh, ripping through the armour and biting deep into the muscle. The First Disciple dragged them back in a transverse slash aimed for

Dumah's throat. The Chaplain swung backwards, barely avoiding it. Every parry cost him ground, his feints and counterstrikes ignored or contemptuously deflected. Frustration balled in his chest, gnawing away at his self-control. It was so tempting to surrender, to cede control to his father's rage, to feel it roil through his veins, a ghost of the Great Angel returned to the material realm. But he was a Chaplain of the Blood above all else.

Chaplains did not slip so easily into the Black Rage.

A glancing blow shattered his jaw, and tore the right cheek of his helm open. Tendrils of actinic power peeled flesh from muscle, warm air stinging the exposed meat. Blood filled his mouth, and the Chaplain hawked a thick gobbet, and several broken teeth, onto the warp-flesh at his feet. It absorbed the sticky life fluid, twitching in adrenal pleasure. He slashed at the heretic lord, his maul describing a crackling arc towards the traitor's plastron. A chainfist blocked it, its storm bolter buckling, the rounds cooking off in a rippling series of detonations that split the ceramite along the heretic's arm and cratered his chestplate.

Too late, he realised the counterstrike had been baited.

Red heat swamped his torso, the underbite chainweapon spearing into his side. Blood sprayed from his mouth, carried by a raw, red scream that should never have issued from a human throat. The power fist hammered his ribs, the swelling scream cut by the shattering of ceramite. Skin ripped, and muscles tore. Shallow breaths slipped between his teeth, sharp stabs of pain blossoming in his chest. The pain was incredible. It ground him to his knees, his pharmacopoeia already drained. Red nothingness began to fringe his vision.

It took every shred of focus, all his discipline, just to stay conscious.

The Disciple's voiced breached the haze like a siege drill. 'How Amit would weep to see his legacy corrupted so.'

Dumah did not rise to the bait, and through the crimson haze he saw heavy sabatons striking warp-flesh. They were the soulless black of wilderness space, trimmed with the same corroded gold that framed every section of his warplate and formed the eye that stared in lidless malice from his plastron. The stone deck vibrated with the chained energies of a warship holding in low orbit, and the rolling thunder of its world-shattering weaponry unleashed once more. Seconds slipped away as his perceptions struggled to coalesce around the First Disciple.

Strength of will alone kept him from sliding into madness.

'You are weak,' the heretic chuckled, advancing on the stricken Chaplain. Firelight played across the teeth of his underbite chainblade, and lethal energies crackled around his power fist. The other was broken, the blade snapped halfway along its length, the power field completely silent. 'Pathetic. Unworthy of the sacred rage that runs in your veins. The god of war covets your line, wretch, and yet you squander the mightiest of his gifts.'

'Our wrath is the wrath of Sanguinius, pure and untainted. We desire nothing from your vile master,' Dumah spat, unable to manage the roar that would have better conveyed his revulsion. 'The sons of the Great Angel will never bow to Khorne.'

The heretic's amusement had not dimmed. 'All say that, and yet they carve his mark into their armour, and take skulls for his throne. You will serve, Flesh Tearer. For your kind, the lure of the Eightfold Path is impossible to resist. Even Amit saw that, eventually.'

'Lies! Blasphemy! You know nothing of my Chapter's founder!'

'I know more of Amit than you.' The heretic grinned. 'I crossed blades with him more than once, and I witnessed his fury unleashed many times more. You are a pathetic shadow of what he was, and even he succumbed to the fate that awaits all your bloodline!'

Dumah lashed out with his crozius, channelling every ounce of strength and hate into the blow. He ignored the agony of his broken bones, the torn muscles and reopened wounds that ignited every nerve in his abused body. The holy rage of a murdered angel propelled him, flowing through him. His crozius moved with blinding speed, a blur that struck the First Disciple's breastplate with a thunderous peal. Weakened by the storm bolter's destruction, the ceramite cracked.

The First Disciple, surprised by the sudden assault, took a single step back.

Dumah launched himself at the traitor, allowing him no time to regain his composure. Wrath lent fresh vitality to his limbs, the need to spill the heretic's blood ending all thoughts of restraint. Pain washed through his body, undimmed by the synthetic stimulants produced by his Belisarian Furnace. His crozius carved through the air between them, trailing lightning and runnels of aerosolised blood. Pain coursed through muscles and meat as he twisted around the Disciple's clumsy swipe, but Dumah welcomed it.

It fuelled strength, feeding his fury.

The Disciple tried to parry, driving the damaged power fist into the path of Dumah's strikes, but without its disruptor field it was merely a ceramite glove cast over servo-joints and cabling. Dumah worked that side of the heretic's guard, driving his crozius harder, faster, its speed and sheer violence ratcheting upwards. Sparks rained from the damaged joints, and the Chaplain laid his full weight into each blow, howling in savage abandon. He did not care that each blow heightened his pain, inflicting as much damage on him as it did on the heretic lord. That did not matter to Dumah. Only the traitor's death mattered now.

The damaged arm seized, its pistons fused and its servos shattered.

The Disciple howled in frustration, smashing his remaining power fist into the Flesh Tearer's side. Ceramite split with a terrible crunch, and Dumah staggered, fresh pain spearing his ribs. Shards of shattered bone ground together, and the sudden struggle to draw a breath meant something had punctured a lung. Warm, wet blood soaked his bodyglove. He tasted it in the back of his throat and felt his strength slipping away, felt his body failing him.

No. The word rose unbidden from his subconscious, barbed with animal fury.

Dumah pushed himself back into the fight, chastising himself for the momentary lapse in faith. Neither fear nor doubt would infect his thoughts. If this fight were to be his last, then he would not greet death with defeat staining his thoughts. He deflected another blow with a two-handed swipe that pulled at his broken ribs, tearing an agonised roar from his lips, almost making a lie of his vow. Yet what he saw was balm to his soul, strengthening his resolve.

The Disciple was struggling, his damaged arm slowing him by degrees.

Dumah weaved around the slow, clumsy swipes of the heretic's remaining power fist, striking like a serpent for the Disciple's armour joints and chest, for the weakness exposed or created by his earlier strikes. Sparks vomited from the Crimson Plate in golden cascades, its joints groaning like a chained ghast with each movement. The traitor blocked where he could, his range of motion limited by the damage. Conflicting energy fields released blasts of power that keened like a banshee's tortured wail.

Pistons buckled in the heretic's knees, his joints and fibre bundles fusing, locking him in place. Dumah ducked under blows, or parried them with two-handed blocks. The traitor's attacks were becoming wilder, more desperate, less considered. The Chaplain hammered his crozius into the breastplate. It buckled inwards, ceramite falling away in thick sheaves, blood weeping from the cracks. Black smoke belched from his crozius' power unit, and its dispersal studs glowed a bright orange, threatening to overheat. Dumah paid no attention, raining blow after blow onto the heretic until the crozius' field gave out with a thunderous boom.

The Disciple sank to his knees, his armour protesting at the unfamiliar motion.

Dumah straightened up, panting heavily. Black smoke framed his vision, and his ears snagged the cries of the damned, carried like a distant shout on a light breeze.

'Perhaps you are a Flesh Tearer after all,' the heretic sneered, but Dumah heard the bravado behind it. 'Why then deny your true nature? You could be the greatest of Khorne's chosen, the most glorious avatars of his pure rage!' Through shattered lenses, Dumah met the Disciple's strange red eyes, swollen by fury and pain. 'You were made to walk the Eightfold Path!'

'That path will never be ours,' Dumah spat, driving his crozius into the blunt-snouted helm. It buckled, and there was the sickening crack of breaking bone. 'We may be cursed to live with battle's roar in our veins, but we are not enslaved to our fury, as you are.'

Another blow. The helm buckled again.

'We are the Angel's loyal sons.' Another blow, another crunch. 'By his Blood are we elevated.' Another blow. The helm was severely buckled, one of the heretic's murder-red eyes a pulped ruin of jelly and meat. 'By his Blood do we serve.' Another blow, and a wet rasp scraped through the voxmitter. The heretic swatted at Dumah with his power fist. It narrowly missed, his depth perception skewed by the loss of his eye. Dumah raised his crozius for the death blow, completing the catechism. 'By his Blood do we surrender our lives in service to Sanguinius, to the Emperor, and to the Imperium of Mankind!'

The death blow fell. The helm cracked, ceramite shards blasting outwards.

The heretic slumped, then fell forwards, life fluid leaking onto the warp-flesh.

One task yet remained, the purpose for which Dumah's flock had given their lives.

He limped towards the crystal construct he had spied earlier, each step driving another lance of white-hot pain through his side. The discorporate daemons brayed, demanding more blood to feed their hunger, their immaterial claws raking at his breastplate, serpentine voices seeding his mind with visions of skulls taken in glorious slaughter, and vast oceans of sweet, sticky blood to slake his unending thirst. Catechisms spilled from Dumah's lips, entreaties to the Emperor and Sanguinius to ward his soul. The unholy fury of Khorne called to the Angel-planted rage that burned like a supernova in his chest, teasing it, tormenting it.

He reached the crystal construct, his breath catching.

It was human in shape and stature, the tattered rags of an armsman's uniform clinging to its torso. Its features were distinctly male, milk-pale flesh hanging in loose wattles from its cheekbones and chin, the muscles beneath severely atrophied. Dry breaths wheezed from its moisture-starved lips as the red crystal closed about its throat, its life unnaturally sustained by the whims of Chaos. Beneath the neck, its body was consumed by the crystal, and small ruby tears wept from its palm, the unhealthy pulse strengthening with each new droplet.

Eyes of white pain and black fire met Dumah's.

Visions of carnelian-skinned monstrosities unleashed against the Emperor's domain ground through his mind like migraine flashes. Entire planetary populations were harvested, their skulls piled in offering to the foul deity that lurked behind skies of liquid fire. Twisters and tempests formed of impure rage ravaged earth watered by innocent blood, baked to dry clay by the sun's merciless heat. Greater daemons lounged in thrones of filthy brass, ruling the slaughter with axe blade and whip, while the creature of living crystal lingered above it all, the vector, the herald, and the witness to the crimes of Sanguinius' second sons, Flesh Tearers no more, now merely the newest host amongst the Disciples of Rage.

'This future will not pass,' he said.

Understanding flickered in the creature's eyes.

Dumah hefted the crozius above his head. Pain sang along every muscle and tendon, but he forced it to remain aloft, channelling everything he had left into a single mighty blow. The weapon screamed downwards, a roar of agonised effort ripping itself from Dumah's throat. The crozius shattered on impact, fragments of sanctified metal lodging in his ruined breastplate and spraying across the quivering warp-flesh like droplets of silvery blood.

White lines spidered through red crystal, the air around the construct shivering with the sudden spike in power. Dumah took a step back, then another, instinct compelling him to distance himself from the foul thing. Panic, or something close to it, crashed against his mind. Had he failed? Had enough blood been spilled here to finish its transformation? He raised the broken haft of his crozius, determined to meet whatever came as a warrior.

The construct fragmented, then shattered. Shards disintegrated before his eyes.

The effect was instantaneous and incandescent.

The vortex began to collapse on itself, its revolutions cycling up to nauseating, eye-watering speed. The Neverborn slinking on its edge shrieked in terrible, anguished rage. It drew on them, on the corruption around it, peeling back the carpet of flesh and bone fittings, reducing them to hissing traces of ectoplasm on the original furnishings. Thunder split the Cretacian skies, the unnatural storm ravaging the fortress-monastery and the surrounding forests beginning to recede. White starlight bled through from the heavens, no longer stained crimson by the storm. Dumah had no time to rejoice. The warp portal dragged at him, pulling him closer. It screamed for his soul, desperate for anything to deny its dissolution.

It snapped shut an instant later, and quiet settled on the reliquaria.

His duty done, Dumah allowed himself to sink into a seated position, relief a warm and welcome flush in his veins. He leaned against a ruined plinth, dragging the untainted air of Cretacia into his lungs. A ragged banner, sewn from the remnant of three older banners – a chalice, an angelic executioner and a saw-toothed blade – was locked in the stasis field.

The first Chapter banner, he recalled numbly, unconsciousness beckoning him.

Boots hammered the thick stone, coming to a stop before him. The tip of a force blade buried itself in the stone, and sky blue could be made out beneath the blood and grime.

'The upper fortress is cleansed, brother,' Paschar said, his voice notably less strained. Dumah smelled the battle stimms still coursing through him, and the blood weeping from his numerous wounds. 'Our brothers sweep the lower levels now. None shall escape.'

Dumah nodded numbly. Unconsciousness still pulled at him.

'Unleashing the damned was a risk,' the Librarian continued, shifting aside slightly to permit a second Flesh Tearer's approach. His armour was crimson, and similarly stained, the tools of an Apothecary at his wrist and waist. Dumah did not move as Thuriel set to work, the young medicae plugging data-probes into his neural connectors. 'But it was a well-considered one. We would not have victory without them, and they fell in the glory they had earned.'

Dumah snorted. He needed no approval, especially from the Librarian. Pain shivered along his nerves, and he bit back a wince as Thuriel sprayed counterseptic on his side.

'Teman?' The name emerged as a dry-throated rasp. He suspected the answer, but the rolls of honour demanded certainty. Rites would be required for all the fallen.

'Dead, my lord, retaking battery command with Raziel's squad.'

Dumah accepted the loss with a nod. He knew the butcher's bill would be high, but they had won, and every brother that yet lived was another to ensure their Chapter's legacy endured on Cretacia. He snorted weakly. The butcher's bill would have been much higher if the generatorum had not been destroyed. An unsettling thought nagged at him.

He lifted his head, meeting Paschar's gaze.

'Where is Barachiel?'

EPILOGUE

Dumah watched the sun rise from the Black Tower.

Red light tinted with glowing orange and pastel pink crept across the burned tracts of field and forest surrounding the Chapter fortress. Vegetation was a thin band of green across the distant horizon, a promise of life that framed the desolation. Sound swelled with the rising light, the chitters, roars and calls of the native beasts reclaiming their fire-scoured territory. Stone trembled beneath his feet: though the largest creatures were still miles out, they were drawing closer. A flight of ranodon slid across the heavens, their cawing high-pitched and piercing, a sharp contrast to the chitters and guttural roars of the forest beasts.

Dumah allowed his eye to wander across the fortress-monastery, its walls and towers swaddled in makeshift platforms and plastek sheets, and the construction materials piled at their feet. Several sectors were closed off by his order, until Adeptus Astartes purgation teams had cleansed the corruption. Those districts deemed irrevocably tainted were forbidden to the Chapter and guarded by psy-warded servitors. His brothers patrolled the walls, their armour bedecked in the trophies taken from the Disciples, and the *Cretacian Justice* lingered in low orbit.

Chains clinked, and another's breath sliced through his reflections.

'Cretacia belongs to the Flesh Tearers once more,' Dumah said.

He moved away from the embrasure, the sun's warmth washing across his back. He forewent armour for simple duty robes and a coat of black ring mail, his weapons and badges of office borne at his waist and back. One was a serrated flensing knife, a relic forged from the shards of his crozius, while the second was limbered across his back, a war-maul with a head forged in the image of a skeletal angel on the cusp of flight. The weight of the relic weapon was reassuring, as was the faith his Chapter had shown in allowing him to bear it.

The Chaplain hoped he would prove worthy of its legacy.

Dumah approached the cell's occupant, his armour freshly lacquered black and marked with red saltires. Its power plant was disconnected, binding him in place as much as the chains and manacles leashing his arms and waist to the three stakes set in the stone floor. Baying cries echoed beyond the cell's iron door, the other inmates of the Tower roused by the promise of life in their midst.

'Thuriel grows well into his new duties,' Dumah continued, placing his right hand on the warrior's shoulder. The chromite augmetic had yet to fully bond with his nervous system, and there was a delay of several seconds between impulse and action. Tension coiled muscles tight. 'He estimates the first Cretacian aspirants will be viable for induction within a year.'

Ceramite scraped on stone, and Dumah flinched involuntarily, surprised the occupant could move while so heavily bound. He withdrew the hand, shamed by his weakness.

'That would not have been possible without you, brother.'

Another series of metallic clinks, followed by the dull scrape of stone.

'You have my gratitude, and the gratitude of the Chapter and Lord Seth.'

A growl ground free, the sound almost strangled by wrath.

Dumah chuckled wryly, though from sorrow more than amusement. He was deluding himself in believing he could reach his damned brother, yet he had to speak his truth.

Drawing a deep breath, the Chaplain let the words well from his soul.

'I know what you sought in the monastery's depths, brother. I saw it myself.' His lips twisted in a sorrowful smile, and he paused, choked up with a nameless emotion. 'You should have heeded my words, and not pinned your hopes on lost causes and flights of fancy. The Rage will never be cured.'

The Death Company warrior growled, acid hissing on his void-black breastplate.

'We knew this truth from the start, but you refused to see it. All I did was to protect you from that blindness.'

Silence stretched. Even the other inmates fell quiet.

'I will honour what you strove for,' he said quietly. 'Though it will not be the vision you clung to. The Flesh Tearers will flourish on Cretacia, and we will honour the Angel with each life we take.' He paused, the words lodging in his throat. 'As for you, my brother, you will taste sweet absolution, and you will die on the battlefield in honour and glory.'

He paused before he closed the cell door. 'I failed the Chapter, and I failed you, my brother.'

Bound in chains of meteoric iron, Barachiel screamed in mindless hate.

'I will not fail again.'

ABOUT THE AUTHOR

Chris Forrester lives and works in his home town of Wolverhampton. A lifelong science-fiction fanatic, he has been an ardent fan of Warhammer 40,000 for over half that time. His work for Black Library includes the short story 'Postulant', featured in the *Cthonia's Reckoning* anthology, and the novel *Wrath of the Lost.*

YOUR NEXT READ

AVENGING SON
by Guy Haley

As the Indomitus Crusade spreads out across the galaxy, one battlefleet must face a dread Slaughter Host of Chaos. Their success or failure may define the very future of the crusade – and the Imperium.

An Extract from
Avenging Son
by Guy Haley

'I was there at the Siege of Terra,' Vitrian Messinius would say in his later years.

'I was there...' he would add to himself, his words never meant for ears but his own. 'I was there the day the Imperium died.'

But that was yet to come.

'To the walls! To the walls! The enemy is coming!' Captain Messinius, as he was then, led his Space Marines across the Penitent's Square high up on the Lion's Gate. 'Another attack! Repel them! Send them back to the warp!'

Thousands of red-skinned monsters born of fear and sin scaled the outer ramparts, fury and murder incarnate. The mortals they faced quailed. It took the heart of a Space Marine to stand against them without fear, and the Angels of Death were in short supply.

'Another attack, move, move! To the walls!'

They came in the days after the Avenging Son returned, emerging from nothing, eight legions strong, bringing the bulk of their numbers to bear against the chief entrance to the Imperial Palace.

A decapitation strike like no other, and it came perilously close to success.

Messinius' Space Marines ran to the parapet edging the Penitent's Square. On many worlds, the square would have been a plaza fit to adorn the centre of any great city. Not on Terra. On the immensity of the Lion's Gate, it was nothing, one of hundreds of similarly huge spaces. The word 'gate' did not suit the scale of the cityscape. The Lion's Gate's bulk marched up into the sky, step by titanic step, until it rose far higher than the mountains it had supplanted. The gate had been built by the Emperor Himself, they said. Myths detailed the improbable supernatural feats required to raise it. They were lies, all of them, and belittled the true effort needed to build such an edifice. Though the Lion's Gate was made to His design and by His command, the soaring monument had been constructed by mortals, with mortal hands and mortal tools. Messinius wished that had been remembered. For men to build this was far more impressive than any godly act of creation. If men could remember that, he believed, then perhaps they would remember their own strength.

The uncanny may not have built the gate, but it threatened to bring it down. Messinius looked over the rampart lip, down to the lower levels thousands of feet below and the spread of the Anterior Barbican.

Upon the stepped fortifications of the Lion's Gate was armour of every colour and the blood of every loyal primarch. Dozens of regiments stood alongside them. Aircraft filled the sky. Guns boomed from every quarter. In the churning redness on the great roads, processional ways so huge they were akin to prairies cast in rockcrete, were flashes of gold where the Emperor's Custodian Guard battled. The might of the Imperium was gathered there, in the palace where He dwelt.

There seemed moments on that day when it might not be enough.

The outer ramparts were carpeted in red bodies that writhed and heaved, obscuring the great statues adorning the defences and covering over the guns, an invasive cancer consuming reality. The enemy were legion. There were too many foes to defeat by plan and ruse. Only guns, and will, would see the day won, but the defenders were so pitifully few.

Messinius called a wordless halt, clenched fist raised, seeking the best place to deploy his mixed company, veterans all of the Terran Crusade. Gunships and fighters sped overhead, unleashing deadly light and streams of bombs into the packed daemonic masses. There were innumerable cannons crammed onto the gate, and they all fired, rippling the structure with false earthquakes. Soon the many ships and orbital defences of Terra would add their guns, targeting the very world they were meant to guard, but the attack had come so suddenly; as yet they had had no time to react.

The noise was horrendous. Messinius' audio dampers were at maximum and still the roar of ordnance stung his ears. Those humans that survived today would be rendered deaf. But he would have welcomed more guns, and louder still, for all the defensive fury of the assailed palace could not drown out the hideous noise of the daemons – their sighing hisses, a billion serpents strong, and chittering, screaming wails. It was not only heard but sensed within the soul, the realms of spirit and of matter were so intertwined. Messinius' being would be forever stained by it.

Tactical information scrolled down his helmplate, near environs only. He had little strategic overview of the situation. The vox-channels were choked with a hellish screaming that made communication impossible. The noosphere was disrupted by etheric backwash spilling from the immaterial rifts the daemons poured through. Messinius was used to operating on his own. Small-scale, surgical actions were the way of the Adeptus Astartes, but in a battle of this scale, a lack of central coordination would lead inevitably to defeat. This was not like the first Siege, where his kind had fought in Legions.

He called up a company-wide vox-cast and spoke to his warriors. They were not his Chapter-kin, but they would listen. The primarch himself had commanded that they do so.

'Reinforce the mortals,' he said. 'Their morale is wavering. Position yourselves every fifty yards. Cover the whole of the south-facing front. Let them see you.' He directed his warriors by chopping at the air with his left hand. His right, bearing an inactive power fist, hung heavily at his side. 'Assault Squad Antiocles, back forty yards, single firing line. Prepare to engage enemy breakthroughs only on my mark. Devastators, split to demi-squads and take up high ground, sergeant and sub-squad prime's discretion as to positioning and target. Remember our objective, heavy infliction of casualties. We kill as many as we can, we retreat, then hold at the Penitent's Arch until further notice. Command squad, with me.'

Command squad was too grand a title for the mismatched crew Messinius had gathered around himself. His own officers were light years away, if they still lived.

'Doveskamor, Tidominus,' he said to the two Aurora Marines with him. 'Take the left.'

'Yes, captain,' they voxed, and jogged away, their green armour glinting orange in the hell-light of the invasion.

The rest of his scratch squad was comprised of a communications specialist from the Death Spectres, an Omega Marine with a penchant for plasma weaponry, and a Raptor holding an ancient standard he'd taken from a dusty display.

'Why did you take that, Brother Kryvesh?' Messinius asked, as they moved forward.

'The palace is full of such relics,' said the Raptor. 'It seems only right to put them to use. No one else wanted it.'

Messinius stared at him.

'What? If the gate falls, we'll have more to worry about than my minor indiscretion. It'll be good for morale.'

The squads were splitting to join the standard humans. Such was the noise many of the men on the wall had not noticed their arrival, and a ripple of surprise went along the line as they appeared at their sides. Messinius was glad to see they seemed more firm when they turned their eyes back outwards.

'Anzigus,' he said to the Death Spectre. 'Hold back, facilitate communication within the company. Maximum signal gain. This interference will only get worse. See if you can get us patched in to wider theatre command. I'll take a hardline if you can find one.'

'Yes, captain,' said Anzigus. He bowed a helm that was bulbous with additional equipment. He already had the access flap of the bulky vox-unit on his arm open. He withdrew, the aerials on his power plant extending. He headed towards a systems nexus on the far wall of the plaza, where soaring buttresses pushed back against the immense weight bearing down upon them.

Messinius watched him go. He knew next to nothing about Anzigus. He spoke little, and when he did, his voice was funereal. His Chapter was mysterious, but the same lack of familiarity held true for many of these warriors, thrown together by miraculous events. Over their years lost wandering in the warp, Messinius had come to see some as friends as well as comrades, others he hardly knew, and none he knew so well as his own Chapter brothers. But they would stand together. They were Space Marines. They had fought by the returned primarch's side, and in that they shared a bond. They would not stint in their duty now.

Messinius chose a spot on the wall, directing his other veterans to left and right. Kryvesh he sent to the mortal officer's side. He looked down again, out past the enemy and over the outer palace. Spires stretched away in every direction. Smoke rose from all over the landscape. Some of it was new, the work of the daemon horde, but Terra had been burning for weeks. The Astronomican had failed. The galaxy was split in two. Behind them in the sky turned the great palace gyre, its deep eye marking out the throne room of the Emperor Himself.

'Sir!' A member of the Palatine Guard shouted over the din. He pointed downwards, to the left. Messinius followed his wavering finger. Three hundred feet below, daemons were climbing. They came upwards in a triangle tipped by a brute with a double rack of horns. It clambered hand over hand, far faster than should be possible, flying upwards, as if it touched the side of the towering gate only as a concession to reality. A Space Marine with claw locks could not have climbed that fast.

'Soldiers of the Imperium! The enemy is upon us!'

He looked to the mortals. Their faces were blanched with fear. Their weapons shook. Their bravery was commendable nonetheless. Not one of them attempted to run, though a wave of terror preceded the unnatural things clambering up towards them.

'We shall not turn away from our duty, no matter how fearful the foe, or how dire our fates may be,' he said. 'Behind us is the Sanctum of the Emperor Himself. As He has watched over you, now it is your turn to stand in guardianship over Him.'

The creatures were drawing closer. Through a sliding, magnified window on his display, Messinius looked into the yellow and cunning eyes of their leader. A long tongue lolled permanently from the thing's mouth, licking at the wall, tasting the terror of the beings it protected.

Boltgun actions clicked. His men leaned over the parapet, towering over the mortals as the Lion's Gate towered over the Ultimate Wall. A wealth of targeting data was exchanged, warrior to warrior, as each chose a unique mark. No bolt would be wasted in the opening fusillade. They could hear the creatures' individual shrieks and growls, all wordless, but their meaning was clear: blood, blood, blood. Blood and skulls.

Messinius sneered at them. He ignited his power fist with a swift jerk. He always preferred the visceral thrill of manual activation. Motors came to full life. Lightning crackled around it. He aimed downwards with his bolt pistol. A reticule danced over diabolical faces, each a copy of all the others. These things were not real. They were not alive. They were projections of a false god. The Librarian Atramo had named them maladies. A spiritual sickness wearing ersatz flesh.

He reminded himself to be wary. Contempt was as thick as any armour, but these things were deadly, for all their unreality.

He knew. He had fought the Neverborn many times before.

'While He lives,' Messinius shouted, boosting his voxmitter gain to maximal, 'we stand!'

'For He of Terra!' the humans shouted, their battle cry loud enough to be heard over the booming of guns.

'For He of Terra,' said Messinius. 'Fire!' he shouted.

The Space Marines fired first. Boltguns spoke, spitting spikes of rocket flare into the foe. Bolts slammed into daemon bodies, bursting them apart. Black viscera exploded away. Black ichor showered those coming after. The daemons' false souls screamed back whence they came, though their bones and offal tumbled down like those of any truly living foe.

Las-beams speared next, and the space between the wall top

and the scaling party filled with violence. The daemons were unnaturally resilient, protected from death by the energies of the warp, and though many were felled, others weathered the fire, and clambered up still, unharmed and uncaring of their dead. Messinius no longer needed his helm's magnification to see into the daemon champion's eyes. It stared at him, its smile a promise of death. The terror that preceded them was replaced by the urge to violence, and that gripped them all, foe and friend. The baseline humans began to lose their discipline. A man turned and shot his comrade, and was shot down in turn. Kryvesh banged the foot of his borrowed banner and called them back into line. Elsewhere, his warriors sang; not their Chapter warsongs, but battle hymns known to all. Wavering human voices joined them. The feelings of violence abated, just enough.

Then the things were over the parapet and on them. Messinius saw Tidominus carried down by a group of daemons, his unit signum replaced by a mortis rune in his helm. The enemy champion was racing at him. Messinius emptied his bolt pistol into its face, blowing half of it away into a fine mist of daemonic ichor. Still it leapt, hurling itself twenty feet over the parapet. Messinius fell back, keeping the creature in sight, targeting skating over his helmplate as the machine-spirit tried to maintain a target lock. Threat indicators trilled, shifting up their priority spectrum.

The daemon held up its enormous gnarled hands. Smoke whirled in the space between, coalescing into a two-handed sword almost as tall as Messinius. By the time its hoofed feet cracked the paving slabs of the square, the creature's weapon was solid. Vapour streaming from its ruined face, it pointed the broadsword at Messinius and hissed a wordless challenge.

'Accepted,' said Messinius, and moved in to attack.

The creature was fast, and punishingly strong. Messinius parried its first strike with an outward push of his palm, fingers spread. Energy crackled. The boom generated by the meeting of human technology and the sorceries of the warp was loud enough to out-compete the guns, but though the impact sent pain lancing up Messinius' arm, the daemon was not staggered, and pressed in a follow-up attack, swinging the massive sword around its head as if it weighed nothing.

Messinius countered more aggressively this time, punching in to the strike. Another thunderous detonation. Disruption fields shattered matter, but the daemon was not wholly real, and the effect upon it was lesser than it would be upon a natural foe. Nevertheless, this time it was thrown backwards by the blow. Smoke poured from the edge of its blade. It licked black blood from its arm and snarled. Messinius was ready when it leapt: opening his fist, ignoring the sword as it clashed against his pauldron and sheared off a peeling of ceramite, he grabbed the beast about its middle.

The Bloodletters of Khorne were rangy things, all bone and ropey muscle, no space within them for organs. The false god of war had no need for them to eat or breathe, or to give the semblance of being able to do so. They were made only to kill, and to strike fear in the hearts of those they faced. Their waists were solid, and slender, and easily encompassed by Messinius' power fist. It squirmed in his grip, throwing Messinius' arm about. Servo motors in his joints locked, supplementary muscle fibres strained, but the White Consul stood firm.

'Tell your master he is not welcome on Terra,' he said. His words were calm, a deliberate defiance of the waves of rage pulsing off the daemon.

He closed his hand.

The daemon's midriff exploded. The top half fell down, still hissing and thrashing. Its sword clanged off the paving and broke into shards, brittle now it was separated from its wielder. They were pieces of the same thing, sword and beast. Apart, the weapon could not survive long.

Messinius cast down the lower portion of the daemon. There were dozens of the things atop the wall, battling with his warriors and the human soldiery. In the second he paused he saw Doveskamor hacked down as he stood over the body of his brother, pieces of armour bouncing across the ground. He saw a group of Palatine Sentinels corner a daemon with their bayonets. He saw a dozen humans cut down by eldritch swords.

Where the humans kept their distance, their ranged weapons took a toll upon the Neverborn. Where the daemons got among them, they triumphed more often than not, even against his Space Marines. Support fire rained down sporadically from above, its usefulness restricted by the difficulty of picking targets from the swirling melee. At the western edge of the line, the heavy weapons were more telling, knocking daemons off the wall before they crested the parapet and preventing them from circling around the back of the Imperial forces. Only his equipment allowed Messinius to see this. Without the helm feeds of his warriors and the limited access he had to the Lion Gate's auspectoria, he would have been blind, lost in the immediate clash of arms and sprays of blood. He would have remained where he was, fighting. He would not have seen that there were more groups of daemons pouring upwards. He would not have given his order, and then he would have died.

'Squad Antiocles, engage,' he said. He smashed a charging daemon into fragments, yanked another back the instant before it gutted a mortal soldier, and stamped its skull flat, while switching again to his company vox-net. 'All units, fall back to the Penitent's Arch. Take the mortals with you.'

His assault squad fell from the sky on burning jets, kicking daemons down and shooting them with their plasma and bolt pistols. A roar of promethium from a flamer blasted three bloodletters to ash.

'Fall back! Fall back!' Messinius commanded, his words beating time with his blows. 'Assault Squad Antiocles to cover. Devastators maintain overhead fire.'

Squad Antiocles drove the enemy back. Tactical Space Marines were retreating from the parapet, dragging human soldiers with them. An Ultramarine walked backwards past him, firing his bolter one-handed, a wounded member of the Palatine Guard draped over his right shoulder.

'Fall back! Fall back!' Messinius roared. He grabbed a human by the arm and yanked him hard away from the monster trying to slay him, almost throwing him across the square. He pivoted and punched, slamming the man's opponent in the face with a crackling bang that catapulted its broken corpse over the wall edge. 'Fall back!'

Mortal soldiers broke and ran while Squad Antiocles held off the foe. Telling to begin with, in moments the assault squad's momentum was broken, and again more bloodletters were leaping over the edge of the rampart. The Space Marines fired in retreat, covering each other in pairs as they crossed the square diagonally to the Penitent's Arch. The mortals were getting the idea, running between the Adeptus Astartes and mostly staying out of their fire corridor. With the fight now concentrated around Squad Antiocles, the Devastators were more effective, blasting down the daemons before they could bring their weight of numbers to bear upon Antiocles. Sporadic bursts of fire from the retreating Tactical Marines added to the effect, and for a short period the number of daemons entering the square did not increase.

Messinius tarried a moment, rounding up more of the humans

who were either too embattled or deaf to his orders to get out. He reached three still firing over the parapet's edge and pulled them away. A daemon reared over the parapet and he crushed its skull, but a second leapt up and cleaved hard into his fist, and power fled the weapon. Messinius pumped three bolts into its neck, decapitating it. He moved back.

His power fist was ruined. The daemon's cut had sliced right through the ceramite, breaking the power field generator and most of the weapon's strength-boosting apparatus, making it a dead weight. He said a quick thanks to the machine's departed spirit and smashed the top of his bolt pistol against the quick seal release, at the same time disengaging the power feeds by way of neural link. The clamps holding the power fist to his upper arm came loose and it slid to the floor with a clang, leaving his right arm clad in his standard ceramite gauntlet. A century together. A fine weapon. He had no time to mourn it.

'Fall back!' he shouted. 'Fall back to the Penitent's Arch!'

He slammed a fresh clip into his bolt pistol. Squad Antiocles were being pushed back. The Devastators walked their fire closer in to the combat. A heavy bolter blasted half a dozen daemons into stinking meat. A missile blew, lifting more into the air. Messinius fell back himself now, leaving it to the last moment before ordering the Assault Marines to leap from the fray. Their jets ignited, driving back the daemons with washes of flame, and they lifted up over his head, leaving four of their brothers dead on the ground. Devastator fire hammered down from above. Anti-personnel weapons set into casemates and swivel turrets on the walls joined in, but the daemons mounted higher and higher in a wave of red that flooded over the parapet.

'Run!' he shouted at the straggling human soldiery. 'Run and survive! Your service is not yet done!'